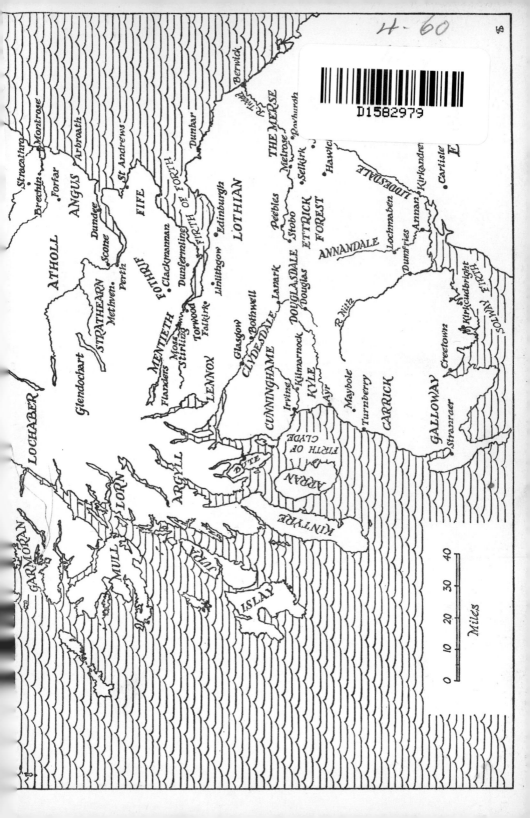

Miles
0 10 20 30 40

A. WILLIAMSON   4TH DECEMBER 1971

THE PRICE OF THE KING'S PEACE

BANNOCKBURN was far from the end, for Robert Bruce and Scotland; not even the beginning of the end—only the end of the beginning. There remained fourteen years of struggle, savagery, heroism and treachery before the English could be brought to sit at a peace-table with their proclaimed rebels, and so to acknowledge Bruce as a sovereign king.

In these years of stress and fulfilment, Bruce's character burgeoned to its splendid flowering. The hero-king, moulded by sorrow, remorse and a grievous sickness, equally with triumph, became the foremost prince of Christendom—despite continuing Papal excommunication. That the fighting now was done mainly deep in England, over the sea in Ireland, and in the hearts of men— his own not the least—was none the less taxing for a sick man with the seeds of grim fate in his body, and the sin of murder on his conscience. But Elizabeth de Burgh was at his side again, after the long years of imprisonment, and a great love sustained them both.

Love, indeed, is the key to Robert the Bruce—his passionate love for his land and people, for his friends, his forgiveness for his enemies, and the love he engendered in others; for surely never did a king arouse such love and devotion in those around him, in his lieutenants, as did he—even though, in the famous Declaration of Independence, at Arbroath in 1320, the same devoted comrades swore that they would put even their Lord Robert from them were he to fail in his adherence to the burning concept of freedom.

Freedom, then, with love—here is the theme and trumpet-call of this, the final volume of Nigel Tranter's trilogy about Robert the Bruce.

ROBERT THE BRUCE

The Price of the King's Peace

THE THIRD OF A TRILOGY OF NOVELS

by
NIGEL TRANTER

HODDER AND STOUGHTON

Printed in Great Britain for Hodder and Stoughton Limited
St. Paul's House, Warwick Lane, London, E.C.4, by
T. & A. Constable Ltd., Hopetoun Street, Edinburgh

PRINCIPAL CHARACTERS

In Order of Appearance

ROBERT BRUCE, KING OF SCOTS; Three weeks after Bannockburn.

SIR JAMES DOUGLAS: "The Good Sir James", Lord of Douglas. Friend of Bruce.

LADY ELIZABETH DE BURGH, the QUEEN: Wife of Robert the First, and daughter of the Earl of Ulster.

SIR GILBERT HAY: Lord of Erroll, High Constable of Scotland. Friend of Bruce.

SIR NEIL CAMPBELL OF LOCHAWE: Chief of Clan Campbell.

LADY MARY BRUCE: third sister of the King.

SIR HUGH ROSS: elder son of the Earl of Ross.

LADY MATILDA BRUCE: youngest sister of the King.

SIR THOMAS RANDOLPH, EARL OF MORAY: the King's nephew by a half-sister.

SIR EDWARD BRUCE, EARL OF CARRICK: the King's only surviving brother.

ANGUS OG MACDONALD: Lord of the Isles and self-styled Prince.

CHRISTINA MACRUARIE, LADY OF GARMORAN: Chieftainess of branch of Clan Donald; widow of brother of late Earl of Mar.

SIR HUMPHREY DE BOHUN, EARL OF HEREFORD: Lord High Constable of England.

SIR WILLIAM IRVINE OF DRUM: the King's Armour-bearer.

LADY CHRISTIAN BRUCE: the King's second sister, widow of Earl of Mar, and of Sir Christopher Seton.

LADY MARJORY BRUCE: the King's daughter, by Isobel of Mar.

LADY ISABEL MACDUFF, COUNTESS OF BUCHAN: sister of the Earl of Fife, and widow of the Comyn Earl of Buchan.

WILLIAM LAMBERTON, BISHOP OF ST. ANDREWS: Primate. Friend of Bruce.

MALCOLM, EARL OF LENNOX: Great Celtic noble, and friend of Bruce.

WILLIAM, EARL OF ROSS: Chief of Clan Ross, betrayer of the Queen.

BERNARD DE LINTON, ABBOT OF ARBROATH: Chancellor of Scotland.

SIR ALEXANDER COMYN: brother of Buchan, Sheriff of Inverness.

WALTER STEWART: 6th Hereditary High Steward of Scotland, the Queen's cousin.

MASTER ROBERT DE WHELPINGTON, PRIOR OF HEXHAM: prominent English cleric.

PATRICK, EARL OF DUNBAR AND MARCH: great Scots noble, formerly on the English side.

SIR ALEXANDER FRASER: High Chamberlain of Scotland.

SIR ROBERT FLEMING: Lord of Biggar; Bruce supporter.

MALCOLM MACGREGOR OF GLENORCHY: Chief of Clan Alpine.

SIR ROBERT BOYD OF NODDSDALE: veteran Bruce supporter.

JOHN MACDOUGALL THE LAME, LORD OF LORN: son of the Chief of MacDougall, Lord of Argyll.

ROBERT STEWART: infant son of Marjory Bruce and Walter Stewart; to be King Robert the Second.

SIR WILLIAM DE SOULIS: Lord of Liddesdale; Hereditary Butler; friend of Edward Bruce.

SIR COLIN CAMPBELL: son and heir of Sir Neil. Stepson of Mary Bruce.

O'NEIL, KING OF TYRONE: Irish prince.

MACCARTHY, KING OF DESMOND: Irish prince.

MASTER ADAM DE NEWTON: Prior of Berwick.

SIR ALEXANDER SETON: Seneschal of Scotland.

DAVID DE MORAY, BISHOP OF MORAY: Uncle of patriot, Andrew Moray.

DEWAR OF THE COIGREACH: Hereditary Keeper of St. Fillan's staff.

DEWAR OF THE MAIN: Hereditary Keeper of St. Fillan's left arm-bone.

MAURICE, ABBOT OF INCHAFFRAY: friend of Bruce, later Bishop of Aberdeen.

SIR DAVID DE BRECHIN: nephew of Bruce by another step-sister.

SIR INGRAM DE UMFRAVILLE: uncle of Earl of Angus; one-time Guardian.

JOHN OF BRITTANY, EARL OF RICHMOND: English commander; nephew of Edward the First.

SIEUR HENRI DE SULLY: Grand Butler of France.

SIR ANDREW HARCLA, EARL OF CARLISLE: English commander.

DAVID BRUCE: infant son of the King. Later King David the Second.

SIR HENRY PERCY, LORD OF NORTHUMBERLAND: son of Bruce's late foe, of same name.

For
ANDREW HADDON
who, too late, pointed out to me that
the English monarchs only became
majestic from Henry the Eighth's time,
an eminence to which their merely
gracious Scots counterparts never
aspired.

THE HOUSE OF BRUCE

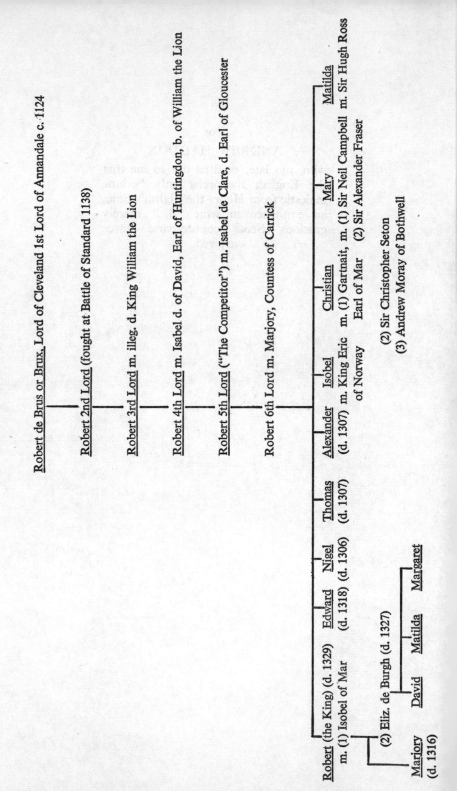

THE SCOTS SUCCESSION

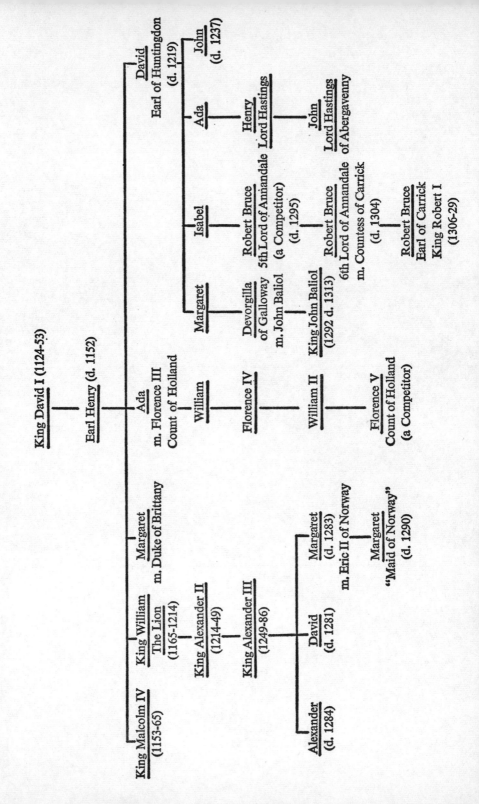

PART ONE

ROBERT BRUCE chewed at his lip—partly to hold back hot words. Already he had all but bitten the head off not only this wretched Englishman, but off his own good friends James Douglas and Gilbert Hay. Which was quite uncalled for and deplorable, he well knew. He kicked gold-spurred heels into his magnificent horse's flanks — there was a plethora of both magnificent horses and golden spurs in Scotland, since Bannockburn—to urge his mount a little way forward, ahead of his companions, where at least he might be spared their inanities.

And immediately, of course, the others spurred after him.

"That ridge ahead, Sire," Sir Roger Northburgh said, gesturing. "It will make a good viewpoint. We may see something from there."

"Good God, man—think you I need to be told that!" the King burst out. "Need I schooling from you that ridges provide viewpoints?"

Abashed, offended, the Englishman closed his lips tightly and stared straight ahead of him at the rolling Cumbrian foothill landscape, southwards.

Sir James, Lord of Douglas, thirty-one and looking younger, with the dark, almost gentle good looks which so strikingly belied his reputation, coughed. "Shall we ride ahead, Your Grace? Prospect . . . ?"

"No!" That was a bark, vehement as it was unkind. Bruce kicked his horse again, from a fast trot to a canter. And promptly, inevitably, the ivory-headed if splendidly dressed group of his close companions did the same, to keep up, unable to understand when a man desired to be alone with his thoughts. Even the King of Scots was entitled to that, on occasion, was he not?

Behind them, at a short distance, the heavily armed and armoured force of some 200 knights and men-at-arms urged their more burdened mounts to maintain approximately the same position, and the entire brilliant company pounded and clanked its way up the long tussocky whin-dotted braeside of Banks Fell, which flanked the fertile Vale of Irthing in North Cumberland. It was almost two years since Bruce had last climbed this ridge, and with a sword in his hand. Gibbie Hay, Lord High Constable of Scotland, had been

13

there too, though Jamie Douglas, as Warden of the West and Middle Marches, had been otherwise engaged.

On the gentle crest of the hill—although it was not what the Scots would call a hill, at all—the King reined up behind the same scatter of wind-blown, stunted ash trees which had shielded them from observation last time. There was no need for such hiding today—but old habits died hard, and this was the automatic reaction of that man on any skyline. He peered down into the fair wide dale beyond, narrow-eyed.

"There they are!" Northburgh exclaimed, pointing. "Down by the river. Beyond that farmstead, this side of the Roman wall . . ."

"I have eyes, sir," the King snapped. A pulse was throbbing where his hard lean jaw-line met his temple.

It was absurd, of course, but the warrior King of Scots was nervous. The veteran of seventeen long years of savage war; the leader of more forlorn hopes than he, or any man, could count; the man whom Christendom had called its second-greatest knight, and now was calling its first; the victor of Bannockburn but three weeks previously—this paladin was nervous, agitated, as any callow youth, and, aware of it, irritable, despising himself. Yet, nevertheless, that throbbing pulse was beating out a very different tattoo in his mind and heart, a fierce exultation such as he had never known at Bannockburn or before.

"Sire—the trumpeter?" Hay suggested. "A flourish? They are little more than a mile away. They would hear . . ."

"No! No trumpeting. Think you we are bairns at play?"

"I will go down, Sire. To prepare them," Northburgh said. "To acquaint them of your royal presence . . ."

"You will not, sir. You, nor any. I go alone."

"But, Your Majesty—it is not fitting. And these are my people. I left them only to find you, to bring you to them. It is my responsibility, until, until . . ."

"Quiet, man! Of a mercy! Wait you here—all of you. This is *my* concern." And kicking his mount into action again, Robert Bruce spurred on alone down the south-facing slope, a brilliant figure in blazing gold and scarlet.

Now there was no holding back, no restraint. In this, at least, he could allow his pent-up emotions release. Beating his beast's rump with clenched fist, he drove headlong down through the slanting grassland and scattered hawthorns, turfs flying from drumming hooves.

The company ahead was not so large as that he had left; but it was a sizeable party nevertheless, of perhaps 100 men-at-arms, steel-girt, led by three or four gaily-clad leaders. No more than Scotland,

14

Northern England was not a place where travellers might safely go less than well protected, in that first quarter of the fourteenth century.

When he was yet perhaps a quarter-mile from the oncoming party a rider left the group at its head, and came fast to meet him, long flaxen hair escaping from a fillet to fly in the wind.

As they neared, Bruce suddenly altered course somewhat. There was a clump of thorn trees a little way to the right. That man was still preoccupied with cover. The other rider followed suit at once.

The man reached the slight shelter of the scrub thorn first, and reining up abruptly, jumped down, so that he was standing wide-legged, tense-faced, waiting, when the woman rode in. She drew up a few yards from him, panting a little, and so sat, staring.

For long moments they gazed speechless, hungrily searching each other's faces with an intensity that was painful; the medium tall, wide-shouldered but lean man, with the ruggedly stern features and fiercely keen blue eyes; and the achingly fair woman, superbly mature in person, her facial lines at once delicate and strong, her beauty proud yet gentled with the lines of sorrow and adversity. So they stared, utterly lost in each other, until the woman slowly reached out her hands to him.

"My dear! My dear!" she managed to enunciate, chokingly.

He ran to her then, stumbling amongst the fallen cattle-barked thorn boughs, and threw himself against her flank, arms reaching up to her waist, face buried against her thigh, shoulders heaving under the gorgeous Lion Rampant tabard, emotion released at last in scalding tears.

Tears had never come readily to Elizabeth de Burgh. Often she had wished that they might. Now she stooped to kiss that bent head, her trembling fingers running through his thick wavy auburn hair. It was the sight of the few strands of silver in that thatch which caught her throat and let her weep.

"Oh, Robert, my heart!" she cried. "The sin of it! The sin of it!"

He looked up, wet-cheeked. "Forgive me, lass. I am sorry. It is joy, not sin. Not tears. Dear God—at last!"

Then she was down beside him, on the grass, in a single lissome movement that blotted out the years for Robert Bruce. Always she had been a magnificent horsewoman. They came into each other's arms.

They had only moments, of course. Then the English party came jingling up, and though they halted at the edge of the hawthorn clump, its trees were small and scattered and privacy was gone. Sighing, the man released her.

15

"Care nothing," she whispered. "We have the rest of our lives, my love." She drew back just a little. "Wait, you."

"I have waited . . . eight years . . . for this!"

"Two thousand, nine hundred and twenty-seven days!" she amended, nodding.

"And yet—you are more beautiful than even I remembered you. Or ever knew you."

"My sorrow, my Lord King—your sight must be failing you!" she got out a little unsteadily, smiling through her tears.

They took stock of each other a little longer, wordless, before the Queen turned and gestured towards the waiting horsemen.

"Here is Sir William de Hotham, who has been my . . . my host these many months. And who, with Sir Roger Northburgh, has conducted me to Your Grace safely and without delay."

The handsome elderly Englishman inclined his grey head. "You are kind, lady. I but did my duty."

"Duty can be done in more ways than one, Sir William."

"I have ever sought to do mine fairly, lady. Without fear or favour," the other gave back stiffly, a little warily.

"Lady . . . ?" Bruce barked. "You are addressing a queen, sir. Do you address Edward of Carnarvon's wife as lady? Do you?" The transformation in the King was quite dramatic.

"Er . . . no, sir. No."

"And do you sit your horse, sirrah, when in your own monarch's presence, and he standing? Get down, man!"

As Hotham hastily dismounted, and his three stylishly-dressed companions with him, Elizabeth looked thoughtfully at her husband, and saw anew what eight years had done for him. The sheer authority of the man was almost frightening. She said nothing.

Belatedly Hotham doffed his velvet cap, for good measure. "Your . . . Your Majesty's pardon," he muttered.

"I understand that you, none of you, have ever acknowledged Her Grace's royal style. In all her years in England. You will do so now, sir, before you take leave of her."

"We had our commands, Sire. From King Edward. The late King . . ."

"Aye. Well, you have different commands now. Make your proper duty to Her Grace, sir—and be gone!"

Frowning, the Englishman came forward and sank on one stiff knee before Elizabeth. He took her hand, to kiss it, though sketchily. "Your Majesty," he muttered.

"We say Grace in Scotland!" Bruce said harshly.

"Your . . . Your Grace's servant," the older man amended, unhappily.

16

"Yes, Sir William," the Queen acknowledged quietly. "You may rise."

As the other Englishmen came to follow their leader's example, Bruce asked, coldly formal, "Has Your Grace any matter you would wish to raise before I let these go? These, your late gaolers? Any matter for which you would have them held personally accountable?"

The woman looked from one to the other, and shook her fair head. "No, Sire. The times of my complaint are past and done with. Better forgotten. Go, Sir William—without ill will. There has been enough of that, God knows!"

It was Bruce's turn to eye his wife keenly. That had been said mildly, almost gently—and Elizabeth de Burgh, whatever else, had never been a markedly mild or gentle woman. What had the years done to *her*, other than enhance her beauty?

"You may go," he said to Hotham, with a brief gesture of dismissal. "Come, my dear." And he held out a hand to aid the Queen into her saddle again.

As the others bowed low, expressionless, the King vaulted on to his own horse with notable agility for a man of forty, and without a backward glance at them, led his wife at a quiet trot northwards.

Some way up the hill Bruce, spurring close, reached out a hand to squeeze her arm, unspeaking.

They smiled, and continued to ride closer together, and more slowly.

At the crest of the ridge a long line of bare-headed men awaited them, on foot, Douglas, Hay and Northburgh in the centre. As the pair drew near, two trumpeters sounded a long and stirring fanfare that went echoing over and around all the soft green hills. The trio in the centre came pacing forward. But still a dozen yards from the royal couple, Sir James Douglas could no longer restrain himself. Abandoning the dignified pacing, he broke into a run, and flung himself onwards to the Queen's side. He reached up for her hand, and at the same time sought to fall on his knee. This being something of a physical impossibility because of the height of her horse, he had to content himself with an odd bent-kneed posture while he clutched and kissed her fingers.

"Your Grace! Your Grace! Dear my lady!" he cried. "God be thanked for this! It has been so long, so very long. Here is joy, indeed . . ."

"Jamie! Dear Jamie—my good friend! My true knight still!" Elizabeth said a little unsteadily. "I might have known that you would come to meet me. And . . . and looking scarce a day older, I vow!"

17

"A laddie still," the Bruce's voice commented quietly, deeply. "But, by his deeds, a man!"

"I have heard of the deeds of Sir James Douglas, never fear," the Queen agreed. "All England has! The Black Douglas has been a name to tremble at these past years." Smiling, she released her hand from the younger man's eager grip. But she gave his own a little stroke in the process, that brought a flush of gladness to those almost delicate boyish features which so many men feared, as she turned to Gilbert Hay.

That man, ever quiet, a little hesitant of speech, retiring save in the face of the enemy, took that hand silently. But his grey eyes, upturned to hers, were full.

"Sir Gilbert—Gibbie Hay, my friend! You also. Another paladin! Renowned Lord High Constable of Scotland, no less! My two most fond and favoured knights. I thank you—in the name of sweet Jesu I thank you both. Not to have . . . forgot me!"

"Forgot!" Hay all but choked. "Did you think . . . ?"

"No, no, friend. But it has been so long. And you with so much else to consider than an Irishwoman captive in a far land . . ."

"You might well have believed yourself forgot!" Bruce interrupted, almost harshly. "That in eight long years these paladins, your husband and your so leal knights, could not come for you! Could not, in all their warfare and victory, lead an expedition into England to release their Queen! God knows, we thought of it, talked of it, enough! Sought to plan it. But . . ."

"My dear—how could you! Think you I did not know it was impossible? I am a soldier's daughter, you will recollect."

"And yet—you must have hoped, lass? I swear you did. Even I did that! Deceived myself. When we won as far south as Durham two years ago . . ."

"I knew. I knew it could not be. Even then. To get so far as Durham was a wonder. And a terrible hazard. How it warmed my heart to know you so near. If more than a hundred miles be near!"

"If they had not held Your Grace so far to the south," Douglas said. "On the Humber. All great Yorkshire in between. A populous land, of great lords, great castles, large cities. Northumberland, Cumberland, even Durham itself—these are different. But great Yorkshire to cross. We would never have won back to Scotland."

"Do not vex yourselves," Elizabeth pleaded. "All this I knew. As did the English! That is why they placed me there. Just beyond your reach. Yet sufficiently near to Scotland to tempt you. So that perchance you might attempt a rescue—and be trapped. That is why I was not sent to London, to the Tower, like Marjory. Is it not so, Sir Roger?"

18

Northburgh, the English hostage knight, prisoner at Bannock-burn and sent south by the Earl of Hereford, England's High Constable, and the vast company of captured lords, to effect this part of the exchange, shrugged. "His Majesty scarcely takes *me* into his royal confidence, Madam," he said.

"This William Lamberton told us," the King acceded. "But even so . . ." He sighed. "I was sore tempted, many times. But—I was a king. Not just a husband. With a realm, a people, to free. Not just a wife!" That was said hardly, deliberately. "You understand?"

"I understand," she agreed quietly, but as firmly as he. "I heard you swear your coronation oaths, you will mind. As I swore mine."

"Aye. Well, then—enough of this. It is fifteen miles to the Border. Thirty yet before Annan, where we lie tonight. Time we rode." He turned. "You, Sir Roger Northburgh—you have other duties to perform. A-many. My daughter. My sisters. The Countess of Buchan. Bishop Wishart of Glasgow. All these captives to bring to me, before your lords at Stirling go free. See you to it. And quickly."

The Englishman bowed and took his leave, to ride on alone downhill towards Hotham's waiting company.

To ringing cheers and acclaim the royal group rode up to the main body of the Scots, the most lovely Queen bowing and smiling. When the remaining knights and captains had been presented and had kissed the Queen's hand, many of them renowned veterans of savage warfare, and all of whom had sought eagerly for the honour of making up this escort, impatient to be off, the King signed to a trumpeter.

With the bugle-notes neighing, the whole company turned to face Scotland. And biting her lips, Elizabeth de Burgh looked back over her shoulder for a last look at the land which had held her captive for what should have been the best years of her life and the productive years of her marriage.

.   .   .

In the much-battered redstone castle of Annan that night, Robert Bruce, waiting with such patience as he could muster for the hour when he could decently announce his own and his wife's retiral from the convivial but maddeningly protracted scene, was unexpectedly involved in another reunion. The clatter of many hooves in the courtyard below intimated the arrival of another party, thus late in the evening. And a little later, two figures appeared in the doorway of the Great Hall, weary, travel-worn but glad-eyed—a man and a woman.

Had it not been for the fact that the dark, saturnine man was Sir Neil Campbell of Lochawe, chief of his clan, whom he had sent to collect her, the King would scarcely have recognised the woman as one of his own sisters. Eight years had dealt a deal more drastically with the appearance of the Lady Mary Bruce than with that of the Queen. He had last seen her, a plump, laughing tomboy of a girl of seventeen, in the woods of Strathfillan, after the rout of Dail Righ; now he saw a haggard, thin, great-eyed woman of fine but ravaged features, obviously desperately tired and leaning on her escort's arm.

"Dear God!" her brother breathed, rising.

All others rose, likewise, in that crowded hall. But though it was the monarch who moved towards the pair at the door, his wife out-paced him.

"Mary!" the Queen cried, and ran to the other woman, arms outstretched, all formalities abandoned.

The two women were embracing, murmuring incoherencies, as Bruce came up. He glanced at the Highlander, brows raised.

"The accursed English!" Campbell all but snarled. He was ever a man of strong feelings and few words.

"Mary, lass!" the King said. "What . . . what have they done to you!"

"Robert! Robert!" His sister turned to him, still clutching Elizabeth. "Praise God! I never thought . . . to see you . . . again."

"Praise! *Praise*, you say?" her brother barked. And then softened his voice and forced a smile. "Aye, praises be, lass. Welcome home, Mary."

"Home, yes." Her voice cracked and broke on the simple word, and with them she was in his arms, sobbing. "Home, Robert! But where . . . where is Nigel? And Alex? And Tom?"

He swallowed, and found no words. Annan Castle was indeed home to Mary Bruce. Here, third daughter of the fifth Robert Bruce, Lord of Annandale, she had been brought up. And when, with endless invasion and terror come to Scotland, her Celtic mother having died, her rather feckless Norman-Scots father exiled to die in England, and her three older brothers away at the wars, she had kept house for her two younger brothers, Alexander and Thomas, a gay and youthful establishment despite the constant alarms, assaults and intermittent flights to safety elsewhere. Now she was back to where she could see, just across Solway, where those two young men had been hanged and disembowelled by Edward of England, following all too exactly in the footsteps of the third brother, Nigel, a year or so before.

They led Mary Bruce to the table between them, as she sought to staunch and dry her tears—and it was notable how close Neil Campbell stayed to her, gently taking her travelling-cloak. While his sister recovered herself, the King questioned his friend.

"You had no trouble, Neil? No challenge to your mission?"

"None, Sire. Since Bannockburn, a hundred of them run from a couple of Scots! Our hostage, Heron, was well known in Newcastle, and made his own and his lord's needs very clear! Henry Percy himself delivered the Lady Mary into our hands. And . . . as God is my witness, I near cut him down there and then at the sight of her!"

"Aye. Well I can credit it! They . . . they still ill-used her?"

Mary Bruce herself answered that, having pulled herself together with a major effort. "No. No, I was no longer ill-used. After . . . after Roxburgh, they shut me up in the Gilbertine nunnery at Newcastle. I was kept alone. By myself. For near four years there. But treated not unkindly. The sisters were not harsh. After Roxburgh it was . . . a kind of heaven!"

All that company, listening keenly, was silent. None would dare ask this gaunt woman of twenty-five years of the fifth of her life which she had passed at English-captured Roxburgh Castle near the Border. There, on the late King Edward's command, she had been immured in an open cage of wood and iron, day and night, summer and winter, hanging over the outer walls of the castle, like a wild animal for all to see and mock—as also had the young Countess of Buchan at nearby Berwick Castle. How these two women had survived such appalling and long-continued savagery, none knew— and could by no means ask, yet awhile.

Neil Campbell growled in his throat.

"God be thanked, all that is now past, Mary," the Queen said. "We can start anew. A new life. Prayers answered. At last. Free again. As is Scotland. Thanks to . . . thanks to . . ." She looked at the sternly-frowning man who was husband and brother.

That frown, so permanently there these last long, terrible years, faded momentarily to a smile of great warmth, almost sweetness, strange in that rugged face, the blue eyes gleaming—for Robert Bruce had been a gay and laughing character once, whom not only his enemies had labelled irresponsible. "Thanks to every man in this hall," he finished for her. "And so many others. Living and dead. I have been blessed in my friends."

The deep murmur from all around was no mere polite and courtly acknowledgement of a royal compliment. There was not a real courtier present—and the Bruce did not pay compliments.

"God be thanked indeed," Mary agreed. "I grow hoarse thanking Him, and all saints. But . . . Christian?" she asked, after her elder sister. "And little Matilda? And Edward? Aye, and your poor Marjory, Robert? How is it with them?"

"Edward you will meet in Stirling. He is well. And, it seems, contemplating marriage at last! Of all women, to Ross's daughter,

Isabella. The man who betrayed you to the English, at Tain!" A shrug, and another brief smile. "Pray God she may tame him somewhat! Matilda is well also—and none so little now. Indeed, she looks for happiness already—and towards that same family, strangely. To Sir Hugh Ross. Who has proved a better man than his father! Christian and Marjory are still in England, prisoner—but likewise to be exchanged for these English lords at Stirling. Of whom we have a-plenty! I have sent for them. But they are held further south . . ."

Although it was not long before Elizabeth led her sister-in-law away to see her bedded, it was a deal later that, at last, the King could take his wife's arm and withdraw in becoming fashion from the bowing, excited company. Wordless, they climbed the winding turnpike stair together. In the lofty but modest tower chamber which had been his bedroom as a boy, the King closed the door behind him with a sigh, though of something other than relief.

"By the Rude—to be alone!" he said. "It is easier, I swear, to lead an army, to win a battle, than to gain a little solitude! For one who wears a crown. Always others there, thronging."

"That has scarcely been *my* burden, Robert," she observed.

"Ah—forgive me, my dear. Of course. You have been kept solitary. Fool that I am! Years alone . . ."

"Years, yes. So that now, Robert, you will understand—I am a little . . . strange. In company."

"To be sure. I should have thought of it, lass. But now, at last, we are alone. That is by with. The company. Care for nothing . . ."

"I will try. But the company I spoke of is not just those . . . others, I fear. You must be patient with me, my heart."

"You mean . . . ? That I—I *myself* trouble you ? You find me . . . find me other than you did ?"

"Dear Mary-Mother—no! Oh, Robert—bear with me. I am become a weak and foolish woman . . ."

"That, I vow, you are not! Weak you never were. Or of us two, the fool! Do not fear, Elizabeth. I shall not trouble you . . ."

"Oh, Robert—hear me. What have I said ? It is nothing so. This, I think, is the most happy day of all my life! It is but that . . . eight years is a long time. With no man near my bed. Scarce a man to speak to, but some sour gaoler. Or a priest. And, on occasion, William Lamberton. My dear, I have longed for this night. And yet dreaded it. Lest . . . lest I fail you, in some measure. No longer please you."

He went to grip her arm. "Save us—is this Elizabeth de Burgh! Is this the woman I took, yon time, by Linlithgow Loch ? Aye, and who took me! And the hundreds of times thereafter, through years of marriage ?"

"I was younger then, my dear. And . . . and a nun since! Whereas you—you will have had women a-many."

That was a statement and no question. Nevertheless it gave the man pause. Still holding her, he eyed her from under down-drawn brows. "Tell me, Elizabeth—what do you desire?" he asked. "Believe me, it shall be as you say."

"You are kind. And I a fool, as I said. It is only this, Robert—woo me a little, this night. As though . . . as though I was a virgin. Your bride. Though I was no virgin when you wed me, to be sure! A little patience, my love. Of your mercy."

"Mercy!" he repeated. "You do not know what you say, lass. I it is who should ask for mercy. Of you. Since I have been no monk! Have known other women. Have failed you . . ."

"Do not say it, Robert. Let us have no talk of failure. Lest I seem to fail you now."

"Foolish one indeed! How could Elizabeth de Burgh fail Robert Bruce! You love me still?"

"I do love you. Not still, but more than ever I dreamed possible. And want you—want you with all my heart. Only—only this body I am afraid of, a little . . ."

He took her in his arms, then, and ran a gentle but strong and knowledgeable hand over her comprehensively, from the smooth crown of her flaxen head, down the tall white column of neck, over the rich, bounteous swell of bosom, down to the long flanks of hip and thigh, and felt her quiver as comprehensively to his touch.

"This body," he said, deep-voiced, "need not be feared for, I warrant! Now, or ever. It is the most splendid, the most challenging, that any man could ever have under his hand. Under his whole person! What ails you at it, woman?"

"I do not know." She sounded, and felt to his touch, breathless. "Only lack of use, it may be. And years. I am thirty-five, Robert. And feel . . . more!"

"Now? Do you feel so old, this moment? With my hands on you?"

"No-o-o. But . . ."

He stopped her mouth with his own. And after only a second or two, her lips parted.

Even as they kissed, his hands were busy with her gown, probing, loosening, sure hands, confident as they were unhurried, masterful but yet coaxing.

Soon her bodice slipped down, to uncover white shoulders. He left her mouth, to plunge his lips down into the noble curves of those magnificent breasts, urgent but tender.

She moaned a little, but neither urged him on nor held him back.

23

He had to hold himself back, indeed, with a stern curb; but sought that no hint of it should evidence itself, even though his breathing deepened. As the rest of her gown fell to the floor, he stooped and scooped her up in his arms, and carried her to the bed. She was no light armful – but that would serve to account for his disturbed breathing.

"There," he panted. "Lie you there . . . and let me tell you how beautiful you are."

"As well the lamp is low!" she got out. But she stroked his face.

"That is the second time this day that you have impugned my eyesight. Do you think *me* so old ? At forty, woman ?"

"I think you . . . besotted. With love, it must be!"

"So be it. I shall recount my love's loveliness. Here and now. She is tall, see you – tall, and proudly made, comely of feature and of form." Pressing her back on the bed, he ran a discerning finger down from head to toe. "Her hair is heavy as spun and shining gold, and has the colour of ripest corn." He lifted a long coil of it and kissed it, running its strands through his lips. "Her skin is honey and cream admixed, yet softer than either and firmer than both." He laid his rough cheek against her smooth one. "Her face is fine-wrought yet strong, clean-cut yet so fair as to break a man's heart. And her lips – ah, her lips are kind and warm and wide and open to all delight!" He covered her mouth with his, and sank his tongue to hers.

When she could speak, breathlessly, she gasped, "Since when . . . has Robert Bruce . . . turned poet!"

"No poet," he assured. "All this I have but rehearsed. On my bed so many nights. In camp and cave and heather. Going over every inch and line and joy of you. In my mind. So that I am expert. As thus." He touched the tall column of her neck. "Her throat is smoothest marble, but alive, warm, strong. Her shoulders are whitely proud, turned to perfection. As for her breasts, they are all heaven in their twin loveliness, rich and round and rose-tipped, bold, beautiful, frank and firm." He was moulding and caressing, thumbing, stimulating the awakening, rising nipples. "But – save us, the tongue of man should be better employed than parading mere words for such delights!" And he closed his lips to better effect on fair, throbbing, thrusting flesh.

Whatever sweet confusion he aroused in that superb bosom, Bruce was all too aware now that his own arousal was all too potent, and time running out. He dared not linger, then, as he would, and as the woman's reaction invited. Biting his own lip rather than her swelling flesh, he raised his head, hand drawing down the linen shift that still part-clothed her, spread fingers smoothing.

"Her belly is polished ivory. With a central well of sheer enchantment. Her bush a golden thicket of happy entanglement guarding the valley of . . . of paradise. In sweet delay."

But he did not delay there, a man all but in extremity. His touch on the soft insides of her thighs, he got out, "Thighs . . . thighs satin-smooth . . . long . . . long . . . smooth . . ." He smothered the rest against her breast, wordless, tense, no longer stroking.

"Robert, my dear," she whispered. "Have done, my heart. Yield you. Yield. Do not distress yourself. Come—yield now, Robert."

But whether she had thought of it or not, that was a man to whom the word yield had become, above all others, anathema. Whatever else, he was no yielder. Now the very sound of it seemed to give him new strength and control. Between clenched teeth he found more words.

"You are . . . altogether beautiful. Desirable . . . beyond all telling. A woman fairer than any . . . that man could dream of."

"Oh, my love! My love!" she breathed. "I pray you—do not wait. Do not withhold. For *my* sake. Not yours! Quickly. Come—come into my love, Robert. Mine! Mine!"

"Is it true? Not for me? You do not cozen me? True that you *want* me?"

"Yes, yes. Quickly . . ."

He held back no longer from entry to her warm embrace. Yet still, even on the delirious tide of satisfaction, achievement, triumph, he did hold back, in some degree controlled himself with fierce effort, sought to contain himself, determined as ever he had been in all his struggling, that Elizabeth should know fulfilment at last. This he could do, must do, owed to her . . .

When at last, with a strangled cry, she reached her woman's climax, it was nevertheless not a moment too soon for Robert Bruce, as, thankfully, he let nature take its thwarted course. He had seldom fought a more determined fight. It was indeed sheer thankfulness, not any masculine triumph with which he let himself sink into the damned-back surging tide.

It was the taste of salt tears on his lips against her hot cheek which presently revealed to his returning awareness that Elizabeth was in fact quietly weeping.

"What now?" he mumbled. "Tears? Surely not. Why so, lass . . . ?"

"Tears—but only of joy, Robert. I thank you—oh, I thank you. Dear heart—you have made me whole again. My brave, true, kind knight—you have rescued me indeed! Lifted my fears from me. I was afraid that . . . that never again would I know this joy, this oneness with you. That the empty years had made me less than woman . . ."

25

"I' faith—if you are less than woman, then I am less than half a man!" he exclaimed. "A callow boy, no more! Who could not handle a full woman. Have mercy on me, lass!"

"I shall make up to you that sore trial, Robert. I shall . . ."

"You shall indeed. But give me a little time—just a little time! Have mercy on my forty years!"

"Sleep, then . . ."

"Sleep, no! I have had nights a-plenty for sleeping. To have all this splendour beside me in my bed, and to sleep—that would be sacrilege, no less! I can still . . . appreciate, woman, even when . . . a little spent!" And his hands began to prove his words once more.

Her chuckle was warm and throaty, and all Elizabeth de Burgh again.

After a while, out of the desultory talk and enriched silences, she spoke, without any change in tone or stress. "Christina MacRuarie?" she asked. "Tell me of her."

The man drew a long breath, and on his part at least, tension came back. "You know of her?"

"Think you that was a name of which my gaolers would leave me unaware?"

He moistened his lips. "Christina of Garmoran was—is—my friend. My good friend."

"Friend, yes. And lover?"

"Friend, I said. Lover only in so far as she gave me her body. From time to time."

"That was friendly, to be sure. And could conceivably be more than that!"

"Could be, but was not, Elizabeth. That I assure you." He raised himself on an elbow, to address her. "See you, lass—only you I love." That was urgent. "Only you I *have* loved. That I swear."

"Yes, Robert—I believe you. I know you love me. Have given full proof of it. But she? How is it with the Isleswoman? When a woman gives herself, not once but many times, over years—then more than friendship is there, I think! Do not mistake me. I am lying here, in your arms, and joying to be so. Fresh from your loving. Not here playing the jealous wife. God knows I have no right to that role, even if I thought to play it. Which I do not. But—I would know what I have to face, in this. Will my husband's friend Christina be *my* friend? Or my enemy?" This was very clearly still the old Elizabeth de Burgh.

He shook his head. "Your friend also, I do believe. But, if she is not—if she becomes your enemy—then she becomes mine also. That I promise you. But why should she be your enemy?"

"When a woman loves a man, she will fight for him. Husband or other. Does this woman love you, Robert?"

He frowned. "No. Not as you mean love. As *we* mean it. We have never spoken of love, Christina and I. When . . . when she first came to me, at Castle Tioram, after we had rescued her from the Rossmen. When she came, she said that I had need of a woman. A woman, not a lover. That, being deprived, I was showing it. Less than the man I should have been—therefore less the king also. I came to accept that as true. And . . . and she could lend me many Highland broadswords, as well as her body!"

"Aye—that is one way into a man's bed! But it could also be the way to his heart. Was she content with the bed, think you?"

"I believe so. *I* was, at least. She was a woman of experience. Widow of Gartnait of Mar's brother. Your own age, or older. Proud. Hot of temper. A fighter . . ."

"As Elizabeth de Burgh once was! And as beautiful?"

"No. By no means. Different in all ways. But kind. When I needed kindness. And you not there. She said . . . she said that one day you would thank her. For me. That you would want a man returned to you. Not a half-man. Or an ailing cripple . . ."

"She said that, did she! I see. I think I have something of the measure of your Christina now! The Lady of Garmoran. And shall deal with her accordingly!" She gave a little laugh. "But, in this she was right, at least. It is a man that I have returned to—no half-man. I can feel it now!"

"Aye—enough of Christina! And enough of talk . . ."

And now Robert Bruce did not have to hold back. Nor yet to coax and gentle. Elizabeth, it seemed, was thus abruptly herself again, vehement, zestful, far from passive. Joyfully, the man proceeded to lose himself in her returning passion.

In time, drowsily, he spoke. "What ails you at, Elizabeth de Burgh? Myself, I find no fault. Now you it is who makes *me* feel my years!"

"Years . . .?" she said. "What then are years? Time? In these last minutes you have given me more of true time and being than in all those lost eight years. I have begun to live again, my Robert . . ."

CHAPTER

2

STIRLING so throbbed with life and activity as to all but burst its
bounds. The great castle on top of the towering rock; the grey,
red-roofed town that clustered and clung round all the folds and
skirts of that rock; and the handsome Abbey of Cambuskenneth
with all the spread of conventual and domestic buildings that filled
the wide near-island in the coiling, shining Forth below both–all
were so full that lords and ladies roosted in attics, knights and
lairds were thankful to share cot-houses, and bishops and mitred
abbots must perforce occupy holy men's bare cells and the like
which they had long since thought to have outgrown. Even the
host of English prisoners from Bannockburn still unransomed, were
packed and herded still more tightly into deeper pits and prisons,
even dovecots, that their vacated accommodation might house their
captors. Scarcely within living memory had the royal Court of
Scotland taken up full residence in this its so royal and ancient
citadel–though King John Baliol had held a hurried and furtive
convention here in 1295. That August of 1314, Stirling was the
centre and heart of Scotland in more than geography, after being an
enemy-held canker for eighteen years.

The atmosphere quivered, as it were, with more than just the
numbers and the noise and the August warmth. There was a great
sense of celebration, of relief, of achievement, in the air. After all
these years of outright war, invasion, and usurping tyranny and
terror, the land was free again, with no single English garrison
remaining. After almost thirty years of weak rule, near anarchy, or
foreign domination, Scotland had a strong king again, a firm hand
at the helm. There was a vast amount to be done, a whole nation to
build up from the ruination and savagery of the past; but the way
seemed reasonably clear ahead, the task their own to handle or mishandle. Six weeks after one of the greatest and most significant
battles of history, this was the celebration of victory.

Strangely enough, it was with the victor himself, and those
closest to him, that this attitude of celebration was least evident. For
Robert Bruce realised as did few others that, substantial and
seemingly overwhelming as was that victory, it was in fact incon-
clusive, partial, even dangerously illusory. A round had been won in

this tourney, that was all. And there were still all too many in Scotland, and of the ruling class, who wished him less than well, and bided their time.

Nevertheless, it was right to celebrate, even wise, so long as the hazards were not lost sight of or minimised. This programme indeed was all of the King's own devising. But he hoped that even in its festive activities the lesson might be brought home in some measure—that the enemy was bloodied but unbowed.

The afternoon's tournament and games could be made fairly apt to his purpose. The theme and background was still warlike, competitive, challenging. And deliberately Bruce had made it more so by freeing, temporarily and on parole, not a few of the English prisoners, to take part. Some of the most renowned knights in Christendom had fallen captive at Bannockburn. The victor would use them, not to make any sort of Roman holiday, but to remind his own people that the foe was still potent, a force to be reckoned with.

The huge tilting-yard that lay just below and to the east of the castle proper, on a broad terrace of the rock, was the scene of the day's major activities. The English garrison had long used it for horse-lines and even cattle-courts, for the maintenance and provisioning of some hundreds of men. Bruce had had it cleared and cleaned up, and great quantities of dried peat brought from the nearby Flanders Moss to carpet it thickly. Lists had been enclosed, a great railed-off jousting-ground and arena, surrounded by hoardings and tiered timber seating, with a handsome royal box and gallery, the whole brilliant with colourful heraldic achievements and decoration, standards, flags and banners flying everywhere, by the hundred. Gaily-hued and striped tented pavilions had been set up, as undressing and arming rooms, and all around saints' shrines, and the booths and stalls of pedlars, chapmen, hucksters and entertainers proliferated. The clamour was deafening—minstrels played, merchants proclaimed their wares, mendicant friars touted supposed relics, children screamed, dogs barked and horses whinnied, all against the roars of acclaim, advice or disgust of the watchers towards the contestants in the arena.

Robert Bruce loved it all, for this was the heady, rousing clamour of peace, not war, something which had not been heard for long in this land. Up on the royal dais beneath the huge Lion Rampant standard of Scotland, where he stood beside the ornate throne, he gazed round on it all with satisfaction, if tempered with a kind of caution.

That the Bruce's place was to stand beside the single throne, today, not to sit in it, was because this was Elizabeth's day. In that throne she sat, radiant, Queen of the Tournament as well as the realm's queen. Dressed all in white and gold, golden circlet around her heavy flaxen hair, she looked regal, supremely lovely and supremely happy—and the man at her side as often glanced down at her for his satisfaction as at the stirring scene and activities, proud to pay her his own tribute. Occasionally she reached over to touch his arm lightly, and their eyes would meet.

As well that the Queen's beauty was thus supreme and quietly assured this day; for she was surrounded by beauty and good looks which might have proved a sore embarrassment to one less well endowed than Elizabeth de Burgh. A goodly selection of the fairest in the land were present today, and a surprising number seemed to have managed to insert themselves into the royal gallery. Moreover, all had somehow contrived to dress themselves, after long deprivement, in the height and extreme of fashion, so that the enclosure was a blaze of colour and pulchritude, with the women for once rivalling their knightly escorts, whose brilliant heraldic surcoats and coat-armour was so apt to steal any such scene.

Nevertheless it required all this beauty and colour to counter and balance the all but overpowering loveliness of the scene and setting itself. Surely nowhere could such an occasion have been so spectacularly placed as here, high on the flank of Stirling Rock. For this, the very key to Scotland, was also one of that most scenic land's most dramatic viewpoints, where the Highlands abruptly met the Lowlands, where the great estuary of the Forth became a river, where the noble vistas spread far and wide before the constrictions of the mountains. This terrace above the teeming town was so drenched in light and colour and vivid, challenging scene, as almost to be painful to contemplate. From the silver serpent of the Forth, coiling through the level carselands, to the thrusting green heights of the Ochils; from the vast rolling canopy of the Tor Wood to the village-strung shores of the Lothian coast; from the grassy glades of the royal hunting-park to the loch-strewn infinities of the Flanders Moss—all against the tremendous ramparts of the blue-shadow-slashed giants of the Highland Line, the eye of even the least perceptive was all too apt to be distracted from the small doings of men, however positive and spectacular.

A spectacle of some compulsion was indeed proceeding in the great arena. It was the final round in a prolonged contest between teams of wrestlers, four men to a team, each put forward by some great lord or other. Bruce himself had fielded a group from his own bodyguard—to see them soundly defeated in the second heat. Now, in this final round, the eight men who struggled there, all but naked save for the distinctively coloured drawers, represented, of all things, the Abbey of Inchaffray and the English prisoners. Egged on, implored and berated by their panting and gesticulating if non-playing captains, the Abbot Maurice and Sir Anthony de Lucy, the mighty but wearying musclemen were obviously nearing the limit of their efforts, their greased and shining bodies now so slippery and sweat-soaked as to prevent all gripping. Two pairs were already reduced to a merely formal and slow-motion pawing.

"Poor men—they are done, quite," Elizabeth declared. "There is no sport left in this. As Queen of the Tourney is it not in my right to call a halt? To declare the contest over and each side equal? And so spare us all more of this?"

"It is in your right and power indeed, my dear—if you would have both sides decrying you! Most of this assembly, indeed!" her husband told her, smiling. "Halt them now, and both sides will conceive themselves stripped of the laurels. And some of the crowd saying that you chose to spare the English, others that you chose to spare Holy Church! Either way, *you* lose! But have it your own way, lass—you are mistress here, today."

"Here is foolishness . . ." she said. But did not interfere.

Sir Hugh Ross, son and heir of the Earl thereof, who had once been Bruce's deadly foe, came up with the Lady Matilda, the King's youngest sister, a pair now all but inseparable.

"Your Grace," he put, to the Queen, "the English grow over-sure, I vow! They claim that they have as good as won this wrestling bout. And now they challenge us to a jousting. One, or many. Single combat, or massed fight. They would try to wipe out the shame of Bannockburn, I think. Have I Your Grace's permission to break a lance with their challenger?"

"Mine, Sir Hugh?" The Queen looked doubtful. "Must I so decide?" She glanced over at her husband. When the English prisoners actually started to initiate challenges, it was perhaps time to pause and consider.

Bruce took over. "Who is this bold challenger, Hugh?"

"There were many in it. But the spokesman, the true challenger, was Sir John, the Lord Segrave."

"Segrave! That man!" The Lord Segrave was a senior English captain, brother to one Sir Nicholas who had once been as good as Bruce's gaoler. He had been Edward the First's Lieutenant in Scotland in 1303 when Comyn and Simon Fraser had ambushed the English army at Roslin, and he had barely escaped with his life—to make Scotland pay for his fright thereafter, to some tune. He was therefore one of the most important captives of the late rout. This might well pose a problem. To refuse the challenge of an eminent veteran could look unsavoury, playing safe; on the other hand, for Scotland to be beaten in so notable an encounter, in one single combat fight, would be unfortunate. And Hugh Ross, although a sound wartime fighter, was untried in the tourney. Yet the King could by no means put it to this eager young man that he might not be of the calibre required.

Matilda Bruce, now twenty-one and full of spirit, sensed her brother's doubts. "Let him fight, Sire," she pleaded. "He will carry my glove to victory!"

"Much good that will do him!" To allow him time for thought, the King turned to his nephew, Thomas, Earl of Moray, who stood behind, and who was friendly with Ross. "How think you, Thomas? You know Segrave. You worked with him, once. His was a hated name, when he lorded it here. Is he one whose challenge we should accept?" He could hardly ask Moray outright whether he thought Ross fit and able to do battle with the Englishman; but his nephew would not wish to see his friend bested too easily. The Earl had sided with the English for a while, against his uncle, and probably knew both possible contestants better than any other man there. Thomas Randolph was a tall, dark, splendidly handsome young man, possibly the best-looking man in Scotland, despite his serious expression and noble brow. It was strange that he was not more popular; he was one of the heroes of Bannockburn—but he lacked humour, and was too patently upright for many lesser mortals. Bruce had come to esteem him highly.

"He is a stark fighter, and a hard man to best, Sire. And sore over our victory, I think. Sorer than some. But he will fight fairly."

"M'mmm. Hugh—do you think . . . ?" The King was interrupted by a shouting from all around, mixed with laughter. Down in the arena the wrestling seemed to have come to an end at last, with three of the brawny fighters in various recumbent attitudes, the victors either sitting upon them or otherwise expressing exhausted triumph. The last pair were down on their knees, growling at each other like angry dogs—but doing no more than growl, in the interests of economy. The scene was comic rather than dramatic, but the laughter was occasioned mainly by the fact that one of the victors was seen to have had his scarlet drawers torn right off him in the proceedings and was now standing, reeling, and grinning sheepishly, stark naked but notably well endowed, while the English knight, Sir Anthony de Lucy, had grabbed the said scarlet rags for want of better banner, to wave in exultation. It did not demand great arithmetical prowess to establish that, despite this misfortune, the red pants team had won, with two of the prostrate bodies blue, one kneeling, and only one Scot on his feet.

A trumpet fanfare preceded the Master of Ceremonies' declaration that England had won the wrestling match. The winning team should proceed to the royal gallery to receive the congratulations of the Queen of the Games.

While not a few Scots were consoling each other to the effect that wrestling had never been really a Scottish speciality, as it was in England, and some of the ladies were gigglingly wondering whether the winning team would in fact present themselves up here in the precise state of undress they were in at the moment, Hugh Ross reiterated his request to the King.

"You cannot deny me the joust now, Sire!" he exclaimed. "To reject the English challenge now would seem as though we feared another defeat."

"Aye. No doubt." Bruce shrugged. "Very well. But, Hugh— arrange it with Segrave that there be more bouts than just the one. Lest all stand or fall by the one throw." That seemed to be the best that he could do in the circumstances.

De Lucy and the four grinning, panting and strongly-smelling champions—one with a towel of sorts hastily wrapped round his middle, to the manifest disappointment of some of the company— were conducted to the royal box, where they bobbed bows to the Queen and King and were presented with red roses by Elizabeth. They were receiving suitable praise and admitting that the conditions of their captivity had at least not emasculated them, when another trumpet neighed imperious summons from down in the lists, drawing all eyes.

Two mounted men had ridden out into the centre of the arena, a gorgeously tabarded herald wearing red and gold arms quartered with red and silver, and lowering a trumpet; and a magnificent figure in shining black gold-inlaid armour part-covered by a colourful surcoat of heraldically-embroidered linen and carrying in the bend of one arm a great jousting helm sprouting ostrich plumes. This eye-catching personage, bare-headed, dark-haired and smiling from a narrow tense hatchet face, sat an enormous destrier or war-horse, also black-armoured and with flapping mantling of the same colours as the herald.

The King drew a deep breath.

"The most noble, puissant and renowned Sir Edward Bruce, Lord of Galloway and Earl of Carrick!" the herald cried, into the hush his trumpet had achieved.

The black knight raised his steel gauntleted arm. "I, Edward of Carrick, hereby declare," he shouted in ringing tones, "that the English are thinking to try their skill, in tourney if not in war! I do hereby challenge to single combat any soever they may put up. Hear you, English—I challenge your best!"

Hugh Ross's spluttered curse resounded in the pause thereafter.

Bruce drew a hand over his mouth and chin, uncertain whether to curse also or be relieved. Probably his brother, more experienced, would make a better showing than young Ross. And now the challenge came from the Scots, as was more suitable. But the thing raised other problems. None so lofty as the King's brother ought to be involved—it gave such contest altogether too great a prominence. Edward had not sought the Queen's permission, as he ought to have done—yet to forbid him now, before all, would be an intolerable affront, and to one of the most popular figures in the realm, a bad start for the so-long-absent Queen's new image. Moreover, his supercession would be bound to give great offence to Ross—where offence could well be done without, for he was heir to one of the greatest earldoms in the land, and already Edward was in bad odour in that quarter, having recently abandoned the Lady Isabella Ross after getting her with child—as he had indeed previously abandoned the Lady Isabel de Strathbogie, Atholl's sister, thereby throwing that powerful earl into the English arms. The Earl of Carrick was a brilliant commander of light cavalry, and courageous to a fault—but he gave his elder brother more headaches than he relieved.

"Sire—I sought this first!" Ross was protesting. "I told Segrave that I would fight him. If I gained your permission . . ."

"My lord of Carrick has not named Segrave," the King pointed out.

"But it was he who challenged . . ."

A new stir heralded the appearance of another figure, only partially armoured, who strode out into the arena, waving arms for silence. "I, John, Lord Segrave, accept the Earl of Carrick's challenge," he shouted. "He, or Sir Hugh the Ross, or any other. By lance, sword, mace or axe. To the fall, or *à l'outrance*!"

"A plague on him!" Ross growled. "Hear that?"

"Not *à l'outrance*!" Elizabeth exclaimed. "Not that. No killing. Has there not been enough of death?"

"I agree," her husband said, grimly. "My brother and I do not always see eye to eye. But I am not prepared to lose him yet! Nor am I prepared to forfeit Segrave's ransom! They must be told so."

"But, Sire . . .!" Ross objected. "Do you rule against me?"

"I have no choice, lad. Can you not see it? To deny my brother, now, in front of all, is inconceivable. He does amiss in this—but he is still the second man in this kingdom. I am sorry."

Matilda made a most unsuitable face at the monarch.

The Master of Ceremonies, after some brief instruction, made loud announcement that the Queen of the Tourney graciously permitted, despite improper procedure, that the Earl of Carrick and the

34

Lord Segrave ride a joust together, Sir Hugh Ross having nobly yielded a prior right. The joust to be for a fall, an unseating only, and no à l'outrance. There would be no fighting to the death at this tournament. Let the champions prepare themselves, and might the best man win.

In the interval of waiting, and while sundry presentations were being made to the royal pair, a new sound above all the cheerful clamour caught Bruce's ear—the thin high squealing of bagpipes. In a flash he was transported back to that day six weeks before, when, in so very different circumstances but only a mile or so away from here, he had listened for and relievedly heard that same sound coming from the west round Stirling Rock. He raised his head.

"Hear that!" he cried. "It is Angus, for a wager! The Lord of the Isles arrived to greet you."

"Scarcely to greet me, I think," Elizabeth said. "From all accounts your Angus of the Isles rates women but lowly! It will be your Council he comes for—to make sure that his peculiar interests do not go by default!"

A great Council of State had been called for two days hence, to plot and steer the nation's course in the new circumstances. A parliament would have been better—but a parliament constitutionally required forty days' notice of calling, and Scotland had matters to settle which could not wait for six weeks.

"He will not rate you lowly, I swear! Or he ceases to be my friend," her husband declared dutifully.

She smiled. "Am I then to be kind to him? Generous? Aloof? Proud? Or cautious?"

"Be but yourself, lass—and you will have Angus in the cup of your hands in short minutes! He is very much a man, and so the more in danger from you!"

"I wonder! But I am agog to meet this Hebridean paladin who denies you his due fealty while accepting your friendship! This rebel whom you have made your Lord High Admiral."

"Angus Og is no rebel, Elizabeth. He but reserves his position as an independent Prince of the Isles. For which who am I to blame him? I have suffered sufficiently from would-be Lords Paramount of my realm! I owe Angus more than I can ever say. Without his great fleet of war-galleys we could not have freed Scotland. He gave us control of our seas, when none other could."

Now everywhere the throng was making way for the newcomers —who obviously accepted all passage and deference as their right. And if the company had been colourful before, it was doubly so now. For the piper-escorted party which came stalking up was so vivid in every respect as to bemuse the eye. About twenty strong—for Angus

MacDonald, though a strangely modest man in his person, never moved abroad without his own court of chieftains, captains, seannachies, musicians and the like—these all were clad in saffrons and tartans and piebald calfskin jerkins, bristling with arms, glittering with barbaric jewellery, their heads mainly covered with the great ceremonial helmets that bespoke the Scandinavian background superimposed on their Celtic blood, outdated casques which sprouted at each side either curling bull's horns or whole erne's pinions, symbols that these were the representatives of a Norse sea-kingdom and no integral part of the Scottish realm.

Most of this alarming company were huge, raw-boned, rangy men, affecting long hair, only rudimentary beards, but lengthy down-curving moustaches reaching to the chin, which imparted a notably cruel and savage impression. But he who strode a pace in front was quite otherwise, a stocky man in his late thirties, dark, almost swarthy, but of open features, clean-shaven, and dressed most simply in a long saffron kilted tunic gathered at the waist by a heavy belt of massive gold links, from which hung a jewelled ceremonial dirk. Bareheaded and otherwise unarmed, he scarcely looked one of the boldest and most ruthless warriors Scotland had ever thrown up, a man whose name spread terror round every coast of England, Wales and Ireland—and not a few of Scotland's own, also.

"Angus!" The King went forward, hands outstretched, to greet him. "So again you come to Stirling! To my joy, if not this time my rescue! Greetings, friend. And to all your company, friends all. Come—here is my lady-wife. Elizabeth—this is Angus, son of Angus, son of Donald, Lord of the Isles and Lord High Admiral."

"The Lord Angus is known to me, as to all Christendom, by repute," the Queen said gravely. "King Edward kept me far from his coasts, I vow, lest the Lord of the Isles should come to rescue me!"

The other considered that, and the speaker, unhurriedly for a few moments, before inclining his dark head. He reached out to take her hand and kiss it.

"Would that had been my lot, lady," he said, then, equally gravely, and despite all the fierceness of his entourage, the West Highland voice was soft and gentle.

She smiled. "So do I! Though, mind, I am Ulster's daughter. And we in Ulster have not always had cause to welcome the Black Galley of the Isles!"

"Had I known of you, lady, you would not have remained in Ulster long, Richard de Burgh's daughter or none!"

"Save us!" Bruce exclaimed. "If that's the way of it, then I needs must keep an eye on my queen, now!"

The Islesman gestured, to include every male present. "That would be the act of a wise man, my Lord King," he agreed. "And no trial, at all!"

"As Queen of this Tournament, I give Your Grace leave to depart," Elizabeth mentioned. "I am sure that something requires your royal attention somewhere! My Lord Angus and I have matters to discuss."

Bruce was about to reply, in kind, when the words faded from his lips as he perceived who was standing amongst the press of Angus's men, a tall striking-looking woman, raven-haired, handsome, dressed none so differently from the others, in saffron tunic, short skirt and soft doeskin thigh-high riding boots.

Elizabeth, noting his expression and following his glance, spoke silkily. "You have a lady in your train, my Lord Angus. Not your wife?"

With a look shot at the King, that man shook his head. "No, lady — my cousin. The Lady Christina MacRuarie of Garmoran, chief of that name."

"I have heard of the Lady Christina also," the Queen said quietly. "Acquaint us, sir."

Bruce recovered himself. "*My* privilege," he said. "Christina — welcome back to my Court. You greatly grace it. Elizabeth, my dear — this is she of whom I have told you."

The two women eyed each other, while all around held their breaths and wondered what this totally unexpected confrontation might portend.

Elizabeth held out her hand. "His Grace's friends are my friends," she said. "I have heard that we both owe much to the Lady Christina."

The Isleswoman came forward to dip a deep curtsy. "Your Grace is kind as you are fair," she said. "As His Grace told us all. But even he could not say how kind, how fair! Accept my duty and esteem, Madam."

It was an odd speech from a female subject, but the Queen found no fault with it. Raising her up, she searched the other's dark eyes with her blue ones. "Yes," she murmured softly, slowly, "I understand much. Now."

"I came unbidden. Believing it my duty. To pay my respects to you, the Queen. Believing that I perhaps owed it to you."

"Yes. I am glad that you came."

Bruce endeavoured to disguise his sigh of relief. "I also am glad, Christina. Angus — present your company to Her Grace . . ."

Soon the trumpets drew all eyes to the lists again, as the two mounted champions came trotting out from either end, to meet in

37

the centre, turn their beasts side by side to face the royal enclosure, and to raise their pennoned lances high. Understandably the Lord Segrave was less splendidly turned out than Edward Bruce, and his charger, though fine, was less heavy; on the other hand it would probably be the more nimble. After bowing formally to each other, they turned and trotted back each to his base, where esquires waited with spare lances, equipment, towels and the like.

"Your brother looks sure of himself, Sir King," Angus Og MacDonald declared. He was no friend to Edward, who despised Highlanders and was not at pains to disguise the fact.

"Edward is always sure of himself!" Bruce grunted. "Would I had his single mind. Or yours, Angus!"

"You are sufficiently well with your own," the other returned. "My lord of Carrick's sureness of mind is that of a captain, not a prince." He did not comment on his own.

"Yet, my friend, that is one of the important matters before this Council," the King said, low-voiced. "Edward is determined that he be appointed, formally and before all, heir to my throne. I cannot longer withhold it, I think."

"So much the worse for that throne, then. And your kingdom."

"What choice have I? Placed as she is, could Scotland survive with a young woman as monarch?"

"A regency? To rule in your daughter's name. Your brother not Regent, but one of a joint regency."

"This land has had its bellyful of joint Guardianship. It will not serve, Angus. Jealousy, intriguing for power, a divided realm. And think you Edward would be content to be one of two or three? He is a man who must dominate, or be kept under by a strong hand. Whose hand would be strong enough, in Scotland, to dominate the Queen's uncle? He would rule, whatever his title. I fear my daughter would live happier with Edward king than with Edward regent. And, my sorrow, there is now no other heir to the throne."

"*Dia*—you talk as though you were a man dying!"

"No—not quite that. But . . . I am not the man I was, Angus . . ."

The single bugle-blast interrupted him, as the two knights below drove forward into action. It would be dramatic and telling to say that they hurtled forward at full gallop. But great destriers do not go in for galloping, especially when burdened with many hundred-weights of their own armour-plating, to say nothing of their riders'. A heavy lumbering canter is as much as they can rise to—and even that takes a little time to achieve.

But at least they thundered towards each other, the ground positively shaking at the weighty hoof-beats. Lances levelled, the visors of their helmets closed, the contestants urged tons of steel and

38

flesh on a collision course. In this sort of fighting there was little room for finesse; iron nerve, almost equally iron muscles, superb horsemanship and split-second timing—these were the prerequisites. And no weakness towards claustrophobia.

Since all might well end with the first headlong encounter, neither wasted any time on feints and gestures. Straight for each other they pounded, eyes busy behind the visors' slits. The least movement, change of position or attitude, cock of the head even, could give some indication of the vital information—just where the lance-point would be aimed—and great heraldic-designed shields over left arms were ready to react.

They met with a splintering crash which made even seasoned watchers wince. It seemed impossible that either of the mounts, or riders, could survive that impact. The horses struck at a slight angle, but near enough head-on to bring them both to an immediate standstill. But split-seconds before that the lance-tips had crossed—and in that instant both men rose in their stirrups for better control and avoiding action, altering the pitch of the said lances. Edward's, shrewdly aimed, struck home full at the other's breast—but by that time the Englishman had his shield up. It took the blow solidly, and the lance's timber shaft snapped clean in two, with the force of it. Segrave's own point, in the clash, missed the Scot's shoulder by a hair's breadth.

For strange moments time seemed to stand still, the tableau motionless. The two combatants were almost in each other's arms, Segrave thrown forward by the impetus and sudden halt of his mount and the failure of his lance to contact more than air. Carrick's position was different. The impact of his lance tended to throw him back, but his charger's abrupt stoppage countered this. Standing in his stirrups as he was, almost he was unseated, to fall sideways. But he was held upright, for the moment, by the pressure on his right leg, held between the two horses. So, poised, they glared into each other's visors, while the panting horses scrabbled great hooves to retain a footing. Then, recovering equilibrium and control simultaneously, they broke apart and went circling ponderously away.

A great corporate sigh rose from the crowd.

"What now?" Elizabeth demanded, breathlessly. "Edward had the best of that. Yet now he has no lance. While Segrave has. What now?"

"It is the fortune of the tourney," Bruce told her. "It has left the choice with the Englishman. He can ride Edward down—if he may! Edward will not run from him, that is certain! Four-foot sword against nine-foot lance! Or he may be chivalrous and allow Edward to collect a second lance."

Segrave did neither. Raising his undamaged lance, he cast it from him. Then he drew his sword, and waved it at his opponent invitingly.

"Ah—that is noble!" the Queen cried. "He rejects his advantage."

"Noble!" Hugh Ross exclaimed disgustedly. "No nobility there. He perceives that the Lord Edward is better than he with the lance, that is all. No point in allowing him another lance. So he will try the sword."

"That may very well be so," Bruce acceded.

Edward had drawn his own sword, and now the champions circled each other warily, while the watchers yelled encouragement or advice. Then Edward took the initiative and, holding his blade straight out before him like another lance, spurred directly for the other.

Segrave stood his ground until the other was almost upon him. Then he jerked his mount away to the right, the wrong side for the Scot's sword, and slashed his own in a sideways swipe as Edward swept past him. This was the classic move, and the other had anticipated it. By standing up and leaning as far to his own right as he could, he avoided that blow by inches. Thereafter he immediately pulled his destrier's head round viciously, hard round to the left and still round, sending the great brute rearing up and pawing the air, until it was completely turned and at the other's back. The Englishman perceived his danger, and spurred away—but just in time. Edward's blade struck a glancing blow, expending most of its force on the great wooden saddle behind the other. Segrave's slightly lighter horse enabled him to draw away.

"Another point to Edward!" the King cried. "That was featly done."

It was Segrave's turn to surprise them. He had only ridden away some twenty yards when abruptly he reined his mount directly round in its tracks, with more pawing of the air. His opponent was unprepared for this, and could not get his heavy charger out of the way in time. He took, in consequence, a heavy blow partly on his shoulder—fortunately not the sword-arm—and partly on his shield, before the other was carried past, and reeled in his saddle.

Everywhere Englishmen shouted hoarsely.

Their champion was quick to exploit his advantage. Swiftly he reined round once more, to drive in whilst the other was part numbed by the blow.

Edward, with only the briefest of seconds to take avoiding action, did not do so. Instead, he spurred to meet the challenge, canted over to his left side in pain as he was. And just before the attack was upon him, with a major effort he wrenched back his destrier's head with

40

almost unbelievable savagery and at enormous cost to himself, so that he swayed dizzily in the saddle with the shock of it. The horse rose high on its hind legs, squealing its fright and hurt, great shaggy forelegs lashing directly in the face of the other charging animal.

Somehow the Scot managed to retain his seat, or rather his stance, for he was standing upright. The other mount, faced with those weaving iron-shod hooves only inches from its face, flung itself aside as abruptly, almost falling over in the process. Segrave was all but thrown, his aimed sword jerked aside as he sought to save himself. And leaning far forward and over, Edward brought down his own brand in a mighty sledgehammer, pile-driving stroke, rough, ungainly but irresistible, which smashed flat-sided across the other's neck, shoulder and chest, and literally lifted him out of his saddle.

Segrave toppled, steel-clad limbs flailing, and crashed to the soft peat with a crunch which drew gasps from all around. He lay still.

After the moment or two of shock, the entire castle precincts rang with shouted acclaim, admiration, and groans. Edward, looking very unsteady, and still obviously twisted with pain, spared no glance at his victim, but raising his sword high towards the Queen, turned his snorting steed and walked it ponderously back to his own base.

Segrave's esquires ran out to the aid of their fallen champion.

"Your realm's credit was safe with your brother, this time, my Lord Robert," Angus Og observed. "It was a notable bout."

"Aye. Edward lacks nothing in courage. And daring. Even skill of sorts. It is judgement he lacks."

"He judged well enough there, did he not?" Elizabeth asked. "I think you are too hard on Edward, Robert."

"Perhaps. Many, I know, think so. Women, in especial! Though some have been known to change their minds!"

"Too hard or not, the Lord Edward will never change," Christina MacRuarie put in. "Men must accept him as he is, I say. And women rejoice—and watch their virtue!"

The Queen considered her. "I think some women may be a match for even Edward Bruce!" she said, smiling a little.

They exchanged appreciative glances.

Presently, Edward himself arrived, shoulder still hunched a little, bare-headed now, but grinning, debonair. In his mid-thirties, he was dark, slenderly built, a much slighter man than was his brother, but tense as a coiled spring. Handsome in a sardonic fashion, he had a roving eye, a wide twisted mouth and a pugnacious jaw. But there was no doubt but that he was a Bruce.

"Bravely done, Edward!" Elizabeth greeted him. "You fought well."

"I fought to win," he told her briefly. "And now I come to claim my reward. From the Queen of these games."

"Far be it from me to withhold it, sir. What do you seek? A white rose? Or a red? A glove? A ring from my finger, perhaps? Or a pearl from my ear?"

"None of these," he declared. "I seek and I crave a kiss. A queen's kiss! And pray it be none too sisterly!" And he cast a fleeting glance at his brother.

"Why, my lord—that you shall have! And with my pleasure!"

He stepped forward, to stoop—even though he grimaced at the pain of it—and planted a smacking kiss full on her lips. Then, his good arm circling her to press her close for another and longer embrace, he drew back—but only for a little, preparatory to a third assault. The Queen's hand went up to take the lobe of his ear between thumb and forefinger, and to nip it hard, so that he yelped—without however any change of her own expression.

"Greedy, sir!" she said. "Would you shame me in front of my liege lord? And yours?"

"If needs be!" he asserted, caressing his ear. "But, save us—I'd prefer to do it more privately! Yours is the choice, woman!"

"Has a husband no say in such matters?" the King asked, but mildly.

"Ask that of the Queen of your realm, brother. Today this Elizabeth is Queen of the Tourney, and not troubled with a husband!"

"I am never troubled with my husband," the woman observed. "My trouble is to see sufficient of him!"

"Were I your husband, you would see sufficient of me, I vow!"

"Too much, perhaps, my brave lord! Like some other ladies say!" That was also a woman's voice, but different, softer, more sibilant.

Edward Bruce's head jerked up, to stare. "You! You here again! The Isleswoman! I' faith—here's a pickle! Christina of Garmoran come back to . . . confront us! What now?"

His brother frowned. "Christina's presence is welcome. As always," he said shortly.

"As always . . .? Ooh, aye!" Edward looked back at Elizabeth assessingly.

"Welcome," she nodded. "The more so, that she will perhaps help to keep such as the Earl of Carrick in their place!"

"Ha . . .!" Edward got no further. A trumpet blast heralded another announcement.

"The most noble the Earl of Hereford, Lord High Constable of England, craves the Queen's leave to speak."

42

Surprised, the occupants of the royal gallery looked at each other. "Bohun! What does *he* want?" Bruce asked. But he nodded to Elizabeth. "We cannot withhold permission to the Constable."

At Elizabeth's wave of acceptance, another voice called. "I, Humphrey de Bohun, Earl of Hereford, do require satisfaction. Robert de Bruce, lately Earl of Carrick, who calls himself King of Scots, did fight and slay my nephew, Sir Humphrey de Bohun, Knight, before the past battle. For the honour of my name and house, I Humphrey do hereby challenge the said Robert to single combat as fought with my kinsman that day."

"A plague on the man—hear that!" Edward exclaimed, into the buzz of comment and astonishment. "A wretched prisoner—challenging the King! Insolent!"

Everywhere the shouts and growls of the Scots showed that they agreed with this judgement.

"Robert—you will not do this?" the Queen asked.

"You are not afraid for me, my dear?"

"Afraid, no. But . . ."

"Your Grace—Sire!" a voice called from some way off. "Allow *me*. That I meet Hereford's challenge." It was Gilbert Hay. "As Constable of Scotland, let me deal with this Englishman."

Bruce frowned. If the other English challenger had presented a problem, how much more did this. Had it been any other than Bohun who made it, there would have been little of difficulty—he would have rejected it out of hand. As King, he could do that without loss of reputation. Indeed, he would have felt almost bound to do so. But the Earl of Hereford was in a special category. As Lord High Constable of England he ranked next to King Edward himself. His capture, fleeing from Bannockburn, must have been a bitter blow indeed. Taken in the field would have been bad enough, but, like his monarch and so many other great lords, he had bolted before the end, and had been pursued and captured as far away as Bothwell, on his flight to England. Now he would be concerned to wipe out that stain. But, more than this, before the battle proper he had seen his nephew cut down in single combat with Bruce, and however much he might have wished to avenge that rash young man there and then, had in fact, despite overwhelming superiority in numbers and arms, withheld—as probably was no less than his duty as a responsible commander. But here too he must have felt his honour to have suffered. Now he required to make a gesture. And Bruce felt some sympathy.

The King waved a negative hand to Hay. "*My* concern," he said.

"You are not going to oblige this presumptuous captive?" Angus Og exclaimed. "You!"

"It is customary at a tourney, when one side has lost a bout, to allow them opportunity to redeem themselves, should they so challenge."

"Aye—but not the King."

"It was I who slew young Humphrey de Bohun. Besides, it was my brother who put down Segrave. Think you Segrave's superior should fight with my brother's junior?"

"And if you fall . . . ?"

"Then Hereford will have proved himself the better man!" Bruce raised his hand. "I accept my lord of Hereford's challenge," he cried. "What weapon does he choose?"

Clear and cold the answer came from below. "You slew my nephew with a battle-axe. So be it. I choose the axe!"

"No!" As clear, ringing, came this denial. "No—I will not have it!" Elizabeth cried, rising from her throne. "I said there will be no killing. As Queen of this tournament, I forbid it! There will be no axes, I say."

Her husband smoothed hand over mouth and chin.

"As Your Majesty wishes," the challenger acceded thinly. "The mace, then. Will that serve?"

Bruce nodded. "The mace, yes." He turned to his wife. "Blunt enough, my dear?"

She bit her lip, saying nothing.

A hand touching her shoulder, and pressing, the King turned and strode off, calling for his armour-bearer, young Sir William Irvine, knighted after Bannockburn.

When at length the monarch rode out into the lists, clad now in splendid armour and with the Lion Rampant vivid scarlet on his yellow surcoat and horse-trappings, it was seen that he had chosen no destrier as mount, but the same grey light garron which he had ridden that day when he had fought Hereford's nephew. It lacked height and weight but its wiry nimbleness and sureness of foot were the assets he coveted today. Men noted the fact. De Bohun, given choice of the vast pool of captured horseflesh, had selected a mighty black charger—which might well have been his own.

Making their bows to the Queen, Bruce looked almost laughably lowly, under-horsed, by comparison, but none there thought to smile, even Edward. The King spoke to Hereford, voice hollow inside his jousting helm.

"My lord—why did you choose the axe? When I am accounted a master with it?"

"For that very reason," the other returned curtly. "And because, with the axe, you killed my nephew."

44

"He died honourably, in fair fight. No call for you to risk your life, proving your house's honour."

"You will allow me, sir, to be custodian of my own honour."

"Aye. But to choose the axe there, means that you meant to kill. Or be killed. And your ransom near paid. Why?"

"Need I account for my actions to you, sir. A rebel?"

"Ha! So it is still the same! You have learned nothing, my lord? The bitter English pride! I am sorry for you . . ."

Abruptly the other wheeled his charger round, and rode back to his base.

However blunt an instrument, the mace required considerable skill for effective use in mounted warfare. Like the axe, it was short in haft, but its knobbly head was heavier, and in consequence, less well-balanced. It was therefore notably short in range and hard on the wrist, and against armour demanded very shrewd placing.

At the trumpet's imperious signal, the two contestants rode at each other, a seemingly ill-matched pair, Bruce having to restrain his lighter mount. Hereford, with superior height, and therefore reach, but a horse which would tire more quickly, was out for a quick decision. He wasted no time on preliminary skirmishing, but drove straight at the other.

Bruce knew that he would be expected to dodge and use his agility. He therefore waited until the other was all but on him; then, as the Earl raised his mace high, ready to smash it down on whichever side his foe decided to veer, he jerked his pony right round in what was almost a full half-circle, under the very nose of the black charger. He achieved it with only bare inches to spare, and went trotting off a yard or so in front of the lumbering destrier whose rider was leaning forward over its neck, flailing furiously but quite ineffectually, the King not even turning his head to look back.

Oddly enough, this manœuvre, which might have looked like the craven shirking of an encounter, did not; rather it gave the impression of cocky and quite insolent confidence.

The great shout of laughter from all around—which was partly what Bruce was playing for—revealed the appreciation of at least a majority of the company.

It was easy to keep just the right distance ahead of the challenger. The King kept it up for just long enough to make it clear that he was in command of the situation. Then, spurring, he cantered away for seventy yards or so, before flinging his beast round once more and sending it headlong towards the other.

This time Hereford was more wary, however angry. He slowed his destrier somewhat, and standing in his stirrups, mace swinging, waited for Bruce to make the move.

The other did not disappoint him now. Straight as an arrow he came, at full canter, almost a gallop. As the distance closed, at that speed it was clear that he could by no means repeat the previous manoeuvre and draw up. Hereford was poised, ready.

The King drove in. At the very last moment he achieved the unexpected in two ways. The first was not so very unusual; he twitched his mount's head so that it bore down on the enemy's left side, not his right, thereby spoiling the reach and stroke of both of them, since the maces were in their right hands. The second was altogether more dramatic; instead of standing, to gain height, he flung himself forward, almost flat along his garron's outstretched neck, and so lying low, half-turned to his left, shield up to take the other's mace-blow.

The Englishman's was a botched stroke, inevitably. He was too high, and his weapon on the wrong side—and in heavy armour a man does not twist and bend with any great suppleness. Only a glancing blow struck the swift-moving shield, and then they were past. Bruce slamming in an unhandy sideways swipe over his horse's ears in the by-going, more as a gesture than anything. It contacted Hereford's leg-armour—but only just.

Again the laughter rose in great waves. This was clowning rather than true jousting, deliberately making a fool of England's High Constable.

If anyone doubted this interpretation of the King's purpose, they did not do so for long. He proceeded to make circles round his less nimble opponent, without ever coming close enough for a blow. Time and again the Earl had almost opportunity to use his superior height and range, and then was denied it. More than once, as the other swept past, he heard Hereford shouting wrathfully within his helm for him to stand and fight like a man.

Even the crowd grew a little tired of this, and offered some positive advice to both contestants.

Bruce had not come into the arena to fight in this way. But the Englishman's arrogant words, his insolent naming of him as a rebel, demanded different treatment from sporting gallantry and knightly behaviour. He fell to be humiliated rather than just defeated.

So Hereford was made angry, resentful, outraged—and tired. Tired as his heavy war-horse was already growing tired. And then, in one of his innumerable darts-in and drawings-off, Bruce did not draw off. Instead he swung round hard in a tight circle, his garron rearing, almost walking on hind hooves, to come down immediately at the rear of the other beast, all but pawing its back. And before either horse or rider could twist round, Bruce rose this time in his stirrups and stretching his fullest reach, smashed down his mace

46

between Hereford's armoured shoulder-blades. The Earl pitched forward, toppled from his seat, and fell in clanking ruin.

Without any of the usual flourishes and bows towards the royal box, or any acknowledgements of the crowd's applause, the King turned and trotted out of the arena.

Armour discarded, with Irvine, he made his way back to the gallery, rather shortly rejecting the plaudits of those he passed. Sir Gilbert Hay came to meet him.

"Let that teach overbearing Englishry to challenge the King of Scots, Sire!" he exclaimed. "Here was pretty fighting."

"That was not fighting, man!" Bruce snapped. "Mummery, play-acting, call it what you will—but it was not fighting. He required a lesson, that is all."

"Nevertheless, it was notably well done."

"You think so? I do not."

Mounting to the royal enclosure, the King paused in his steps. The gallery was a deal more crowded than when he had left it. And markedly quiet, silent. He stared.

A new party had obviously arrived in the interim, dusty and travel-stained, half of them women. All looked towards him, and none spoke.

He recognised his sister Christian. She was older, of course, with grey in her hair—but hadn't they all? She was smiling, and though drably dressed, still looked remarkably unlike a nun despite all her years shut up in an English nunnery.

"Christian!" he cried. "Praises be—here's joy! For a wonder! Welcome! Welcome home." And he started forward.

Her smile fading, and the jerk of her head to one side, gave him pause. He glanced quickly towards where she had indicated. A young woman stood beside Elizabeth, thin, anxious, shrinking almost, great-eyed. Two great tears were trickling down the Queen's cheeks.

"Sweet Christ-God!" Bruce gasped, and stood, for once utterly at a loss.

None there could find words to help the moment past. And Christian and Edward Bruce, at least, were seldom at a loss for words.

It could only be Marjory, his own daughter. His only child. And he had not known her. He had welcomed his sister, but not his child. But . . . how could he have known? He had thought of her always as last he had seen her, a child of eleven. His mind knew that she would have grown up, in eight years; but his inner eye had still looked for the child he knew. Not that he knew her very well. In all her nineteen years he would not have totalled three passed in her

47

company, more was the pity. But this sad, pallid, ravaged and unhealthy-looking young woman—this to be Marjory Bruce, the chubby child he once had discovered to be a poppet . . .

She was gnawing her lip, her huge eyes never leaving his face. Not realising himself how stern was Robert Bruce's face now, in repose, they confronted each other.

It was Elizabeth's open hand, upraised and held out, that saved him.

"Marjory! Marjory, lass!" he cried chokingly, and strode towards her, arms wide.

At the last moment, stumbling, features working sorely, she ran into that embrace, coughing.

"Girl, girl!" he got out, clasping her frail shaking body. "Lassie— my own daughter! Dear God, Marjory—together again! At last. Och, och, lass—all's well now. It's all by with. You are safe. Safe again."

A young-old bedraggled waif, the Princess of Scotland wept on her father's splendid shoulder, wordless.

Elizabeth came to them. Her quiet strength helped them both. They managed to master their painful emotion.

"Here is another you should greet, Robert," Christian said. "Who crowned you once!"

Again Bruce would not have known that the emaciated, raw-boned, hard-faced woman who waited there was Isabel MacDuff, Countess of Buchan, the sonsy girl-wife of his late enemy Buchan, who had played truant to place the gold circlet on his brow at Scone, at his coronation, as was the MacDuff privilege. The years in the cage on Berwick walls had left their indelible mark. Unlike Mary Bruce she had toughened to it, coarsened, become a lean, stringy woman of whipcord and iron, instead of the eager, high-coloured, laughing girl.

As she dipped a stiff curtsy, he raised her up, taking both her hands. "Isa," he jerked. "What can I say? What words are there? To greet you. To welcome you back. What words are there for what lies between us?"

"None, Sire," she answered, level-voiced. "Words are by with. Only deeds will serve now. As ever. Deeds."

He eyed her a little askance, at her tone of voice. "Aye, deeds. It has to be deeds, in the end. It took . . . too long, Isa."

"Aye, But there is still time."

"For what, mean you?"

"Vengeance," she said. "I want vengeance."

"M'mm. To be sure. Some vengeance you have had already, I think . . ."

48

"Not sufficient."

"No. Perhaps not, Isa. But—we have had more to do than just seek vengeance." He turned, gesturing. "At least I have been humbling one of their arrogant lords, their Constable . . ."

"That is not how the English humble their prisoners!" the Countess said thinly.

"No. No—I am sorry." He moved back to his daughter's side. "You will be tired, lass. With your long journey. This is no place for you—a tournament! No place for any of you. Come—we will go in. We are very grand, in Stirling Castle now! Elizabeth, my dear . . . ?"

"I shall stay, Robert. A little longer. Queen it here. Many would be disappointed if we both leave now. Go you. With Marjory. I will come later."

"My thanks." Holding his daughter's arm, he looked at the other returned prisoners, set-faced. "Thomas!" he called. "Where is my lord of Moray? Ah, Thomas—those English lords. The captives. I will not have them near me, now. Hereford and the rest. Send them away. Ransoms paid or no. I would be quit of them. Before I am constrained to use them as they have used these! You understand? Off back to England with them."

"But—much of the money is as yet unpaid, Sire. The return of these *your* captives was but to be Hereford's ransom. The rest . . ."

"Money! Think you I care for their money? Now! Seeing my daughter . . .! Get them away, I say. Before I further stain my honour and do them the mischief they deserve. See to it, my lord."

"Is this the King of Scots' vengeance?" Isabel MacDuff demanded.

"It is the King of Scots' royal command!" he returned. And then, more kindly. "We shall pay our debts otherwise, Isa. Never fear. Come you, now, Marjory . . ."

49

3

THE vast Council Chamber of Stirling Castle, true seat of government of the realm, was fuller than it had been for many a year. It was the first Privy Council that Bruce had held here—the first full Council that he had ever held, many as he had attended, one even in this great hall, summoned by John of Brittany, Edward the First's nephew and Governor of Scotland, to hear, amongst other things, the ghastly details of William Wallace's death at Smithfield, London. A number then present were here again now, and, like the King himself, must have been very much aware of the shadow of that great and noble man whom the Plantagenet had butchered in his insensate hate, and who had contributed so much to make such Council as this possible.

Not all there, however, would have the man Wallace at the backs of their minds. Indeed, not all present were inclined to look upon today's as at all any sort of celebratory occasion; but rather as a making the best of a bad job. For this was the first Council of a united Scotland—and the Scotland which had fought the English for so long had been far from united. Whether it was so now, for that matter, remained to be seen: though the monarch had done all in his power to make it so—more in fact than most of his close associates, of the mass of the people even, deemed either prudent or right. The unity of the kingdom was almost entirely Bruce's own conception; just as the idea of patriotism, the love of Scotland as an entity, a nation, for its own sake, had been almost solely Wallace's. If the ancient realm now stood free, and facing the future with at least a semblance of confidence and unity, it was the work of these two very different men with their differing visions.

It had never been easy, any part of the forging of those visions into reality. And it was not easy now. Since other men, through whom it all fell to be achieved, saw the visions only dimly or not at all. The clash of outlook, temperament, interest and will was unending. The Scots were ever a race of inveterate individualists and hair-splitters. With men such as the Earl of Ross, Sir Alexander Comyn, Alexander MacDougall of Argyll and Sir John Stewart of Menteith—all of whom had fought against Bruce—seated round a table with such as Edward Bruce, the Earl of Lennox, the Lord of the Isles, Sir James Douglas and Sir Neil Campbell, it required a strong hand to control them. But a great deal more than merely a strong hand.

"Do I have it aright?" Angus of the Isles was demanding. "Edward of England, despite his defeat, refuses a treaty of peace on all terms? Or just the terms we offer?"

"On all terms, my lord." Bishop William Lamberton of St. Andrews, Primate of Scotland, had just returned from a brief embassage to London. "He still names us rebels, His Grace an imposter, and will consider no treaty. I did what I could to persuade him, and his Council, but to no purpose. To my sorrow."

"The war, then, goes on?"

"In name, yes. Since they will not make peace."

"Our terms were easy, generous," Lennox said.

"Too generous!" Campbell jerked. "I said we should have invaded England after the battle—not sought to treat. Given them no rest. We had the advantage."

"We still have," the King pointed out, from the head of the long table. "Nothing is lost. But . . . I had hoped that they would have learned their lesson."

"The English never learn," old, blind Bishop Wishart of Glasgow said.

"Any more than do we!"

"What do we do now, then?" Hay the Constable asked.

"Muster to arms—what else?" Edward Bruce declared strongly. "Do what we should have done six weeks ago—invade. In this, at least, I am with the Campbell." He and Sir Neil had never been friends.

"Aye! Aye!" Many there undoubtedly agreed with this course. But some did not. "It is peace we need, not war," Lennox insisted. Essentially a gentle man, it was his misfortune to have been born one of the great Celtic earls of Scotland; and so, willy-nilly, a leader in war. "The English may be too proud to treat with us. But they are nevertheless sore smitten, and cannot be looking for war. Meantime. They need peace. But, I say, *we* need it more!"

"I agree with Malcolm of Lennox," the Earl of Ross, his fellow Celt put in, a huge man, with something of the appearance of an elderly and moulting lion. "Our land is in disorder. We have had enough of fighting."

"Hear who speaks, who fought nothing!" That was Angus Og MacDonald. The Highlands were no more united than were the Lowlands—and Ross and the Isles had been at feud for centuries. "If it is fighting you want, Islesman—I am ready to oblige you, whatever! And gladly . . .!"

"My lords," Bruce intervened patiently. "May I remind you that we are here discussing the English peace treaty. Our terms are rejected. They were honest terms – not hard. Merely that the English should renounce all their false claims of suzerainty over Scotland, assumed by the present king's father. And that they recognise myself as lawful king here. This, in their pride, they will not do. We are still their rebels! So peace is not yet, whatever we may wish. So we plan anew. I seek your advice, my lords. That only."

None there were abashed by any implied reproof, being Scots.

"How does my lord of St. Andrews gauge the English mind in this matter?" Sir James Douglas asked. "The English Council, rather than King Edward? Since they sway him greatly. Is it only pride and spleen? Or do they intend more war?"

Lamberton shrugged wide but bent shoulders. Like so many men there, he was aged before his time, only in his mid-forties but looking a score of years older, his strong features lined and worn. The years of war and captivity had left their marks – and the Church was far from spared.

"Who can tell? With the English. As a people they are assured of their superiority over all others. Nothing will change them. Now they are struck in their pride – which is their weakest part. Galled by their defeat, who knows what they will do."

"But that very defeat! Surely it must give them pause?"

"Pause perhaps – but little more, I fear. If England was governed from York, I'd say we should have peace. But from London . . . !"

"Why say you so?"

"Because the South is too far from Scotland and their warfare. Shielded from war and its pains, the Southrons are the arrogant ones. Their armies are mainly of Northerners, or Welshmen, or mercenaries. With these they will fight to the last! The southern lords are beyond all in pride. And they are rich – we here cannot conceive of their riches. And there are so many of them . . ."

"Here's a sorry tale, i' faith!" Edward broke in. "Must we sit here and bemoan our lot? We, the victors! We beat them, did we not? And shall do so again. Enough of such talk. I say, muster and march!"

"What my lord Bishop says is wise," the King declared, the more sternly in that it was his brother whom he contraverted. "I, who also know the English south, take his meaning. He says, in fact, that the English will not make peace until their southlands suffer. How to make them suffer, then? Here is our problem."

"How can we reach them, Sire? They are safe from us," Douglas said.

"Directly, yes. But there may be other ways."

"What has Your Grace in mind?" the warrior Bishop of Moray asked.

"Not outright war. But enough to make them fear war. And its hurt. To *them*. On more sides than one. The French threat, again. We are still in treaty with France. There is a new king there, now that Philip the Fair is dead. Louis is weak, perhaps, and may not act—but he mislikes Edward of England and grudges him his French possessions. He could be persuaded to threaten, if no more, I think. Across the Channel."

"Little that will serve us!" Angus Og commented. Although one of Bruce's most formidable and valuable supporters, he always required to assert his cherished status as a semi-independent princeling, and frequently chose to do so by way of criticism and by never using the normal honorifics of the other's kingship, to imply fealty.

"Aye, my lord—of itself. But taken with other measures. As, let us say, your own! How far south, on the English coasts, would my Lord of the Isles venture his galleys?"

"Ah—now you talk good sense, Sir King! My wolfhounds will raid right to the Channel, to the Isles of Scilly, if need be. There is naught on the seas to stop them!"

"The English have many stout ships, friend."

"Stout, it may be—but slow. They have no galleys. My galleys are faster than any other ships that sail the seas."

"So be it. You will go teach the proud Southrons what war means! Raiding their coasts. My lord of Ross has galleys also—as I know to my cost! He can serve their east coast, while you the west and south."

The two chiefs glared at each other.

"At the same time, there should be raiding all along the North of England. That is easy. But one fast-moving strong column to drive south. Its flanks and retreat covered by others. To strike fear—nothing more. Deep into the soft Midlands. As far as may be, and return safely. How far, think you, it might win?"

"London!" James Douglas exclaimed, amidst laughter. "*I* will frighten London for you, Sire!"

"Scarce that, Jamie! But, moving fast enough, you could win far, I believe. Well below Yorkshire."

"Far further than that . . ."

There was much spirited agreement now.

But Lennox was doubtful. "This is war, Sire. Will it not but provoke retaliation? It is peace we need, I say, not such prolonging of the war."

"To be sure, my friend. It is for peace I plan this. For permanent

53

peace. Not merely a pause in the fighting. Somehow we must win that peace treaty out of the English—or Scotland will never be able to use her freedom, to gain the benefits of her long struggle. We must make them desire such treaty. I think we shall not do it if *we* do nothing. So we must strike fast now, whilst they are still licking their wounds. Not full invasion. That would cost us too dear. Especially at harvest time. We need this year's harvest indeed. But sufficient to alarm them, down there in their south. How say you, my lord Primate?"

Lamberton, his most trusted friend and councillor, former Chancellor of the realm, raised his brows. "It is worth the trial, Sire."

"You say no more than that?"

"I do not know, Sire. It would have to be done at once. Before representatives could be sent to the French. If there was something else that we might do . . ."

"Ireland," Edward Bruce said shortly. "Threaten them from Ireland, instead of France."

"You mean . . .?"

"I mean use Ireland. The Irish hate their English oppressors near as much as do we. They have risen against the English many times. Always they are doing so. Invade, and they will rise again. Together we shall drive the English into the sea! Then, from the South of Ireland, we shall offer a threat that will make the English tremble in their beds!"

There was much acclaim and support for this bold programme and for the dashing Earl of Carrick. It was not a new idea, of course. Bruce and his associates had often discussed it in the past, as a means of reducing the pressure on Scotland. This was but a fresh aspect of its possibilities.

"That would entail a major campaign, brother," the King objected. "Much time. Many men. Too great an undertaking . . ."

"Not so. Give me but 5,000 men and I will win Ireland for you. And quickly. Our own Galloway, Carrick and Annandale men, and some chivalry. Have the MacDonald put us over the water in his galleys, before he goes raiding."

"I say this is folly, my lord," his nephew Thomas Randolph, Earl of Moray, contended, the most level-headed as well as the most handsome young man in the kingdom. "A new war. Across sea. This would be a mighty adventure. But is that what we would have today? To win Ireland could take years. A sink for men and ships. When we require swift results . . ."

"I tell you—give me but 5,000. Less. And I will have an Irish host facing the South of England in but weeks."

54

"There is sense in this," Angus Og asserted. It was not often that the Lord of the Isles and the Earl of Carrick agreed. "At such invasion, Ulster would rise, you may be sure."

Bruce smoothed hand over mouth. Angus and Edward made a formidable coalition: and the Islesman knew Ireland better than any there, since it was in Ulster that he was apt to earn his living, with his broadswords and galley-fleets hired for the interminable clan wars.

"Ulster is not Ireland," he mentioned. "The south is very different. And it is the south which would count, in this. Besides, brother—you it is who I would look to lead this dash deep down into England." This, in fact, had by no means been the King's intention, for Edward was far too rash a commander to entrust happily with so disciplined a thrust as this must be; but the command would undoubtedly appeal to him—that went without saying—and would probably wean him away from his Irish ambitions.

The other looked thoughtful.

"This we can do, then," the monarch went on. "At no great upset to our realm. The Irish adventure can wait. My brother of Carrick, and Sir James, Lord of Douglas, to make the dash for the south, my Lord of Moray at their backs to guard their flanks and retreat. Sir Gilbert, the High Constable, and Sir Neil Campbell of Lochawe, with Sir Robert Keith, the Marischal, to command more general and shallow raiding into the English North. While the Lord of the Isles, Lord High Admiral, and the Earl of Ross, harry the coasts southwards. Is it agreed?"

"At least it could be noised abroad, in the North of England, that the French are like to invade across the Channel," Lamberton suggested. "No harm in that—and it would add to alarm. Soon reach London's ears."

"When do we ride, Sire?" Douglas asked.

"So soon as we can muster the men."

"Numbers?" Edward jerked.

"For your company? How many do you want? To make a swift, tight, manageable force? Strong, but not too large."

"Six hundred. Well mounted."

"Very well. And you, Thomas?"

"More, Sire. Since I will require to divide, flanks and rear. And hold a corridor secure. Two thousand."

"Yes. As I would have said, myself. So be it."

There was excitement in the great chamber now, men stirring in their seats. Bruce had to call for silence. "My lord Chancellor," he said, "the next business?"

55

At a parliament the Chancellor acted as chairman, with the monarch merely present in a presidential capacity; but a Privy Council was the King's own meeting, and the Chancellor only acted as secretary. Bernard de Linton, Abbot of Arbroath, was young for such an appointment, young even to be an abbot; but he had one of the shrewdest brains in the kingdom, and Bruce had never regretted his choice of him, even though it had offended more senior clerics who coveted the position of first minister. A long-headed, lantern-jawed man, with hair receding and smouldering dark eyes, he sat at the King's left hand.

"My lord of Carrick's claim to be appointed heir to the throne, Your Grace," he said, tonelessly.

The stir round the table now was different, with new elements in it, discomfort, some resentment, as well as tension. All eyes were on the two brothers.

"Ah, yes," the King nodded. "This matter has been raised before. But without decision. You would speak to it, my lord?"

Edward cleared his throat. "You all know the position," he said abruptly. "This rejection of our peace treaty makes it the more urgent. The King is no longer young. He has these bouts of sickness. And war is still our lot. The succession must be assured—and he has only a daughter. The Lady Marjory has now returned to us. We all esteem her well. But she would make no monarch for Scotland—any can see that. This realm requires a king, and a strong king—not a weakly lassie as queen. In peace as in war. None can gainsay that. As next male heir, I say that, for the good of the realm, the succession should be settled on myself. Herewith." He ended as abruptly as he had begun.

"You have heard, my lords. The situation is known to you all. I shall value your advice."

"Your Grace, it is not for us to decide this matter," David, Bishop of Moray objected. "Only a parliament may change the succession. With your royal approval."

"True. But a parliament will need guidance. I believe the next parliament would approve the decision of this Council."

"If, as God forbid, our liege lord was to be taken from us," Lamberton observed, "would not a strong regent serve the Queen and the realm almost as well as a strong king?"

"No!" Edward barked. "There is a world of difference."

"Admittedly, my lord. But that difference need not be to the hurt of the realm. Or to the hurt of an already much-wronged young woman!"

"Aye! Aye!" That evoked considerable agreement.

"She may marry. What then? How would the Queen's husband

esteem a regent over them? There would be factions, divisions, parties. This kingdom is sufficiently divided. I say only a king's strong hand can unite it."

"With all respect to the Earl of Carrick," James Douglas said, "I hold that it is wrong, shameful, even to consider this change. The throne is the Lady Marjory's birthright—unless a son be born to His Grace. What right has any, save God, to take it from her?"

"Well spoken, Sir James!" Hay supported.

"Nevertheless, it could be the kindest course," Sir Alexander Comyn, Sheriff of Inverness, pointed out reasonably, an elderly grave-faced man. "The princess might well be the happier. Would the position of a young and inexperienced queen be so enviable? This kingdom will not be a sure and settled one for many a year. Let us hope King Robert is spared to see it so. But, if not, how would it be for the Lady Marjory? Even with a strong regent. She might thank you to be spared the crown, I think."

Men considered that, thoughtfully.

"Surely, above all, the desires of two persons require to be considered in this," the Earl of Moray put in. "Those of the lady herself, and of His Grace. Lacking that knowledge, how may we decide?" He looked at his other uncle.

Thus appealed to, the King sighed. "It is a hard matter. My personal desires, my love and affection for my daughter, my duty to the realm—all are here at odds. My daughter has suffered terribly. I would now deny her nothing. And yet—could her hand steer this realm? As to her wishes, it is too soon to have put it to her. For my own desire, then I would say—if she marries and bears a son, I would wish that one day he wore my crown."

A murmur of understanding and sympathy greeted that.

"It could be so," Edward took him up. "The Act of Succession passed at a parliament could be so written. Myself as king. The Lady Marjory's son, if such should be, thereafter king."

"And if *you* had a son, brother?" The King did not add the adjective 'lawful', there, as he was tempted to do—for Edward had indeed recently had a son by the Lady Isabella Ross, whom he had omitted to marry. The wronged lady's father's snarling noises from down the table made the point for him, however.

"*My* son would, by decree, take second place to hers."

Many looked at him doubtfully, wondering how likely any of them were to see such a thing happening.

"Let us leave it so, then," the King suggested. "I will ask my daughter her wishes. Consider this matter well, my lords, before the next parliament. Remembering that all must be decided for the best weal of this realm which we have fought so long to free and save." He drew a long breath. "Is there other business, my lord Abbot?"

"Only this of the awards, appointments and grants of lands, following upon the recent victory, Sire. The forfeited lands and positions available for distribution," the Chancellor said. "A long list."

"Ah, yes. Long, indeed. As is only fit and proper, since so many fall to be rewarded. But, happily, it is all set down, is it not? But requires reading over. My will in this matter. Do so, my lord, for this Council's approval—and let us be out of here, this warm summer day . . ."

. . . . .

That evening, in his private quarters of the castle, Bruce broached the matter with his daughter.

"As my only child, lass, you have all along been heir to Scotland's throne," he told her. "Now that you are a woman grown, and home again—how do you esteem it? How do you feel?"

"Feel? I feel no different than ever I have felt, Sire. I pray that I may never have to be queen."

"M'mmm. Why, my dear?"

"You would be . . . dead."

"Aye. But death comes to us all, one day. It may be a long while yet. But, in that day, you should be queen."

"Unless I die before you!"

"Marjory!" Elizabeth protested. "Such a thing to say, at your age! Not yet twenty years. At the beginning of your life."

"Many a time I wished myself dead. In London Tower," the girl said. Hollow-cheeked, pale, she looked a sad creature.

"But that is all past now, my dear. You must try to forget it."

"Yes. I am sorry. But it is not easy. To forget. So long . . ."

"To be sure, lass," her father said. "We know. We will do all in our power to help. But meantime you are heir to Scotland."

"Must I be so? Could it not be . . . another, Sire?"

"Is that your wish? Your considered wish? And . . . must you Sire me, girl? Can you not name me Father?"

"Yes. Yes—I am sorry."

"No, no. But—I would take it more kindly, lass. Now, this of the throne. All it means. Have you thought well on it?"

"I do not know. All that it means. Save that I have no wish to rule a nation."

"What *do* you wish for, Marjory?"

"Only . . . I think . . . to be left . . . in peace."

He sighed, and looked at Elizabeth, who spoke. "How can she

know, Robert? Think you for her. She has been home only two days. If you can name this home. She has had no home, ever. No father, no mother. A captive for eight of her nineteen years. Long years held solitary, confined in London Tower. None permitted to speak with her. Then in a nunnery, alone again. Shut away from the world. If *I* near lost my reason, I, a grown woman, how would she, a child, fare? How can she tell you what she will wish, as heir to the throne?"

"To be sure, yes . . ."

"I had time and enough to think of it, Madam," the girl said. "This I do know—that I have no wish to rule. Is there no other? Must it be I?"

"Aye. Your uncle. Edward would have it, if he could. But yours is the right."

"Let him have it. I want nothing of it."

"It is less simple than that, girl. Edward, I think, would make but a poor king for Scotland. He acts first and thinks after."

"My dear—must we talk of this? Now? As though you were as good as dead!" Elizabeth protested. "You are but forty. Twenty years hence, perhaps, such might be needful. Not now."

"With a realm at war, see you, the succession is important. And we are still at war, more's the pity. Edward demands a decision. The matter will come before the next parliament. It is necessary that I know my mind, in this. And Marjory's."

The great-eyed girl looked from one to the other. "You . . . you could yet have a son, could you not?"

Her father drew a long breath. "That is in God's hands, lass."

Elizabeth spoke quietly. "It is our prayer, Marjory. But it seems less than likely. At my age. When no children came before. I fear that I am . . . barren!" What it cost Ulster's magnificent daughter to make that declaration, Bruce could only guess at.

"Say it not, my dear!" he exclaimed. "One so strong, so fine, so lusty as you! Here is nonsense. We have been parted long. But there is time yet."

"Perhaps. But I think we should not cozen ourselves. The chance of a prince is small. From me."

Her stepdaughter bit her lip. "Then . . . do you mean . . . would you have me . . . to marry? To beget a prince?"

Bruce cleared his throat. "That would be best. Advisable. A blessing for all. But—we would not push you. Into marriage. There is time."

"I do not wish to marry."

"Perhaps not. Yet. But, in time. It is expected. In your position. You know that."

59

"Who?" she demanded, baldly.

"Eh? Save us, Marjory—not so fast! You could have your choice. Of almost any unwed man in this land! Always remembering that he should be of a quality and name to father an heir to the throne. To choose one of lesser estate and fame could cause jealousies, offence, you understand . . ."

"I am not like to choose any," she said.

"You may change your mind, my dear," the Queen observed gently. "Once young men come wooing you!"

"Who would come wooing *me*?"

"Plenty, lass!" her father told her grimly. "But not all for the right reason. To be husband of the reigning queen, father of the king-to-be, many would be ambitious."

Distastefully Marjory Bruce screwed up her features. "I would have none of them. Find another monarch, Sire. Father. I am sorry. If not my Lord of Carrick, some other."

Exasperatedly Bruce gazed at her. "See you, girl—there is more to life, for a king's daughter, than saying you do not want this and you will not have that!"

"I am sorry . . ."

"And for all saints' sake, do not keep saying that you are sorry for everything! You are a Bruce . . .!"

"Robert," Elizabeth intervened, "the hour is late. We are all tired. Another time. This great matter of the succession need not be settled tonight?"

"No. That is true. Time enough . . ."

Later that night, Bruce and Elizabeth lay in each other's arms in the sweet exhaustion of love.

"By the Rude," the man murmured, running a caressing hand over the rich satisfactions of her person, "what ails us that we cannot make a child, sweeting? Between us. Our flesh is as one, if ever man's and woman's was. Is it so much to ask? That we achieve a son? A thing any scullion and kitchen-wench can do, with all the ease in the world! What ails us? When a son would banish so many of our troubles."

"Nothing ails *you*, my dear. That is proven! Other women have not failed you in this respect!" That was true. More than one of the ladies with whom he had consoled his manhood during those long years had produced sons which they proudly proclaimed were the King's.

He shrugged. "Is it that we are not suited, then? Each to each? 'Fore God—I *feel* suited to you, woman! As to none other."

"It is a strange thing. *I* could not feel more truly a woman, and giving."

"Giving, yes. None give as you do. Nor take! Bless you."

"Giving. Taking. But not making!"

"At least, the giving and taking is no burden, no hard task, lass!"

"Ah, no. No! The trying is joy! Joy!"

"Joy, aye. Then, shall we try once more, my love? Try . . . ?"

"With all my heart!"

CHAPTER

4

IT was surely as strange a sight as those quiet, green, south-facing
Cheviot valleys had ever witnessed. As far back as eye could see,
along the narrow winding floor of Upper Redesdale, was a dazzling
mass of colour and stir in the mellow autumn sunlight of an October
early afternoon. The place was in fact packed full of men and horses,
richly caparisoned, armour gleaming, painted shields, heraldic
surcoats and trappings, banners by the hundred. Women too added
to the colour—for although the men greatly predominated, and
mostly wore breastplates of steel or shirts of chain-mail, they were
none of them in full heavy armour. At the head of this so strangely
located and holiday-minded host, facing into the wider reaches
where the Rede suddenly opened out of its hill-bound constrictions
just north of Otterburn, and Lower Redesdale expanded into more
populous territory, was still more colour and brilliance; for here the
King and Queen and almost their entire Court waited and watched,
while an impromptu archery contest proceeded. Bruce was anxious
to encourage archery and bowmanship amongst his people—for it
was an arm in which the Scots had always been weak, and had paid
dearly for their weakness.

If this joining of green valleys was a strange place to be practising
archery, it was a still stranger place to look for the royal Court of
Scotland, fourteen miles into Northumberland, and facing south.
Yet they had been here for a couple of hours already, and the long
column, however vital and active seeming, was stationary.

Bruce himself, like most there, was not wholly preoccupied with
the bows and arrows. His glance was apt to stray away southwards,
down the widening vale ahead, eyes screwed up against the slanting
yellow sunlight. And when he did not see what he wanted there, he
tended to look over to where his daughter sat, drawing grass-stalks
between her fingers. Marjory was never alone; yet somehow she
gave the impression of being alone. Men eddied around her, young
and not so young, the most gallant in the land. She was quietly civil
towards them all, and equally—but that was all. None received
encouragement to linger.

Three months had done much for Marjory Bruce, physically. She
had filled out not a little, the hollow cheeks and bent shoulders were

largely gone. Indeed she was no by no means unattractive. But the great eyes were still anxious, wary, her whole attitude tense, reserved. Men she obviously distrusted; women she kept at a distance. And she still had grievous coughing bouts.

"Walter is attentive," the Queen said, following the direction of her husband's gaze. "Of them all, he is the most . . . determined."

"And gaining little advantage, I fear!"

"Fear? Would you wish Walter success, then?"

"Why not? He is young. Honest. And looks well enough. I think he would be kind. And he is already kin. To you, at least." Walter Stewart was indeed Elizabeth's cousin, his father, James, the previous High Steward, having had to wife the Lady Egidia de Burgh, the Earl of Ulster's sister.

"She shows no fondness for him."

"She shows no fondness for any! Is he ambitious, do you think?"

"To be more than Steward? Who knows. At least he is loyal, and always has been. And of as good blood as any in Scotland." She paused. "Keith, there. The Marischal. What of him? He also dances attendance."

"A sound man," Bruce acknowledged. "Sober. But older. And less illustrious of lineage. And was not always my friend. I would prefer young Walter."

"And Marjory? Which would *she* prefer?"

"Neither, it seems. None, indeed. I fear that if she is to marry, we will have to choose her husband for her. It is strange—the Bruces were ever a lusty race. The Mar blood it must be."

"Or the life she has had to lead. You must bear with her, Robert."

"Aye—but something must be contrived. I had hoped this adventure would have brought her out."

A shout of acclaim indicated that once again Sir Neil Campbell had won the archery by a clear lead; and none was louder in praise than the Lady Mary Bruce—nor more demonstrative in her whole-hearted kiss of approval. Her brother grinned.

"There is how Bruce women are apt to behave! Mary, God be thanked, has made a good recovery." It was certainly scarcely believable that the haggard, gaunt wreck of a woman of three months before could have been restored to this laughing, lively creature. Thin she still was, and was likely to remain; but vigour and the joy of life had returned.

"Mary would compound these last years, I think," Elizabeth said. "Will you let her wed Sir Neil, Robert?"

"To be sure. He is my very good friend. I have given him all

63

Argyll, on the forfeiture of Lame John MacDougall of Lorn. Which makes him a very great lord. And a sound support of the crown in the Highland West. Such match pleases me well."

"I am glad. For they like each other assuredly, and will make a good couple. As, I hope, will Matilda and Sir Hugh. When he is at home!"

The King smiled a little. "Aye—Matilda is a born flirt. Young Hugh will have his hands full with that one. But she is not truly wanton, I think. At the test, she will be true."

"To be sure. And meanwhile, young Menteith makes haste to test!" Hugh Ross was still away with his father and the Lord of the Isles, raiding in their galley fleets the English southern coasts. The Earl of Menteith, not yet of age but the more eager to play the man, was not letting the grass grow.

"No harm in that. My sisters can well look after themselves, the saints be praised!" And he jerked his head towards where Christian, Lady Seton, erstwhile Countess of Mar, held her own court of slightly older men. Christian had always been a woman who needed men about her, and her years of confinement in the nunnery must have taxed her hard. Now she was making up for lost time.

The Queen smiled. "I think, perhaps, it is some of your young men who need the taking care of! Sir Andrew Moray of Bothwell, for instance. How old would you say he was?"

"M'mm. His father, my friend, was slain at Stirling Bridge. That was in 1297—seventeen years ago. That one was a boy of eight, then. That makes him twenty-five. Old enough to know his own mind! And to need no protection from me!"

"Christian is a year older than yourself, is she not? Forty-one!"

"What of it? There is much life in her yet. If only my daughter was as my sisters!"

On the fringe of the Lady Seton's group, a tall, serious but good-looking young man lingered, much junior to the others, the son of a hero, of the man who had done most to bring Bruce and Wallace together. His fascination with the King's elder sister was something of a joke at Court—but there was no doubt that Christian Bruce was not averse to Andrew Moray's attentions.

"And there is Isobel. In Norway. Is she of a like humour?" The eldest of the Bruce family was Queen of Norway.

"The good Lord knows! I have not seen her since I was a laddie. But she was beautiful—I remember that. The best looks of the family. And married very young. I have no doubt but that she sets the Court of Norway by the ears!" He sighed. "I wish that Isabel MacDuff could so find an interest in men. To take her mind off her hurt. She used to be spirited enough."

"Your Christina MacRuarie seems to have taken her under her raven wing! I wonder why?"

The Countess of Buchan, sour-looking, stern, did not so much avoid men as repel them. She had insisted on coming on this expedition, in her search for vengeance, that was all; Bruce would have left her behind, if he decently could, sympathetic as he was towards all that she had suffered in his cause. She was now sitting a little way apart, set-faced, eyes part-hooded, while Christina of Garmoran chatted to her.

"Christina is kind in more ways than one! I thought that you would have learned that, my dear. Clearly she feels for Isabel."

"Do not we all. But she will not be comforted . . ."

Shouts interrupted her, and turned all heads southwards. From the direction of Otterburn, banners, many banners, were showing above a low grassy ridge. More than rivers were joining in Redesdale that day.

As the heads of men and horses appeared, nodding plumes, gleaming lance-points and tossing manes, it could be seen that three great banners dominated all—those of Bruce, Douglas and Moray. The impression was of a triumphant host.

The King, with Lennox and Hay and a few other lords, strode out a little way to meet the newcomers. Cheering arose from both hosts.

James Douglas flung himself down from his horse, armour notwithstanding, and ran to fall on his knees before the monarch. "Sire," he cried, "Greetings! I rejoice to see you. Well met. Your message reached us at Simonburn. Last night. To our great good cheer."

"Aye, Jamie—it is good to have you back. And you, Thomas." His nephew, Moray, was not far behind Douglas. Edward Bruce remained in his saddle, grinning his mocking smile.

"What is this? Another tourney?" he exclaimed. "Have you brought all Scotland to meet us, Robert?"

"Call it a progress, brother. With a purpose. Has all gone well?"

Edward shrugged. "Well enough. It would have gone better had our nephew here not interfered."

"That is scarce fair, my lord!" Douglas protested. "The decision had to be Moray's."

"He was welcome to decide for his own force. Not mine."

"My decision could not but effect both forces, my lord," Moray conceded. "Yet it fell to me to make it. Mine was the responsibility."

"The command was mine . . ."

"My friends—I asked if all had gone well," the King cut in, only a little sharply. "I expected an answer—not a dog-fight!"

"Your Grace's pardon," Douglas hastened to apologise. "It is a foolish bicker, no more. We won as far south as the Humber. Beverley and Holderness, on the east. Richmond on the west. Then my lord of Moray, keeping our rear, sent word that the Yorkshire lords were gathering men in great numbers, that he could not much longer promise to hold our rear secure. He said we must retire."

"Fleeing from shadows!" Edward scoffed. "I would have driven on. Cut my own way back and through, when I was ready. If Moray was so fearful, and must retire. But Douglas, on the east, played his game and turned back. I could not go on . . ."

"And by the Rude—why should you, man? At Beverley you were near 200 miles deep into England. More than half-way to London! Eighty miles further than ever before. That is magnificent, I say. Not a cause for quarrel! That you got so far was a wonder. And I thank you all."

"I would have reached the other Richmond. On the Thames!" Edward declared. "Even without this fine nephew of ours! Scared the Plantagenet out of his catamite's bed! But when Douglas deserted me . . ."

"My lord—you will take that word back!" Sir James cried. "On my oath, you will! I desert none. His Grace told me, before we started—told *you*—that we were to be guided by Randolph, in our rear."

"I was given the authority in this . . ." Moray asserted.

"Not over me, Carrick, by God! You were not . . ."

"Silence!" the King cried, suddenly furious. "All of you. Not another word of this. It is unseemly. In my royal presence, and before all these. My lord Constable. And Sir Robert the Marischal. See that all are marshalled. Ready to move. The two hosts as one. Sir Neil Campbell to command the rearward. See you to it."

"Where go we now, Sire?" Edward demanded, unabashed.

"Down Redesdale to the North Tyne. And we burn Redesdale as we go—in the hope that we need not burn Tynedale."

"You make for Tynedale? With all this company? And intend to spare it? *We* spared nothing that we had time to burn!"

"Perhaps. But Tynedale is an ancient fief of the Scots crown. I go to resume suzerainty over it." He shrugged. "You were not pursued? No? Then, since you are good at burning, brother, will you aid with this business? Redesdale to be a balefire, to warn Northumbria that the King of Scots approaches!"

"As you will . . ."

So, as the royal cavalcade slowly made its colourful way southwards towards the great valley of the North Tyne, it did so down a corridor of fire and billowing smoke, a new and unwelcome experience for the ladies present—save perhaps for the Countess of Buchan who would fain have used a torch herself—however used to it were most of the men. In a belt some two miles wide, every manor and farm, every cot-house and barn and mill, went up in flames; all stacked grain and hay likewise, all cattle, horses and sheep driven off and sent herded back on the road to Scotland, with such booty as was readily transportable. All less mobile stock, pigs, poultry and the like, was slaughtered and added to the flames. The unfortunate inhabitants themselves were not physically maltreated, unless they made actual resistance—which few indeed were unwise enough to attempt. Pathetic parties, groups or families, either fled apace into the hills, left and right, or stood afar off and watched their homes and livelihood devoured. Only churches were spared, and to these many of the refugees flocked, amid lamentations.

The Queen and her ladies had been brought up in a hard school, and did not complain. Indeed, they knew that they would have to put up with this, before they left Stirling. But they did not enjoy it, and were notably silent throughout. Fortunately the wind, from the south-west, blew up the valley, largely carrying the smoke away from them.

"Unhappy Redesdale," Elizabeth said, "that it should lie north of Tynedale, and so be used as warning and example. When any other might have served."

"Aye, it is hard. But there is more than that to it," her husband told her. "Redesdale was paying its tribute. These last two years. To be spared our raiding. Like so many others. But at this last collection, they refused to pay. They fall to be taught another lesson."

"No doubt. But still, I say, poor Redesdale!" She glanced over her shoulder. "Robert—have pity on James Douglas," she urged, low-voiced. "He rides behind, there, a picture of woe. Edward, even Thomas Randolph, can take your strictures and be none the worse. But Sir James is otherwise. And surely he deserves well of you?"

"To be sure. But Jamie ought to know me better. We have been close for ten testing years. I could not berate my brother alone, before all. So I needs must seem to blame Douglas and Moray equally with him. They know that. But likewise, Jamie should have known not to persist with that bicker, as he did."

"He was so anxious to tell you all. How well they had done, how far they had won. And then, this!"

"Aye, Well . . ." Bruce half-turned in his saddle. "My Lord of Douglas to ride with the Queen and myself," he called clearly.

Eagerly the younger man spurred up. "I am sorry, Sire," he

burst out. "It was ill done. I forgot myself. Your pardon, of a mercy! I shamefully forgot myself."

"The fault was scarcely yours, Jamie. But you know, better than most, that I cannot too openly chastise the second man in the kingdom, seem to take sides against my own brother. Even when it is clear that he is in the wrong. As here. Think no more of it. My sorrow that I had to speak as I did. When I so greatly esteem what you all achieved. You did very well. Better than I could have hoped. At what cost? In men, Jamie?"

"Very little, praise be. Scarce any, indeed. We fought no single battle, nor even a major skirmish. The English seem to have lost all spirit, since Bannockburn. A hundred will flee from two or three Scots. The terror of us went before us, melting the sinews of men. We burned so many towns that we lost all count. Their castles we could not spare time to assail; but manors we laid waste by the hundred. Most left abandoned before us. Surely we taught the English a sufficient lesson."

"Let us hope so. If it will but persuade King Edward to sign a peace treaty. Somehow he must be forced to it, if we are ever to build the Scotland we should have, the Scotland we have bought so dearly." The King shook his head. "That is why I make this progress to the Tyne. Something more that Edward Plantagenet cannot ignore. I go to assert my ancient overlordship over Tynedale. No King of England could accept that, I think, and still face his people. Either he must fight on again, or come to terms. And he is in no state to resume the war. Not for some time." Bruce paused. "These Yorkshire lords that Moray feared? How great a force did they assemble? And do they follow on, northwards?"

"They mustered a great host, yes. Many thousands. But of no great quality, and lacking in spirit. They did not attack us, either before or after we turned back—although our scouts told us that we passed within a few miles of their camp. They followed on after, but at a careful distance. How far, we could not tell, for our rearward lost touch with them. They are no danger, Sire—that I am certain."

"Good. I would prefer no battle with the ladies present . . ."

Lower Redesdale converged on the wider vale of the North Tyne near Bellingham, some ten miles down. Here, that evening, opposite the hamlet of Redesmouth, the Scots halted for the night, leaving a wide trail of complete devastation behind them. But no burning and ravage went on into Tynedale. Instead, many splendidly attired heralds and couriers, well escorted, were sent out, east and west, to make summons and proclamations.

The tented camp Bruce set up was deliberately magnificent,

rivalling the tourney-ground cantonments of Stirling, with multi-hued pavilions, silken awnings, heraldic banners, and colours everywhere. In contrast to the grim business of burning and spoliation, a picnic and holiday atmosphere now prevailed, with feasting, music, even dancing on the greensward. Nevertheless pickets maintained a sharp watch around a wide perimeter—to the occasional discomfiture of sundry highly-placed love-makers and philanderers.

The King was in no hurry to move off, next day, to give his heralds—and the stern warning of burned Redesdale—time to make their maximum and widespread impact. It was noon before they started, and now a large company of mounted musicians led the way, dispensing sweet melodies. High officers of state, bishops and senior clergy, even three of the newly-arrived foreign ambassadors, from France, Norway and Hainault, came next, before the royal party, all clad in their most brilliant. The solid ranks of armour and men-at-arms kept well to the rear. The sun failed to shine, unfortunately, but at least it did not rain.

Five leisurely miles brought them to Wark, now only a village but formerly a place of some size and importance, chief messuage-place and administrative centre of one once-mighty Lordship and Honour of Tynedale. Here Bruce left most of the baggage and a substantial number of men, to erect a more permanent camp in the level and readily defendable haugh between the Wark and Dean Burns and the River North Tyne. Here they would return.

Another seven miles or so, by Chipchase, Simonburn, Humshaugh and Chollerford, brought them to Hexham, at the junction of the North and South Tyne. They met with no opposition—and if their reception by the country-folk was scarcely rapturous, at least some people did peer from windows and doorways and pend-mouths. Tynedale waited, tense, watchful—but it did wait.

At the famous and ancient ecclesiastical town of Hexham-on-Tyne, dominated by its great Priory, larger than many a proud abbey, it was Robert Bruce's turn to wait, outside the massive walls, while the Prior was summoned with the keys. It was not much more than a year since Bruce had last been here, and in a different mood, and Master Robert de Whelpington came in fear and trembling. But he was greeted genially.

"A good day to you, my lord Prior. I hope that I see you well? And your Priory and town prosperous?"

The cleric, a stocky, red-faced man, young for so eminent an office, swallowed. "Aye, Majesty. Or . . . no, Majesty," he stammered. "Not . . . not prosperous. No. Not that. In these hard times. We are poor. Much impoverished . . ."

Bruce, glancing over the other's rich clothing and beringed fingers, smiled. "Come, come, Master Whelpington! Surely you mistake? This is one of the richest foundations in the North of England. Unless . . . unless you are so sore hit by raising and equipping your steward and the men you sent to fight against me at Bannockburn! And paying their ransoms thereafter!"

The Prior positively gobbled. "No, no, Sire—not so! It was not me. It was my Lord Percy. My lord of Northumberland. He it was. He insisted that we provide a troop of men. Under his banner. He is a hard man . . ."

"I know Henry Percy passing well, Sir Prior. But also I know your Priory's banner and livery! I hold that banner, sir, a Saltire Or on Azure, captured amongst a thousand others. It lies at Stirling still. Perhaps I should have brought it back to you?" He shrugged. "But that is not my concern today. I am here on kindlier business. My herald would inform you, last night? I am come to lift the burden from your shoulders. The burden of Henry Percy and his like! You say that he is a hard man. Then, my friend, you may find me kinder! For I have come to resume this Honour and Lordship of Tynedale into the Scots crown. Percy is no longer your lord. I am. The King of Scots."

The Prior stared, biting his lip. But he risked no words.

"How say you, sir? Is not this good news? A king to protect you, not a robber lord who cares nothing for Holy Church!"

"Ah . . . yes, Sire."

"Is that all you can say, my Lord Prior?"

"No, Sire. I . . . I am overwhelmed. It is too much for me. Give me time, Your Majesty . . ."

"Aye. But only until tomorrow. Tomorrow you, and all Tynedale, shall swear fealty to me. Not here. At Wark, the ancient seat of this lordship. You will see to it. You understand. You and yours. Meanwhile—my lord of Moray, take these keys. I place the town in your charge. See that my lord Prior, the magistrates, and all men of substance, present themselves before my royal presence at Wark by noon tomorrow, to take the oath of fealty. No excuses will be permitted. Bringing their tokens of service and allegiance. Detach sufficient men for this duty, nephew. The Prior will give you all aid. I will not enter Hexham today. When I do, I expect to be received fittingly. Bells ringing, streets garlanded, townfolk out and in their best. Is it understood? Very well. Let us return to Wark, Your Grace, my lords and ladies. We rest there hereafter."

With no further leave-taking of the unhappy Prior, the King led his great company round and back whence they had just come, northwards. He signed to the instrumentalists.

70

"Let us have music . . . " he called.

. . .

Back at Wark, the Scots settled in for a stay of days. The working-party had been busy erecting streets of tents, field-kitchens, horse-lines and watering-points, a tourney-ground, even a temporary market-place—since the existing one in the village was small and inadequate—on the level meadows to the south of the township. For a few days at least, little Wark was to become a worthy capital of the historic and once illustrious Honour and Liberty of Tynedale—in the interests of political strategy.

The Tynedale lordship was important from any point of view. For one thing, it comprised no fewer than thirty-eight manors, many of them rich ones, and included its own royal forest and numerous special and hereditary privileges. Its significance as a Scottish crown holding within the realm of England was self-evident. Alexander the Third, of blessed memory, had almost come to blows with the young King Edward the First over it, in 1277; and, as events turned out, it might have been better had he in fact done so, while he and Scotland were still strong, and his realm united, and Edward was not yet intolerably puffed up with grandeur and successful conquest in France, Wales and Ireland. As it was, to keep the peace and promote good relations, Alexander had consented, against better judgement, to do fealty to Edward for this ancient Scottish crown heritage, inherited from an ancestress, Matilda of Northumberland, wife of David the First and grand-niece of William the Conqueror. Alexander, needless to say, had drawn the line at going in person and kneeling before Edward to take the feudal oath of homage, and had actually sent Robert Bruce, Lord of Annandale, Bruce's grandfather, to do it for him—one of the few weak and unwise acts of a puissant monarch; though it falls to be remembered that Scotland and England were then on excellent neighbourly terms, with no bad blood between them. Edward Plantagenet changed all that. Consumed by his ever-growing lust for power and domination, he used this proxy act of homage for the Tyndale lordship, and other of Alexander's English estates, as excuse for the subsequent claim for overlordship over all Scotland. When Alexander fell to his untimely death over Kinghorn cliff, and his grandchild heiress, the Maid of Norway, died on her way to Scotland to take up her kingdom, Edward declared that he was suzerain of all Scotland, Lord Paramount, since the King of Scots had done homage to him, the King of England. The fact that the homage had been done only for lands in England, and that Alexander had proclaimed that Tynedale was a detached part of Scotland and therefore not a subject for homage anyway, was ignored. Edward used one of the greatest armies in Christendom to back up his claim. Tynedale, then, was one of the basic causes of the long and bloody Wars of Independence.

Bruce now planned to give a different twist to the screw.

That evening was passed in feasting, music and a torchlight and bonfire festival of dance and song, after the Highland fashion that Bruce had learned to appreciate during his campaigns in the North. Sundry of the local folk were constrained to attend, and treated kindly—to their manifest wonder and suspicion. Tynedale, these last twenty years, was more used to being a battleground than a royal playground.

In the morning, happily, the sun shone. All forenoon, while a programme of horse- and foot-racing, wrestling and manly sporting contests proceeded, people kept arriving from all the castles, manors and villages of the lordship, doubtfully, reluctantly, in obedience to the imperious summons of heralds and messengers. All were courteously received by various officers of state, dined and looked after—but none were presented to the King and Queen, however lofty their status. The royal family kept their distance in a special elevated enclosure of silken awnings and banners which crowned a green mote-hill where once the timber castle of Wark had risen.

A carefully-calculated few minutes before noon, the Prior of Hexham arrived, in very different state from his yesterday's appearance. He came in full canonicals, under a resplendent cope, at the head of quite a lengthy procession, with singing choristers and men-at-arms, mounted on a white jennet and with a silken canopy of the Priory colours of blue and gold held over his head by four mounted acolytes. Holy Church had apparently decided that some display was in order.

The Church had dominated Tynedale, of course, since Alexander's day. On King Edward's unilateral assumption of suzerainty over Scotland, he had casually handed over this lordship to Anthony Beck, Bishop of Durham—whom he had promoted to that princely see from being one of his wardrobe clerks. And that bullet-headed militant clerk had naturally used Hexham, the ecclesiastical centre, rather than Wark, to control his new domain, ruling Tynedale through the Priors thereof, and with a rod of iron as he did all else. So, for twenty years, successive monkish incumbents had lorded it in the name of their episcopal master, as well as owning great Church lands of their own—and scarcely gained in local popularity in the process.

At midday exactly, a fanfare of trumpets gained silence for the herald King of Arms, who then called on all present to draw near, in

72

orderly fashion, to the mote-hill, into the presence of the most puissant and mighty prince, by God's grace, Robert, King of Scots. Thereafter, himself proceeding half-way up the grassy mound, he declared:

"Hear me, King of Arms and Grand Seannachie of the realm of Scotland. In the name of His Grace, our liege lord Robert, I do now declare, affirm and pronounce that he, the said Lord Robert, hereby resumes and takes unto himself, this his Honour, Liberty and Lordship of Tynedale, justly and duly by his inheritance, edict and law, to have and to hold for all time coming as a royal patrimony and as an integral part of his realm of Scotland, as did his ancestors before him, and as is duly documented, signed and sealed in the Assize Roll of this the county of Northumberland of the year 1279, and otherwhere, acknowledging the said Lordship of Tynedale to be outside the Kingdom of England and within the Kingdom of Scotland. Moreover, all grants, charters, detachments and privileges in the said Lordship, wrongously and unlawfully given by the Kings of England, Archbishops of York, Bishops of Durham, or any other whatsoever, of late years, are hereby cancelled, withdrawn, nullified; and only those grants, charters and privileges granted by the said gracious Lord Robert, King of Scots, his heirs and successors, shall stand and hold good for all time coming. In token whereof it is required that all occupiers, holders and tenants of lands, office and privileges in the said Honour, Liberty and Lordship of Tynedale do herewith come forward, in due order, and do homage for the same, as is just, lawful and proper, to the said Robert, as liege lord, taking the oath of fealty on their bended knees, renouncing all other. This in the name of Robert, King of Scots. God save the King!"

The flourish of trumpets that followed this peroration was drowned in the great shout of acclaim from thousands of Scots throats—if from few English.

"To present himself first before the King's Grace," the speaker went on, when the noise had abated, "I call upon Sir John de Bellingham, Hereditary Forester of the Royal Forest of Tynedale, to make homage."

After a little initial shuffling and delay, an elderly man came limping forward from the long file of Englishmen, to climb the mound, flanked by two Scots esquires. He bowed before the King, shook his head as though recognising that protest was pointless, and sank down on stiff knees, holding out his hands. He did not once raise his head.

Bruce extended his own hands, palms together, for the other to take within his.

"Repeat the oath of fealty," the King of Arms commanded. "In these words. In the sight of God and all these present, I, John de Bellingham, knight, do acknowledge . . ."

"In the sight of God and all present," the older man mumbled, "I, John de Bellingham acknowledge . . ."

"Speak up, man! Do acknowledge the noble and mighty Robert, King of Scots, to be my liege lord . . ."

"I cannot, Sire!" the Englishman burst out. "I cannot take you as my liege lord. King Edward is my liege, and to him I have sworn my fealty."

"Silence, sirrah!" the herald barked. "Or do you wish to lose your lands and your liberty both ?"

"One moment, my lord King of Arms," Bruce intervened. "Sir John—King Edward of England is indeed your liege lord in matters pertaining to the realm of England. This I do not gainsay. But for the lands you hold in Tynedale, pertaining to the realm of Scotland, *I* am your liege. You are at liberty to refuse fealty therefor; also for the office of Royal Forester of Tynedale, with all its rights and profits. But, if so, you lose the said lands and office forthwith, I promise you. Choose you, my friend."

The other moistened his lips and glanced up at last at the King, swiftly, briefly. He nodded, unspeaking, submitting.

"Proceed, King of Arms," Bruce murmured.

"Do acknowledge Robert King of Scots, to be my liege lord, for the lands of Bellingham and Henshaw, and for the office of Keeper of the said King's Forest of Tynedale, with all its pertinents and profits."

The knight muttered the required words.

"Speak plain, man. And say further—in pursuance of which oath, I do swear to uphold the said King Robert with all my strength against all and any who may hereafter hold contrary interests, so help me God!"

". . . so help me God!" the other ended, unhappily.

"I accept your fair oath of fealty, Sir John, and rely upon your good support hereafter," the monarch acknowledged gravely. "Also I shall require account for your stewardship of my Forest of Tynedale over these years past, and payment of what is mine by right and law. See you to it. You may retire, and hereafter be my guest in the festivities that are to follow. Next, my lord ?"

"I summon Sir Adam de Swinburne, Sheriff of Northumberland," the herald cried.

A big, florid, bull-like man came striding forward, by no means hanging his head. Handsomely clad in velvets and fur, he gave no impression of submission. He drew himself up before the King, and bowed briefly.

74

"I am prepared to offer a limited form of homage for my Tynedale lands, Sir King," he jerked. "As to yourself, as lord of these manors."

"On your knees, fellow!" the King of Arms rasped.

Bruce waited until the other was approximately and awkwardly down on one thick knee.

"It is not for you to offer anything, Sir Adam!" he said. "I *command*. Command fullest fealty and allegiance. If you choose not to yield it—why, I understand you have still large lands outside Tynedale. You may repair to them! And leave Tynedale to others."

"Sire—you would put a noose round my neck, in this! I am King Edward's sheriff of this county."

"Not I, my friend. *I* do not put a noose round any man's neck. You do, of yourself. Yours is the choice."

Swinburne cleared his throat. "Then . . . . I must accept. Under protest, Sire."

"No. *I* do not accept. I accept nothing under protest. You make the full oath freely, or none at all. Nor do I debate further with such as you, sir!"

Wordless, the other held out his open hands for the King's.

"Proceed, my lord King of Arms."

The next to be called up was one Sir William de Ros of Yolton, for the manor of Haltwhistle. A diffident and nervous youngish man, he made no fuss nor protest about the oath-taking, however much he stammered over the words. When he had hurried off, the herald asked whether he would now call the churchman.

"Not the Prior, no. Not yet. Master Whelpington, I think, will be none the worse of a little more waiting!"

Undoubtedly the Prior of Hexham would have expected to be the first to be summoned to the royal presence, however reluctant he might be to make any vows of fealty. The Church's holdings in the lordship were greater than any other, and its senior representative a power to be reckoned with.

A succession of smaller men were called out and made their obeisance and allegiance without demur, as a gabbled formality, only anxious to be back into a safe anonymity. Prior Whelpington fretted under his splendid awning.

At length the King of Arms pronounced his name and style. Frowning, he came forward, still under the canopy, although the acolytes were now, of course, on foot. The King raised a single eyebrow towards the herald, who promptly flicked a dismissive hand, and two of his minions stepped out in the Prior's path and peremptorily ordered the acolytes back. Less assuredly the cleric came on, alone.

"So, my lord Prior," Bruce greeted him, "do you find the sun trying?"

"The sun . . . ?"

"Your canopy. I hope that you may subsist without it, at least while you take your vows of fealty."

"Your Majesty—I pray to be excused. Any taking of vows. It is not right and proper. That I should kneel before you. I am the representative of Holy Church, here in Tynedale. My allegiance is not to an earthly king . . ."

"It is not as representative of Holy Church that I summoned you here, Master Whelpington. It is as holder of large lands in this my lordship."

"But the lands are held by Holy Church, not of myself."

"To be sure. But if Holy Church elects to hold large lands and temporalities, collect rents, extort dues and service, and so to act the temporal lord, then Holy Church must pay the price. You are here to do feudal homage to me, as feudal lord and superior, for lands and privileges which the Church hold of me in feudal tenure. It is simple."

"But, Sire—the Church is different. It is not as these others. It is Christ's own Body. His divine substitute, here on earth."

"I do not recollect hearing that Christ was a holder of great lands and privileges when He was on earth, sir!"

"The Church is in the world, and so must act as in the world. It cannot be otherwise . . ."

"Precisely, Sir Priest! Therefore, in your worldly capacity as Steward of the Church's worldly gear, tenancies and lands, you will do homage for those that stem from my lordship, like every other worldly tenant. Unless, to be sure, you prefer to relinquish them. That course is open to you, and no oath-taking necessary."

The Prior twisted the glistening rings on his fingers. Then he jutted his plump chin, and stared at a point somewhere above the King's head. "I cannot swear fealty to you, Sire," he said in a strained voice. "It is not possible. You are . . . man excommunicate!"

Bruce said nothing for long moments. When he spoke, his voice was level. "You say that? You are bold, at least! Then, if you cannot render what is due to a man excommunicate, neither can you accept from him such lands, titles and tenancies. I must needs withdraw them, therefore, for your sake and mine. And bestow them elsewhere. Others will be glad to have them. My lord King of Arms— how many manors of mine does the Priory of Hexham hold in fee? Not Church lands, but manors of which I am the superior?"

"Nine, Your Grace. Nine entire manors, besides rights of pasture, turf-cutting, millage, water and the like, over much other land."

"Aye. Then we shall find new vassals for all such, on the resignation of the Prior of Hexham. Let it be so proclaimed."

"No, Sire—no!" Whelpington cried. "I do not resign them. I cannot!"

"If you are not prepared to make fealty for them, you must." Bruce was suddenly stern, patience exhausted. "But enough of this, sirrah. It is not my habit to debate with vassals! You have my royal permission to retire."

"Majesty—of a mercy! Not that. I will do homage. Whatever you say." He plumped down on his knees. "My lord Bishop—and the Archbishop—they would be wrath. Exceedingly. If the lands were lost. I would be dismissed. Let me take the oath . . ."

"Very well, my lord Prior. I will overlook your ill-spoken words. On this occasion. But not again. Say on."

Not waiting for the herald's prompting, the cleric launched into the fealty formula, clutching the King's hand between sweating palms.

The entire distasteful business over, Bruce rose, wiping his hands. He turned to his wife and daughter who had sat throughout just behind his chair. "So much for the delights and majesty of kingship!" he said wryly. "A huckster, I have something to sell, and must needs drive a hard bargain! Men are scarce at their noblest when chaffering. I hope that you have been entertained, if not elevated?"

"Better this than swordery and bloodshed. Or burning," Elizabeth commented. "Think you this will bring Edward of Carnarvon to the conference table?"

"If it does not, nothing will!" He shrugged. "But that is the worst of it done with, God be praised! Now for better things—the tourney, games, feasting. Be gracious to these English now, my dear—but not too gracious! They must learn who is master here. And tomorrow we will enter Hexham . . ."

77

5

TURNBERRY, in spring, was a fair place, all shouting larks and wheeling seabirds, great skies, spreading sandy machars, blue seas, white waves and magnificent vistas across the Firth to the soaring, jagged mountains of Arran. The castle itself, above the shore, was less daunting than many, a wide-courtyarded place of mellow stone with walls which, because of its low protective cliffs on three sides, did not require such lofty and prison-like masonry as was usual. It was Bruce's birthplace, chief seat of his mother's Carrick earldom, and his memories of it still tended to glow with the light and lustre of boyhood's carefree days—even though there were now apt to be occasional shadows from the grim night of massacre, eight years before, when he had returned here from his Hebridean exile, to make his first bloody assault on an English-held fortress of his mainland realm.

But, this breezy, bright morning of billowy white cloud galleons and the scent of clover, seaweed and raw red earth, the man's thoughts were concerned with the future, not the past, as he picked his way alone down over the rocks, sand-slides and crevices of the shore. It was good to be alone for a little; yet he frowned as he went. Elizabeth said that he frowned too much, these days . . .

He was seeking his daughter Marjory. Elizabeth said that she came down here, to the shore, a lot, to sit, also alone. With any other young woman of her years, status and looks, such withdrawals could be looked upon as far from unnatural—and the parallel absence of one or more young men could be looked for also. Not so with Marjory Bruce. If one thing was sure, it was that his only child *would* be alone, despite the plenitude of escorts who would have jumped at the opportunity to accompany her.

He found her in a hollow of the broken cliff-face, dabbling her feet in a clear rock-pool, and gazing out across the sparkling Clyde estuary to the blue, shadow-slashed mountains. She withdrew and hid her white foot hastily at sight of her father. Bruce shook his head at that automatic, almost guilty gesture, but restrained his tongue.

"I used to know every inch of this shore," he told her, casually. "I played here, as a boy. And found it a deal more kindly kingdom than that I now cherish!"

"Yes," she said.

He sat down near her, and began to loosen his boots. "A pool, replenished by the tide, is a world in itself, is it not? A different order, of time, strength, beauty. A starfish for king! These winkles, in their shells, for knights and lairds in their castles. Clinging little limpets who cleave to their patch of stone, for the humble folk—for it is all they have. Scurrying, fearful creatures that hide in the waving forests of weed. Hunters or hunted? All conforming to some laws and order we know not of. Until some uncaring, heedless god puts in his great foot—so! And all seems changed. For a moment. And only seems so. For all is everlastingly the same." And he dabbled his own bare foot in the cold water.

She did not comment, nor ventured her own foot back again.

"Each creature's world is, in the end, what he makes of it," he went on. "The heavy feet of fate disturb the surface, yes. But underneath, the inner life is our own. To make or to mar. I have marred much of mine. Shamefully, terribly marred. But I have made something, also."

"Yes."

"You, lass, esteem this world but little, I think? And would make your own? Withdraw from the one, into the other. Is it not so?"

The inclination of her head was barely perceptible.

"That is well enough. As an escape, a refuge. But not as a world to live in, my dear. We must live in the world into which we were born. And make what of it we may."

"What are you seeking to tell me?" she asked then, level-voiced. "That I must do better? That I must laugh and sing and dance? That I must find all men a joy and a delight? And all women, too?"

"Scarce that, lass. I would but have you to understand that your life can still be full and rich. Rich, for you. That although you have suffered grievously, that time is past. You are young, and have most of your life to come. You can still make much of it. Being my daughter is not all trial and sorrow. You can have . . . almost anything that you ask for. Anything you may wish."

The look she turned briefly on him, then, shocked him.

He bit his lip. "Marjory—I know that, for my sake—or because you were my daughter—you suffered intolerable things. Were for years shut up, alone, first in that Tower of London, then in a nunnery. Kept alone, spoken to by none. God knows I do not, cannot, forget this. Part of the price I paid for this kingdom! But . . . you must seek to put the ill past from you. As I seek to do. As the Queen seeks to do. And your aunts. I have much to put behind me, sweet Christ! I, who murdered a man at Christ's own altar. Who have condemned three brothers, by my actions, to death most shameful—three brothers, and friends innumerable. The guilt of it comes to me, often. In the night, especially. But, see you, I do not, must not, dwell on it. *You* have no guilt; the guilt is mine. But the weight of woe is ever with you. You must put it from you, lass—I say, you must!"

Marjory only shook her head. "You do not understand," she whispered.

"Then tell me. Tell me, your father."

Helplessly she spread her hands. "How can I? It is not possible." Her eyelids drooped. "I wish that I had died. In the Tower. Almost I did. They wished that I would. As did I. But I did not die. It would have been better . . ."

"Dear God, girl—never say it! Not that."

"Why not? When I think it, know it. What is wrong with death?"

Almost he groaned, as helplessly he looked at her. "What . . . what have they done to you?" he said.

She made no answer.

Bruce fought down the rising tide of anger, frustration, apprehension. Determinedly he steadied his voice. "See you, daughter—I ask you to turn your mind to this matter. This matter of the realm. Of today's parliament. It is necessary that we speak of it. Now. I have tried to speak with you on it, so many times. But you would not. The succession. Today it will be decided. You are listening? Today's parliament must decide the matter."

"Is it not already decided?" she returned listlessly. "My Uncle Edward is to have the succession, is he not?"

"It is less simple than that, Marjory. Edward desires it, yes. And I hear must have it. Many will support him. But he will not make a good king. He is rash, headstrong—and his very rashness poses a further problem. For he is unmarried, and has no heir—however many bastards! He is, indeed, more like to die a sudden death than I am! The wonder is he has not already done so! Leaving none to succeed him. The succession could scarce be in worse hands."

She shook her head, as though deliberately disassociating herself from responsibility.

"Any Act of Succession, therefore, by parliament, must declare a second destination. Should the first heir to the throne die without lawful issue. It must, can only, be yourself, Marjory. After Edward. Whether you wish it or no. There is none other."

"What are you telling me, Sire?"

That word sire rankled. Bruce frowned. "This, girl. That the throne's succession is of the greatest importance for the realm. A continuing succession. If it is to be saved from internal war and misery, and the evils of rival factions fighting for the crown. It is my

80

duty, as monarch, to ensure that succession to the best of my ability."

"Yes."

"Therefore, Marjory, since it seems that you will make no move in the matter, I intend to announce to this afternoon's parliament at Ayr that it is my decision to give your hand in marriage to Walter Stewart, High Steward of Scotland. And that, failing other heir of my own body, the succession, after Edward, shall devolve upon you, my daughter, and thereafter on any issue from such marriage." Robert Bruce did not realise how sternly, almost harshly, he had made that difficult pronouncement.

The young woman, after an initial catch of breath, made no comment whatsoever.

"You hear? Walter Stewart."

"Yes."

"Save us—have you nothing to say, girl? When your husband is named for you?"

"Only that I guessed it would be he."

"You did? How so?"

"From the way you spoke to him, these last months. Looked at him. Left us together."

"So! And what have you to say? Of Walter Stewart?"

"As well he, as other."

"Of a mercy! Is that all?"

"What would you have me to say?"

"At least, how he seems to you as a man, a husband. He is handsome, well-mannered—but no pretty boy. Younger than you, but able with a sword, sits a horse well, can wrestle. He is a great noble, with large lands, head of one of the most illustrious houses in my kingdom."

"Yes. So you would have him for your good-son. Have his child heir your throne."

"No! Or . . . i' faith, girl—you are sore to deal with! It is necessary that you wed. You know that. You could have your choice of any in the realm. But you would not. Would choose none. So I must needs choose for you. Walter Stewart asked for your hand. I know none better. Do you?"

"I have said, as well he as other. What more do you want from me? I shall obey you."

"From my daughter, my only child, I look for more than obedience."

"Your only child born in wedlock," she corrected.

His brows shot up. "Ha—does that gall you, then?"

"You must wish that it had been otherwise. That one or other of these had been my mother's child. And I had been born bastard. It would have spared us both much."

He stared at her nonplussed, at a loss. "I never wished you other than very well," he said. "As a child, I found you . . . a joy."

"When you *saw* me, came near me."

"I was fighting, girl! Fighting for this kingdom. For eighteen years I have been fighting."

"Yes," she nodded. "You have your kingdom."

Sighing, he began to pull on his boots. "I have my kingdom," he agreed heavily. He stood up. "Was I wrong to believe that I could have my daughter also?" When she made no response, he went on, "I go back to the castle. It is a dozen miles to Ayr, and we leave at noon. Do you attend the parliament?"

She shook her head. "Only if you command it."

"I command nothing of you, lass."

"Save that I marry. And produce you an heir."

He spread his hands in token of resignation, or possibly defeat, and left her sitting there.

. . .

The Ayr parliament of April 1315 had much to discuss besides the question of the succession. Foremost came the peace offensive, the great endeavour to bring the English to negotiate a firm and lasting peace, not just another temporary truce in this unending warfare; and part and parcel thereof, their recognition of Bruce's kingship and the essential and complete independence of his kingdom. This was elementary, basic to all settlement; yet strangely, though the English claim to overlordship, suzerainty, was only some twenty years old, and the product of one man's megalomania, this was the stumbling block holding up all agreement – despite Edward the Second's hatred for his late father and all his works.

But before this vital issue, there was a symbolic item to be staged, a mere ceremony but significant of much, in the Great Hall of Ayr Castle, the same slightly smoke-blackened hall, built by the English invaders, where once William Wallace had hanged the fatly obscene nude body of the sheriff, Arnulf, and his two chief henchmen, before burning all. This afternoon, Abbot Bernard of Arbroath, in his capacity of Chancellor of the realm and chairman of the assembly, after bowing to the King and opening the proceedings, called the name and style of the most noble Sir Patrick Cospatrick, 9th Earl of Dunbar and March.

There was a hush, as everywhere men eyed the side door which opened to reveal the slender, darkly handsome person of a proud-featured middle-aged man, splendidly attired. Looking neither right nor left, this newcomer strode firmly down the long aisle between the ranks of Scotland's great ones, unhesitant, straight for the dais, which he mounted, to bow before the throne.

"Your Grace, my lord Robert, I, Patrick of Dunbar, humbly crave leave to make my due homage to yourself as liege lord," he announced in clear, almost ringing tones.

Bruce, in his gorgeous scarlet and gold Lion Rampant tabard, permitted himself just the glimmer of a smile. There was nothing humble about the voice or attitude, nor in the level glance of those dark arrogant eyes. Nevertheless he inclined his head, graciously, as though well satisfied. "Welcome to my Court, Cousin," he said.

The fact of the matter was that this represented victory, undeniable victory. This man, perhaps the greatest in power of all Scotland's thirteen earls, and second only to the absent Fife in seniority, had been the most unswervingly of all on the English side. Which was scarcely to be wondered at, since his lands, such as were not in Northumberland and further south, were all in the Merse, the East Borders, in Berwickshire and Lothian, areas which had been wholly and consistently in English occupation, almost defenceless against invasion. This man's father, dying five years before, had fought boldly with the English on every major battlefield of the wars, from the very first, that of Dunbar itself. And the son it was who had aided Edward the Second to escape James Douglas and his other pursuers after Bannockburn by providing a boat to take him from Dunbar to Bamburgh. Now this confirmed Anglophile had decided that it was time to change sides. Nothing could more plainly underline the fact that he believed that Bruce's hold on Scotland was secure.

Taking the King's hands in his, the Earl repeated the oath of fealty as forthrightly as he had done all else. Bruce nodded.

"Your homage I receive gladly, Cousin," he said. "We shall let the past be past, for our mutual weal. And that of this realm. Your lands and estates are herewith returned to you." This was said more loudly than the rest, and was aimed at the ears of those who believed still that the King was over-kind and gentle to traitors. For Patrick of Dunbar could still indeed have represented much danger to Bruce's throne.

This was not only for geographical and strategic reasons, important as these were. It was what was in the Earl's veins that represented the greater menace. For his line was royal, descending directly—more directly than Bruce's own—from the ancient Celtic monarchs. The first of the line had been Malcolm, a grandson of Malcolm the Second, and the brother of Duncan the First whom MacBeth had murdered. The descent had been from father to son since then. Moreover, this same first Malcolm had married a grand-daughter of Ethelred, King of England: while the 4th Earl had wed an illegitimate daughter of King William the Lion. In the great competition for the Scots crown, after the Maid of Norway's death, this man's father was one of the competitors. In the end he had thrown in his weight behind Bruce's grandfather's claim. But the fact remained that here was an alternative line to the Scots throne, which could be used against Bruce and his successors. This oath of fealty, pronounced before an entire parliament, was a major insurance against trouble.

As Dunbar stepped down from the dais and proceeded to the earls' benches, amidst mutterings from sundry present, led by Edward Bruce, the Chancellor raised his voice again.

"The matter of the recent negotiations at York relative to a peace between this realm and that of England. My lord William, Bishop of St. Andrews, who led His Grace's commissioners, to speak."

William Lamberton rose, at the head of the bishops' benches. Last time he had sat in this castle of Ayr, he had been a hunted refugee, dressed in ragged, nondescript style, and hungry, seeking to persuade Robert Bruce to accept the Guardianship along with John Comyn. His great gaunt frame had a permanent stoop to it now.

"My lord Chancellor, we have little good to report. After the raids deep into England, and His Grace's resumption of the Tyne-dale lordship, King Edward was forced to take measures. He appointed Aymer de Valence, Earl of Pembroke, to be governor of all the North of England, between Trent and Tweed, wielding viceregal power and authority—a thing unprecedented in England while the monarch is himself in the country. But Pembroke, although a hard man and an able soldier, found both lords and people in no mood for fight. Or, let us say, in no mood to fight the Scots, since they were scarce loth to fight amongst themselves. Indeed, defeat in the field, at Bannockburn, and weak leadership, has brought the English to do what they have ever mocked the Scots for doing—fighting each other instead of the enemy! There was, and is, near to civil war in the North of England, with large bands, often led by lords and knights, harrying the land. Some even claim that they do so in the name of the King of Scots!"

There was some laughter and acclaim at this picture of their enemy's discomfiture, but Lamberton held up his hand sternly. "If this is of no credit to the English, nor is it of any benefit to us," he declared. "It but creates confusion, and distracts King Edward from the true issue—coming to terms with His Grace. He did go so far as to agree to talk with us. At York. On the subject of a peace. His Grace sent four commissioners, myself honoured to be one. We went to York, to treat with the English commissioners. And did so treat. For weeks. With little result. The English would not concede our terms. Even the most modest."

"How modest, my lord Bishop, were your terms?" the Earl of Dunbar and March asked, not aggressively but not diffidently either. Obviously he was going to be no cypher in the realm's affairs.

"Questions may be asked only through myself, my lord," Abbot Bernard reminded, but not objectionably.

"Entirely modest," Lamberton answered. "We demanded the recognition of this realm of Scotland as the independent kingdom which it always was; and that our Lord Robert was our lawful and rightful king. And, secondly, that the English troops be withdrawn from Berwick-on-Tweed, the only Scots fortress they still hold. This, and assurances of no further interference in the affairs of our realm. Sundry other small matters, but these were the main requirements. None can say that they are not modest. We could demand nothing less. Yet it is these that King Edward will not accept. The independence of Scotland, and the suzerainty of King Robert. He still claims to be Lord Paramount of Scotland, as did his father. Despite all. Despite defeat, raids, and His Grace's homage-taking in Tynedale."

"Then we must teach him otherwise!" Edward Bruce cried. "I have said all along that we were too gentle, too soft. The English understand only one argument—force. Naked steel. Show them that, and they will bargain. If I had but been allowed to drive on to London, last June . . .!"

There was a growl of approval from many throats.

"My lord Bishop—have you finished?" the Chancellor asked.

Lamberton nodded. "Save only to say that though we talked for weeks, we could move them nothing, in this. King Robert is a rebel, they said. The English have an arrogant assumption of authority that is beyond all debate. I do believe that they conceive it God-given! Certain subjects are not for discussion. One is that the Scots are an inferior people. As are the Welsh and the Irish. They cannot be other than subject. Possibly the French also. Save that there are more Frenchmen!" That the stern and statesmanlike Lamberton spoke so, was eloquent testimony of his frustration and helplessness.

Sir Neil Campbell, who with the Earl of Lennox and Bishop Balmyle of Dunblane had been Lamberton's fellow-commissioners, stood up. "My lord Chancellor," he said, "it is my belief that we but waste our time seeking this treaty of peace. The English have no

85

intention of making such. And even if they signed some form of words, it would not be worth the paper on which it was written. They lick their wounds, yes—but only that they may be able to strike back. It is not peace they seek. One of their lords, at York, told me that, now that the former King John Baliol is dead, in France, King Edward is cherishing his son. In London. The English king, who hated the father, has taken the son into his personal care. For what purpose, think you?"

Bruce was struck anew by the sad change in his old friend and companion-in-arms—who was now his brother-in-law, having recently married the Princess Mary. Campbell, although still on the right side of forty, had grown thin and hollow-cheeked of late, a man fading before their eyes. Wags put it down to marriage with the over-sexed Mary—but Bruce knew that it had started even before Bannockburn. One of his original band, the King grieved for him sorely; also for his sister, who had surely suffered enough.

Lennox spoke up, amidst the exclamations at this revelation. "My good friend, the Lord of Lochawe, takes too gloomy a view, I say. This of Edward Baliol could be only a bargaining gesture. To win better terms by the threat. Such as we ourselves make, with the raids and the Tynedale progress. The English are sore troubled. They have lost much faith in themselves. All that has been done—the expedition of my lord of Carrick, the raids on their coasts of my lords of Ross and of the Isles, Your Grace's move in Tynedale—all this has indeed struck them hard. They are, perhaps, nearer to yielding than we think. Pembroke himself confided to me, at York, that King Edward scarce knew where to turn, he has so many problems. And he is unpopular with his people. He is blamed for the defeat at Bannockburn—although I think the fault was more Hereford's and Pembroke's own. I say, let us have patience. Keep up our present tactics. King Edward may be nearer breaking than we know."

"Patience!" Edward Bruce burst out, from almost the next seat on the earls' benches. "There speaks folly! Patience! Do nothing! And give the English time to recover. That way, we will have to fight another Bannockburn before long. By being patient! Campbell, for once, was right!" These two had never been friends. "Patience is no way to deal with the English. Only force do they heed. The harder you strike them, the more ready they are to talk. So, I say, let us strike them hard. And where they are weakest. In Ireland."

That gained a mixed reception, cheers and objections, both. The King frowned.

"Ireland is where we can do most damage with fewest men," his brother went on. "The Irish chiefs are ready to revolt. They have gallowglasses by the thousand. Properly captained, and with an armoured host of chivalry to lead them, they could drive the English out of Ireland in weeks. Then astride the Irish south, we threaten the *English* south. Across their channel. The Welsh, too, would rise at that stage. They love the English no more than we, or the Irish, do! Give me a few thousand men, and I will win Ireland for you!" Edward looked directly at his brother now.

All others, the Chancellor included, perforce did likewise.

The King took his time. This was serious, he recognised. Edward had long cherished the notion of invading Ireland. But to raise it, like this, in parliament, where he could demand a vote—and quite possibly command a majority from frustrated members—put the project into a different category. He knew that he, Robert Bruce, was against it; therefore Edward must be fairly sure of himself, sure of large support.

"My lord of Carrick's proposal is not new," he said. "It has been discussed many times. And always the decision has been against it. Because it must amount to a major campaign of war. It cannot be otherwise. And we have had more than sufficient of war. It is peace Scotland needs now, not more war."

"The King says that we need peace," Edward took him up promptly. "But my lord Bishop, and these others, tell us that the English will not make peace. Not yet. We must force them to it. We can do that only by making them choose peace rather than war. *I* would say that, while they are in defeat, at odds with each other, licking their wounds as the Campbell says, we should invade them. Invade England with all our power. Not just raids. I say that we could be hammering at the gates of London within a month! And then they would be praying on their knees for peace—their bended knees! But, if that is too great a venture for those of you who are so weary of warfare—then, I declare to you, this Irish venture should commend itself. My royal brother says that it would be a major campaign of war. Yes—but not for the *Scots*. Only for the Irish. All I need is a spearhead. A small force, to give them a lead. Five or six thousand men. Of these, I will take 3,000 of my own. From my Lordship of Galloway and earldom of Carrick. So I ask this parliament for a mere 2,000. To purchase an English peace for you. And, moreover, to make an ally of Ireland instead of an English province."

This was heady stuff, and for the victors of Bannockburn dangerously so. Bruce could sense how a large part of the assembly rose to it.

"Will my lord of Carrick tell us what makes him so sure that the Irish will rise in large numbers?" he asked, evenly. "The English have a strong grip. The Anglo-Irish lords are powerful, and notable fighters. They have had to be! Witness my own good-father, the Earl of Ulster. They will not be so easily broken."

"Ulster and many others are still in England. And the Irish chiefs will rise. O'Neill. O'Connor. O'Brien. Sorley McDonnell. Young MacQuillan. MacSweeney. Forty thousand men are committed, for the start. If we land before May is out. Twice that within two weeks of landing."

There was absolute silence in Ayr Castle hall now, at what Edward had said and what it implied. All eyes turned on the King.

The knuckles gleamed whitely on Bruce's clenched fists as he fought to control his hot temper. For long moments he did not risk words. When he did, they came jerkily, almost breathlessly.

"You . . . have done this! Written to them? These Irish chiefs. Planned a campaign. With them. Gone so far. Won promise of support. Numbers of men. Without . . . without my authority. Without so much as informing me! The King!"

Even Edward Bruce was abashed in some measure by his brother's obvious tight-chained fury. He spread his hands. "Not so, Sire. I but sounded them. Sought opinions as to the chances of success. Made enquiries, as would any prudent man. Before I raised the issue here . . ."

"Prudent man! By the living God . . .!" In his extremity, Bruce gripped the arms of his throne with a force almost enough to wrench them apart. Somehow he managed to master himself. "Continue, my lord."

"Because there had been talk of this before. And no true decision. I deemed it right to make such enquiries. To bring to this parliament. So that you, and others, may judge aright. The worth of it. Surely that is no fault?"

"You named these chiefs as committed. To whom committed?"

His brother hesitated. "To myself. At this present. But to Your Grace, as King. when the matter is settled and the invasion begins."

"So! Meantime, they are committed to you, the Earl of Carrick! But great chiefs such as these do not commit themselves and their thousands to war without prior commitment being made to *them*. For the matter to get thus far, *you* also must be committed. How far?" That was a bark.

"I . . . I have promised to go. With my own force. From Galloway and Carrick. Whatever you do. Before May is out." That admission came in a rush, but forcefully, defiantly, not conceding anything. And then, as the merest afterthought. "With Your Grace's permission."

So it was out. Plain to all men. The King's brother, the second man in the kingdom, entering into secret warlike negotiations with the leaders of a neighbouring realm. It could be called *lèse-majestié*. Even high treason. Or just plain, insolent contempt of any authority other than his own.

Bruce's every impulse was to hit back, to assert his own overriding authority, to show who was master in Scotland, brother or none. But the long hard years of self-discipline, of taking the long view, of thinking for the realm rather than for himself, triumphed. A public break between himself and his brother could do untold damage—especially if indeed many supported Edward's project. Moreover, this was a parliament, not a council, convened to hear the will of the community of the realm rather than that of the monarch. And there was the matter of the succession, which was due to come up hereafter, and which any drastic break with Edward would throw into confusion.

When Bruce spoke, he had himself in hand. "It was not well done, my lord," he said severely. "The secrecy. This of committing yourself, without my knowledge and assent. For whatever reason. This is the King's business, and his only. But . . . since the policy behind it affects the whole realm, I would hear the will of this parliament. How do you say, my lords?"

There was a long pause, with some shuffling of feet. Few there could fail to recognise the awkwardness of the situation; that an expression of approval for the Irish venture could be taken as a gesture against the monarch. Yet obviously, not a few were in fact in favour, even amongst the most loyal.

Well aware of their predicament, Bruce spoke again. "My friends —in a parliament, all should speak their minds. Their true minds. For the weal of the realm. It is your duty to give me guidance. Without fear or favour."

Lamberton rose. "I am against such adventure, Sire," he said. "Ireland could become a bleeding wound in Scotland's side. As it has been in England's. I say no."

From the nods of the six other bishops present, it was clear that the Lords Spiritual as a body were with the Primate.

Edward's snort was eloquent of his contempt for all such.

"I also am against," the Earl of Lennox said.

"As am I," Patrick of Dunbar declared. "The English hold on Ireland is stronger than my lord of Carrick deems it."

"I believe it rash, to the point of foolhardiness," Randolph, Earl of Moray, said.

"That you would!" Edward exclaimed. "All of you!"

There was a shocked hush, at this discourtesy, and the King wondered whether his brother was going to destroy his own case.

89

Then, unexpectedly, and out of due order, Neil Campbell spoke—although, not so much out of order as it seemed perhaps, for Sir Neil was now the King's kinsman by marriage, and moreover had been promised the earldom of Atholl, which was in process of forfeiture, David de Strathbogie being still sufficiently offended over his sister's betrayal to remain in England and in enmity.

"I do not often agree with my lord of Carrick," the Campbell declared. "But here I do. I believe invasion of Ireland will alarm the English more than anything else we may attempt, barring invasion of England itself. Possibly even more so. For the southern English care nothing for what goes on in their North, where we would be fighting. As we have seen. But many southern lords have great lands in Ireland. I say, let my lord of Carrick have his 2,000 men. It will not sorely hurt the realm. And may win us much."

The elderly Earl of Ross, who had seemed to be asleep throughout, suddenly raised his nodding leonine head. "I agree," he said briefly, and let it sink again.

Thus encouraged, others spoke up.

"So I think," Sir Alexander Fraser announced.

"As do I," Sir Robert Fleming nodded.

"It can do no harm," the Lord of Crawford said. "So long as we keep it to small numbers."

"I agree," Malcolm MacGregor, chief of his name, gestured, with the dramatic flourish with which he did all things.

"And I," the veteran Sir Robert Boyd of Noddsdale put in—and Bruce valued his decision more than most.

The King drew a hand over his mouth. These were the fighters, his late colleagues of desperate days, speaking now, men close to him by every bond men can forge between them, the loyalest of the loyal. Many of them, he knew, were no friends of Edward's, however much they might admire him as a brave man and noted leader of light cavalry. Yet they were supporting this Irish venture. Almost involuntarily he glanced across to where James Douglas and Gilbert Hay sat, on the benches of the great officers of state, Warden of the Marches and High Constable respectively. These two, closest of all . . . ?

Jamie was looking unhappy. Seeing his friend and liege lord's gaze, he rose. "I . . . I say against," he jerked, and sat down.

"I also," Gibbie blurted, as briefly.

There were a few more, for and against, after that. But Bruce paid little attention now. He perceived how it was, and accepted that he must change his position. The discomfort on the faces of Douglas and Hay left him in no doubt. These two leal friends, whom he knew loved him beyond all telling, would not for anything on earth seem to take part against him; but he knew that were it not for that, they would have decided for the Irish project. So be it.

"My lords," he said, when there was a pause. "I am grateful for your advice and counsel. Your guidance. It is clear that there is much division on this matter, but that many whose opinion I value greatly do commend the Irish adventure. My lord Chancellor need not, I think, put it to the vote. Unless so my lord of Carrick demands. As is his right. I am agreeable that a limited expedition shall go to Ireland. I will double the numbers that my lord of Carrick raises from his own lands. He shall lead the project, as it seems, he has arranged. But my men, the realm's men, shall be under the command of my nephew, the Earl of Moray, whose ability, most certainly, will be of the utmost benefit to his uncle."

There was a great indrawing of breaths as all considered this. The monarch, Bruce the hero-king, had given in. But only so far. And he had appointed Moray, the level-headed and imperturbable Moray whom Edward hated, perhaps the one man within the kingdom who could cope with his fiery uncle, as watchdog.

Edward glared from his brother to his nephew, gulped, but nodded. "So be it," he repeated. "No vote."

The audible sigh of relief from all around was interrupted by the King himself. "One further matter, before I ask my lord Chancellor to proceed with the business. Five or six thousand men cannot be carried over to Ireland without a large fleet. My lord of Ross, who favours this venture, will no doubt lend his galleys. But that will not serve for half of it. There will be required my lord of the Isles' galley fleet."

That gave all pause—as it was meant to do. Angus Og was not present. On principle, he avoided parliaments, as his attendance might be construed as in some measure admitting that his lordship was a constituent part of Bruce's kingdom, a contradiction of his notional independence. And Angus Og cordially loathed the Earl of Carrick.

Edward looked put out. "Angus of the Isles will not refuse? Will not withhold his galleys?" That was a question rather than one of Edward's confident statements. "He is the Admiral. High Admiral of Scotland. He will do as you say."

"The galleys are his own, not the realm's. And Angus of the Isles is . . . Angus! If he disapproves of this venture . . .!" Bruce did not need to enlarge on that. "But I will speak with him."

The King paused, and all recognised that he remained the master. That he could prevent the expedition from sailing, if he would, without having to order it. He went on.

"There is another matter to be considered. In this. It was next on my lord Chancellor's list for discussion. But it has relevance now. Lame John MacDougall of Lorn, in rebellion, whom King Edward made his Admiral of the Western Sea, to harass us, has returned to the Hebrides. In force. So the Lord of the Isles sends me word. And urges a campaign against him. He by sea, myself by land. MacDougall has a large fleet. Part his own, part English, part Anglo-Irish. I need not tell you what he could do against any invasion fleet for Ireland, carrying thousands of men. Across the Irish Sea."

There was silence now. Even Edward looked thoughtful at the prospect.

"It would be better, then, if we dealt with Lame John first. Before my lord of Carrick's venture."

Edward Bruce was looking anxious. He shook his head. "No," he cried. "It must be in May. That was the agreement. With the chiefs. O'Neill in especial. Before their hay-harvest, he said, when the men return to their crofts. After the end of May it will be too late. I am committed to a May expedition."

"Then, my lord, I say that you should have thought more fully on how you were to carry your thousands to Ireland!" The King had his headstrong brother now. But scoring points off Edward was not Bruce's main concern. It was the maintenance of his own magnificent team of lieutenants and friends in harmony, as one of the most effective fighting units in all Christendom. Much was worth sacrificing for that. He shrugged.

"The safety of my own realm is paramount, and must come first," he went on. "I must deal with John MacDougall. But it may be that this can wait until, let us say, the end of June. I shall speak with the Lord of the Isles. I may be able to persuade him to come here to the South-West, in mid-May, a month from this. With his galleys. To carry the Irish expedition across. And then to return for the assault on MacDougall. This I will seek to do. Is it agreed?"

Heartfelt applause greeted this suggestion, this gesture, from all parts of the hall, so that Edward was constrained to join in. He was aware that he had been in some measure out-manœuvred, made to look slightly foolish, and put in his brother's debt. But at least his project could go ahead.

"My lord Chancellor," the King turned. "My regrets that I have for so long obstructed your place and function. To the next business."

Bernard de Linton bowed. "I declare the matter of the Act of Succession to the Throne, to be decided by this parliament. It has long been His Grace's concern that in the event of his death, without a son, the succession should be secured, in proper fashion, for the due maintenance and good governance of the kingdom. Since Almighty God has seen fit, in His infinite wisdom, to deny His Grace such lawful son, the King has hereby sought to make such provision, and now declares the matter for this parliament's acceptance, or otherwise." He paused.

"Hear, then. It is the King's wish and proposal that, in the event of his own death without a son being born to him in wedlock, his right noble and well-beloved brother Edward, Earl of Carrick and Lord of Galloway, does thereupon succeed to the throne as lawful King of Scots. And should the said Lord Edward die without lawful son, before or after, the said succession shall revert to His Grace the Lord Robert's daughter, the Lady Marjory, and any heirs to her body. Is this accepted and agreed?"

There was a mixed reception and little enthusiasm. Few there, even amongst those who most admired his dash and spirit, considered that Edward would make a satisfactory monarch. Yet the alternative was a spiritless girl who most clearly desired no part in kingship. A regency, to rule, while Marjory reigned, might have been better—except that the regent would have to be Edward, and if he was going to rule, he might as well be the King. And, if there was suggested a triumvirate of regents, say Moray and another, Edward would seek to dominate, inevitably; all the troubles of the old Guardianship days would be renewed. The assembly signified assent, that was all.

The Chancellor nodded. "It is the King's added proposal that in the Act to be drawn up to make this parliament's decision lawful and binding, it should be stated that, if the said Lord Edward, or the said Lady Marjory, should die leaving a male heir who is a minor, in that event the most noble Thomas, Earl of Moray, His Grace's sister's son, should administer the governance of the realm until such heir reached due age. Is this agreed?"

There was more general applause for this.

"Furthermore, and related to this matter, it is His Grace's royal pleasure and satisfaction to make known to his loyal lieges of all Estates here assembled, that he has decided to bestow the hand of his daughter, the said Lady Marjory, upon his leal and true councillor and friend, the noble Lord Walter, High Steward of Scotland. Which match he believes will well serve the realm and well please all those here present."

The shout of acclaim which greeted this announcement proved that belief true, at least. Everywhere men cheered. It had been feared that Marjory would never marry; and Walter Stewart was well liked, of good blood and sufficiently lofty in rank to satisfy all. Or nearly all. The young Earl of Menteith looked glum, as did his

93

uncle, Sir John Stewart. The Earl of Strathearn, though not quite so young, was unmarried and had had his eye on Marjory likewise; he did not look overjoyed. Nor, for that matter, did the Earl of Carrick himself. But such doubtful looks were confined to the earls' benches.

At the King's signal, Walter Stewart rose in his seat amongst the great officers of state, and bowed modestly, flushing a little. It was a notable moment for the House of Stewart.

Eyes rose to search the minstrels' gallery, on this occasion reserved for a few privileged lady spectators, in case the bride-to-be had slipped in to join her stepmother and aunts, there from the beginning. Such searchers were disappointed.

"What have you for us further, my lord Chancellor?" Bruce asked.

"Certain forfeitures, grants and appointments, Your Grace . . ."

The drama was over for the day—and men were only anxious to escape from the over-warm hall to discuss it all. The remainder of the programme was rattled through in record time.

After his formal retiral, the King summoned his brother to a small private room of the castle. There they faced each other alone.

"Edward," Bruce said shortly, "you will now give me such explanation as you may."

"Is any required?" the other demanded, equally brief. "I would have thought the matter sufficiently clear."

"I had hoped, for your sake, that there might be some reason, something I knew not of. To excuse you a little."

"I do not look for excuses," Edward returned. "You should know me better."

"I it was who sought excuses for *you*. For my brother."

"Then spare yourself, my good Robert! And me. I did what I did because it was the only way to force your agreement. To the Irish project. You would not have it, otherwise. I knew it to be the right course. To bring the English to heel. But you would have none of it. So I forced your hand. You will thank me, one day!"

"I do not thank you now. Think you I have not considered this Irish matter as deeply as you have done? And decided against it, with good reason. It is too dangerous. Its success depends on others than ourselves. There lies the greatest danger. That, and maintaining supplies by sea. Remember it. But—you have, as you intended, forced my hand. You have set up your judgement against mine, and acted in secret to enforce it, to constrain me. That is neither the action of a brother, nor yet of a loyal subject."

"Of a mercy, Robert—forget that you are a king, for a moment! Remember that you are just your father's son, as am I—save that

94

you happened to be born first! And *he* was a fool! We are not play-acting now, before your parliament or Court. Have I not as much right to do as I believe to be right, as have you?"

"I would remind you, brother, that you took your oath of fealty to me, as your liege lord."

The other snorted. "I did as much to Edward Plantagenet, once! As did you!"

"So! Loyalty means nothing to you? As brother *or* subject!"

"It means that I shall serve you, and the realm, to the best of my ability and my wits. As I have done. *My* ability. And *my* wits. And, for a while, in Ireland!"

"I see. So now we have it. I marvel that you dare to speak so. To me. Even you, Edward. When I could have you silenced so easily. Clapped in the pit of this castle, to wait until you learned your duty."

"Could—but will not. Will not, Robert! I know you too well. To do that you would require to be a different man from what you are. And a fool, into the bargain—which you are not. For many think more of me than you do!"

"I will not, no. You are right in that. I will let you go to Ireland. But . . . I will never trust you again, Edward. Remember it."

"Have you trusted me, for long? Setting your tame watchdogs on me—Thomas Randolph and the Douglas! Always watching me, holding me back. You have never trusted me, Robert."

"I have ever known you headstrong. Rash. And taken precautions. That is all. As was my duty."

"Duty . . . !"

"Edward—God help Scotland when you are King!"

Laughing suddenly, cheerfully, uninhibitedly, the other clapped his elder brother on the shoulder. "At least I will be a less solemn and sober monarch, man! You will see." And still laughing, he flung out of the little room.

Frowning perplexedly, Bruce stared after him.

It was two months to the day later, and Ayr was the scene of a very different activity, the bustling excitement and noise of an army in embarkation. The entire town was like a disturbed ant-hill of armed men. But like the ant-hill, there was method, order, in the seething and at first glance aimless commotion. Angus Og MacDonald and his captains and clansmen were getting used to embarking armies.

His great galley fleet, one of the most significant weapons in Bruce's armoury, however independent its master claimed to be, covered not only all the harbour and jetty area but also the sand and shingle beaches for half a mile—for galleys were constructed for drawing up on the open strands of their home islands and sea-lochs. In their scores they lay, long lean greyhounds of the sea, high-prowed and high-pooped, low-waisted, banking twenty, forty, sixty oars, single masts with their great angled booms rising like a forest. These were the swiftest, most savage and dangerous ships in the world—and amongst the most comfortless to sail in.

So Edward Bruce's 6,000 had found, nearly a month before, when they had been ferried across the Irish Sea, from Ayr to Larne, in Ulster, in unseasonable weather, with MacDougall of Lorn's craft lurking hull-down to the north, afraid to attack while the Lord of the Isles was there in force. Angus had seen the invaders safely landed and consolidated, indeed win their first small battle against only moderate opposition at Carrickfergus, and then had returned here to Ayr, on the King's business.

The royal army now assembling, despite all the activity, was in fact a modest one, by kingly standards, although hand-picked. Most of the host for the Highland expedition had been gone for two weeks, horsed, by land, around the innumerable sea-lochs and estuaries between the Lowlands and Argyll. Bruce was transporting a bare 1,000 men by sea, and with a special objective.

There had been a great splitting up of forces and captains. As well as Moray, Bruce had sent Sir Robert Boyd, Sir William de Soulis, Sir Hugh Ross, Sir Philip Moubray and others, to back up Randolph as much as to support his brother. At home the Earl of Lennox, Neil Campbell and Alexander Fraser were commanding the main host marching north-west. James Douglas, Keith the Marischal, Robert Fleming and young Scrymgeour were to keep up a series of hit-and-run raids into England, and to collect the mail, or protection money therefrom, which had become an ever more important item of the Scots revenues. William Lamberton and Abbot Bernard would see to the rule and governance of the realm in the interim. While Bruce took his new son-in-law and Gilbert Hay with him in the galleys.

Walter Stewart had been married, three weeks before, to Marjory Bruce, amidst great pomp and ceremony. He was nowise averse, however, to this interruption of the honeymoon period; indeed, his father-in-law feared that he had been positively relieved. The bride showed no signs of distress, either.

They sailed on Midsummer's Day, a stirring sight, the Queen and her ladies waving them off in fine style, into the west. The King did not go in Angus Og's galley, as was usual, but in a command craft of his own. His thousand men were not evenly disposed over the fleet, but concentrated less than comfortably in a mere dozen vessels.

There was grumbling amongst the men at this overcrowding; even some recognition of danger, when the fleet should reach the open sea and the notorious hazards of rounding the Mull of Kintyre. For these galleys had very low freeboards, and moreover were already well filled with their own double crews, with two men to each oar and the spare team required to maintain high speeds and act as boarding crews. The largest were already carrying 250 Islesmen, without passengers – although none of Bruce's dozen craft were of that size.

It was not long, however, before all concerned perceived the reason for this crowding. Off the south tip of Arran, with a freshening breeze and the long Atlantic swell already beginning to make the overloaded craft pitch and roll alarmingly, the fleet split up, and into very unequal squadrons. Angus Og himself, with about thirty ships, continued on course for the open sea, south-westwards now. While the King's galley, with its tail of heavily-laden followers, swung off to starboard in a fully ninety-degree turn, to proceed due northwards up the narrow Kilbrandon Sound, between Arran and the eastern coast of long Kintyre.

Quickly the breakwater effect of Kintyre became apparent, and the ships gained speed and comfort both. The south-west breeze, funnelling round the Mull, now much aided them, bellying out the great single square sails, which each bore the proud undifferenced device of the Black Galley of the Isles. With the long oars sweeping rhythmically, to the squeal of rowlocks, and the gasping, unending chant of the crews, they thrashed up-Sound at a speed fast horses

D
97

would have been unable to maintain, exhilarating, scarcely believable. The smell of sweat was almost overpowering, as strong men purged their bodies with vast exertions after the over-indulgences in the taverns, alehouses and brothels of Ayr.

By evening they had left Arran behind and were into the lower reaches of Loch Fyne, one of the longest sea-lochs in all Scotland. It probed for forty miles deep into the mountainous heart of Argyll. But the King's squadron was not going so far; not half-way in fact, to where, a mere dozen miles up, a small side-loch opened off to the west—East Loch Tarbert.

In June it is never really dark in Scotland, and the galleys drove on through the half-light confidently, even in these narrow, skerry-strewn waters. Before dawn they turned into the side loch.

It was only a mile long, and at its head was a settlement where a new stone castle was being built—Bruce's own, the result of an understanding with Angus of the Isles, who was also Lord of Kintyre. Below these unfinished walls the galleys moored.

But there was no rest for the crews or passengers. Immediately all were set to felling trees, in which the area was rich, choosing straight pines. Oatmeal and water, laced with strong Highland spirits, served for breakfast, eaten as men laboured.

By early forenoon all was ready. The logs, trimmed and smoothed, were in position on the shingle beach. Long ropes were run out from the first two ships, and hundreds of men attached themselves thereto, like trace-horses. Crews waded chest-deep into the water to push. Then the King's trumpeter blew a long blast that set the echoes resounding through the enclosing hills.

As more than a thousand men took up the strain, and heaved mightily, the two vessels began to move forward, up out of the water like leviathans. Under the tall thrusting prows teams pushed the round logs to act as rollers, a team to each log, positioning them, guiding them beneath the keels, catching them as they came out below the sterns, and then picking them up and hurrying to the bows again. The galleys moved up the slope, heavily, but went on moving. Bruce led the way, encouraging the long lines of haulers, taking a hand frequently at the ropes himself.

He had remembered what the chief of MacGregor had told him, long ago when he was a hunted fugitive, how from time immemorial the proud Clan Alpine had been wont to drag their chiefly galleys across that other *tairbeart*, the narrow isthmus of land between Loch Long and Loch Lomond, from sea-water to fresh; and how King Hakon's son-in-law Magnus, King of Man, had heard of the device over fifty years ago, before the Battle of Largs, and had surprised the Scots by appearing without warning in the Clyde estuary, from the Hebridean Sea, by crossing this more westerly tarbert. For here also was only a mile-wide isthmus. Just over the intervening low ridge, *West* Loch Tarbert struck inland for ten miles from the Sound of Jura and the Western Sea.

The ascent was stiff for such heavy loads, and taxed all the muscle and determination. Then Bruce realised that, as so often of a summer morning, there was an onshore wind. This, sweeping down Loch Fyne's cold-water surface, blew on to the warmer land here from an easterly direction. Hurrying back to the leading galley, he yelled to the few men still on board to raise the great sail. It was worth trying, and could do no harm.

The moment that the sail began to open, the effect was felt by every man pulling and pushing. The wind seemed to take half the weight off the vessel. Speed increased dramatically. Quickly the other craft hoisted sail likewise. Everywhere men laughed and cheered, however breathlessly. Here would be a tale to tell, a great song to sing, something to twit Angus Og with—how the Lowland king sailed from Loch Fyne to Jura Sound!

They did not in fact sail all the way; for once the crest of the ridge was passed, the east wind died away, and any breeze there was came from the west. However, it was now downhill and easier going. In little more than two hours after leaving the East Loch, the first two vessels were dipping their forefeet into the West.

There was no triumphant pause in the men's Herculean exertions. Without delay, all but a few turned back, to repeat their performance.

They improved on their methods, their route and their expertise, but it was early evening nevertheless before all the galleys were safely into the West Loch, with men exhausted and tempers frayed. The King himself had been seeking to hide his fretfulness for hours. It had all taken longer than he had anticipated, and he was working within narrow time limits.

Whenever the last keel was in the water, and despite the grousing of tired and hungry men, he gave the order to sail. Down the long narrow loch they sped, in line astern, through the low Knapdale hills, into the eye of the westering sun.

In ten miles the wide waters of the Sound of Jura opened before them, ablaze with the sunset. Only a few miles ahead, to port, lay the small isle of Gigha, with beyond it all the long unbroken line made by the great islands of Jura and Islay, purple against the evening light.

Walter Stewart, who did not know the Hebrides well, standing beside the King on the high poop of the foremost galley, stared. "A goodly sight, Sire," he said. "Fair. But . . . where is John of Lorn?"

Bruce pointed southwards. "Between us and Angus Og, I think!"

he said. "It is my prayer that he will learn the fact before long. And too late!"

MacDougall was, in fact, using the narrow seas of the Sound of Jura as a fortress area, guarding his own territory of Nether Lorn. It was ideally suited for this purpose, skilfully used. A great funnel fifty miles long, a dozen miles wide at its base between Kintyre and Islay, it narrowed in to a mere couple of miles between the Craignish peninsula and the northern tip of Jura. By massing his fleet at the southern end, and stretching a boom across the narrows at Craignish, with guard ships, the rebel Lord of Lorn, whose mother was a Comyn, could turn this whole great area into an inland sea; and even though the islands to the west were Angus's, his ships of war could dominate all therein. Only the one alternative water access was available, the narrow gap lying between the north end of Jura and the next island of Scarba. And this was the famous Sound of Corryvrechan, with its menacing whirlpools and tidal cauldrons, better guard than any boom of logs and chains.

Angus Og's information had been that MacDougall was using the Isle of Gigha as headquarters and base. On Gigha, therefore, the King's flotilla bore down.

As they approached the green, rock-bound and fairly low-lying isle, a mere five miles long and a quarter of that wide, all aboard the royal squadron, who were not working the sweeps, stood to arms. There was only the one effective landing-place of Gigha, the small shallow bay of Ardminish two-thirds of the way down the east side, and it could be seen that it was packed with shipping. But experienced eyes quickly discerned in the level beams of the setting sun, that these were not fighting ships, galleys, galleasses, carracks, sloops, but rather supply vessels, transports, shallops, and the like. As might be expected, the fighting force would be at sea, somewhere to the south, facing the threat of Angus Og's fleet.

"We leave this for later, Sire?" Gilbert Hay asked. "Go seek Lame John, while there is yet light?"

"I think not, Gibbie. It will be a clear night, never truly dark. John MacDougall can wait a little yet. I told Angus to give me until dawn tomorrow. Then to do as he would, lacking us. We will take this island, behind MacDougall. Give our force a taste of fight, to rouse and inspirit them. And these ships anchored there—we might put some of them to use. Aye—we will assault Gigha."

It was eloquent of the sense of complete security of whoever commanded on the island that no alarm was taken at their approach, no postures of defence made. Bruce had ordered his own galleys' sails to be furled, so that the black device painted thereon would not be visible from land, and they drove on under oars only. No doubt they would seem to be no more than a detachment of MacDougall's fleet returning to port for some reason. At any rate, as they beat round the little headland of Arminish Point, wary of the skerries, the twelve galleys encountered no sort of opposition. The newcomers were drawing in alongside the craft already ranked there, and armed men in their hundreds pouring over the side, before anybody on Gigha realised that there was an emergency.

As an armed assault the occupation of Gigha was laughable; but as a strategic exercise it could hardly have been more successful, or more speedy. There was a little fighting, but of so sporadic and minor a nature as scarcely to be worth the title. A few men were slain and some seriously injured, admittedly—but such casualties were mainly the work of angry islanders themselves, MacDonalds—for this was of course one more of Angus's many territories—who had suffered much at the hands of the invaders and were not slow to take this opportunity for revenge. Bruce had to clamp down swift and stern discipline, to prevent a general massacre. Nearly all the prisoners were English sailors and their Irish women campfollowers. He left a small garrison under Sir Donald Campbell, Sir Neil's brother, and sailed away before the islanders or his own people could organise the inevitable celebration. As it was, a lot of strong liquor came aboard the squadron with the returning warriors. They were not quite so cramped for space now, for Bruce ordered the addition of a number of the captured ships to their strength temporarily. There were murmurs at this, for these were slow non-fighting vessels, which could only be a weakening influence. But the King was adamant.

It was nearly midnight, and they drove southwards over a smooth, quiet translucent sea which looked like beaten pewter. Visibility was good for that hour, but provided little definition beyond a mile or so.

Bruce had few doubts as to where to look for John MacDougall. Just a few miles ahead, beyond the islet of Cara, the coast of Islay, to the west, became much littered with a host of outlying reefs, rocks and skerries, south of Ardmore Point; and thereafter swung away westwards towards the Oa, vastly widening the mouth of the funnel-shaped inland sea. The line for MacDougall's fleet to hold was obviously one stretched between these Islay skerries and Glencardoch Point on Kintyre. Patrolling a ten-mile belt, his vessels could act as an almost impassable barrier, giving each other mutual cover and support. Angus Og was bold, and probably had slightly the larger fleet; but he would be rash indeed to try to break through such a barrier head-on. He might succeed, but hardly without heavy losses; and even so would be apt to find not a few of his craft trapped thereafter in the Sounds of Gigha and Jura, facing unknown odds. Hence Bruce's manœuvre.

Sure enough, look-outs from two or three leading vessels shouted almost simultaneously their sighting of ships ahead. The long low craft did not stand out very clearly against an uncertain horizon, and they were probably not more than two miles off.

"Many of them, Sir King," the MacDonald shipmaster of Bruce's galley reported, from some way up the mast-stay. "A great host of ships. Sails furled, mostly. Beating to and fro. But, if we can see them, they can see us better. The light is behind us."

That was true. Sunset in these latitudes is almost due north at midsummer, and it is the northern sky which remains lightest until sunrise. Bruce's squadron would probably have been visible to MacDougall for some time, and would inevitably be causing major astonishment and speculation.

"Aye. Then let us give them something to fret over. Trumpets to sound the signals for line abreast. And for the torches to be lit."

And so the trumpets neighed shrilly out over the summer sea, and their martial notes could not fail to be heard by the patrolling fleet. As the King's vessels moved up into a long line, red flame blossomed aboard each, as the pine-branch torches, contrived from selected material from the tree-trimming operations at East Loch Tarbert, were set alight.

Quickly the entire scene was transformed. The night, from being one of quiet luminous peace, became angry with the crimson murky flame of smoking pitch-pine. Hundreds of the torches flared, and stained sea and sky.

Bruce's reason for bringing along nearly a score of the anchored vessels from Ardminish Bay was now clear. He had almost trebled the size of his fleet, and this would be all too evident from the enemy's standpoint. Yet the half-light would prevent it from being apparent that these were not fighting ships. John MacDougall could not be other than a very alarmed man.

Bruce kept the trumpets blaring, a martial challenging din, as they drove down upon the patrolling squadrons on a two-mile-wide front.

Then the pinpoints of red light began to break out far to the south. One or two, wide-scattered, quickly multiplied into scores, winking, flickering, growing. Cheers rose from the King's ships. Angus Og was there, and responding.

MacDougall of Lorn was no craven; but nor had he the rash, headlong gallantry of, say, Edward Bruce. And his role here, any-way, was to harry the Scots' flanks, to seek to prevent major opera-tions against England, not to fight pitched battles against odds. He could not know whose was this northern fleet; but clearly it was in league with Angus of the Isles. He had to accept that his present position was untenable, and took steps to alter it.

He had not much room for manœuvre. The very strength of his former situation, in the narrows, was now its weakness. He had three choices. Either he sought to break through to the south, or to the north; or else tried to escape to the west, into the open Hebridean Sea.

That he chose the third was hardly to be wondered at. Angus's power he knew, and feared. What threatened from the north was a mystery—and therefore the more alarming. An escape round the west of Islay would give him the freedom of wide waters, and the possibility of communicating with his base of Gigha, from the north.

Bruce was far from blind to these alternatives. He himself would probably have chosen as did MacDougall, in similar circumstances—especially as the loom of the great island of Islay would provide a dark background against which shipping would not be readily visible.

The King was ready, therefore, for the first signs of a sustained westerly movement amongst the ships ahead. Swiftly he sent orders to his fast galleys to swing out of line to starboard at fullest speed, west by south, torches doused.

It became a race, a race which the King could not really win, clearly, since many of MacDougall's ships were already to the west of his own. Some inevitably would escape; but he might trap much of the centre and east of the enemy line.

The breeze was south-westerly, and of no use to either side. It was now a case of sheer muscle and determination, the oars lashing the water in a disciplined frenzy of urgent rhythm, the panting refrain abandoned now for the clanging beat of broadsword on metal-studded targe, faster and faster. Each galley surged ahead in a cloud of spray raised by its scores of oars.

Soon it was evident that at least some of Angus Og's ships were on the same mission, on an intercepting course. The three groups, or rather lines, of galleys, approximated to an arrowhead formation with an extra long point.

Inevitably, it was a short race, of only three or four miles, and for the last of them the leading ships were within hailing distance of each other—near enough for Bruce to try to pick out flags and banners, the sail devices being meantime hidden. There seemed to be two or three of the fleeing line wearing flags of various shapes and sizes.

"Which will be MacDougall's own?" the King demanded of his shipmaster.

"Who knows? Angus Og flies always a long whip-pennant at his masthead. But Ian Bacach . . . ?"

"He will be proud to be the English king's Admiral of the West," Gilbert Hay suggested. "He will likely fly a large flag of that traitorous office, as well as his own banner of Lorn."

"Aye, you are right. Two large flags . . ."

The trouble was that there seemed to be two vessels wearing two large flags each, sailing close together. Perhaps King Edward appointed a deputy admiral to keep an eye on MacDougall? It would be typical English practice.

There was not much time for any decision. Ardmore Point of Islay looked very close, half-right, and the profusion of skerries and reefs would be closer still. Details were hard to distinguish in the half-light. Any action would have to be taken quickly now.

"Cut in between those two," the King jerked. "Can we do it? A last spurring of speed. Are they able? The rowers?"

"Clan Donald are always able! Most of all against MacDougall. Murtach – the pipes!"

So, with the bagpipes screaming and sobbing their high challenge and the oarsmen miraculously redoubling their huge efforts – aided undoubtedly by the High Steward of Scotland who went along the benches with a great flagon of the islanders' whisky, proffering each open, gasping mouth a swallow – the King's galley swung to port and hurled itself across the intervening quarter-mile of sea, at a steepening angle, to head in between the two fleeing beflagged craft in a burst of speed that had to be experienced to be believed.

Now it was possible to distinguish banners. Both ships ahead flew the Leopards of England; but, while that in front also flew a blue and white device of three boars' heads, two and one, the second flew also the emblem of a galley, not unlike Angus Og's own. Only this galley was on gold, not silver, and with dragon heads at stern and prow, and a cross at the masthead. It was the Galley of Lorn. The similarity was not so strange; for Clan Donald and Clan Dougall were descended from brothers, Ranald and Dougall, sons of the mighty Somerled. The fact made their descendants only the more bitter rivals, especially as Dougall had been the elder brother.

There was no need for Bruce's command to turn in. The MacDonald skipper was already steering a collision course, and every man not at the oars, save those who had grabbed grapnels and ropes, had swords, dirks, or axes in hand. The piper, Murtach, blew his lustiest.

The oarsmen on both vessels were equally expert. They kept up their deep driving strokes until the very last moment, when another second's delay would have meant rending chaos, the snapping of long shafts, men broken as well as oars. Up in the air the inner teams of each raised the sweeps, in a rippling progress. Then the two galleys crashed together.

Instants before that even, the grapnels were flying, with their snaking cables to warp the craft securely. Men were leaping, from the moment of impact.

Walter Stewart was one of the first over the side, sword held high.

Bruce touched Hay's arm. "After him, Gibbie. See that he comes to no harm. He is keen—but I do not want to lose a good-son so soon!"

The King himself waited, however contrary to inclination. Indeed, when at length he leapt, battle-axe in hand, he was one of the last to leave the galley. But he was able to jump straight on to the other vessel's high poop, from his own. And it was on that poop that John MacDougall was likely to be found.

This manœuvre, although logical, had its own danger. For it ensured that the King stepped almost alone into the thick of the enemy leadership. Sir William Irvine, Bruce's armour-bearer, who never left his master's shoulder during active service, was close behind; but nearly all the others had already gone.

In consequence, Bruce found himself hotly engaged from the moment of jumping. Many of the poop's former occupants had already leapt down into the well of the ship to help repel the mass of the boarders; but half a dozen or so, of chiefly or knightly rank, extra to the shipmaster and helmsman, still remained. These, with one accord, hurled themselves on the royal intruder with eager swords.

Robert Bruce had fought on a galley poop before, and knew its hazards and limitations. Indeed it was on such a constricted, crowded, lofty and slippery platform that he had first made the acquaintance of Christina MacRuarie, amidst flashing steel. He had chosen the battle-axe now, deliberately—and he was a renowned master of that difficult weapon. Irvine, behind him, and lacking the experience, bore the conventional sword—and quickly learned his error.

In the confused mêlée which immediately followed, three swordsmen vied with each other to strike down the King—and thereby got not a little into each other's way. Two others circled, to get behind Bruce, and these Irvine made shift to deal with.

Bruce's shield jerked up to take the first clanging sword stroke. The second, a sideways swipe, he drove down and away with a blow of the axe. The third, impeded by the other two, was off-true and slightly short, merely scraping the King's chain-mail and achieving nothing. Seeing his opportunity, with the three men bunched together and for the moment off guard, Bruce hurled himself bodily at them, using shield as battering-ram. He sent them spinning like ninepins, their long swords a handicap now. One crashed all his length, the battle-axe smashed down to fell another, and the third, a knight in full armour, went staggering backwards, retaining his feet on the heaving deck only with difficulty. After him Bruce plunged.

Behind, Will Irvine was discovering the disadvantages of a full-length sword in a confined space. Admittedly his two opponents were similarly handicapped; but even so he had not space to wield the weapon effectively. Bruce's lunge forward had left his back unprotected. Irvine had to keep close. After a couple of abortive thrusts in the general direction of the assailants, he fore-shortened his weapon by grasping it one-third of the way down the blade, and flung himself after his master, turning so that they were approximately back to back. Only just in time. As one sword came jabbing viciously, he beat down on it blindly with all his strength, using his weapon purely as a weight. Both swords clattered to the deck.

The hapless armour-bearer snatched out his dirk, all he had now to face the other two. "Sire! Sire!" he yelled. To give him his due, that was all warning and no cry for help.

Bruce, flinging himself after the staggering knight, had perceived as he did so that, in the limited space of the poop-deck, one of the men dodging aside to avoid the rush did so with a limp. Immediately the King changed direction. Lame John, for a wager!

It was at that moment that Irvine's cry sounded in his ear. Biting off a curse, he whirled round. He recognised the situation in a moment—one man driving in with a sword, another reaching for his dagger, and his armour-bearer swordless. He leapt for the first, leaving the other to Irvine.

The swordsman had to change his target and tactics hurriedly—and such slight hesitation was fatal in face of the Bruce with a battle-axe. The shorter-handled, more adaptable weapon, which was effective as a blunt instrument almost any way it might strike, greatly outclassed in speed and wieldiness the long, heavy sword which had to use point or cutting edge. A quick feint with the axe to the thigh area brought the sword sweeping down in a defensive stroke—and a still quicker and explosive upward jerk drove under the man's sword-arm. Though he was armoured in mail, the fierce impact of it cracked the shoulder-blade above with an audible snap. Limply the arm sagged and the sword fell. Bruce, who saw that one of his earlier toppled foes was now on his feet again, dirk in hand, did not waste more time on the shocked swordsman, only using his shield to give the man a violent if contemptuous push that sent him reeling back, while he swung the axe on the dirker. That unfortunate went down for the second time, and stayed down.

The King turned to find Irvine and his original opponent grappling, seeking to invalidate each other's daggers. He raised his axe once more—then, ever mindful of other men's *amour propre*, desisted. His armour-bearer would not thank him for a rescue in equal combat. Only brief seconds had elapsed, as he swung back on his former objectives.

Four men only remained before him now, clustered around the helmsman—the armoured knight, one who was almost certainly the shipmaster, and the limping individual.

"John MacDougall—submit you!" the King panted. "I, Bruce, demand it."

The Lord of Lorn did not lack courage, but he had been lame from birth and so inhibited from personal armed prowess. He did not fling himself forward, therefore, to contest that challenge, but jerked a word to the others. The knight moved out, but warily. Then the shipmaster, quick as a flash, drew a dirk and flung it, spinning through the air.

It was a wicked, accurate throw, with only two or three yards to cover, and had Bruce not been wearing a chain-mail jerkin he would have been transfixed. As it was, striking him on the chest with considerable force, the weapon's impact made him catch his breathing, and he knew a burning pain. But, axe swinging, he came on. And now he was angry.

Almost casually he brushed aside the less than enthusiastic knight, keeping his eye on the skipper—for a man who could throw one knife could throw another.

"John MacDougall," he cried again, "I am waiting."

There was no reply.

The shipmaster had something else in his hand now. It looked like a spike rather than another dirk. MacDougall also held a sword, but looked not in a posture to use it.

"Lord of Lorn," the King barked, "do you wish to live? Or die? Choose quickly." Seeming to look only at the chief, now but a pace or two in front of him, all his attention was nevertheless concentrated on the shipmaster.

"On my ship, *I* command, Sir King!" the other threw back, in his sibilant West Highland voice, so misleadingly gentle.

Then Irvine was at Bruce's side, and sword in hand again. "Let me deal with this dog!" he gasped.

Even as the shipmaster hesitated between targets, Bruce leapt.

107

It was a violent sideways jump, like the release of a coiled spring. And it was at the captain, not at Lame John, that he leapt. Before the other's arm could adjust to a jabbing instead of a throwing position, the King's axe smashed down. The man dropped like a slaughtered stirk.

The helmsman had a dirk, but seemed doubtful about using it—as who would blame him. Bruce gestured his reddened axe round at the chief.

"You are my prisoner, MacDougall. Yield you!"

For answer, the other made use of his sword, at last, in a savage despairing poke.

Bruce eluded it with ease, and slapped down the flat of the axe on the outstretched sword-arm—which broke like a dead stick. The man squealed with pain.

"Fool!" his monarch told him, breathlessly. "You are fool . . . as well as traitor! I could have slain you. Tell me why . . . I should not . . . even now?"

Nursing his arm, and gritting his teeth, MacDougall found no words.

Walter Stewart came bounding up the poop-steps now, Hay following. "The ship is ours! The ship is ours!" he cried excitedly. "We have them. Have you seen MacDougall?"

His father-in-law smiled. "He is here. I fear that he has hurt himself a little. We must ensure his comfort, now. His close comfort, see you!"

All resistance in this galley was soon over. Bruce took stock of the wider scene. Pairs of ships seemed to be fighting it out over a wide area of water, and in the half-light it was almost impossible to decide which side had the advantage. The only clue was that few vessels seemed now to be heading westwards. Some of the enemy had undoubtedly escaped past Islay. But with the Lord of the Isles' fleet now fully engaged, it seemed improbable that many more would do so. There was no sign of the beflagged galley which had formerly been so close.

"It is enough," the King decided. "Leave the rest to Angus. He would have it so, I swear. Gibbie—find means to send him a message that I have this Lord of Lorn. Walter—have our foolish friend back to our own galley. He is almost the last of my rebels. Will—see that this craft is taken back to Gigha. Find sufficient rowers. And the wounded seen to. I return there, hereafter. Now, Sir Knight—your name? An Englishman, I think . . . ?"

CHAPTER

7

THE sudden and unexpectedly swift collapse of the MacDougall-English naval threat left Bruce, for once in his career, almost at a loose end—and in quite the most beautiful part of his kingdom, in high summer and fine weather. All his affairs elsewhere were under control, in the short term, with his disturbing brother away in Ireland, Douglas keeping the English North on the hop, Lamberton and the other churchmen in firm and effective control of the kingdom's essential governance. There was a certain amount of mopping-up and example-making to be done in the Clan Dougall lands, but there was more than sufficient men to see to that. A unique holiday spirit seemed to develop in Argyll and its adjacent isles. Instead of returning forthwith to Ayr or Stirling, therefore, the King decided to send for Elizabeth and the Court to join him in a Hebridean idyll.

Such an expedition, of course, would take a little while to mount, if he knew anything about womenfolk, and their ideas and priorities. While he waited, Bruce thought up an interim and more personal design. It was only some seventy or eighty miles north from Gigha, as the crow flies, to Moidart and Castle Tioram, beyond the Ardnamurchan peninsula. He felt that perhaps he owed a visit to Christina MacRuarie—owed it to himself, as well as her. So, one early July morning of blue skies, high fleecy clouds and sparkling waters, a single galley flying no banners, royal or otherwise, slipped out of Ardminish Bay northwards up the amethyst, green and azure Sound of Jura. It left behind the High Steward of Scotland, the High Constable of Scotland, and the Lord High Admiral of Scotland, to see to affairs in Argyll. Surely that should be sufficient.

By the narrows of Craignish, boom now removed, the Isles of the Sea, the Ross of Mull and fabled Iona, the ship threaded the colour-stained Hebridean Sea in as joyous and carefree a voyage as this essentially lonely man had ever known. He decided that he must bring Elizabeth to see Iona, and the tombs of his Celtic ancestors, the semi-legendary royal line of which he was the heir. Meantime, he had other business.

On he sailed, by pillared Staffa and the Treshnish Isles, up between long Coll and the Cailleach Point of huge Mull, with the thrusting promontory of Ardnamurchan, the most westerly point of the mainland of the British Isles, seeming to bar the way ahead. Then, beyond its white-fanged snout, with all the spectacular loveliness of the jagged mountains of Rhum, Eigg, Muck and the saw-toothed Black Cuillin of Skye, opening before them, they swung in eastwards to a great bay, lined with silver cockle-shell sands, towards the wooded narrow jaws of Loch Moidart. And there, on a rocky half-tide islet in the green throat of the loch, the mighty Castle Tioram rose, aglow with the westering sun, seat of the MacRuaries, the children of Rory or Roderick, another of great Somerled's sons.

Here the dark and fiery Lady Christina ruled supreme. A dozen of her own galleys and birlinns rode at anchor in the loch.

The King's unheralded arrival created less stir at Castle Tioram than it would have done at most houses. Christina treated it as a perfectly normal development, and with no Court or strangers to consider, behaved towards Bruce as she might have done to a brother—and a younger brother at that. He had spent weeks in this castle when his fortunes were at their lowest ebb, and none were likely to forget.

But after a great meal, with music and saga-telling in the High-land fashion, in the Great Hall, Christina took her guest up to the castle battlements, to watch the blazing spectacle of the sunset over the isle-strewn sea. Eyeing the ever-changing wonder of it, she spoke her mind.

"I think you will not come seeking my bed tonight, Robert," she said. "Not now. Why, then, have you come to Moidart? You do not need men. Nor ships. Nor, I scarce think, counsel. What brings you?"

"Think you I must only come to you needing something, Tina?"

"It is the way of men."

"You think less than highly of us, if you say so."

"I am not a girl, Robert. I was wed at fifteen, near twenty years ago, and widowed three years later. I have had much experience of men."

"You have had much experience of *me*, lass. Yet you still believe I must only come to you in my need?"

"I will tell you that when you tell me why you have come."

"Could I not have come for love of you, Tina?"

"So it *is* my body? My bed?"

"I have not said so. But . . . if I did come knocking at your door— would you accept me? Tonight?"

"Have I ever turned you away, Robert?"

"Not yet."

"Nor would I." She looked at him, in that strange painted light. "Yet you will not come, I think. Now that you have your Elizabeth. I believe I know my Robert Bruce! That is not why you have come."

"No," he admitted. "That is true. Although . . . I am tempted! But, nor is it true that I came seeking your aid, your help."

"Why, then?"

"What I said, woman. I came for love of you," he insisted. "Can you not conceive that a man can see a woman as a friend? Not only desire her body? Even when her body is desirable indeed. I came as a friend, Tina. Is it so strange? You are my very good friend. Have been for long years. Is that not sufficient reason to come visiting you?"

She reached out to touch his arm. "Robert—I believe that you mean it. That you do not cozen me!"

"Why should I cozen you? You, of all women. You, who have cherished me, nursed me, sailed with me, fought with me . . ."

"And lain with you! There is the heart of the matter, Robert. A man and a woman who have lain together can never be . . . just friends. It is not possible."

"You say so? I do not see why not. They but know each other the better. You are no less my friend, Tina, that we have bedded together."

"No less, but more. Different. Otherwise."

"As you will. Whatever you say, I have come to Castle Tioram kindly affectioned. I never might speak with you fairly, at the Court. Speak as now. Alone, for any time. To thank you for how you were kind with Elizabeth. When you could well have been other. For much patience. Understanding. And you not a patient woman, as I know well! So I came. From Gigha. In friendship."

She smiled, now. "Then I thank *you*. From my heart. You are a strange man, Robert Bruce. But you are very welcome to Castle Tioram. Whatsoever your reason for coming. And you keep your own chamber, this night?"

"God aiding me, woman!"

"Oh, and I shall aid you also, never fear! With a locked door, no less!"

He looked a trifle put out. "No need for that. You may trust me, I think. And no need to sound . . . so keen!"

"You would have me temptress, Sire?"

"No-o-o. But you can still be friendly, Tina." It was his turn to reach out a hand. "A chaste kiss now, would harm none . . ."

"I do not give chaste kisses, friend! I am Christina of Garmoran! One way, or the other. Mind it, sirrah!"

"Why are women ever so difficult?" he demanded, of the last rays of the sunset.

"Women are women," she returned. "Not half-creatures. Not Isleswomen, at least! Come you, and I will show you to your lonely chamber."

He grinned. "Elizabeth, I think, would scarce believe this . . .!"

. . .

Five days of hunting, hawking, fishing and sailing at Castle Tioram, and much refreshed—and still his own man—Bruce sailed south again. He would have taken Christina with him, to Gigha, but she declared that it would look a deal better if she appeared, a day or two later, in her own vessel.

In the event, Christina and the Queen arrived at Gigha on the same day. Elizabeth was enchanted with all she saw, falling in love with the Hebrides at first sight. Even Marjory appeared to be less abstracted and withdrawn than usual—although Walter Stewart took credit for that.

Gigha was much too crowded now, and a move was made to Angus Og's "capital" of Finlaggan, on Islay, where, on islands in the freshwater loch of that name, he had a large castle, chapel, hall of assembly, and burial-place. This was the seat of government of the Isles lordship, princedom, or as it still called itself, kingdom—and Angus was at pains to demonstrate to his visitors something of the princely state he still maintained. He called a Council of Sixteen, consisting of four thanes, four Armins or sub-thanes, four great freeholders or lesser lords, and four knights; these, advised and guided by a large number of people whose right it was—judges, seannachies, chiefs, the Bishop of the Isles and seven senior priests, plus numerous hereditary officers such as MacEachern the sword-maker; MacArthur the piper, MacKinnon the bow-maker, and MacPhie the recorder, sat at stone tables round a central flat rock on which sat Angus himself. All this on the not very large Council Island, and in the open air, so that the place was already overcrowded before the distinguished visitors got a foothold. The proceedings were formal and merely ceremonial, a strange admixture of the purely Celtic and the Norse.

Thereafter, however, in his own house, Angus played host in truly princely and utterly ungrudging fashion, almost to the exhaustion of his guests. Every conceivable aspect and speciality of the Hebridean scene was exploited, and day after day of brilliant sunshine and colour was succeeded by night after night of feasting, dancing, music and story-telling. Practically every major island of both the Inner and Outer Hebrides was visited—and under the Lord of the

Isles' protection the holiday-makers were safe from the attentions of even the most notoriously piratical chieftains, like MacNeil of Barra, MacMath of Lochalsh and MacLeod of the Lewes. Iona was the favourite with the ladies; and Staffa, with its caverns and halls like cathedrals of the sea, a close second. So taken was Marjory Bruce with Iona that she insisted on being left on that sacred isle of the sainted Columba, with or without her husband. Certainly it was beautiful, its white sands a dream, and its little abbey a gem; but the King feared that his death-preoccupied daughter was perhaps morbidly concerned with the serried tombs of her royal ancestors— allegedly no less than forty-eight kings of Scotland, eight Norse, six Irish and even an Englishman, Ecgfrid, King of Northumbria, lay here. Nevertheless, at least she had found an interest in something. Walter and she were left to work it out.

Nearly four weeks of this pleasant lotus-eating existence had passed, when one sultry August day the peace of it was shattered. A small fast galley arrived at Islay from the south, an Irish one this time, one of O'Neil's. It brought Thomas Randolph, Earl of Moray.

Moray was an able, clear-headed, unexcitable man, the last to raise hares or scares. That he should have left his command to come all this way was indicative of some major development. Bruce, about to set out on a deer-driving expedition on neighbouring Jura, drew his nephew aside when he had raised him from knee-bent hand-kissing.

"Well?" he demanded.

"Less than well, Sire."

"Is it defeat? Disaster?"

"Not that. Not yet . . ."

"What, then? My brother—is he well?"

"Well, yes. Very well . . ."

"Then why are you here, man?"

"I was sent. The Lord Edward sent me. Commanded me to come."

"You went to Ireland, Thomas, under *my* command. Not Edward's."

"Aye, Sire. But—in Ireland *he* commands. Commands all. He is master there. Much the master. And Your Grace is far away."

Keenly Bruce eyed his nephew. "This is not like you, Thomas," he said. "I sent you, as the one man whom my brother might not over-awe and browbeat. To curb and restrain him, should need be. And I put all but Edward's own levies, from Galloway and Carrick, under your command. Yet you let him send you back?"

Calmly the other nodded. "All true, Sire. But I came not only

113

because my uncle sent me. I came because I believed it best. That you should know what transpires. With the Lord Edward."

"M'mmm. Very well, Thomas. Say on."

"It grieves me, Sire, to speak so, Of my uncle and your brother. To seem the tale-bearer. But I believe the Lord Edward works against your interests, not for them. Always he was headstrong, going his own way. But this is different. Now he seeks power. In Ireland. Rather than to defeat the English. And no longer talks of the threat to the English South. Or of forcing a peace treaty. Now he talks of uniting Ireland."

Bruce, well aware of all the eyes that watched them closely, and the minds that would be wondering, putting their own construction on secret converse and grave faces, mustered a sudden laugh, and slipped an arm around his nephew's shoulder.

"Come, Thomas—you ever were a sober fellow!" he exclaimed, loud enough for many to hear. "Here's little cause for gloom. So it ever was. Come—tell me of the campaigning. How far south you have won . . ." And he linked the arm now through the younger man's, and led him away along Finlaggan's loch shore.

"Your Grace is pleased to laugh," Moray said stiffly. "But there is little laughter in Ireland, I promise you . . . !"

"Tush, man—that was for these others." The King's voice was lowered again. "It will serve our purposes nothing to have men construing trouble. And women turning it into catastrophe. Now—apart from this of Edward, what of the campaign? What of our arms?"

Moray shrugged. "As to soldiering, we have done well enough. But at a price. We have won many battles and lost none. In Ulster at least the Irish have risen well in our cause. O'Neil, O'Connor, MacSweeney are never out of the Lord Edward's presence. We overran the provinces of Antrim, Down, Armagh and Louth, even Kildare and Meath. We defeated many English captains and magnates, and many of the Anglo-Irish lords. But at Dundalk, in Louth, we turned back, instead of pressing on. Back to Ulster to Connor, in Antrim. From whence I came here, on my uncle's command."

"Back to Antrim? Giving up all that you had won in the south? Why?"

"Well may you ask, Sire. As did I! But it was the Lord Edward's decision. And he commands not only his own troops, but all the Irish also. Morever, most of our Scots knights look to him, rather than to me. Even those supposedly under my command."

The King looked thoughtful indeed. "But this is not like Edward," he objected. "Edward was ever for pressing on, not for turning back.

There must have been a reason? You were winning—yet he retreated?"

"There was a reason, yes—but not sufficient. Not sufficient for *me*, let alone my headstrong uncle! There is famine in Ireland, see you. Living off the country is hard indeed. Our men were hungry, our horses weak, many dying. There is disease also. We have lost more men from sickness than from battle. Even so, better to have pressed on—for the famine is less grievous the further south you go, the country ahead less devastated than that we had already fought over. We could have taken Dublin, where the English have much food stored. We were but thirty miles from it, and the English there in panic. Said to be fleeing southwards. But—we turned back."

"And Edward's reason? His proclaimed reason? He must have had one."

"To consolidate Ulster, he said. To make the North a secure base for further drives southward. To gain reinforcements. More men. That is why I am sent here—that, and to get rid of me, I think! To seek more men from Your Grace."

"God's mercy! I told him. Three thousand only I would give him. *Lend* him. Said before parliament. No more. Less than three months past. And now he sends for more? Knowing my mind full well. Yet . . . you say the Irish have risen well? In Ulster, at least. What needs he with more men, then?"

"He uses the Scots as his spearhead. Always. As would any commander. Our men, trained in the long wars against the English. The Irish gallowglasses are brave, good fighters. But they lack discipline, one clan at feud with another. They are less than reliable. And they fight on foot. It is our light cavalry that ever leads. And so suffers most."

"Our losses *have* been heavy, then?"

"Not heavy, as war is reckoned. For what was gained. Half the men you sent are no longer effective. Either from battle, sickness or hunger. Horses worse."

"I see. But, still—you have not given me reason for Edward, of all men, to retire. From Dundalk to Antrim. When he was winning."

"That is why I consented to be sent home, Sire. I believe that the Lord Edward—and O'Neil and O'Connor with him—is winning Ulster for himself. Is more concerned in setting up a government for Ulster than for forcing the English to a treaty. He is summoning all chiefs and landholders, appointing officers and sheriffs, acting viceroy rather than commander."

Bruce shook his head. "*You*, Thomas, I could have conceived might act so. You—but not Edward. So—he now waits, for you to return with more men from me?"

"I do not know if *that* is why he waits, Sire."

"What mean you?"

"Perhaps he does not expect you to send him more men, in truth. Or me to return!"

"Ha! You think that?"

"I do not know. It may be so. Or I may be wrong. Certainly he *wants* more Scots light cavalry. But whether he truly expects it, knowing Your Grace's mind, I know not. Any more than I know his true purpose in Ireland."

For long moments the King was silent. At length, he spoke thoughtfully. "My brother is not a devious man. He ever prefers to act, rather than to plan. I conceive, Thomas, that you may be attributing to him something of your own mind and mettle. Seeing deeper into this than does he. You would not act so without careful intention and purpose. With Edward it could be otherwise. He could be merely gathering strength for a greater, stronger thrust to the south. And making sure of a secure base behind him, in truth."

"It could be. I know it. So I have told myself many times. And yet—somehow, he has changed. He acts the governor, not the commander. For weeks I have been ill at ease. It came to me that I must tell you. I could not tell you all this in a letter. Nor by the lips of any messenger. Even my own lips falter over it. Perhaps I did wrongly to come, Sire—to leave Ireland. But . . ."

"No, Thomas—not wrong. You knew that I trusted you, relied on your judgement. It was right to come to me. But this is *all* a matter of judgement, is it not? Of interpretation. Of one man's mind, by another and very different man."

"Your Grace thinks me in error, then? In my judgement. Such as it is!"

"I do not know. You have been with Edward, close, these last months. Heard him, seen him. But I *know* him better than you do. Have known him since a child, grown up with him. And he has never been . . . devious."

"Save before the Ayr Parliament. When he admitted to secret correspondence with these Irish chiefs."

"True. True. That was not very like Edward, either," Bruce shrugged. "It is difficult. What would you advise that I do, nephew?"

Without hesitation the other answered, "Send me back. With more men. Enough men, under my close command, to ensure that my uncle heeds my voice! With orders, strict orders, for me to prosecute the war southwards. With all speed."

Impulsively the older man clapped the other's shoulder. "I' faith, lad—we may on occasion differ in judgement! But our minds think alike when it comes to strategy! That was my own design. You shall go back. And I shall send with you more men of substance. Lords, committed to *your* support. Now that we have disposed of MacDougall, men and captains are available. So be it, Thomas—you shall return to Ireland with another 2,000 men . . ."

They turned back.

That finished holiday-making for Robert Bruce. In two days, most of his company were on their way southwards, leaving the painted paradise of the Hebrides to its own colourful folk. There was work to do elsewhere.

ELIZABETH DE BURGH stood beside the great bed, rocking the tiny red-faced morsel in her arms as it snuffled and wheezed and whimpered. Softly she crooned to it, her voice alive with the aching longing of the childless woman. But her eyes never left the white, grey-streaked, strained face on the pillow below.

She had stood there for half an hour now, in the tower-room of Turnberry Castle, waiting, a prey to so many and conflicting emotions. The physicians, midwives and other serving-women she had long since banished from the chamber. Only the Queen herself, her stepdaughter and the new-born infant remained in the tapestry-hung, over-heated apartment, with the flickering firelight and the smell of sweat, blood and human extremity.

Marjory Bruce's breathing was quick and shallow, her lips blue, her closed eyelids dark. For long she had lain so, unmoving save for the light uneven breathing. Since the afterbirth indeed. It was nearly three o'clock of a wild March night, and the waves boomed hollowly beneath Turnberry's cliffs, seeming to shake the very castle.

The Queen's patience was inexhaustible, her cradling and whispering continuous.

Without a flicker of warning the heavy eyelids opened and the dark eyes stared up, deep, remote, expressionless, unwinking.

Elizabeth held the baby out, and so that those eyes could see it.

They changed neither in direction nor in their lack of expression. "All is well," the older woman said quietly.

The other closed her eyes again.

There was another long interval, silent save for the muted thunder of the waves, and the creak of the dying log-fire as the embers settled deeper in the glowing ash.

When the girl opened her eyes again, the Queen was still there, and in the same position and attitude. Once more she held out the child.

After a while, and without turning her glance on the infant, the blue lips moved, almost imperceptibly.

Elizabeth leant closer, to hear.

"It is . . . complete?" the faint words whispered. "Sound? No . . . monster?"

"It is a fine boy. Small, but perfect. See. A boy. An heir. And well. You have done so very well, my dear."

There was the tiniest shake of her head.

"It is true. All is well, Marjory. Look—see for yourself."

Still the girl did not look at the child.

"Shall I put him here? Beside you. In your arm?"

"No." That was certain, at least. She turned her head away, and the eyelids closed again.

Elizabeth bit her lip, and sighed, but waited still.

Presently, seemingly out of great depths, the other spoke, her voice little more than a breath. "A boy. He . . . will be . . . glad. As am I. Now . . . I can die . . . in peace."

The older woman gasped, with the shock. "Ah, no, child—no!" she said. "Do not speak so. All is well, now. You will see. You will soon be well again. And so very happy."

There was no least response from the bed.

"Hear me, Marjory," the Queen persisted, strangely uncertain for that assured and beautiful woman. "You should rejoice, not talk of dying. Now that you have something to live for. A child. A man-child." And as an afterthought, "And a husband. This fine boy—he needs his mother."

Silence.

"He is yours. All yours. An heir, yes—but also a part of yourself. To cherish and nurture. To watch grow into a man. To love and guard and guide. A man-child . . ." The older woman's voice broke. "Oh, God!" she said.

She might not have spoken.

The Queen began to pace up and down the room, still holding the baby. Every now and again she came to stare down at the ashen face, so still, so death-like. And each time it was with a stoun at the heart. For here was the shadow of death indeed, called for, besought, and approaching near. Elizabeth de Burgh could feel its chill hand, there in that overwarm chamber.

Her fears were not all fancy, an overwrought imagination born of weariness, distress and the small hours of the morning—just as Marjory Bruce's talk of death was not just the near-hysteria of a young woman new out of the ordeal of childbirth. For it had been a bad birth, a terrible birth, with the child six weeks premature added to a breach presentation. It had gone on for fourteen evil hours, and Marjory, never robust nor inspirited, had screamed and begged for death. Grievously torn and with internal haemorrhage, she had lost a great deal of blood—was probably still bleeding under all the

119

physicians' bindings, for they had been unable to staunch the flow, try as they would. Death was no figure of speech in that apartment. And the girl had no wish to live.

Bruce and Walter Stewart had been sent for immediately after Marjory's fall from the horse which had touched off this emergency. She ought not to have been riding, of course; but she had all her family's stubbornness, and found a horse's saddle one means of attaining the solitariness which she seemed to crave. If anything could be called fortunate about the entire unhappy business, it was that she had been thrown not far from the castle, and her fall seen from a cot-house; otherwise she might well have been dead by now.

The King and her husband, as it happened, were not so very far away as they might have been, since they were soldiering again—besieging Carlisle, some ninety miles away, at the request of James Douglas, who was finding its English garrison a thorn in the flesh for his campaigning over the Border. Carlisle and Berwick were now the only enemy-held fortresses north of Yorkshire. Walter, if not the King, would almost certainly leave all and come hot-foot the moment the news reached him; but even the fastest and best-founded horses would take many hours to cover 180 miles across the Border hills and mosses. A galley would have been quicker—but not in these March equinoxial gales. Riding all through the night as they probably would, they could scarcely be at Turnberry before daylight.

Elizabeth was intensely weary, anxious and at a loss. She had never left that bedside since the younger woman had been carried to it, still in her disarranged riding attire. But she would not, could not, abandon her vigil. She would not even lay down the child. Endlessly, patiently, she walked and watched, hushed and mur-mured.

The long desperate hours passed. On the bed, Marjory Bruce did not stir, scarcely seemed to breathe.

How many inspections of that slight, motionless figure the Queen had made she did not know, when she noticed the single gleaming tear-drop on the pallid cheek. The sight of it moved her almost intolerably. It was long since Marjory had been seen to weep. Hers had been a dry-eyed ordeal and agony. Elizabeth sank down on her knees beside the bed, child still in her arms, and sank her head on the soiled coverlet. Almost she beat it there.

"Oh, lassie, lassie!" she cried brokenly. "How they have hurt you! Injured you. Men! Men, with their evil passions, their blind pride, their selfish folly! They have spared you nothing! Nothing!"

Long she crouched there, the baby part-supported by the bed. Perhaps, in time, she dozed a little. For when she became aware again it was with a jerk. The tear-drop was gone, evaporated. But the eyes were open. So was the mouth, slightly.

She stared, as her mind grappled with what her eyes told her – the ashen pallor waxen now, the dark glance fixed, glazed, the parted lips stiff. And looking, she knew, and a great convulsive sob burst from her. She clutched the morsel of humanity in her arms almost to suffocation.

After the first onslaught had worn off, Elizabeth's impulse was to run for the others, the physicians, midwives, courtiers, anyone to take the burden from her shoulders, the burden of what she alone now knew. But she told herself that was folly. Marjory was dead, undoubtedly. No one would bring her to life again. And, for herself, she wanted no strangers intruding on her grief.

She closed those glazing eyes, but otherwise did not handle the body. For a while she could not bring herself to lay down the baby, moaning over it in an extravagance of sorrow for the motherless mite, saying to it what she could not say to Marjory Bruce. But at length she placed it in the handsome cradle Stewart had had made before he went to the wars. Then she went and sat, crouched, gazing into the smouldering fire. She tried to pray for the departed, but could not. Her mind sank away into a grey vacancy of regret and fatigue.

It was thus that Robert Bruce and Walter Stewart found her when, between five and six in the morning, they came storming into that fetid chamber out of the blustering night, covered with mire and the spume of foundered horses, urgent, vehement, demanding, sweeping aside the servitors and others who cowered outside.

The hush and atmosphere of that room, with the drawn, almost blank face that the Queen turned to them, hit them like a mace-stroke. Each halted, drawing quick breaths.

There was no other sound but the snuffling from the cradle.

The men reacted differently. Stewart strode straight to the cradle. Bruce, after a long look at his wife's strained and warning face, went to the bed.

For long moments he stood staring down, fists clenching. Then a great shuddering groan racked him. "Dead!" he cried. "Dead! Oh, God, oh, Christ-God – dead!" And he raised those clenched fists high, up above his head, towards the ceiling, beyond, towards heaven itself, and shook them in a raging paroxysm of grief terrible to behold.

Elizabeth came to him then, to reach out a tentative hand to him. Walter Stewart came, faltering-stepped, gulping, looking askance at the bed, his normally ruddy face suddenly pale.

Bruce saw neither of them. "I am accursed! Accursed!" he

ground out, from between clenched teeth. "All that is mine, rejected of God! Now my daughter, my only child. Dead. Slain. Slain by myself! Who forced her to marriage! One more. One more to pay the price of my sin. My brothers. My kin. My friends. Now, my daughter." He gazed around him wildly, although he saw none of them. "Why these? Why not myself? God, in Your heaven—why not myself?"

"Not your sin, Robert," the Queen said, level-voiced. "If this was for the sin of any, it was Edward Plantagenet's sin. Who ruined her young life in hatred and vengeance. Vengeance on you. Here was the sin."

"*I* defiled God's altar, woman! *I* slew John Comyn, in passion, in the holy place. I, excommunicate, who presumed to this unhappy throne, with a murderer's hands. *I* desired an heir from my own loins. I, not Edward Plantagenet. I slew my daughter as truly as I slew the Red Comyn!"

The woman shook her head, but attempted no further comfort. Her weariness and pain were such that she drooped as she stood, the proud de Burgh.

Walter Stewart turned and strode to the window without a word. He stood blindly staring out into the darkness, his face working. He had not so much as touched the bed.

The King's wide shoulders seemed to sag and droop, likewise. He sank forward on to the bed, arms outstretched over that still, slight body. "Marjory! Marjory!" he whispered. "Can you forgive me? Where you are now. Can you forgive? The father who brought you to this? Can you, girl? Of your mercy!"

Silence returned to that chamber, save for the child's little noises.

At length, heavily, Bruce rose, and looking round him as though a stranger there, paced across to his son-in-law who still stood at the window like a statue.

"I am sorry, lad," he said. He laid a hand on the other's shoulder. "Sorry. It may be that I need your forgiveness also. I ask it of you." Though his voice quivered, all was quiet and sane again.

The High Steward of Scotland shook his fair head, helplessly. "Have I . . . Your Grace's permission . . . to retire?" he got out. And without waiting for an answer, turned and hurried from the room.

Bruce looked over to his wife by the fire. "How was it?" he asked, evenly. "How did she die?"

Slowly, carefully, Elizabeth told him the grievous tale of it. But she spared him not a little.

He heard her out, silent. But he asked no questions. Indeed, he scarcely seemed to listen, his mind plumbing depths of solitary despair.

Finishing, she took his hand and led him over to the cradle. "A boy," she told him. "A boy, perfectly formed. A fine boy. And well. Your . . . grandson."

For long he looked down at the shrivelled, red-faced little creature.

"Aye," he said, at length. "This . . . this is all! All for this. This puny scrap is destiny! The destiny for which I have fought and schemed and struggled. For which countless men have died. For which a realm waits. The destiny for which my brother seeks to conquer Ireland, MacDougall languishes in Dumbarton's dungeon, Douglas hammers Durham city and I besiege Carlisle. For this handful of wrinkled flesh!"

Elizabeth opened her lips to speak, but could not. She busied herself instead with smoothing the baby's coverings, and sought to still her quivering mouth. "Carlisle?" she got out, aside. "Is it well, there? The siege? Does all go well? Sending for you was no hurt? That you should leave . . . ?"

"No. It mattered nothing. I was gaining nothing. This siege is a folly. Carlisle will not fall. It is too strong. Its walls and towers. Without siege-engines we can do nothing. We sought to make a sow, to take us close to undermine the walling. But it sank into the earth made soft by these rains. Too heavy. They indeed have better machines than have we. Their governor, Harcla, can snap his fingers at us. I should never have begun it. But I promised Douglas. The least I could do, when he was hazarding all, deep in England. To protect his rear. But I will raise it now. End it. Assail Berwick instead, where we have more chance . . ." His voice tailed away, and the soldier was quickly superseded by the man again. "But what matters Carlisle! Or Berwick either. With what this room portends. Destiny is here, not in Carlisle. Here is the prize! That! And here the price paid!" Bitterly he said it.

She shook her head, and took his arm. "Your grandson," she reminded. "And motherless. Helpless."

"Aye." Nodding, he stooped then, to reach out and pick up the closely bundled infant. "So be it. This, then, is my heir. Scotland's heir. One day this will wear my crown!"

"Perhaps," the Queen said, strangle-voiced. "Perhaps not, Robert."

"If God has any mercy for me, he will. Is it too much to hope? You say that he is well-made? Healthy?"

She moistened her lips. "He is a fine boy, yes. But still, he may not wear your crown. Who knows? For I . . . I am pregnant,

Robert! At last. At my age! Sweet Jesu—I am pregnant . . .!" Her voice broke.

For moments he could not so much as speak, lips parted. Then, "Dear God of all the saints," the man gasped. "Christ, Son of the Father—pregnant! You! It is true?"

Dumbly she nodded.

"You are sure? Not some false sign? Some cozening of the body . . .?"

"No. It is sure. Oh, Robert . . .!"

Hurriedly but gently, then, he laid his grandson back in the cradle, and turned to take his wife in his arms. "My dear, my dear!" he said. "Here is wonder. Here is miracle. Here, here . . ." He wagged his head. "Lord Jesu, woman—what are we? What are we, I say? The playthings of God? Playthings, no more . . .!"

"Say it not, Robert—say it not!" she urged, chokingly. She turned her face and buried it in his chest, clutching him convulsively, half-sobbing, half-laughing.

Two months later, almost reluctantly, the King was besieging Berwick-on-Tweed instead of Carlisle. He was against siegery, on principle. Being almost wholly devoid of the necessary engines for the business–mangonels, trebuchets, ballista, rams, sows and the like– where fortresses could not be successfully assaulted, stormed or infiltrated, or their water-supplies cut, he was left with the wearisome business of starving them out. And this was quite foreign to Bruce's vigorous, not to say impatient nature. The siege-maker has to have special qualities–and this man just did not have them.

But pressure to invest Berwick had been strong. It was the only Scots soil still in enemy possession, and as such a standing reproach, a denial of their limited victory. Moreover, it had usually been the headquarters of the English administration over Scotland, and for it still to be in Edward's grasp was galling in the extreme. Now that MacDougall was put down, this assault was the only action the King could take, within his own realm, to hasten Edward's acceptance of the peace treaty. Also James Douglas, Warden of the Marches, saw Berwick as a perpetual challenge to his authority, and claimed that he could not go raiding deep into England with any peace of mind leaving this occupied stronghold, which could be reinforced by sea, behind him. Douglas, of course, had a sort of vested interest in Berwick. Here his father had been governor, in 1296, had gallantly withstood Edward the First's siege throughout the terrible sack of Berwick town, had been tricked into terms by the English, and then shamefully betrayed and sent walking in chains, like a performing bear, down through England to imprisonment in the Tower. James was concerned to avenge his father.

He was, in fact, the moving spirit in this siege, the King, though present, being less than well. Since his daughter's death he had been moody, at odds with himself and others, dispirited for so purposeful a nature. It was not that he was actually and recognisably ill. He went about, if somewhat lethargically, and indeed denied that there was anything wrong with him. But those close to him knew well that he was not himself, and veterans like Gilbert Hay and Lennox claimed that they recognised the same symptoms that had laid him low at Inverurie in 1307, and at Roxburgh in 1313–though, they admitted, with much less virulence. Certainly Bruce itched a great deal, his skin hot and dry, and of an evening was apt to be flushed with a slight fever. Elizabeth, who had little objection to camp-life and had accompanied her husband to Berwick, was anxious – but Bruce was not a man to fuss over and she had to content herself with small ministrations and watchfulness.

This was the situation one evening of late May when the burly, grizzled and tough Sir Robert Boyd of Noddsdale was ushered into the royal presence, from long travelling. He found the King and Queen, with Lennox, Hay and Douglas, in the vicarage of Mordington a mile or two north-west of the walled town, which had been Bernard de Linton's pastoral charge before he became royal secretary, Abbot of Arbroath and Chancellor of the realm. It was a small house for so illustrious a company, and plainly plenished, but the nearest stone and slated residence left intact near the beleaguered citadel.

"Welcome, Sir Robert," Bruce greeted him. "Here's an unexpected pleasure. Have you fallen out with my brother? Or have you come to aid us in this plaguey siege? You have the soundest head for such matters in my kingdom, I vow." News of late from Ireland had been good, and he had no reason to anticipate ill tidings.

"Your siege I know not of, Sire," the other returned. "I came at the command of my lord of Moray. And in haste. To outpace another. From your royal brother. Another courier, from the Lord Edward. My lord of Moray conceived that you should have warning."

"Warning of what, man? Not defeat? Only a week past we had word of victories, progress . . ."

"No defeat, no. Quite otherwise. The Lord Edward has assumed the crown. Has been enthroned King of Ireland."

"Wh-a-t!" Not only Bruce but all other men in the room were on their feet at this bald announcement.

"King, no less. Crowned and installed. At Dundalk. Ten days past. King."

"But . . . great God – how came this? Is it some mummery? Some foolish play-acting?"

"Not so, Sire. It was a true coronation. He was solemnly led to the throne by O'Neil, King of Tyrone. And supported by many sub-kings and chiefs. All assenting. Crowned High King of All Ireland."

"It is scarce believable. My brother. To do this . . ."

"Only Edward would do it!" Elizabeth said. "Only he would conceive it possible. The bold Edward!"

"Bold, woman! This is . . . more than boldness. This is folly, beyond all. Treason indeed – highest treason."

126

"You say so? How can it be treason, Robert? Against you? You are not king in Ireland."

"Do you not see? Edward went to Ireland as my lieutenant and representative. Leading an army of my subjects. On a campaign to advance the interests of my realm of Scotland. Now, he has thrown all that to the winds. He has made himself a monarch, and therefore no subject of mine. He thus rejects both my authority and my interests. The campaign to win a peace treaty."

"But may not this but aid in it? In bringing the English to treat? If he unites Ireland, as its king . . ."

"Save us—*you* should know the English better! This will end all possibility of a treaty. For us to defeat their minions, in a rebellion. To drive many of their captains out of Ireland—that might have served our purpose. But to set up Edward as King of All Ireland— that is no mere rebellion. That is the greatest challenge to England's might and pride. For to them Ireland is a province. They will, and must, treat this as fullest war. To the death. They will now muster all their power, to keep Ireland. And because this new king is my brother, with Scots troops aiding him, they will conceive me as behind him. And refuse to make any peace treaty. With this one stroke Edward has destroyed all we have worked for, since Bannock-burn."

There was silence in that room for a little, as all considered the implications.

"Why? Why did he do it?" Bruce went on. "He is rash, yes. But this is not the result of a sudden whim. This he must have planned."

Boyd coughed. "My lord of Moray believes that he intended this, before ever he went to Ireland. That he had O'Neil's, and the others', offers of the throne, secretly, all along. That this was the real reason for the Irish adventure—not the English treaty. So my lord said, to tell Your Grace."

"Aye. I can see it now. Was I blind? How could I tell that he, my own flesh and blood, could so intend?"

"Edward was ever ambitious," the Queen reminded. "Chafed under authority. Yours or other."

"He was not content to be named as heir to your throne," Lennox put in. "He required a throne *now*!"

"Once I heard him say that there was not room in Scotland for both Bruces!" Douglas added.

"He said that . . . ?"

"Aye, Sire. I did not tell you. But he said it."

"He thought me hard on him, yes. But was I so? He seldom obeyed my orders. Chose his own way. But there can only be one king in a realm, one master, not two. I' faith, I learned that lesson sufficiently in the Guardianships!"

"So now he has gone to be king in a realm of his own, Robert," Elizabeth said soothingly. "Is that so ill, in the end? For you? At least Edward cannot now afflict you by his disobedience and resentment. As King of Ireland he will no longer trouble you. And will be a sore thorn in the English flesh."

"Your Grace's pardon," Boyd interjected heavily, "but I fear that it is less simple than that. The Lord Edward sends a courier, Sir William de Soulis, the Butler, to inform His Grace of all this. And to seek more men. Aid. Money. Food. Horses."

"Mother of God—he does?" Bruce cried. "After this, he turns round and seeks my help!" The King actually barked a harsh laugh. "Edward! Edward would! Save us—that is my brother, to be sure!"

"What will you do, Sire?" Hay asked.

"What *can* I do?" Bruce took a pace or two back and forth. "The deed is done. I cannot undo that. I can refuse him aid. Recall all Scots forces from Ireland. Leave him to his Irish. That, yes." He paused. "But . . . will it serve me any advantage? Serve Scotland's cause? Good, or ill?"

"You will not further support him, Sire!" Douglas exclaimed. "Now! After this . . . ?"

"Let me think, Jamie—let me think, a mercy's sake. I *must* think, even if Edward does not! Poor Ireland, with an unthinking king!" He looked up. "Sir Robert—how does my nephew say? My lord of Moray? His judgement in matters of state I ever esteem. Did he reveal his mind to you?"

"He did not make so bold as to send advice, Your Grace," Boyd answered carefully. "But he did say that, though you would be angry, wrathful, he did not believe that you would break with the Lord Edward. That though your cause suffers set-back in this, all may not be loss. That you may still use him, and the Irish, to your advantage."

"Aye. So I begin to think also. He is a long-headed wight is Thomas! And how think yourself, man? Your counsel also I value."

"Since you ask, Sire—I say likewise. Send him support. Possibly but little. But promise more later, on condition that he moves south forthwith against the English, with all speed and strength. Before they can learn of this, and send reinforcement from England. Since you cannot unmake this king, use him while you may. It will not bring about your peace treaty. But it could weaken your enemies. Which is always profitable."

"There speaks good sense. I thank you, friend." Bruce smiled grimly. "Was that why you came so fast? From Ireland. To reach me first. So that I should not, in my wrath, say what could not be unsaid? Refuse all support? And so, in haste, injure my cause?"

The other looked uncomfortable. "Not so, Sire," he said gruffly. "Or . . . but little. I came swiftly that you should have the tidings from your own friends. The more so in that I mislike William de Soulis!"

"Ah. Very well, Sir Robert. I thank you, whatever your reasons. Now, refreshment . . ."

* * *

So Bruce was well prepared when, two days later, Sir William de Soulis, Lord of Liddesdale and Hereditary Butler to the King of Scots, nephew of the late Guardian, came riding into the camp outside the walls of Berwick with quite an imposing cavalcade, all under a great banner bearing the three golden crowns of Tara, on blue—a device not seen in Scotland for centuries.

The King received him in a grassy hollow at a bend of Tweed. But however ready he was for the other's mission, he was scarcely prepared for his manner and style.

"Greetings, Sire!" the newcomer called, after the considerable trumpet flourish. "I, William de Soulis, Lord of Liddesdale in the Kingdom of Scotland, and Earl of Dundalk in the Kingdom of Ireland, bring greeting and God-speed from the mighty, puissant and gracious Lord Edward, by God's grace High King of All Ireland, to the illustrious Lord Robert, King of Scots. Hail!"

Bruce blinked. "All that?" he wondered. "Between brothers, Sir William, is that not . . . too much?"

It was the other's turn to blink. But he was a suave and quick-witted man, handsome, florid, courtly and not easily put out. "Your Grace has heard?" he wondered. "Heard that His Grace your royal brother is now King of Ireland?"

"Aye, friend—I have heard. Though not that he had started to make earls so soon!"

De Soulis bowed. "My poor worth over-valued," he agreed smoothly. "But the greetings I bring are none the less hearty. I bring them with love and esteem."

"I would esteem them more, sir, if they were offered in more seemly fashion. I am not used to receiving greetings from seated subjects, while I stand!"

Hastily de Soulis dismounted, and his entourage with him. "Your Grace's pardon. I was conveying greetings from one monarch to another. As envoy."

"Sir William, on Scottish soil you are the servant of one monarch only. Lord of Liddesdale—nothing else. Save my household butler! Remember it!"

"Yes, Sire. To be sure. I crave pardon."

"As you ought, sir. Now—deliver my brother's message. But as *my* subject."

"H'mm. As you will. His Grace of Ireland sends royal greetings and fraternal affection. He informs you that he has accepted and assumed the crown of All Ireland, duly offered and presented by O'Neil, King of Tyrone, with the Kings of Munster, Leinster, Meath and Thomond, and other sub-kings and lords of that realm duly assembled. For the welfare of that kingdom, the better prosecution of the war with England, and for the good alliance and support of your realm. To such end His Grace offers a treaty of alliance between both equal realms, of mutual support and aid of all kinds, against all and soever. This in love and esteem. God save the King!"

"Indeed! Which king?" Bruce observed mildly. And when the other did not answer, went on. "Why did my royal brother not inform me of such assumption of this throne?"

"Inform, Your Grace? But surely . . . surely you knew? That it was possible. Mooted. Long since. Surely you knew that?"

The King eyed the other searchingly. De Soulis seemed genuinely surprised. It was quite possible, quite in keeping, that Edward might not have informed even his closest associates that he had not told his brother of his monarchial ambitions and secret moves. In which case it might be wisest to let de Soulis remain in ignorance of the fact.

"I should have been informed of the impending coronation," he said carefully. "Who knows, I might have wished to grace it by my presence!"

De Soulis shook his head. "That His Grace did not confide in me. No doubt there was an urgency, Sire. No time. It would have taken many weeks to bring Your Grace to Dundalk."

"No doubt." Bruce let it go. "Well, Sir William," he went on, as though terminating the audience, "you have brought your tidings and my brother's greetings. For which I thank you. I now must needs consider my reply, for you to take back to Ireland."

"But, Sire—there is more." The other looked concerned.

"Ah."

"Yes. In return for this proposed alliance of the two kingdoms, this aid in your war against England, His Grace requires aid also. He requires trained cavalry, with the horses. Arms. Money. Also provisions—for there is famine in Ireland. He requires these from Scotland . . ."

"Requires, sir? *Requires!*"

"Requests, Your Grace. In exchange for Ireland's adherence to your cause."

"So! May I remind you, Sir William, that my brother went to Ireland as my lieutenant. To prosecute the war. To force a treaty from England. He took 6,000 of my subjects—mine, not his. And I have since sent more, with the Earl of Moray. Thus far, I have done the paying, provided all. With little result. Save, it seems, to win a throne for my brother! At my charge. Yet now he *requires* more from me, men and money. In exchange for *his* support! Here seems to me to be strange bargaining, sir!"

"Matters have much changed, Sire, since our expedition left Scotland."

"Seemingly! But not of my will. I still expect my brother's fullest support in this warfare, without any talk of exchange."

"I would remind Your Grace that Ireland is an independent kingdom . . ."

"Ireland is today a conquered province of England. I have had sufficient travail and sorrow in freeing Scotland from a like state, not to take on the reconquest of Ireland! If such is my brother's design, he must needs find Irishmen to do it. Or other allies. My Scots forces are there solely to win a treaty of peace from Edward of Carnarvon."

There was silence while de Soulis digested that.

"Then—you will not send aid to the Lord Edward? To His Grace?"

"I have not said so. But any that I send will go on *my* terms. Not as part of any bargain. They will be sent to the Earl of Moray, under his command. And he will take orders from myself. You understand? All Scots forces will he command, as my lieutenant—since my brother is no more that. And a full offensive southwards will be mounted forthwith. Before the English hear of this and send reinforcement. This is my decision. You will inform my brother."

The other bowed. "And . . . and how many men will I inform His Grace that you will send? Under these conditions."

"One thousand within the week. Light horse. More later, and when I hear that these are being used to good purpose. With silver. And food."

"His Grace hoped for many more than a thousand."

"His Grace will have to earn them, then! He has set back my hopes of a peace treaty, set back Scotland's full recovery, by years. As the price of his crown. This you will tell him. You have it? Then, I declare this audience ended, Sir William. You may retire . . ."

BRUCE, typically, had chosen his own way to counter incipient sickness and debility. He had always claimed that it was the Earl of Buchan's imminent threat, and the subsequent vigorous action of the Battle of Barra, which he had risen from his sick-bed at Inverurie to fight, which had cured him that first time. So, in midsummer of 1316, he had impatiently shaken himself, left the weary siege of Berwick to underlings, and exorcised his ill humours of body and mind by setting off personally, with James Douglas, Walter Stewart and a large, fast-moving force, on a massive, deep-penetration raid into England.

And, surprisingly, it had worked. In the saddle, at the head of an armed host in enemy territory, the hero-king became himself once more.

Now in the golden days of early October, they were on their way home again, a little weary but flushed with success, and with almost an embarrassment of booty and prisoners to delay them. And Bruce was in no mood for a leisurely progress through the English North, however subservient its people. For the Queen's time was due towards the end of the month, and the King was agog, eager, to be back for this momentous event. Also to be with Elizabeth in what could only be an anxious time. A first child, at her age, was bound to be less than easy; and Bruce's first wife, as well as his daughter, had died in child-birth. Moreover, he had delayed a little longer than he had intended, in the south, due to the concomitants of unprecedented success.

They had won as far south as Richmond, again, without major opposition—and even to Bruce it had seemed strange for a King of Scots to be ranging at large so deep into the green heart of England without let or hindrance, entering cities, receiving addresses of reluctant welcome and even more reluctant tribute and treasure. Richmond itself, protected by its great castle, had been almost too reluctant, and had been all but committed to the flames before the unhappy magistrates realised that the castle would not, could not, save them, and had painfully paid up the promptly increased demands. Thereafter a certain amount of organised resistance in the West Riding had required that an example be made, and the Scots had swept through that fair land with fire and sword before, concerned about the time factor and the long journey home burdened with so much booty, Bruce had sent one more letter to an apparently unconcerned London urging an immediate treaty of peace. Perhaps he had waited rather too long for the answer which did not come. Quite unable to understand Edward of Carnarvon's ideas as to ruling a kingdom, it had been the Scots' turn for reluctance as the order for retiral was given.

So it was that, in a mellow autumn noonday, hazy sun, turning bracken and reddening leaves, the long, long, winding column of chivalry, armed might, highly-placed prisoners for ransom, and laden pack-horses by the thousand, had crossed Liddel Water north of Carlisle and was nearing the subsequent crossing of Esk on the line for Annandale, when another and scarcely less impressive, though smaller cavalcade came into sight ahead, over the green Border hills. No great noble or officer of state left in Scotland was likely to travel the land in such style, especially on apparent road to England, and a tremor of excitement ran through the royal host.

When the sound of music and singing reached them on the still air, wonder grew. Admittedly great prelates sometimes travelled the country so with their choirs, acolytes and relics; but this was not Lamberton's and certainly not Abbot Bernard's style, and old Robert Wishart of Glasgow was practically on his death-bed.

Then somebody perceived the preponderance of dark blue about the host of banners, and from that it did not take long to discern the three golden crowns on the greatest.

"By the Rude—another embassage from Ireland!" the King cried. "What will it be this time? More men required? More money? More royal greetings?"

"Sire—is that not the Earl of Moray's banner?" Douglas asked. "Near the front. It is his colours—red and ermine."

"Not under the Irish standard, surely! Not Thomas . . .!"

Then suddenly, as they drew closer, many about the King recognised something about the head-high, shoulder-back carriage of the slender figure in black armour that rode in the forefront of the oncoming brilliant company.

"It is Edward himself!" Walter Stewart exclaimed. "My lord of Carrick. This . . . this king!"

"Aye," Bruce said.

Men stared at each other doubtfully.

The King drew rein. "Let us await His Grace," he said carefully.

To a vigorous fanfare of Irish trumpets they met there on the open side of one of their own Annandale hills. Edward drew up a

133

yard or two away, the others falling back from the two principals. He raised a steel-gauntleted hand.

"Hail, brother!" he said.

Robert smiled a little "Well met, Edward," he nodded. "Here is surprise."

"Yes. I greet you. Greet you in the name of all Ireland."

"Indeed? William de Soulis did that also, if I mind aright. What does it mean, Edward?"

Somewhat taken aback, the other cleared his throat. "It means . . . it means that it is not only as a brother that I greet you now, Robert. But as a monarch. Another king. One realm greeting another. That much, does it not?"

"I do not know. Tell me how much it means. From one to whom words, professions, compacts, mean but little, it seems!"

Edward flushed under his magnificent crested helm. "I was never one for splitting hairs, no," he agreed. "Bartering words. I prefer to act, brother. I find it more profitable."

"Profitable," Bruce nodded. "There we have it, yes. You have an aptitude for profit, Edward!"

His brother frowned. "I do not know what you are at, man. Do not talk in riddles. I could never abide you in such mood. But . . . I had expected warmer welcome than this. After so long a parting. See you—here is no way for kin to meet, after so many months."

"Aye—perhaps I am too sober. You must bear with me. But . . . I cannot forget that at our last leave-taking you promised leal service as my lieutenant and representative, Edward. And then abused my trust. Used my forces for your own ends."

"Not so. What I did was for the benefit of your realm as well as of Ireland. To further the fight against the English. But, i' faith—I have not come all this way to listen to your strictures, Robert! To be hectored by you. I have had enough of that in the past, by God! I would remind you that matters have changed since our last meeting. That although I am still your brother, I am no longer your subject! We are equals, now—equals, do you hear? Monarchs, both. I beg you not to forget it!" That was hot.

As Edward grew the hotter, so Robert became the cooler. "That is exactly the issue, the point I make," he said. "You left here my subject, my sworn servant, owing me and my realm allegiance. And you return quite otherwise. Disclaiming all allegiance, claiming equality. And to win this equality, and throw off your allegiance, you used my power, my name, my trust. Without my knowledge or consent. Knowing that I would not have given it . . ."

"There you have it! Knowing that you would not have given it! Here is the heart of the matter. This thing had to be done lacking your consent, or it would not have been done at all. *You* must ever be master. *You* command. You would never have agreed to have me a king, so that you could no longer command me. I know you, man! You are a notable captain, but you cannot abide that others should rival you. I know you—therefore I acted as I did."

Bruce shook his head. "By each and every word you speak, you prove that you do *not* know me, brother though you are! Neither know nor understand. Nor ever have, I think. I was against the Irish adventure from the start, because it would be like to draw away my strength, Scots power seeping away into the Irish bogs. How much worse that you should become King of that sorry country. With a kingdom to make and unite and hold together and defend. As well as forcing the English to a needless challenge. You must see it?"

"It was to challenge the English that I went to Ireland, was it not? With your agreement."

"To harass, to worry, to hinder. Not to force major war upon them. Think you the King of England can stomach a King of Ireland?"

"I know not, nor care. What is more to the point—it seems that the King of Scots cannot stomach it either."

And Edward Bruce reined round his splendid mount and rode back to his own party in most evident and high dudgeon. All around, men looked askance.

His brother sighed, and beckoned forward the Earl of Moray, to his side.

"So, Thomas, you are returned. With good reason, I have no doubt. I am glad to see you—I am indeed. Yours has been a thankless task, I think?"

"Thankless, Sire. And fruitless, I fear. I have done what I could —but that is little. My uncle now is gone quite beyond me. Only you can affect him now."

"I! Sweet Mary—that seems less than likely! I, of all men, he resents most."

"Yet you, of all men, he requires, Sire. He thinks to need no others. But your goodwill and aid he must have. Else, I swear, he would not be here today!"

"So he comes a-begging, Thomas? Despite all?"

"Yes. Or, he would rather say, a-bargaining, I think."

"And chooses a strange tone to bargain in!"

"Aye. But he will change his tone. If he must. Give him time. He has not travelled these hundreds of miles just to bicker with you."

"M'mmm. Perhaps you are right. And *you* would have me . . . bargain?"

"I believe so, yes. That is why I have come with him. There are reasons."

Moray was proved right about Edward changing his tone, there and then, for now the other was calling back.

"Brother–whither? Where do you make for? Annan? Lochmaben?" He sounded himself again.

"Lochmaben tonight," Bruce answered.

"Then I shall press on. We have been long on the road. I will await you at Lochmaben. And hope for better talking!" And in fine style he swept off, under his forest of banners, whence he had come– although minus Moray.

"His Grace is recovered," that man said dryly. "As he needs must, if he is to gain what he requires from you. He has brought two sub-kings with him, and dare not fail."

"You say so? And what does he want, Thomas?"

"He wants 10,000 men, 100 heavy chivalry and 500 bowmen. He wants Angus of the Isles' galleys. He wants silver enough to pay his Irish host. Also knights and trained captains, veterans, as many as he can win."

Bruce eyed the other for long moments, thoughtfully. "Jesu Son of God and Mary!" he said. "Would he have my crown also?" He gestured to Moray to remount, and turning in the saddle, almost absently waved on the vast column that had ground to a halt behind him.

"Of my brother," he went on. "I am now prepared to believe anything. Anything under heaven! But you, nephew–did I misunderstand? Or did it seem that you would have me listen to these . . . these rantings? Could that be Thomas Randolph?"

"Aye, Sire. It is my belief that you should heed and consider well. You cannot grant him all that he asks, to be sure. But some consent may be to your advantage. Indeed, I see you left with scant choice. The English must now, I think, attempt the re-conquest of Ireland. Nothing less will serve. So, either you hinder them, or you do not. If you do not, the country will fall to them like a ripe plum. I know it. I have made it my business to know it. Your brother is king in name only. Less king than were you at the start–for you at least were of the blood, had been Guardian, and had fought long for the realm. My uncle has none of that. The Irish people know him not, nor care. He is a magnificent captain of light cavalry, but no general. With no notion of statecraft. He has won many small victories, but consolidated nothing. These Irish kinglets and chiefs hate each other. They fight together all the time, like our Highland clans. They made him High King only to spite others–who therefore love him the less. And to gain *your* aid, against the English.

That is why he must win that aid, now. Without it, his kingdom will fall fast. Even faster than it was raised up."

"And you think that should concern me?"

"Aye, Sire, I do. For if the English win a swift and easy campaign in Ireland, you—and Scotland—will suffer. That is sure. Now they are down, licking their wounds, out of faith in themselves and their leaders. But give them a quick and easy conquest of Ireland—as it would be, God knows—and there will be no holding them. They will be up again. And the English, sure of themselves, resurgent, are hard to beat. *You* know that. And there are still ten times as many of them as of us."

Bruce was looking at the younger man sidelong. "My sister bore a son indeed!" he observed. "What has ailed me from doing the same?"

Moray flushed a little. "If I have learned anything of affairs and rule, I have learned it of you, Sire."

"But your wits are your own, lad."

"You take my point, then?"

"I perceive that there is much in what you say, yes. That will require much thought."

"So long as you do not dismiss the Lord Edward's requests out of hand. As they would seem to deserve. And then have to face a triumphant England, in Ireland! Victorious and but fourteen miles from the coast of Galloway!"

"Aye. But what of consuming away my power? The very real danger of wasting my strength in Ireland? Always this is what I have feared in the Irish adventure. Of draining my Scots forces into the bottomless bogs. Already I have sent many thousands. To what end? How many remain? Ill-led, misused, they are squandered. I make no criticism of you, Thomas, who are only their commander in name. I have well understood your difficulties. That it was not for you to devise campaigns and teach your uncle how to fight a war."

"Sire—it is all true. You say that you fear to waste more men, to squander your strength. There is one sure way to avoid that, to make certain that your forces are used to best advantage. Go with them. Come back to Ireland with us!"

"Eh . . . ?" Bruce frowned.

"Do you not see? This could answer all. With you there, my uncle could no longer delay, hold back, and use your forces for his own ends. With your sure hand on the helm, the galley of war would sail straight. Moreover, Angus of the Isles would work with you, where he would not with the Lord Edward."

"But, man—you are asking me to engage in full-scale war. Across the seas. The thing I have ever been most against."

E* 137

"Not full-scale war, no. Not for you. Not for Scotland. For the Irish, perhaps. But for you, only a campaign. Which you can leave when you will, commit such forces as you will. It is your *presence* that is required. That could change all."

"The English are already pouring new forces into Ireland. In the south. You know that? We learned it in Yorkshire."

"No. But I did not doubt but that they would. They must. That is why I say that they will overrun all Ireland, and swiftly. If *you* do not stop them. And if they do, you will have to try to stop them, one day. Somewhere. Better to do it on Irish soil, with mainly Irish levies. Is it not so?"

"I will have to consider this," Bruce said slowly. "Here is a great matter."

"That is all I ask," the younger man acceded. "That you think on it . . ."

Not a great deal of that thinking was done that day, or night. For just before they reached Lochmaben in mid-Annandale, an urgent courier caught up with them, with the news from Turnberry that the Queen's labour had started, at least two weeks early. In a cursing flurry of alarm, Bruce abandoned all else, and leaving the supervision of his army, guests and prisoners to others, spurred off on the sixty-mile road to the Ayrshire coast. On this occasion Walter Stewart stayed behind, but Douglas and Moray, hastily yelling orders and instructions, flung themselves after their liege lord.

They were hard put to it to catch up. The King rode like a madman, taking shocking risks, savaging his horse. If the blight and doom which seemed to hang over his life—or, at least, the lives of those near and dear to him—was to strike again, if he was to fail Elizabeth as, he told himself, he had failed so many, then Scotland truly would have to look for a new king!

Far into the night they rode, through the shadowy hills, with mounts stumbling now, flagging, snorting with every pounding beat of their hooves. Bruce pounded his own mind as relentlessly. What had he done? What had he done? Elizabeth! Elizabeth! A little light-headed, perhaps, he was beginning to confuse this night with that he had ridden seven months before. And the horror grew on him.

When at last he thundered over the drawbridge timbers at Turnberry, the watch shouted down at him from the gatehouse-parapet. But he did not pause. He flung on through the outer bailey to the inner, vaguely aware of all the lights ablaze. It was one of the grooms who ran to catch his steaming, blown mount as he leapt down who shouted after him.

"You have a bairn, my lord King! A bairn. A wee lassie!"

Bruce hardly took it in, as he ran clanking into the keep and up the winding turnpike stairs.

It was not the same room, at least. He knew that it would be their own chamber, up at parapet-level, indeed the apartment in which he had been born. Outside, on the small landing, was the usual group of whispering servants, who fell back at the sight of the frowning, mud-stained monarch. A courtier hurriedly threw open the door.

There was the sound of a child crying—but it came from a little turret chamber off, where lay Robert Stewart, Marjory's child, whom meantime the Queen was bringing up almost as her own.

He strode across to the great bed, and as he came Elizabeth's corn-coloured head, damp a little with sweat, turned. She smiled up at him. It was a good, honest smile, though tired.

"Thank God! Thank the good God!" he gasped. "Elizabeth, lass—praises be! You are well? Dear heart—you are well?"

"Well, yes, Robert. Weary a little, that is all. I am sorry. Sorry that I came before my time. That I brought you hastening. After . . . after . . ."

"I feared, lass. I feared. Greatly."

"I know what you would fear. But you need not have done. You wed a great strong Ulsterwoman, Robert!" She looked down at the infant that slept within the crook of her arm, so like that other wrinkled entity whom he had stared down at in March, and who now cried fitfully in the turret. "I should not say it, my dear. It is unfair to this moppet, who has come to us after so long. Is she not a joy? And so like you, Robert! The same frown! The same haughty disdain of mouth! I should not say it—but I am sorry that I have not given you the son you sought."

"I care no whit! So long as you are well. Nothing else concerns me . . ."

"No—you must not speak so," she chided. "It is not true. Not kind. This little one is a great concern. Part of you, and part of me. The Princess of Scotland. It has taken me long, long to produce her! I will not have her spurned. Least of all by her sire! Take her, Robert—for she is yours. More so than that boy in there, that you dote on! Take her."

"As you will." He lifted up the baby, gingerly, in his arms, steel-clad and spattered with horse's spume as they were. He peered into the tight-closed tiny face. "Another Bruce," he said, gravely. "Dear God—what have You in store for this one!"

"Enough of that!" Elizabeth exclaimed, with surprising strength and at her most imperious. "Such talk I will not have. I am a mother now—and no mere queen! We will have no talk of fate or

139

curse or doom. This is our daughter, not any pawn of fate. Mind it, Robert Bruce!"

He smiled, then, and almost involuntarily jogged the infant up and down. "We shall call her Matilda," he said.

"Matilda? Why, of a mercy? Why Matilda?"

"Because she *is* Matilda—that is why."

"I had thought to call her Bridget. A good Ulster name. Celtic, too . . ."

"Matilda," he insisted. "Just look at her. She could be no other."

"I am her mother. Surely I have some say . . ."

"And I am the King! My word is law. Hear you that, Matilda Bruce? Remember it!" Stooping he laid her gently down within Elizabeth's arm again. "Care for her well, woman. She is the King's daughter." And the hand that replaced the child brushed lingeringly over the mother's cheek and brow and hair.

"Oh, Robert," she whispered. "I am so very happy."

He nodded, wordless.

PART TWO

IT took some six weeks to mount the great expedition, in especial to convince Angus Og to bring his galleys south for a winter campaign. Bruce himself was well aware that he was violating his instincts, not only in going campaigning at this time of year, but in involving himself in the entire Irish project. But he accepted that what Moray had said was true; the dangers of doing nothing were greater than the risks he now ran. And this was the only time when he could contemplate leaving Scotland, when winter snows and floods sealed the Border passes and made any large-scale attack from England out of the question. He was assured that it seldom snowed in Ireland, and though it rained not a little, winter was often the dryest period. Indeed it seemed that it was apt to be a favourite campaigning time in Ireland, once the harvest was ingathered. He must be back, whatever happened, by late spring. So he assured Elizabeth.

So they assembled and embarked at Loch Ryan, in Galloway, in late November—the same place where Thomas and Alexander Bruce had landed ten years before in their ill-fated attempt to aid their brother's re-conquest of Scotland, an attempt which ended in their betrayal and their shameful executions. Angus of the Isles had landed them, and, however reluctantly, once again he was co-operating; but only because Bruce himself was going on the expedition. He certainly would not have done it for Edward. For he was not just acting the transporter, this time; he was taking part with his friend, if not his monarch, and a thousand of his Islesmen with him. Indeed, most of the transporting was being done otherwise, in a vast and heterogeneous fleet of slower vessels drawn from all the South-West, under the pirate captain, Thomas Don—for the narrow, fast, proud galleys were hardly suitable for the carrying of great numbers of horses and fodder and stores.

It was not all just what Edward had asked for, of course. There was a considerable array of knights and captains, yes; some heavy chivalry, some bowmen, and much light cavalry; in all perhaps 7,000. Also many spare horses, largely captured from England, grain, forage and money. All went under King Robert's personal command. Edward indeed was not present, having returned to Ireland weeks before, with his court of kinglets and chiefs, and in a very uncertain frame of mind. He was getting men and aid—but scarcely as he had visualised. Although he could hardly object to his brother's attendance he was obviously less than overjoyed. But at least it had all had already had one excellent result; for Edward, put out and concerned to prove his prowess, had managed to reduce the important English base at Carrickfergus, which had long been a thorn in Ulster's side, in a great flurry of activity on his return. Oddly enough, though Ireland's new monarch would have been the last to admit it, he had to thank his brother's father-in-law mainly for this. Richard de Burgh, Earl of Ulster, sent home by Edward of England to take command of the military side of the reconquest of Ireland, had made a peculiar start by diverting the convoy of ships sent to Drogheda, farther south, for the relief of Carrickfergus, using their stores and arms to ransom his own kinsman, William Burke, or de Burgh, captured by Turlough O'Brien, King of Thomond. Apart altogether from the consequent fall of Carrickfergus, a most strategic port on the north side of Belfast Lough, in Antrim, all this added a hopeful flavour to the venture, the hope of divided loyalties amongst the English and the Anglo-Irish.

Bruce was leaving James Douglas behind, with Walter Stewart, to see to the protection of Scotland, while William Lamberton, Bernard de Linton and the other clerics looked to its administration. Jamie would dearly have liked to accompany them—and Bruce to have had him. But there was no one on whom he could rely so completely in matters military—save Thomas Randolph, who had already returned to Ireland with Edward. Moreover the Douglas had become a legend in the North of England, by his brilliant and unending raiding, so that fathers used his name as a warning for unruly children, and mothers hushed their offspring to sleep with assurances that the Black Douglas would not get them. The young idealist of a dozen years before had become worth an army in himself.

Douglas, then, and the Steward, with the Queen and her ladies, were there at Loch Ryan to see the expedition sail. Elizabeth herself would have accompanied them had it been possible; not only had she a taste for camp-following, but Ulster, after all, was her home, and she had brothers and sisters there. Bruce's intended programme was not one into which a woman with a new-born babe would fit, however tough; and with her father a leader of the enemy, complications would be likely.

Actual sailing was held up, in the end, by the non-arrival of Sir Neil Campbell and his contingent from Argyll. These had by no means the furthest to come, and there was some wonder at this, for Campbell, although in poor health, was not the man to be behind-hand in any adventure. When, at length, with the King ordering no further delay and the Campbells to follow on their own later, the famed black and gold gyronny-of-eight banner did appear on the scene, it was at the mast-head of a single galley, not a squadron, coming from the north. And the man who stepped ashore at Stranraer and came hastening to Bruce was not Sir Neil but his son by a mother long since dead, Colin Campbell, a young man in his early twenties, darkly handsome.

"My sorrow, Sire, that I come late," he cried. "But I needs must bury my father!"

"Bury . . . ? By the Rude—do you mean . . . ? Mean that Neil Campbell . . . is dead?"

"Dead, yes. He died the day after Your Grace's summons arrived at Innischonnel. The Lady Mary, your sister, found him. In the water. At the edge of the loch."

"Drowned! Neil Campbell drowned? I'll not believe it! I have seen him swim a hundred lochs and rivers . . ."

"Not drowned, Sire. He had fallen there. Dead where he fell. Alone. He was a sick man. Had been failing . . ."

"Dear God—Neil! Neil, my friend." Bruce was shaken, and showed it. Not all had loved the Campbell chief, an abrupt, secretive man of few graces, tending to be quarrelsome—who yet had captured Mary Bruce's heart thus late in their lives. But he was a mighty warrior, loyal to a fault, and the King loved him well. One of the original little band of heroes who had shared their lord's trials and perils when he was a hunted fugitive, who indeed had saved them all time and again by his hillman's skill in the desperate Highland days after Strathfillan, he had become the first to die. A thousand dangers, battles, ambushes, treacheries, he had survived— to die thus on the edge of his own Highland loch, a done man. The shock to Bruce, his friend, was partly for himself; for they were of a like age, both in their forty-third year, and the cold hand of the Reaper, in clutching one, momentarily brushed the other's heart also. In that instant the King felt old.

But he pulled himself together, as he must ever do, and put on the stern calm face of the monarch. "I am sorry, my friend," he said. "Beyond telling. Sorry for you and for my sister. Especially for her, who has suffered too much already. Some, it seems, are fated to suffer more than their share in this life. In the next, it may be, they will have their recompense. As for you, you are your father's son. And he ever lived with death, as any knight of mine must. Duly ready to entertain him. Neil Campbell was a noble knight, and many times held my life in his strong hands. Not for you to grieve him. Only to emulate."

"That is my humble prayer, Highness. That I may serve you as he did. To that end I would come with you on this sally to Ireland. In whatever lowly office."

"And so you shall. But in no lowly office, sir. You are a Highland chieftain now, head of a great clan. And an earl's son, in all but the name. I had intended to belt your father Earl of Atholl, in room of my kinsman, David de Strathbogie, traitor. The good Neil is gone to higher honour than I might give him. But to provide for his wife and my sister, I shall appoint her Countess thereof, and endow her with the lands of the earldom. As for you, friend—kneel you!"

And drawing his sword, Bruce there and then knighted the surprised young man, tapping him on both shoulders with the flat of the great blade which had shed so much blood for Scotland. "Arise, Sir Colin. Be thou a good and true knight until thy life's end!"

There was murmured acclaim, and appreciation of a right royal gesture. But some undoubtedly perceived that it was also a shrewd move indeed, binding one more great earldom closer to the crown, as the King had done with Moray and Ross, and territorially isolating the hostile earldoms of Angus and Fife by putting Atholl in the care of the Campbells—but only in the care. The Lady Mary was known to be pregnant, and the earldom was for her, not for her stepson. Elizabeth at least recognised a king's mind at work over a man's heart.

They sailed later, on a calm grey day of leaden seas and chill airs. The galleys took most of the men, leaving the great fleet of assorted slower craft to transport the horses, stores, armour and fodder. It was not a long voyage, with the coasts of Scotland and Ireland only some twenty-five miles apart at this point; but with Carrickfergus to reach, half-way up Belfast Lough, it would be more like a forty-mile sail from Loch Ryan. The Lord of the Isles had scouting galleys out, for there was always the possibility of attack by English ships, but so far there had been no alarms.

In one of Angus Og's sixty-oar greyhounds, Bruce could have dashed across the North Channel of the Irish Sea in three or four hours. But he stayed with his heterogeneous armada, which was soon scattered far and wide over the waters, with impatient scornful galleys circling and herding slow craft, like sheep-dogs, in their efforts to maintain some semblance of order, unity and a protective screen. Fortunately no enemy ships put in an appearance; but it was an uncomfortable interlude for the Scots leadership. And it was cold for everybody but the galley oarsmen.

Edward Bruce, who had an eye for appearances, had sent a squadron to meet them at the mouth of the Lough, under Donal O'Neil, King of Tyrone, no fewer than four of the vessels being packed with musicians and singers; so that the foremost Scots ships went heading up-lough thereafter to the sound of spirited Irish melodies – to the disgust of Angus Og, who considered this an insult and a travesty. Carrickfergus drew near, its lofty, high-set, English-built castle dominating the narrow streets of a walled seaport town.

But when Bruce landed, with the streets and alleys decked with bunting and evergreens, he discovered that little or no arrangements had been made for reception and dispositions of the Scots forces. A resounding committee of welcome was very flattering to himself, but no other provision seemed to have been made for the disembarkation and housing of 7,000 men and almost twice that number of horses. The town was already full to bursting point with the wild followers of Irish kinglets, chiefs and clerics, and the harbour and even the approaches thereto crammed with shipping. Bruce's veterans swore feelingly. Fortunately, as the King was refusing to proceed with the welcoming magnates up to the citadel for the official ceremonies, without first being assured of the proper reception of his army, a harassed Moray made an appearance, with the suggestion that the main mass of the Scots should not disembark here at all, but sail up the lough a further four miles or so, to a level area of meadow and greensward, at White Abbey, where there was space, water and wood for fuel.

Unceremoniously Bruce returned to his ship, leaving his high-sounding escort standing at a loss, and sailed on, to see to the due installation of his troops in the spreading demesne of White Abbey – much to the outrage of its Anglo-Irish abbot.

As a consequence, it was well after dark before the King came back to Carrickfergus, with his lieutenants, through the crazy confusion of shipping that packed the lough, to meet a much reduced and very agitated committee of magnificos, now including de Soulis the Butler. By them he was hastily conveyed, in torchlight procession, through the network of lanes and alleys where pigs, poultry and children got in the way, towards the great castle on its rocky terrace, which Edward was making his capital.

If that proud man was put out by the prolonged delay and implied rejection of his welcome, he did not permit it to divert him. Everywhere around the castle torches turned night into day, bonfires blazed and coloured lights flared. Every tower and turret was stance for a beacon. Probably his display gained in impressiveness thereby, even if choking smoke was the inevitable concomitant. Music resounded, by no means all of it harmonising.

The wide forecourt of the castle had been turned into a great amphitheatre, lined by thousands, while in the centre, jugglers, tumblers, bear-leaders and other entertainers performed by the light

147

of the flames, all to the strains of pipers and minstrels and drum-
mers. Through this the visitors were conducted in procession,
O'Neil pointing out this and that. Across the drawbridge into the
outer bailey, beyond the lofty curving curtain-walls, the scene was
different. Here dancers in strange barbaric-seeming costumes
paced and glided and circled to less lively melodies, while rank upon
rank of personages stood, bowing low as the King's party passed. A
great many of these appeared to be clergy, for Carrickfergus was a
great ecclesiastical centre. Beyond the gatehouse, the inner bailey,
narrower, was full to overflowing with chieftains, seannachies,
knights and captains, drawn up in groups according to their rank
and status. Then up the keep steps, past the yawning guardroom
vaults and dungeons, and up into the Great Hall, a dazzlement of
light and colour, where scores of young women dressed all in white
gyrated and dipped and postured to the gentle strumming of harps,
with great beauty and dignity.

"The daughters of kings," O'Neil observed confidentially. "A
hundred virgins."

Bruce doubted it, somehow. A lot of highly interested, roguish,
not to say downright bold glances were emanating from the ladies;
and his brother was not the man to neglect his opportunities in that
direction. But he nodded gravely.

At the far end of the huge hall was the dais platform, here occupying almost a quarter of the total space. It was more crowded than
the main floor. Massed to the right were standing rows of mitred
bishops and abbots, with unmitred priors, deans, archdeacons and
other prelates, all in most gorgeous robes. On the left were lords and
officers of state of every degree and highly colourful variety of
costume, from wolf-skins and embossed leather to silks, damasks
and brocades. And in the centre, forming a horseshoe, were ten
thrones, two of them empty. The arrangement of these chairs was
almost symmetrical—but not quite. All were gilded and handsome,
with crowns surmounting their high backs, four curving on one
side and four on the other of two at the head of the horseshoe. These
two, although placed side by side, were not quite a pair; one was of
the same size and type as the other flanking eight, while its neighbour
was not only larger, taller and more splendid, but was raised on a
little platform of its own. On it Edward Bruce lounged, magni-
ficently clad in cloth-of-gold and blue velvet, with a great cloak of
royal purple fringed with fur and sparkling with jewels, flung
negligently over one shoulder. The chair beside him was empty.

As the new arrivals came up, trumpeters set the rafters ringing
with an elaborate fanfare which drowned and stopped all the com-
peting music, and the dancers with it. In the silence that followed,

148

O'Neil of Tyrone turned and bowed, wordless to Bruce, more deeply to Edward, and then stalked over to one of the empty thrones, on the right, and sat down.

Another trumpet-blast, and a resplendent herald stepped forward, to intone:

"The mighty O'Rourke, King of Meath, offers greeting to Robert, King of Scots."

A thick-set, grizzled man rose from one of the chairs and held a hand high, unspeaking.

Bruce inclined his head.

Another trumpet. "The illustrious MacMurrough, King of Leinster, offers greeting to Robert, King of Scots."

A giant of a man, but strangely bent to one side from some ancient wound, went through the same procedure.

"The high-born O'Brien, King of Munster, offers greeting to Robert, King of Scots."

A white-haired and bearded ancient, fine featured, serene, but frail, stood with difficulty and raised a quivering arm. Bruce knew him by repute as a sacker of monasteries and ruthless slayer of women and children, but bowed nevertheless.

The next, a kinsman, O'Brien, King of Thomond, was little more than a child, a pimply, fair-haired youth who scowled—perhaps with reason, for his father was alleged to have been boiled to death in a cauldron by the previous saintly-looking welcomer barely a year before.

"The puissant O'Carroll, King of Uriel." A slender dark elegant, who would have been supremely handsome but for a cast in one eye, made flourish of his salute, while Bruce decided that he would not trust him one yard.

The sixth to rise was the valiant MacCarthy, King of Desmond, a man almost as broad as he was high, with long arms which hung to his knees, said to have the strength of an ox. He, certainly, would be an excellent man to have at one's side.

The amiable, red-headed O'Neil, King of Tyrone, was next, and hurried through his performance with some embarrassment, barely rising from his seat.

Last rose O'Connor, King of Connaught, first among equals, who should have been High King—had the others been prepared to accept him. A studious, delicate-seeming man, he looked more of a scholar than a warrior. He alone did not raise his hand, but bowed towards Bruce, stiffly formal.

Then the trumpets sounded once more, louder and longer, and the herald took a deep breath.

"The serene, right royal and victorious Lord Edward, king of

149

kings, by God's grace *Ard Righ*, High King of All Ireland, greets the Lord Robert, King of Scots, and welcomes him to this his realm and kingdom."

Edward broke the pattern. He did not stand up, or raise his hand, or even bow. "Come, brother," he said, conversationally. "You are late. I looked for you hours ago. Have you not some captain, some horse or baggage master, capable of settling your people into quarters?"

Bruce eyed this good-looking, awkward brother of his, biting back the hot words – as seemed to be ever necessary. "I came here to play the captain rather than the monarch, Edward," he said evenly. "I shall continue to do so."

"M'mm." The other considered that. He shrugged. "Come, anyway, Robert. It is good to see you, however . . . delayed. All Ireland welcomes you. Come – sit here."

Bruce nodded, and moved unhurriedly up between the seated kings. He stood, looking down at his brother for a few moments before he sat down in the lesser throne. "You are content, now?" he said, smiling a little.

"Content?" Edward frowned. "How mean you – content?"

"Why – High King! So very high!"

"It is the style. The Celtic style."

"Aye. I seem to have been climbing, ever since I set foot on Irish soil! And now my neck suffers stretching!" The elder brother exaggerated the necessary upward-looking posture somewhat, from his lower chair.

The other ignored that. He clapped his hands. "The music. The dancing. Resume," he called. "You like my dancers, Robert?"

"They are very fair. And doubtless they do more than dance? But I might have esteemed them better as cooks! Or even scullions, brother! We have travelled far, and our bellies in more need of distraction than our eyes and ears!"

"You will be feasting in plenty, anon, never fear. Be patient. As I had to be, awaiting you! Much of my provision was spoiled. By the delay. My cooks are working to repair that delay. We would have eaten well, two hours ago, brother. Roasted peacocks. Breast of swan. Sucking boar seethed in malvoisie. Spiced salmon. Peppered lobster. Woodcock . . ."

"*We* would have eaten well, to be sure. But the men I brought – what of them? I found no provision made for them, cold, tired, hungry. This is the first day of December, Edward – winter is on us. Even in Ireland! To have them lie under the open sky . . .!"

"It is an army you have brought, is it not? Not a parcel of clerks or women! I' faith – in the past, our armies found their own meat and shelter well enough! Did they not?"

Curiously Bruce considered his brother. "*You* say that? You would have me turn my people loose on your land? To do their will? An army foraging! Is that the King of Ireland speaking?"

"From the man who burned half of Scotland, and more than once, you are becoming exceeding nice, I think!" the other gave back.

Robert drew a long breath. "Remember that, Edward, when your Abbot of White Abbey comes making complaint that I have misused his property!" he said grimly. "Now–what of the enemy? The English? Do they press heavily? How far south are your outposts? And where is my good-father, Ulster . . . ?"

Edward was not, in fact, eager to discuss the strategic position; but thereafter, and especially when presently they moved into the banqueting-hall, next to the kitchens across the courtyard, where he found the soldierly MacCarthy, King of Desmond, sitting at his right hand, Bruce did learn sufficient to give him a fair overall picture. Hostilities were at the moment more or less suspended, without there being any accepted truce, while both sides regrouped and drew on their strength–or so Edward described it. He had had to give up Dundalk–where the coronation had taken place–and their furthest south outposts were at Downpatrick and the line of the Quoile River, not thirty miles south of Belfast Lough. North of that was in their hands, although there were one or two Anglo-Irish lords holding out. The entire west side of the country was an unknown quantity, although some of the chiefs there were believed to be in revolt. In fact, only Ulster was secure–and not all of that, it seemed. Edward might be King of All Ireland, but three-quarters of the country had yet to be convinced of it.

Not even all the Irish princes were on Edward's side. O'Hanlon, MacMahon, Maguire and MacGoffey were known to be co-operating with the English meantime, as well as many lesser chieftains. Some would change sides at the first sign of success, no doubt; but the reverse might well apply with others presently accepted as loyal.

However, all the news was not of this calibre. The English leadership seemed to be having its own troubles. Nobody was very sure who was in command. Sir Edmund Butler, the Justiciar, over whom Edward and Moray had won a victory earlier, had been thereafter replaced, on orders from London, by Roger, Lord Mortimer. But at the same time, a tough and militant cleric, John de Hotham, Bishop of Ely, had been sent over as Chancellor of Ireland, and political overlord, and there was bad blood between him and Mortimer. The de Lacy brothers, important Anglo-Irish Lords of Meath, appeared to be offended at both of these appointments, and with their friends and allies were not exactly in revolt but were refusing to co-operate. Most uncertain of all was Richard de Burgh's position. As Earl of Ulster he was the greatest of the Anglo-Irish nobles—indeed the native Irish referred to the Anglo-Irish as the Race of Richard Burke—as well as the foremost commander in age as in seniority and in rank, of any in Ireland; and had more than once acted as commander-in-chief of Irish forces. But he was apparently now only to command in the north—although admittedly that was where the main fighting would be apt to be—and presumably under the authority of both the Bishop and Mortimer. The reason for this was difficult to fathom—although some suggested that it was because de Burgh had been Edward the First's great crony and comrade-in-arms, and Edward the Second, hating his late father and all his works, might not trust him, might even wish to humiliate him.

Whatever was behind it all, it seemed to Robert Bruce a situation which should be exploited, and swiftly. But it quickly became apparent that such was not his brother's opinion, nor that of most of those around him. Let the English squabble amongst themselves, was the reaction. Why interfere, when that would most probably just unite them? Let them grow weaker, while they themselves gathered their strength. Besides, here was no time for campaigning, before the Yuletide festivals were over. Ireland was a notably Christian, not to say, holy, country, the most pious in the western world. They must not offend religious feeling.

Bruce, aware of how much religious feeling his brother possessed, did not take this seriously at first. But as time wore on, he realised that it was no laughing matter. Edward was himself quite ruthless about religious susceptibilities, strong though they were; but he was using them as excuse for delay. He was not ready to move, and he found the peculiar Irish preoccupation with religious form, observance and display convenient to his purpose.

Certainly that of 1316-17 was the busiest, fullest Yuletide Bruce had ever experienced. Every day for weeks seemed to be a saint's day—the names of most of which the Scots had never so much as heard. Not that the consequent celebrations were in the main tiresomely sanctimonious, or even very recognisably sacerdotal. Parades, pageantry, contests, feasting, singing and dancing, even horse-racing, were seemingly all part of the programme of worship, the clerics foremost in promoting all. The rain, which tended to fall daily, did nothing to damp down at least local pious spirits.

Bruce fretted but conformed. He could, of course, have taken matters into his own hands, and led his Scots force southwards independently. But that would have much offended the Irish, and involved lack of co-operation if not actual hostility on the part of the local populations through which they must pass, a serious matter. Irish politics being what they were, and the Church being so all-pervasive and influential, such a move would have been rash indeed.

Not that the period of waiting was wholly wasted. It gave time for Scots captains to get to know their Irish forces, as well as for more men to flood in from various parts of Ulster and the North. Time also for the integration of the army, and a certain amount of training—though this was scarcely popular. Bruce quickly realised that there was little that he could do to make a more unified force out of the Irish legions, neither themselves nor Edward being prepared to tolerate any such interference. He contented himself with picking out men for a light cavalry force—for which, since he was providing the horses and squadron commanders, they could hardly object. This he prevailed on MacCarthy of Desmond to captain, with Angus Og as liaison, who knew the Irish best from his many mercenary campaigns here. These made a dashing, swift-moving force—if only they could be relied upon to do as they were commanded. Working with the Scots, they would form the spear-head of the campaign.

In the end, it was not until the beginning of February, with rumours of de Burgh massing troops at Drogheda, that at long last a start was made from Carrickfergus—inevitably on the Day of the Blessed Brigit, Abbess of Kildare. There were, in fact, two distinct armies—Bruce's light cavalry host of Scots and selected Irish, to the number of about 9,000; and the great composite mass of Irish gallowglasses, kerns and clansmen, stiffened with Scots veteran captains and some heavy chivalry, unnumbered but probably totalling some 40,000. One was fast, to conduct hard-hitting, swift-striking warfare of the sort Bruce had perfected; the other slow, cumbersome, to come along behind, consolidating, occupying, supplying. Edward, of course, should have commanded the second and main army—as he did in name; but he was a cavalry commander above all, and he insisted on riding with the first force. In fact, much of the time he was out in front with the advance guard, however unsuitable in a monarch. He had been reluctant to start—for he had wanted the Scots strength to stabilise his hold on his kingdom and defeat his internal enemies—but once committed, typically, he was all fire and energy.

As much to keep up with Edward as anything else, the cavalry army, after rounding the head of Belfast Lough, dashed the twenty-odd miles south to the limits of their occupied territory on the very first day. Bruce was uneasy at already leaving the main host so far behind—but was more uneasy still when he discovered that Edward's advance party, finding their welcome insufficiently enthusiastic, had burned the church at Bright, and already sacked the monastery of the walled cathedral town of Downpatrick, where they had proposed to spend the night. This in allegedly friendly country. Admittedly there had been some opposition at Greencastle, which had an Anglo-Irish de Courcy lord, and which Edward took with a flourish – but, after all the religious observance, this seemed to be an odd way to start a campaign. Edward had Irish backing, however, for his assertion that this was how wars were conducted in Ireland.

There being insufficient forage for the thousands of horses at Downpatrick, allegedly St. Patrick's burial-place, they moved two miles eastwards to the wide abbey-lands of Saul, flanking Strangford Lough, where St. Malachy had built the abbey on the site of the barn wherein St. Patrick held his first Christian service in Ireland, and where there was grass in plenty. There was no getting away from saints and sanctity in this country. Even the grass, it was alleged, would be the better for the horses, in these holy pastures – although this did not prevent Edward's men from treating the abbot and his monks less than gently. Bruce forbore criticism thus early. Assuming that Edward would remain with his main infantry army, he had underestimated the difficulties of a divided command, and this *was* his brother's country.

Next day they rode so fast and so far that there was little time for adventures on the way, and no real opposition showed itself. They were still near Ulster, of course, County Louth. Leaving unmolested the Knights Templar castle of Dundrum, they went by Castlewellan and Rathfryland, with the mountains of Mourne on their left, through Newry and Faughart until, at dusk, they came to Dundalk itself, the furthest south of Edward's penetrations hitherto, where he had been crowned. Ahead lay the English-dominated territories. They were exactly half-way to Dublin in two days.

The clash of will between the two brothers, which was bound to take place sooner or later, occurred soon after they left Dundalk, on a chill morning of wind and threatening rain. Beyond the ford of the Fane River, the road forked. Edward wanted to drive south-east, straight for Drogheda, the English seaport-base, twenty miles away, while still they held the initiative and at least partial surprise. Robert, ever against siegery and time-consuming attacks on fortresses, said no. They should make for Dublin itself, fifty miles on. That would be totally unexpected, whereas Drogheda might well already be expecting attack. Dublin was far too large to be defended in total, having long outgrown its walls. It was the capital, and ostensible seat of government. Capture of Dublin would rally the whole of Ireland.

It was not like Edward to reject anything so bold and vigorous as this. But having declared for Drogheda, his authority was at stake, and he evidently felt bound to insist.

"Drogheda first," he declared. "What good Dublin if Drogheda remains a threat at our backs?"

"Dublin is worth a dozen Droghedas, man. We will cut the line between the two. Then your Irish army of foot can move down to seal off Drogheda. That is not *our* task. Let them do it."

"No! It is fifty miles to Dublin. All the country will be roused before we get there. Surprise lost."

"Edward—you have the pig by the tail, not the snout! Do you not see? Drogheda is the English base—but Dublin is the government centre for all Ireland. None will expect us to make straight for it. At the speed we rode yesterday, we can be there before tomorrow's dusk. Think of it! Before Bishop Hotham and Mortimer can decide who commands what! Or my good-father Ulster can succour either!"

"*That* is why you will not attack Drogheda, I swear!" his brother cried. "You are afraid to meet Richard de Burgh! Or too nice! Your Elizabeth's sire. Well—I am not! We ride for Drogheda, I say."

"We do not, Edward," Bruce said, softly now. "Or if *you* do, we part company."

"You . . . you challenge my word? Mine? Here in Ireland, I'd remind you, *I* am king, not you!"

"King you may be, Edward—but I command all Scots forces. Not you. On these terms alone I brought them to Ireland. They follow *me*, in Ireland as in Scotland."

"S-o-o! This is your vaunted aid!"

"This is my aid, yes. Though I never vaunted it. Far from it. I would have preferred to stay in Scotland, where there is much to be done. But . . . I warned you. I came as a captain, and will continue to act as such."

Edward twisted in his saddle, a magnificent figure in his dazzling, gold-inlaid black armour and purple cloak, against his brother's somewhat rusty chain-mail, and stared at the group of senior commanders who rode just behind, and who could not fail to have heard this exchange—Moray, Gilbert Hay, Keith the Marischal, Fraser the Chamberlain, Angus of the Isles, de Soulis and MacCarthy of Desmond.

"Well?" he demanded. "Who, in Ireland, obeys the King of Ireland?"

De Soulis moistened his lips. "I do, Sire."

No one else spoke.

"And you, MacCarthy?"

"I must obey my liege lord," the King of Desmond said, all but growled. "Since I am vowed to it. But I agree with the Lord Robert. Go for Dublin, I say."

With a glare at the level-eyed, silent Scots, Edward faced the front again, and dug in his spurs savagely, to race ahead.

Bruce and the others made no attempt to catch up with him too soon. At least he took the road that forked towards Dublin, south-west.

Whatever else, Bruce had thereafter no cause for complaint about the speed at which they made for the capital. A horsed host of thousands travels at the pace of its slowest riders, not its fastest, and there was no keeping up with Edward. But even so the main body had reached Slane, on the Boyne, half-way to Dublin, with dark falling, when Bruce called a halt. He had half expected the river-crossing to be held against them. Here was good grass, and meadow-land for camping, and nearby to the south was the fabled Hill of Tara, site of the ancient capital of Ireland and seat of the pagan kings. That day they had engaged in no fighting, assaulted no castles, by-passed all major towns. They were only twenty-five miles from Dublin, and on the edge of the Pale, level with Drogheda nine miles to the east. To have gone further that night would have been folly. But of Edward there was no sign. Young O'Donnell, son of the King of Tyrconnel, was leading the advance party, with Sir Colin Campbell. Presumably his liege lord had taken over.

Bruce sent a fast rider after him, to inform that he had halted at Slane, in a good defensive position, holding the river's ford. A couple of hours later the courier was back, alone. He announced that His Grace of Ireland was at the small monastery of Skreen, on the side of the Hill of Tara, eight miles on, and entirely comfortable. He would stay where he was.

This would not do. Bruce recognised only too well the dangers of this sort of situation—especially with Richard de Burgh not so far away. Gulping down the last of his meal, dark as it was and raining thinly, he wrapped himself in his cloak, called Gilbert Hay to accompany him, left the army in the care of Moray and told the courier to turn again and lead him to Tara.

It was an unpleasant ride, over benighted, uneven country, with the streams running full. Of Tara's renowned hill they saw only the dark loom as they circled its broken skirts, to come at length to the modest ecclesiastical establishment of Skreen, alleged to have risen on the site of the hermitage of St. Erck, in one of its southern folds. Here, the advance guard of 150 men lay at ease—and no sentry saw fit to challenge Bruce's little party. In the Prior's room—with no sign of the Prior—Edward lounged before a glowing peat fire, with the young Prince of Tyrconnel.

"So you have seen fit to honour us with your royal presence!" he greeted his brother. "Have you eaten? We do very well here."

"No doubt. But I did not come here to eat, Edward. I looked for you, and this forward squadron, at Slane. Not eight miles beyond!"

"Then you should have used your wits, Robert. Where else would the King of Ireland rest, in this corner of his dominions than on Tara's Hill?"

"It matters not where the King of Ireland rests the night! Nor the King of Scots, either," Bruce answered harshly. "What matters is where their army rests. And this small monastery on an open hillside, however notable, is not it."

"The army, you assure me, is your concern! So be it. Rest it where you will. For myself, I am very well here."

Robert bit his lip. He looked from O'Donnell to Hay, and then to the door. "Leave us, if you please," he told them. And when he and Edward were alone, moved to stand at the side of the fire, the steam rising from his cloak.

"Edward," he said heavily, "you know as well as do I that for a small advance column to camp in open enemy country, unscouted country, eight miles ahead of its main force, is folly. And when that small party contains the king of the land, proclaiming his presence and caring nothing for his safety—then that is worse than folly. You could be captured, easily—and where is your kingdom then? Held to a ransom that could spell the end of your ambitions. If the English did not first hang you as rebel!"

"Save us—more fraternal preachings! Spare me that, of a mercy!"

The other shook his head. "No—I did not come to preach, to berate you. To quarrel, Edward. The reverse, indeed. If you and I quarrel on this campaign, it will come to disaster. Nothing surer."

"For once we are in agreement, brother!" Edward conceded, jerking a laugh.

"Yes. Then we must come to terms in this foolish warfare."

"I am glad to hear it. But—whose terms? The King of Ireland's? Or the commander of his host's?"

His brother took a pace or two across the room. "See you, Edward—it is not my purpose to belittle your position. To undercut your authority. As king. You believe that I cannot abide your being my equal, a monarch such as myself. That is not so. I am not such a fool. Your Irish kingship I respect. And am sustaining. And will continue to do. But I was against this whole Irish adventure. I was forced into it against my judgement. Yet it is in the main by *my* power and strength that it is being pursued. You know very well that as a united force to conquer Ireland, all your kinglets and princelings amount to so much wind—swelling names, resplendent titles, brave men enough, but hating each other and with no least notion of discipline. What is happening far behind us even now, in that great rabble of foot, God knows! I would have thought that would have been *your* task, to command and seek to unify."

"I believe you said that you did not come to berate and belittle!"

"Aye. My concern is that my Scots host is used to the best advantage. And for Scotland. To that end I retain full command. But that also serves your interests, Edward."

"On my territory *I* should command. It is intolerable that in his own realm a monarch should see his authority set aside by another whom he brought in to aid him. And that his own brother."

"Two men may not command a host. Nor a kingdom. Once before, I gave you that answer, you will mind! When I was sick, years back, and you proposed that you should share the Crown of Scotland with me! Both kings. I did not love you for that, I do admit! But it would not have served then. And it will not serve now. Committed to this campaign, *I* command."

"And I? What am I? A lackey, for you to order as you will? Great God—I have had enough of that in Scotland!"

"Not so. I have come here tonight with proposals. Either go back to your own great Irish host, and command that as you will—if it will obey you! Or stay with me and the Scots, as my equal in kingship but accepting my command as captain. Agree to be second in the command of the cavalry host."

"Second? When you have our precious nephew Moray, to your hand! And that barbarian Angus Og! And Hay, Keith, and the rest! Do you think that I am witless enough to believe that you may prefer me to any of these? You never have done!"

His brother opened his mouth for a hot reply, then closed it again. He looked instead into the red glow of the fire. "You do not remark on my first proposal? That you go back to your Irish host. So . . . hear what I propose here," he said levelly. "Now that we are like to meet with the enemy at any moment, with de Burgh only an hour or two's ride away, our present headlong riding will no longer serve. We must advance with a deal greater care—though still fast, if we are to surprise Dublin. And in different formation. No longer a small scouting force ahead, and then all the main host. Still we need scouts in front, flanking vedettes, and a rearward. But the main host should now be split into two. Say 3,000 and 6,000. Each to remain near the other for support, but some way apart, for safety, for easier handling in close country, for better observation

158

of enemy forces. You understand? I offer you command for the first host. Of the 3,000."

The other stared. "You mean it? Command? Full command?"

"Full command, under my direction. I retain overall command. But within that, this host will be yours. Mainly MacCarthy's Irish horse, but with a stiffening of Scots. How say you?"

"Why? Why do you do this, Robert? Is it a trick . . . ?"

"No trick. I offer it because we must come to terms, Edward. It this campaign is not to fail. It may be that I keep too much in my own hands, that I assign too little authority to others. I think not – but it may be so. I am willing to try this. For harmony and the sake of our cause."

Edward was on his feet now. "Under your direction I am in full command of this first cavalry force? Is that it? I will not have Moray, or the Islesman, or other of your friends, sitting on my heels? Frowning and reproving . . . ?"

"No. Any Scots veterans that I give you will be lesser men. You will have full command. Only – I expect my directions to be obeyed, Edward. Or else we think again. Or we turn back, here and now – for me, all the way back to Scotland!"

His brother searched his face for a long moment, and then grinned. "Very well, Robert – we shall try it. Try again. On these terms. Here is my hand on it!"

They shook hands there before the Prior's peat fire. It was a long time since these two had made any such gesture.

"Now – to planning," Bruce said briskly, "MacCarthy says that there is much broken, forested country ahead. Mid-Meath. Between Trim and Dunshaughlin. My good-father has a manor and castle at Ratoath, in this part. And Trim is the de Lacys' most powerful castle. We do not know how they will jump . . ."

IT was just after noon next day that the first fruits of the royal brothers' rapprochement became apparent. Bruce, at the head of the main Scots force, now little more than 5,000 men, with detachments well out on the flanks and to the rear, was riding at a fast trot through scattered and broken woodland country south of Dunshaughlin, when young Sir Colin Campbell came galloping back from the forward host.

"His Grace of Ireland, Sire, sends me to inform you that he has captured a kern who declares that the Earl of Ulster is here. Here, not at Drogheda. At his own house ahead. This Ratoath, he names it . . ."

"De Burgh, here? In front? With how many men, Sir Colin? An army?"

"No, Your Grace. Not many, the man said."

"That sounds strange. He can scarce be ignorant that we are near. My brother—what does he do?"

"He rides for Ratoath, with all speed. To capture the Earl."

"He does? Aye, he would!" Bruce frowned. "I do not think that I like the smell of this! How far ahead is he?"

"Four miles. With another three to go to Ratoath, the kern said."

"And the country? What is it like? Is it still wooded, close? As here?"

"Thicker, Sire. More hills. Rocks."

"M'mmm. This kern that you captured? How was he? Did you see him taken?"

"Yes. He was sitting at the roadside, watching us pass . . ."

"Watching! How many of the people here do that? They flee at the sound, much less the sight, of us! Was he armed?"

"No, Sire. Save with a cudgel. He seemed a simple countryman . . ."

Bruce turned to his close lieutenants. "How say you?" he demanded.

"It could be honest. Or it could be false. A trap," Angus Og said.

"I mislike the sound of it," Moray asserted.

"The Lord Edward has 3,000 men now," Gilbert Hay reminded. "It would require to be a large trap!"

"What do you fear, my lord King?" Campbell asked. "What is wrong?"

"Two matters smell wrong. One large, one small. Your Queen's father is no ordinary man, no mere Anglo-Irish baron. He is a warrior, and wily, a veteran trained by that great schemer, the late Edward Longshanks. He cannot but know of our advance. Last night we were only ten miles from Drogheda. If he is indeed in front of us now, is he the man to have left Drogheda with only a few men? For this Ratoath, directly in our path?"

"How do we know when he left Drogheda, Sire? He may have been at Ratoath for days," Hay pointed out. "We have had no sure news."

"Our flank vedettes to the east have sent us no warnings of any movement of men, from Drogheda or anywhere else," Sir Alexander Fraser put in.

"The Earl of Ulster is thought to be at odds with this Bishop and Mortimer," Angus added. "He acted strangely over the relief fleet for Carrickfergus. If they have superseded him as commander in Ireland, it may be that he does not seek to fight you now, but to talk. Parley with his good-son?"

Bruce drummed fingers on his saddle-bow. "It is possible. But . . . this other matter does not smell well, either. This of a knowledge-able kern, who waits to watch my brother's host go by. That metal does not ring true. Had de Burgh wished to parley with me, would he have done it thus? Sent a common kern to let slip that he was in the neighbourhood? However secret, he would have sent me a messenger of quality."

"The kern could still be just a kern, Your Grace. A villager of this Ratoath, who knows the Earl . . ."

"Could be—but may not be! I shall ride the easier when I am assured of it. Meantime, we shall hasten. Four miles is too great a gap, in this close country . . ."

The King's face grew longer, his frown darker, as they drove on, at a canter now, into ever thicker and rougher country, with rocky bluffs, densely wooded and with flooded scrub-covered bottom land. This was the sort of territory in which a cavalry host was least effective, even light cavalry. If an attack was indeed to be made on them, this was the place for it. Yet, no word had come back from Edward that his force was meeting with any difficulties. And Bruce's own flanking scouts sent no warning of anything unusual.

When Colin Campbell at length announced that it was here that the kern had been taken, here that he himself had turned back with his message, his liege lord all but snapped his head off. They were passing through a small open glade with evil swamp on the left and a steeply rising bank on the right.

"Did MacCarthy, did any of the Irish, say what sort of a castle this of Ratoath is?" he interrupted. "I think it cannot be a great place, in this wretched country. I had never heard its name, never heard my wife speak of it."

"The Prince of Tyrconnel named it a small place, Sire. Scarce a castle at all, I think, as we Scots would say. A moated manor, rather . . ."

"Aye. I like this less and less . . ." Bruce chewed on his thoughts for a while. The swamp on the left was drying up somewhat, with more trees; but the bank on the right was growing ever steeper, taller, almost a cliff. Apart from famous death-traps like the Pass of Brander in Lorne, and Glen Trool in Galloway, he had seldom seen territory which he liked less, from a military point of view. He had reduced the pace to a slow trot now. Yet Edward's force had gone through here, only a short time before. There was no least sign of trouble, only recent horse-droppings.

He took a sudden decision. "Campbell," he ordered, "ride you forward, after my brother. Take a small party—a score. My salutations to His Grace—but request him to turn back. Forthwith. Whatever he is doing, besieging this Ratoath, or other. His host to return. To close up, until we are safely through this evil country. It may be little necessary—but we could meet disaster here. We should not be more than half a mile apart. Where each could cover the other. You have it? With my salutations, mind—but it is a firm command." And as the other, nodding, turned to collect his twenty or so men from the first files behind, the King added, "Do not be distracted, left or right, see you. You are not scouts. Ride fast. Press on to my brother. If you get hint of trouble, avoid it. I shall have others out, to scout, behind you."

"Do you but make siccar, Sire?" Fraser asked, as the little party clattered ahead. "Or have you more reason than we here perceive?"

"I smell danger, Sandy," the King answered that implied criticism. "It stinks in my nostrils. Do not ask me for better reason!"

The words were hardly out of his mouth when a scream from ahead, around a bend in the woodland track, was immediately followed by shouting, confused, urgent.

He dug in his spurs. They all did.

Hurtling round the bend, Bruce saw a scene as confused as the noise. One man lay spread-eagled on the road, an arrow transfixing his chest. Two horses were down, hooves lashing. Others were milling about, one with a long shaft clearly projecting from its haunch. Colin Campbell was seeking to marshal his men and lead them off to the left, off the track, down into the boggy woodland.

"Follow me!" he was shouting, "Follow me!"

Cursing furiously, Bruce drove his horse straight for the young knight, shaking a suddenly upraised fist.

Campbell saw him, and mistook the gesture. "I will get them!" he yelled and spurred on.

After him the King plunged, pushing aside two men-at-arms in the way. Coming up with the eager Highlander, he reached over and struck him a resounding buffet with his steel-gauntleted fist, that sent the other reeling in his saddle.

"Fool!" he cried. "Back! Back, I say! If your life means nothing to you, think of these others. *My* subjects! Back, man!"

Shaken, Campbell pulled up, staring as though his monarch had run mad.

"What were my last words? The last I spoke you?"

Appalled, the young man reined round, waving his men back now. "I . . . I am sorry, Sire. I did not think. Or . . . I thought otherwise. To save Your Grace. The next arrow might have struck *you* . . . !"

"When *last* I struck you a blow, man, I said that you should be a true knight until your life's end!" Bruce panted, turning back for the track. The heat was going out of his voice, however. "You were near your life's end there, I swear! But a true knight obeys his liege lord's commands. Remember it. I said turn aside for nothing."

Back at the halted column, Fraser called out. "You have a good nose, Sire! Even for so small a trouble."

"Small, Sandy? What mean you by small?"

"I count but eight arrows. There may be more in the bushes, missed their mark. But no large force would shoot so few."

"But they are English clothyard shafts, see you—not our short Irish or Scots bolts."

"Even so, Sire, but few. And now they have seen how large a force we are, they forbear."

Moray had men dismounted, awaiting his order to slip off into the trees. He looked at his uncle.

"Leave them, Thomas. They will not shoot against us again, I think. Not here. Sandy is right—these must be a small party. But English, mark you. They made a mistake, opening up on Campbell's troop, not knowing that we followed so close. They will have fled now, deep into these fastnesses. Let them go. But—this is not all the danger that I smelt, by the Rude!"

"You think there are more, Sire?" Hay asked. "Yet they have let the Lord Edward's force go past, it seems . . ."

"To be sure there are more. And if my good-father is behind

163

them, many more. A small band of archers would never have risked shooting at Campbell's score if they had not greater numbers near. Besides, what are a dozen English archers doing in such a place? That is not how these fight. They are part of a scouting patrol, I say, sent to watch. Their leader misjudged, that is all. But, if they were sent to watch this road, from these woods, then whoever sent them is expecting us! Yet he has let my brother past. You see the pattern? Remember we are likely dealing with Richard de Burgh, fox as much as lion! I would say that he is waiting for *me*. In ambush."

There was silence, as the leaders of the long column eyed the King.

"And the Lord Edward?" somebody asked.

"The Lord Edward no doubt goes on with a blithe heart! He is likely already besetting an empty Ratoath Castle, waiting for him as bait!"

"You conceive the Earl of Ulster as between us and Ratoath, between us and my uncle?" Moray asked.

"I would judge it likely."

"And we cannot get word to him?"

"We can try. Not along this road. By sending men on foot, back and up by the high ground, to the right. That way they may win through, unseen. Your Islesmen would be best, Angus. But it cannot be other than slow."

"And us? While they do it, dare we go on?" Fraser demanded.

"Yet we cannot wait here. As ill a place to defend as any I have seen. And if we retire, will not de Burgh turn on the Lord Edward's force instead? From behind. Where he will think to be safe, with us at his back."

"We will not retire, no. Edward apart, I did not bring these thousands to Ireland to retire in the face of the first threat. But— I prefer that *I* choose the battle-ground, not my good-sire!"

"How can you do that? Placed as we are?" Angus Og said. "We dare not retire. There is no good ground to fight on for miles back, as we have seen. Since we cannot stay here, we can only go on, de Burgh or none!"

"Aye, my lord—you are right. But we go on warned. Warned, and dismounted. If there is to be fighting, in such country, I would do it afoot."

"Aye! Aye!"

"Is that best, Sire?" Hay wondered. "To throw away our speed. Should we not remain mounted, and charge our way through. Many as we are. Using our speed and weight . . ."

"No, my lord Constable—for that is what de Burgh would expect us to do. If that earl is indeed before us, he will have planned for that, the wrecking of a mounted host. So we go afoot. Horses, in these bogs, are useless. All horses, therefore, to be sent to the rear. Lest arrows get them. We need them hereafter, if we are to conquer Ireland! But not here and now. If Richard de Burgh is here. *If*, I say . . ." The King shrugged.

Metaphorically they all shrugged. It was all supposition, after all. Save for those clothyard shafts and the one dead man. There was nothing hypothetical about them.

With a certain amount of difficulty, and even some grumbling, along the line, the cavalry host there and then converted itself into an infantry host, passing the horses back. Bruce had the men close up into a much tighter and broader formation, as broad a front as the terrain would allow. Also, he insisted that all shields be carried, and on the left arms, not left with the horses—never a popular move with cavalrymen.

And so they moved on southwards, slowly now. And silently, with the command passed down for the maximum of quiet.

It made a strange progress through the early February afternoon, thousands of armed men all but tip toeing, unspeaking, watchful, aware. Bruce had their relatively few archers up near the front. Never for a moment did any of them cease to scan the woodland ahead and to the left.

The King gave his instructions as they walked. "Thomas—our first warning may well be a hail of arrows. They will seek to pick off our leaders first. But if they have any wits, they will let us get well into their trap. Go you part way down the column. If we are attacked from the woodland, have all behind you, save for the horse guard, swing off the track. Down into the wood. A wide sweep, to take the archers in flank. And swiftly. Or we may not survive! You have it?"

"Aye, Sire. But you?"

"We will play the poltroons! We will throw ourselves down. As poor marks for arrows as may be. Covered by our shields. To give you and your men time to get in amongst them. Then we shall up and charge to your aid." He glanced upwards, half-right. "Pray for us that there are no rocks loose, up there!"

The bank above them was steep but mainly of earth and rough grass, with scrub clinging. Higher, perhaps 200 feet above, the slope eased back out of sight, and the lessened gradient permitted taller trees to grow.

"At least it is no place for archers," Moray commented. "They could not shoot down at that angle, without exposing themselves. And it is too steep for men to charge down."

"Aye—as for men to charge up! So long as it remains so. It pens us in, cramps us—but it does not threaten us greatly. Off with you, then, Thomas—and God go with you. If a bend of the track comes between us, three short blasts from my trumpeter means that we are attacked. One long blast, and you hasten directly forward to me. Gibbie—pass the word back. All men to fall flat if the arrows come, and so lie."

They had gone perhaps another half-mile when Colin Campbell spoke suddenly, low-voiced. "I saw something, Sire. Movement. In the trees . . ."

"Where, man? Where?"

"Yonder. Near that white tree. The dead tree. Right of it." He pointed to an area about 250 yards away.

"Do not point, man. That could bring the arrows. Do you see aught . . . ?"

No movement showed.

"It could be a deer. A boar. I have seen droppings," Angus Og said.

"Shall I go search?" Campbell demanded.

"No. That will serve nothing. Send a man back to Moray. Tell him of this. The place. For the rest, move on."

Now the sensation of tiptoeing, of walking on hot stones, was intensified. It would have been a clod-like dolt indeed who could have stalked on unconcerned. Stout warriors found themselves stooping a little, hunching their shoulders, seeking to shrink their persons behind shields and armour.

No attack developed.

Then, round a substantial bend in the road, there was a major change in the scenery. Temporarily the scattered woodland rolled back, to reveal a wide clearing, perhaps a quarter-mile across. Ahead was more forest, but the high bank on the right began gradually to break down and level off.

Bruce drew a long breath. "If I planned an assault, this is where I would choose," he said. "Before this bank ceases to wall us in. With a killing ground, open for archers. Yet cover all round for my forces. It . . ."

"Sire—see! A flash. A flash of light," the keen-eyed Campbell cried. "Ahead. Half-left . . ."

"I saw it," Hay confirmed. "Sun on steel, for a wager!"

"Look—another! Farther over . . ."

"So be it." Bruce was all decision now, raising his battle-axe in his right hand and slamming it downwards twice. "Down!" he commanded. "Down!" And all along the line the cry was taken up, as men fell flat on their faces, shields jerking up to cover them. It was though a giant sickle mowed them down.

"Trumpeter—three blasts!" the King panted, as he himself went low.

166

Somewhat off-note and gaspingly, the trumpet neighed its warning from the mud of the track.

Results were immediate and quite fantastic. As though echoes had gone crazy, other trumpets and horns began to shout and yelp and ululate all around at some distance, in a shrill cacophony. There were urgent cries. And, within seconds, the first arrows began to hiss and twang and fall, raggedly admittedly, but in ever increasing numbers and accuracy.

It is safe to say that never before had Bruce's veterans had a like experience. To lie flat on the ground and allow oneself to be shot at, without any answering gesture, was beyond all belief frustrating, humiliating, as well as alarming. Yet none there failed to realise how much better off they were lying down than standing up. From 400 yards or so lying men make a very poor target, largely invisible as individuals. When there were thousands, as here, the arrows could scarcely fail to find them, but it had to be by dropping shots, not directly aimed. And it is quite the most difficult feat in archery to so direct an arrow, and by your bow-string pull so control its flight, that at a given exact distance it will change its upward course and curve down in a parabola so as to land at a steep angle on even a wide target. This is the science of ballistics, and although the English and Welsh bowmen were apt to be the best in the world, few could be expert at this. Moreover, by its very nature, anything such could only be contrived by effecting a slackening of velocity at the given point; which meant that unless the angle of fire was very high indeed, the fall of the shaft, by the time it reached its target, had lost most of its impetus.

As a consequence, though a great many arrows were shot, comparatively few landed amongst the recumbent Scots at an angle to do any damage; and of these most were of insufficient velocity to penetrate leather, much less armour and chain-mail. There were some deadly hits, some screaming—but for a major archery attack casualties were negligible.

Nevertheless it was not pleasant to lie there, pinned down, helpless. The waiting seemed endless. Not to be hitting back was the worst of it; but there was nothing that men could do in a prone position. The arrows continued to fall. They were tending to come in volleys now.

It was the volleying becoming ragged again, with the change in tenor and scale of the shouting from their hidden assailants, that gave the prostrate host some indication that at last this stage of their ordeal might be ending. The anger, threat and jeering in the chorus of hate was being affected by new notes that spoke of surprise, urgency, even alarm. Moray's people were beginning to concern the enemy's right flank.

167

It was possible thereafter for the Scots to trace the advance of their friends, unseen as they were. The archery became ever more erratic, and died away at the north. But presently the advance slowed, if not ceased altogether. It was obvious that fierce fighting was taking place in the swampy woodland. Bruce counted every second.

The arrows had not stopped their dropping shower altogether, but it was on a vastly lessened scale.

"Will," the King cried. "Now! Cover us." Sir William Irvine, Bruce's former armour-bearer, had been put in command of the six-score or so Scots bowmen.

These now, at Irvine's order, were the first to take the grievous step of rising from the prone. They rose each only on one knee, admittedly – and in this their shorter Scots bows aided them, lacking though they were in hitting-power. But it took a deal of courage for men to hoist themselves up, to make immediate targets of themselves. As swiftly as they might, their own arrows began to fly, practically unseen as *their* targets were. Some few never drew string before they fell back, pierced through.

Although they were shooting blind, even such attack would be alarming for men standing up behind six-foot-long bows just within the screen of bushes. The enemy fire slackened almost to nothing. It was more than Bruce had hoped for.

"Sound the advance!" he jerked. Then, as the trumpeter's unsteady notes rang out, he was the first to his feet. "Up!" he shouted. "Up! A Bruce! A Bruce!" Axe raised, shield held up before him, he leapt forward, down off the track and into the softer ground to the left.

He did not look back, nor did he have to. He did not have to shout for speed, either. No man there was going to linger, with even a few arrows in the air and some 300 yards of open ground to cover. Yelling, the Scots line rose and surged after him, while their own archers raised their bows to shoot above their heads, in their turn having to attempt dropping-shots.

By the noise, Moray's people had redoubled their efforts on hearing Bruce's advance trumpet-call.

What with the return archery, and the twin Scots assaults, the enemy clearly were thrown into considerable confusion. Their own surprise attack had proved no surprise, and the biters were being bitten. Some arrows did still come over at their suddenly mobile opponents – and now with a higher percentage of casualties; but they were no longer volleyed, or anything but individual and spasmodic efforts.

Bruce was fortunate, considering his prominence, foremost

position, and the Lion Rampant of his surcoat and shield. Two shafts did strike that shield, harmlessly, and another ripped along his right forearm, tearing the surcoat's linen sleeve but failing to penetrate the chain-mail beneath. A fourth actually clanged on his helmet, knocking it slightly askew and setting his head ringing, but doing no damage. Then he was close enough to the trees for archers to be considering their own safety rather than throwing good arrows after bad.

Shouting the dreaded Bruce slogan, the Scots flung themselves into the wood, thankful to have covered the intervening open ground alive. It was no conventional woodland, tall trees being fairly wide-scattered; but there was a great deal of low scrub and bush, rising out of undrained boggy ground—difficult country to fight in. But almost certainly less difficult for the Scots than for their opponents, or many of them—English archers with six-foot bows and footmen with long pikes, both of which were of no help to passage through clutching undergrowth.

Immediately the struggle became indiscriminate, utterly confused, catch-as-catch-can. There was no line, no distant prospects, no means of assessing numbers. Each man fought whom he could see—or tried to avoid fighting. And in this again the Scots had the advantage. For archers were precious, highly-skilled folk, and knew it—specialists with a clear-cut role. Not for them the cut-and-thrust of a hand-to-hand mêlée, in bogs and bushes, where their unwieldy bows and quivers of yard-long shafts got entangled in everything that grew. Their duty, most certainly, was to retire—and their protecting pikemen's duty to get them out of a dangerous position, not to engage in needless heroics.

So the mood was sensible retreat on the one hand, and angry advance on the other—a situation liable to develop predictably.

The Scots, however, chased their foes through the scrubland with more sound and fury than actual bloodshed, more shouts than blows, without even having any clear idea how many of them there were, or where their line was, if any. The enemy retiral was in roughly a southerly direction, which was as far as certainties went.

Presently these fleeing men became involved with others fleeing diagonally across their front, south-westwards, left to right. This must mean that Moray's advance was close on the left. In a very rough and ragged fashion the pursuit swung round also, so that all movement was approximately in the same direction.

A number of archers fell, and rather more pikemen. But it could by no means be called a slaughter. The King himself did not achieve a single victory, none waiting sufficiently long for him to get within axe-range.

Ploughing his way through clutching brambles, he found a panting Moray at his elbow.

"Too easy," that man gasped. "They flee . . . too easily."

"They are not the main body."

"They lead us to it ?"

Bruce nodded. "If we let them."

"You suffered badly ? With the archers ?"

"No. Little. Thanks to you."

"De Burgh's position ? Formation ? His main body. How think you ?"

"If he leads this host, they will be a-horse. In that, he is like my brother, a cavalryman. He would never demean himself to fight on foot! I judge him waiting somewhere that he may use his horse. Open firm ground in front of him. The bowmen sent to trap us. Pin us down. On that road. Against the cliff. He and his horse to finish us off. My guess, they must be massed to the south, and so that they can see some way down that road."

His nephew nodded. "He will not expect attack from this flank."

"He *would* not. He will now, with this rabble fleeing back on him."

"He will not know our strength."

"Not in here. But he will know our *total* strength. Less than 6,000. He will have watched Edward ride past, with 3,000 men. He can count, Thomas!"

The trees were thinning before them now and the brittle winter sunlight flooding the area beyond. Into this open space the fleeing archers were bolting, Scots at their heels.

Suddenly Bruce held up his hand, and barked a command to the trumpeter, "Sound the halt! Quickly, man!"

He could see, now, beyond the last of the trees. There, across another 300 yards or so of grassy clearing, were the solid, serried ranks of a great army drawn up, silent, waiting, menacing, horse and foot, banners, trappings, knightly chivalry, helmeted steel-girt infantry and Irish irregulars. Stetching right across the line of vision, each flank disappeared into trees again.

Even Moray jerked a shaken curse.

"So-o-o!" Bruce said. "My good-sire!" He pointed to where, near the centre, the great red-cross-on-gold standard of de Burgh stirred beside that of the Leopards of England.

"God save us there are tens of thousands there!" Hay, at their backs, exclaimed.

The King did not comment. "Have our bowmen forward," he ordered. "Now is their opportunity."

So, in a strange, unequal way, the situation was reversed. The Scots were in cover and the enemy stood as a vast target for archers in open ground. Unfortunately the bowmen were too few to take fullest advantage; nor were they so expert as their English counter-parts—for archery in war had never been greatly practised in Scotland. But they did their best, and soon their shorter arrows were winging their way into the waiting host, scattered and few at first but ever increasing as men came scrambling out of the scrub. And no difficult dropping shooting was required here. Richard de Burgh was no crawler on the ground; his ranks stood upright, or sat their mounts as knights should. The least expert or most breathless marksman could not miss.

However staunchly gallant—and well encased in steel—the Anglo-Irish knights might be, de Burgh's rank-and-file could not stand still and take this for long. Fairly quickly the massive line began to sag and fold and break, as men and horses went down screaming. Obviously the English leaders were seeking to rally and bring back into action their own disheartened archers.

"Will he charge us ?" Moray demanded. "His chivalry ?"

"Would you ?"

The other bit his lip. "I . . . I do not know."

"Nor, I think, can he know. He cannot know how many bowmen we have. It is no lengthy charge—but in face of strong and direct shooting he must lose many. When he reaches here—what? In this scrub forest, heavy chivalry is useless. Horses hamstrung, and out of every bush our people leaping up to pull his knights out of the saddle. No—I think de Burgh will not charge with his chivalry yet. His foot, yes."

Angus Og came stumbling up, cursing the clutching brambles. "A diversion? To turn their flank?" he suggested. "From the east. I could take my Islesmen . . . ?"

"To be sure, friend. Good! To harry them, make them fear for their rear. But . . . I cannot afford you many. Their foot will rush us here, any moment. We are too few already. Three hundred, no more . . ."

Some English arrows were coming back at them now. And some of the Scots were running short of shafts. This could not continue.

"Where is the Lord Edward!" Hay cried, hotly.

None answered him.

"Keith is back with the horse," Bruce said. "Send back to him, Gibbie. Tell him I need a cavalry feint to the right. Along the road. The cliff levels off. To use that. Swing round their left flank. He has not many men, with the horses. But a few score would do. Not to sacrifice them. Only a gesture. To pin down their cavalry there . . ."

"I think their foot are preparing to rush us, Sire," Moray interrupted.

"Aye. Pray they don't send in too many for us, at once! Sir Colin — gather men with horns, trumpets. Send them over into the woodland to the left. To scatter. And blow. Sound as though we have a host marshalling there. Continue to blow. It may trouble de Burgh . . ."

The expected charge of the enemy foot erupted—and the Scots bowmen had but few arrows left for them. It made a terrifying sight, with thousands coming. Bruce drew back his line deeper into the wood, to allow the scrub and trees fight for them, break up the impetus. In a way it paralleled their own first charge from the road— save that they had been charging archers, specialists with a high assessment of their own skins. These would meet a less careful reception.

In yelling fury the enemy foot hit the tangled woodland, pikemen, sworders and dirk-wielding Irish kerns—and the last were the most effective. Utter chaos resulted, in seconds, and continued, a crashing, slashing, cursing, stumbling frenzy, wherein all sense of lines and fronts disappeared and men fought perforce as individuals and little groups—when they could fight at all. Pikes were proved useless, indeed a handicap, and abandoned, long swords being only a little better. Battle-axes, maces, dirks and knives were the weapons that counted—and here the Scots were better equipped and versed.

For once Bruce could partially forget his allotted role of the calm, detached general who stood back and directed. The man was, in fact, a fighter of fierce and terrible effectiveness, especially with his favourite weapon the battle-axe. Seldom indeed in these last years had he had opportunity to indulge this savage prowess. Now he could, and did. Tireless, shrewd, wickedly skilful, he wielded the dripping, slippery axe, and left a trail of felled men behind him.

Time had little relevance in these circumstances, and how long it was before a slackening in the fury of the struggle indicated to the King that this particular stage of the battle was ending, there was no knowing. His personal awareness had been of consistent victory, but as to how his cause had gone, he had only a vague impression. Now he perceived that not only was he, and other Scots, still in sight of the southern edge of the wood, but that they were in fact edging still nearer to it. Which could only mean that the enemy, in general, was retiring.

Presently it became obvious to all, and the retiral turned into headlong retreat, as men turned and ran from those damnable thickets for the open ground and freedom from probing, thrusting steel. The Scots retained possession of the wood.

Breathlessly Bruce took stock, wiping blood-stained hands on torn surcoat. Horn and trumpet-calls were still sounding from the east.

Peering out of the trees, he could see that there was considerable stir on the right wing of the enemy host across the clearing. Angus Og's diversion, plus all the horn-blowing, was evidently preoccupying them there. The Marischal's projected thrust on the other flank could hardly have developed yet; but something had kept the main body of the mounted men inactive and in their place.

"How now, Sire?" Alexander Fraser asked, mopping blood from his jaw. "These are dealt with. But how do we deal with the mounted host?"

"We do not. We leave them to try to deal with us. Are you hurt, Sandy?"

"A thrown dirk. A graze only." He shrugged. "It is stalemate, then? They cannot risk to charge their heavy chivalry into this wood. And we cannot attack them."

"Scarce that, yet. They have still many foot. They will try again."

"If only the others would come back. In their rear. The Lord Edward . . ."

"Forget the Lord Edward's host—as I have done!" That was harsh.

In the breathing-space they regrouped, assessed casualties. On the whole they had got off lightly, so far. The fallen enemy lay thick around them, and not all were dead, by any means—but this was scarcely the time to tend them. Men grumbled, but more at the clutching brambles and thorns than at their hurts.

It could be seen that some proportion of the English cavalry was dismounting. And there was more marshalling of foot.

"Another assault. This time stiffened by armed knights and cavalry on foot. Slower, but harder to bring down," the King said.

"Archers forward, Sire?" Fraser asked. "Few arrows left."

"No. Hold them back. Then, move into position behind the attack. A few shafts at de Burgh, then. To keep him from moving in his mounted host in support. More value in that."

Trumpets blaring, men yelling, the second assault began, though inevitably it came much more slowly. With no arrows aimed at them, many men must have been grimly relieved. But the leaders seemed wary, too.

This time, save for the hundred or so archers, who remained hidden, Bruce withdrew his men before the long enemy line. The deeper into the wood's entanglements, the more broken those ranks must become. But he detached groups under Sir Robert Boyd and Sir Hugh Ross, right and left, to seek to work round behind, both to upset the advance and to support the bowmen.

This battle, as it developed, held a less feverish note. Men were tiring, as well as wary. Towards the end of a hard-fought day, men who have managed to preserve their lives thus far tend to have a growing interest in prolonging them further. This applies to both sides. Moreover, the heavily armoured dismounted chivalry added a new dimension. There could be nothing feverish about their fighting, nor their movement amongst the undergrowth. But they were very hard to lay low. This, indeed, became a ding-dong struggle, dour, hard-hitting, but lacking the fervour of heretofore.

Bruce, well aware of it, recognised its dangers for the side with the smaller numbers. He racked his tired wits and splitting head, even as he fought, for some livener, some new factor – and could think of nothing. That insidious word stalemate had got into his mind. Damn Sandy Fraser for pronouncing it! But the situation did indeed seem to have become almost static, unsusceptible to successful manœuvre.

Who would have prevailed in the end it would have been hard to forecast. But, no thanks to Bruce, or any Scots plan, a new factor did arise. Angus Og and his Islesmen got tired of making gestures and shadow-fighting, isolated on the main enemy's east flank – as fiery Gaels would – and came back to their comrades for some real fighting. They picked up most of the hornblowers in the process, who likewise had become disillusioned. But entry into a wildly confused battle in dense woodland is a dangerous operation, with friend and foe inextricably mixed and not always easily identifiable.

The Lord of the Isles, therefore, had his 300 come in dramatically, vigorously chanting their wild Hebridean slogans, shouting for Clan Donald, and identifying themselves with great success, while trumpets and horns blew varying versions of the Scots advance. Certainly it sounded an infinitely greater influx than any mere 300. Moreover, and perhaps most telling of all, the newcomers sounded fresh, enthusiastic and vehemently aggressive.

Almost everywhere the enemy foot wavered a little.

When the majority of the Highlanders, left with Bruce, heard their fellows' stirring arrival, they raised their own similar yells and slogans, in welcome. This could not but affect the rest of the Scots around them. Everywhere the shouts and challenge arose, with an inevitable if temporary increase in the tempo of the fighting.

It was too much for a foe already weary and lacking confidence. There was no wholesale giving up or retreat; but from that moment the second assault on the wood was lost. The drift back southwards began.

Nothing spreads faster than the aura of defeat. Soon it became almost a rout. Angus Og's fire-eaters were, in fact, balked of their fine fighting.

The Scots leadership, at least, had no regrets. Panting, thankful, they watched the tide ebb. It was not always that they blessed Angus of the Isles.

Whether it was the ignominious return of his second attack, a cavalry engagement which seemed to be developing on his left flank – where Keith the Marischal was at last making his gesture – or merely the accumulated disappointments of a long day, Richard de Burgh suddenly seemed to have had enough. He was not so young as once, of course – now in his mid-sixties – and no doubt the stalemate was even more apparent to him than to his son-in-law. At any rate, to the surprise of the Scots, trumpets began to sound purposefully across the clearing – and these were clearly not for any further advance or attack. There was a marshalling of a screen of light cavalry behind which the main body could retire in good order. Riders went spurring off, right and left, no doubt to order the break-off of hostilities on the flanks. Without haste, with discipline and dignity, the Earl of Ulster turned and left the field in a south-easterly direction. He was no panic-monger, just a realist.

From the woodland the Scots jeered – but none sought more actively to speed the enemy retiral.

Heavily Bruce leaned against a tree. "Praises be to God!" he said. "But . . . what was that? A victory? Or a defeat? Or . . . a great folly? A waste?"

"A victory, surely, Sire," Colin Campbell averred elatedly. "Since we retain possession of the field."

The King looked around him. "The field! Such trophy, lad, for such battle – if you may call it that. Which ought not to have been fought."

"Your Grace is weary, dispirited," Fraser declared. "It is a great victory, by any counting. An English knight we have captured, one Cosby, says that the Earl had 40,000 men."

"Dear God – 40,000? I'll not believe it! Half that, perhaps . . ."

"There were great numbers in the trees to the east. Foot. That you never saw," Angus Og put in. "Mostly these Irish kerns. None too eager to fight for the English, I think."

"Aye. My good-sire no doubt had his problems. And his own doubts. His supersession must injure him. Divided interests. I could conceive that he loves *me* even better than he does Edward of Carnarvon! Or this Bishop!"

There was much to do, with the wounded and the dead of both sides to attend to. Even though the Scots had got off comparatively lightly, considering what might have been their fate, they were not less than severely mauled. And the enemy wounded was legion. The aftermath of battle was, in its way, as taxing, and a deal more distressing, than the fighting. However fierce a warrior, Bruce himself was ever affected by suffering. Not a few, even of his close colleagues, considered him soft, unsuitably weak, in this.

It was some time, therefore, before he moved back to the road, and then on to the open space where de Burgh had waited for them, and where there was sufficient firm ground to set up camp for the night—for the early winter dusk was beginning to fall. It was hardly likely that there would be another attack, in the circumstances, but scouts and pickets were sent out all around.

It was one of these who presently returned to announce the approach of His Grace of Ireland's host, from further south.

Edward rode up in style and flourish, as always. And in some haughty reproach. "I hear that you have had some fighting, brother!" he called. "A victory, of sorts. Over de Burgh. Need you have kept it to yourself? Might you not have deigned to share the honour with me? It is my territory. I had thought that we were to share more equally, henceforth?"

Bruce drew a hand slowly over set features. "You conceive *me* at fault, Edward?" he asked, as his Scots lieutenants growled in their throats.

"Would not any man of honour? You must always retain any glory for yourself. We were beleagureing Ratoath Castle, de Burgh's house. Believing him within."

His brother turned away while he mastered his tongue. "I fear that there was little of glory to share in this," he said stiffly. "Or honour. It was an unnecessary battle. We were in fact ambushed. And yet, we had 3,000 men as advance guard! To protect us from ambush!"

The other drew up in his saddle. " 'Fore God—you are not seeking to lay blame on *me*? For your fault!"

"Fault, man! If there is fault in this, where lies it? In the main host, which rode into a trap? Or in its forward guard, which rode blithely through that trap, unknowing, with no flanking scouts—since such must have discovered a great army there. Some say as many as 40,000, lying close in wait."

Edward stared. "Forty thousand . . . !" he said.

"Myself, I do not believe it was so many. A prisoner says it. But even half as many—what difference?"

"They . . . they must have moved in after we passed."

"To be sure. But since they were largely foot, and we followed you within the hour, they cannot have been far off. I think, brother, that I am entitled to better advance guarding than that!"

"I sent you word, did I not? That the peasant said de Burgh was here, at Ratoath. Not at Drogheda."

"With a small number of men, only! No thanks to you that I did not believe that tale."

176

"If he lied, am I to blame? At least, I informed you . . ."

"Aye." Wearily Robert shrugged. His head was aching, had been since cessation of battle had given him time to recognise it—no doubt the effect of the arrow on his helm. "You informed me. Of that. But . . . let us have done, Edward. It is past . . ."

"You still were at fault in not sending *me* word. Informing me. Of this battle. That I might have my part . . ."

"Christ God!" Bruce burst out. "Are you crazed, man? What think you it was? A tourney? Young Campbell I did send, before the assault began. But he was himself ambushed. Well you know the advance's duty to spy for and protect its rear. In this also you failed . . ."

With a muffled oath, but no other leave-taking, the King of All Ireland wheeled his charger round and plunged off, waving his colleagues after him, to their great confusion.

That night the two hosts camped a good mile apart. The royal brothers were wider apart than that.

THE battle of Ratoath may have been one which should never have been fought, but it proved to be a highly significant turning point, materially affecting more than merely those taking part. Although that was not immediately apparent.

It changed the course of the Scots' campaign in Ireland. Bruce's force had to halt in its drive on Dublin, to lick its wounds and reorganise, and the vital element of surprise was eliminated. Then Richard de Burgh had the trouble which so often follows defeat in the field, having to face near-mutiny from lieutenants and allies who alleged mismanagement and half-heartedness. He retired on Dublin, not Drogheda, presumably with the intention of strengthening the capital's defence. But with unanticipated results. Instead of being welcomed as reinforcement and comfort, he was in fact arrested and warded in Dublin Castle by Sir Robert Nottingham, the mayor, presumably on the orders of Bishop Hotham, the Chancellor, charged with dereliction of duty and succouring the enemy. The Scots did not learn this until later. But they did know that his thousands were now in the city.

Scouts brought back even more significant news, militarily speaking. The citizens, under this Nottingham, had risen to the defence of their town, with spirit. They were abandoning areas which had grown up outside the old walls, and these suburbs, being mainly of timber, had been set on fire, to offer no cover for the attackers. They had even pulled down the great church of St. Saviour's, to use its stones to repair breaches in the said walls, and to extend the defences of the quays, so that reinforcements might come in. Indeed, they had demolished the bridge across the Liffey. If these energetic measures were typical of the determination of the Dubliners, then a new situation had arisen.

While Bruce reorganised and sought news and reports, his brother, hot for action to redeem his name, made a brilliant assault on Castleknock, only eight miles from the city, using MacCarthy's Irish horse. He was successful enough to capture Tyrrel, lord thereof, and burned the town, church and district, sending its smoke billowing up within sight of the Dubliners. This was the sort of swift, individual operation at which Edward excelled. It was questionable, however, whether it did more than stiffen the Dublin people in their determination to resist.

The royal brothers were now on coolest terms, for all to perceive. It could not go on thus.

The third night after the Ratoath battle, Bruce rode with Moray and Angus Og to Edward's camp at Castleknock—where they were kept waiting a considerable time until Edward received them in the castle hall. Robert was primed to set and deadly patience.

"Brother," he declared, when at last they confronted each other. "I have come for a decision. It is time that we took it. High time."

The other looked wary and hostile in one. "Decision? How mean you?"

"Decide how and where we go, now. For no longer is it sound strategy to assail Dublin."

"What! You mean . . . ? You resile? From Dublin? Now, before it. You shirk it . . . ?"

"Call it that if you will. Only by surprise could we have taken it. With our numbers. Ratoath meant that there was no surprise. The city is to be held, and vigorously. To attempt to besiege it would be folly. And give time for our enemies to bring great numbers against us, from all over Ireland. I will not hazard my Scots in such case. A swift-moving cavalry force is not for siegery—as you well know."

"I' faith—*you* it was who must take Dublin! Not Drogheda. Against my wishes . . ."

"That situation has changed. Vastly. We must change strategy accordingly."

"*We* must! I'd mind you who reigns here. Not *Robert* Bruce!"

The other ignored that. "We have three choices. We can turn back to Ulster—but that would look like defeat, and gain us nothing. We can move around Dublin and proceed towards the south—but this leaves the enemy in force between us and our base in Ulster. And the south-east is where the English are strong. Or we can turn west. All the West of Ireland is open to us, save Limerick. There the English are least strong, and your Irish princelings rule. Two-thirds of the land. How say you?"

Edward gnawed his lip, his dilemma obvious. Clearly the last was the best course. But as clearly it was his brother's course.

"I do not say any," he jerked. "I will not be thrown choice of this or that. By you!"

Robert shrugged. "It is not I who offer the choice. I only put it in words. It is there. The facts are there. Only the decision is ours. Have you better choice, Edward?"

"If you fail me over Dublin, the capital . . .!" Edward looked away.

179

"There is famine in the West, my lord King," MacCarthy of Desmond, one of those who stood behind Edward, pointed out.

"I know it, friend. But we have a saying in Scotland that hungry men are angry men. They will rise the more readily against the English. And Englishmen are notable for their great eating! I think the hunger will bear more heavily on their people than on ours. Have you better course?"

"No. Save for the famine, it is the best. We could win the whole West."

"If we could have surprised Dublin I would have preferred to move south and east. With a possible sea descent upon Wales. That was formerly my aim. But that is not possible now, with the enemy well warned. The West alone offers opportunity to us, in this pass."

"You are set to go to the West. Then go alone!" Edward snapped. They eyed each other.

"Your Grace of Ireland—you would not split the host!" Moray put in.

"Ask that of your other uncle!"

"And you? What will you do?" Robert asked.

"I want Dublin. My capital."

"No doubt. But how to win it, and it embattled against us, with a few thousand men?"

"Not a few thousand. I have a great army of foot at my back. Have you forgot? An army that will grow greater."

"I have not forgot it. Nor the pace at which it moves! Nor that it wars in itself. And lacks a commander! It will take two weeks to reach Dublin—if it ever does. By then, the English will have 100,000 in the city."

"And I will have more! I will call all Ireland to Tara. To Tara's Hill, the true heart of this land. They will rally to me there, their King."

Speechless, Robert regarded him, the cynical realist, the hard-bitten cavalry leader. Could a crown do this to a man?

"My lord King—you will not wait here, idle, for weeks?" Mac-Carthy said.

"Idle, man? Think you I am an idler? By the Mass—I will not be idle! While I wait I shall raise my standard on Tara. But I shall do much more."

All men looked from one monarch to the other.

"Very well then, brother," Bruce said at length. "This is the parting of the roads. I have had my bellyful of waiting, at Carrick-fergus. I brought these thousands of picked men for swift warfare. I move west."

"As you will. Better thus, perhaps . . ."

So, two days later, the Scots host turned its face from Dublin and trotted off to the west, without ceremony or formal leave-taking. It would be debatable which brother heaved the deeper sigh of relief. Bruce left Angus Og and his Islesmen with Edward, since that man did not want to go too far from his ships; moreover he understood the Irish best.

They forded the Liffey at Leixlip, the Salmon Leap, and then moved south-west to Naas, in Kildare, meeting no resistance, riding free. Almost a holiday atmosphere prevailed, after the strains and stresses of the last weeks. To be on their own, responsible only to themselves, with the clouds of disagreement and suspicion removed, was as good as a tonic.

Not that it was anything in the nature of a joyride, from the first. At every township they passed, King Edward of All Ireland was proclaimed, and local lords and chiefs urged not only to declare their allegiance but to take or send contingents to Tara forthwith, lest their loyalty be doubted. They took the castles and manors of a number of Anglo-Irish barons who failed to declare their adherence to Edward Bruce, but wasted no time on besieging strong points. Their scouts and flanking pickets fought a number of skirmishes; but the main force was never engaged.

Bruce by no means allowed either this easy progress or the holiday atmosphere to put him off his guard for a moment, to distract him from a commander's duty. He was there, basically, to cause the maximum of concern and difficulty to the English occupying forces; secondly to give armed support to his brother's throne. Both with as little loss to Scotland as might be. To that end he was seeking to draw the English and their allies away from the Pale, and from Eastern Ireland generally, into the native and wilder West where they would be infinitely more vulnerable. But that he was taking risks he knew well, especially in the essential matter of sustenance. Six thousand men and their horses require a lot of food and forage, and in an impoverished and war-ravaged country, such was hard to come by.

So, as they went, Bruce was more concerned with collecting and transporting feeding-stuffs than with actual fighting, at this stage. The area was not actually famine-stricken, but the warnings were that it would get worse as they proceeded westwards. Wherever opposition developed, therefore, they made the people pay, not in blood and treasure but in cattle, horses, grain, meal and hay. And where there was no convenient opposition, supplies were bought from the local population at fair prices—for it was no part of the Scots' intention to antagonise those disposed to be friendly. Herding cattle along with them would have delayed their advance greatly, so beasts were slaughtered, and evening camp-fires were as much for smoking and salting meat for the future as for cooking the day's meal. It was only a very rough-and-ready curative process, but it would serve for men whose standards were not too nice. The season of the year helped, though not really cold as Scots knew cold. Long and ever-growing strings of packhorses followed the host, laden with food for man and beast. This supply-train was not allowed to straggle, and was carefully protected.

From Naas, the seat of MacMurrough, King of Leinster, they went by Castledermot in Carlow to Callen in Kilkenny, de Clare country—where, however, the de Clares remained discreetly out of sight. And ever the face of the land changed. There was no great deal of tillage in the Irish countryside at best, and grain was correspondingly scarce. Gradually even what there was died away. But not only this. The rich grasslands and pastures for which this land was famous were now dwindling also, and moorland, bogs, peat-moss, rushes and outcropping stone became ever more dominant. There were green oases in it all, but the terrain was becoming ever barer. Yet it was not an empty country. There were people in plenty, living in miserable cabins and huts of turf and reeds. The castles and manors and abbeys grew fewer, the townships smaller, the churches less ambitious. Yet it was probably true to say that the population increased as the living conditions deteriorated. And everywhere hunger increased until it became the very taint on the air. From being a faint shadow it became a threat and then an all-pervading aura, a condition of life.

The Scots host's supply-train began to shrink.

There was no problem in recruiting the Irish for Edward's cause, now. The difficulty, indeed, was to prevent thousands from joining Bruce's own company, with immediately available food as added attraction. He had to struggle now to keep down his numbers. This was Munster, where the ancient O'Brien ruled, and he was known to support Edward. But only mounted men were of any use to Bruce—and horses seemed this year to be for eating, in Munster, rather than riding. He found it hard, nevertheless, to reject and drive off hungry men. And, willy-nilly, his train grew. And slowed in consequence.

All this time Bruce saw nothing of the real enemy. But they heard of them, frequently. Sir Edmund Butler, the former commander in Ireland, who had superseded de Burgh, and then himself been superseded by the Lord Mortimer, was still in effective control in Kilkenny, with, it was said, 30,000 men. Hence Bruce's drive in this direction. An interesting report said that the de Clare brothers had joined him there—and the de Clares, related to the English Earls of Gloucester, and therefore distantly to Bruce himself, were amongst the most powerful and influential of the Anglo-Irish nobility known to be highly resentful over the present English demotion of their kind.

Bruce pondered this circumstance not a little. Mortimer himself was said to be on the move, from the east, with a large English force, part of it no doubt de Burgh's late army. De Burgh was said to be still languishing in prison in Dublin Castle; although how rigorous was his captivity would be hard to say, for it was rumoured that the city mob had broken into the castle and slain eleven members of the Earl's staff—which indicated less than solitary confinement.

Out of all this varied information Bruce made what plans he could. He conceived the disgruntled Butler to be the weakest link in the chain. He would concentrate on him, if possible before Mortimer could effect any link-up.

Then, at Callan, only ten miles from Kilkenny, and Butler, chance took a hand. One of the Scots patrols captured an Anglo-Irish knight named de Largie, with a small escort, who turned out to be a courier from Mortimer to Butler. Brought to Bruce he was civilly treated, but his despatches carefully unsealed and perused. He proved to be carrying a peremptory message, in unflattering terms. The Englishman told the Anglo-Irish noble that he was coming south-west to take over his army when he had dealt with the presumptuous Scots rebel Edward Bruce and his Ulstermen; but meanwhile Butler was to hold his hand, do nothing without further orders, and to have no truck with de Clare, who was under suspicion.

Reading this, Robert Bruce slapped his knee and barked a laugh. "The English!" he cried. "Will they never change? Never learn? The blind arrogance of them! This, from a newly appointed commander to the man he succeeds, a man of twice his own years and of prouder lineage!" He tossed the letter across to Moray. "Read it, Thomas—and then have Will Irvine to fasten this seal down as though it has never been tampered with. He has nimble fingers. Then give the letter back to de Largie, and let him go on his way to Kilkenny—with my regrets for having interfered between a courier and his duty!"

"Aye, Sire—to be sure. This will gravely offend Sir Edmund Butler. And the Lord de Clare. Who is his friend, indeed his kinsman, I think. But – what then?"

"Then, Thomas, I too shall write a letter. To Butler. At once. To follow this de Largie. In, say, two hours. That should give Butler time to digest the one and be ready for the other! A much more civil letter."

"Saying, Sire?"

183

"Saying that I regret an honourable man's adherence to the wrong side. That I find him, and his people, an obstruction on my road to Limerick. That I suggest our differences would best be resolved, in true knightly fashion, before Kilkenny two days hence. Say, noon. In honest armed combat, knight to knight, host against host, myself against himself. A challenge, Thomas—the gauntlet thrown down. From the King of Scots. How think you Butler will answer that?"

Moray looked thoughtful. "I do not know."

"How would you yourself, man? In like case. After receiving that insolent letter from Mortimer?"

"I think . . . I think that I would remove myself. Make shift to some other place. Quietly. If I had opportunity."

"Precisely. As would I! That is why I have given him two days. We shall see. Aye—and Thomas, before you let de Largie go, see that he believes us to have more horse than we do. Say, 10,000 . . .!"

Butler and de Clare did, in fact, rather better than Moray's suggested reaction, even though they did not commit themselves to pen and ink. The very next morning they disbanded their entire army, ordered its component parts to return to their homes, and then themselves quietly disappeared. Whichever way they went, they did not go to meet the Lord Mortimer.

The Scots army was astonished—even if their liege lord was slightly less so. It was as good as a great victory, and bloodless. The fact that Butler had been having enormous difficulties in feeding his host no doubt contributed.

The way clear before them, Bruce pressed on westwards.

They came to famed Cashel, in Tipperary, with its cathedral, round tower and abbey, one of the most holy places in a holy land, a rock rising from an extensive plain. Here was also the palace of the Munster kings; but O'Brien was presumably with Edward, and no supplies were forthcoming from either his servants or the monks. The army moved on towards Limerick and the Shannon, with the Western Sea beginning to draw them.

Now, with the elimination of Butler's host, and Bruce's fame spreading, everywhere the Irish rose in support, and in their thousands, their tens of thousands. As day followed day, they came flocking to Bruce's banner, and paid little heed to his instructions to head eastwards to join their own monarch at Tara and Dublin. Instead they attached themselves to the Scots, and came west with them—or at least, travelled behind, an embarrassment and a delay. Yet it was their country and their cause, and Bruce was not the man ruthlessly to spurn and drive them away. Especially as they were almost all hungry and he was known to have food.

184

Unfortunately he had far from enough food for all, and inevitably there was trouble. Moreover, the Irish clans were even more quarrelsome than the Scots variety, and internecine battles of real violence were an almost daily occurrence. Worst of all, these unwanted cohorts raided and pillaged wherever they went, in typical clan-war fashion, not only in the names of their chiefs and sub-kings but in the name of the King of Scots also.

All this was outside Bruce's calculations, and he blamed himself for not having foreseen it. But regrets and recriminations aside, this could not be allowed to go on. Most evidently it was possible to be bogged down in Ireland in more ways than one.

It was, therefore, a vast and sprawling horde, quite unlike any army with which Robert Bruce had ever been connected, which at last reached the Shannon at Castleconnel, a few miles north of Limerick, on the 10th of March, the Feast of St. Bronach. Limerick was the greatest city of the West, the third largest in Ireland, and, with its port, had all along been the Scots objective. It was a fortress-town set on an island in the wide river, and was thought to be fairly strongly garrisoned – but by Anglo-Irish and pro-English Irish under O'Hanlon and MacMahon. Butler's, and de Clare's, disaffection might well have spread here. If it could be taken, the whole of the West ought to fall like a ripe plum.

But a welter of reports reached Bruce concurrently with his arrival at Castleconnel. The most immediate informed that, only a few days earlier, a large English fleet had sailed up the Shannon to reinforce and stiffen the garrison of Limerick. And to feed it, which was more vital still. The second was from the east, from Angus Og, whom Bruce had left with Edward, declaring that Mortimer had trapped the Ulster host in a bend of the Liffey near Naas, with a vastly superior army, and though the position had its own strength, protected by river and marshes, the situation was serious. Edward would never bring himself to ask his brother for aid in it, but he, Angus Og, could and did. He urged King Robert to turn back from the West, and take Mortimer in the rear, to their mutual advantage. But quickly – for the Ulster force had insufficient supplies to hold out for long.

The third report was from O'Connor, the studious King of Connaught, from Athlone, announcing that famine was making terrible inroads in the areas to the north and west, with plague in its wake, and advising Bruce strongly against making any advance meantime into those parts.

These tidings set the King urgently to think.

That same night he was given still further cause for cogitation. Early in the morning there was a great disturbance of shouts and screaming and the clash of arms, at the north part of the camp. The King rose immediately, to learn from the captain of the guard that it was not truly an attack or even one of the typical inter-Irish affrays. It was an assault, yes—but with a difference. The Irish this time were not fighting amongst themselves. The assault was against the Scots lines—not the men, but the horses. They had been driving the beasts off and slaughtering them, there and then, for food.

"How many?" the King rapped out. "How many gone?"

"I fear, Sire, that they may have taken some 200. There were thousands of them, crazy with hunger. The Irish . . ."

Bruce looked from the speaker to Moray and Gilbert Hay, who had joined him. "This, then, is the end of the road, my friends," he said heavily. "Once this has started, it will continue. Starvation is the enemy we cannot fight, and win. Our horses are vital to us. Without them we are lost. I have misjudged. Tomorrow, we turn back."

They nodded, silent.

So next day, to the consternation, reproach, even fury of most of the Irish chieftains—though not all—the Scots disengaged themselves. It had to be ruthlessly done, in the end, and Bruce did not enjoy doing it. But he had made a mistake, and this was part of the price he had to pay. His first duty undoubtedly was to his own people. They rode away fast from Castleconnel, eastwards, leaving Limerick and its investment to the great, quarrelling Irish host. They turned their backs on the enemy, and rode. Robert Bruce who had never done such a thing in his life, was not a man any dared speak to for some time thereafter. It was St. Patrick's Day.

They continued to ride fast, for day after day, eating up the miles —for that was almost all there was to eat. No laggards needed to be reminded that it was a race against time, against growing hunger, especially against the failing strength of the horses—for forage for beasts was as scarce as food for their riders. There were two schools of thought about this—one said that they should not press the animals, use them lightly, so as to cherish their flagging powers; the other that they should drive on at their hardest while any strength remained. The King inclined to the second course, especially in present circumstances, with the Ulster army to relieve if at all possible.

Avoiding all entanglements, fighting and delay, they were at Kells, half-way across the land, by the third night. But this pace could not be kept up, all knew. At least they were facing east—and by contrast with the famine-stricken West, in their hunger-dominated minds they recollected the East as a land of plenty.

Next day another courier caught up with them, about ten miles north of Kilkenny, from Angus of the Isles. He informed that the pressure was off the Ulster force. Mortimer, who appeared to be a quarrelsome man, had fallen out with Sir Robert Nottingham, Mayor of Dublin—and presumably with Nottingham's superior, the Chancellor, Bishop Hotham—for he had now taken sides with de Burgh, and was demanding the earl's release from Dublin Castle, Hotham's headquarters. This having been refused, he had abandoned his assault on Edward's force and marched on Dublin instead. None knew now what went on in the city, and who prevailed.

"My brother scarce needs me to aid him in this Ireland! Or any other," Bruce commented. "These Englishmen that Edward of Carnarvon sends over are all the aid he needs! What does His Grace of Ireland do now, then?"

"He marches, Sire. Northwards. For Ulster. For Dundalk and Carrickfergus."

The King stared. "You mean that he retires? Not just changes position? Retires hot-foot for Ulster?"

"Aye, Sire."

"But why? I sent word that we were returning to his aid. And what of his great host of Irish foot? The host that was marching south?"

"It is said that they are dispersed, Your Grace."

"Dispersed! I' faith—what mean you? Dispersed?"

The messenger shrugged. "That is all that I know. My lord of the Isles said dispersed. The talk is that they quarrelled amongst themselves. The Irish kings. And so broke up. Before Drogheda. But I know not . . ."

"Save us all—if this is how wars are fought in Ireland! It is beyond all belief. Are they all crazed in this island?"

"When men are in doubt for what they fight, this could be the position," Moray suggested. "We, in Scotland, knew for what we fought. Believed in it. Here it is otherwise. And in such case men tend to fight for their own hands. Or not fight at all."

"On my word, you are a sage, Thomas!" the King cried, ruefully but not really unkindly. "But no doubt you have the rights of it. As usual! But—what of us? For what, for whom are *we* to fight? Now? Tell me, you who are so often right, nephew! Tell me. On my soul, I think that we should go home to Scotland! And as fast as we may. What do we here, in the middle of Ireland?"

The heartfelt acclaim of all who could hear the King's voice was interrupted by the Earl of Moray.

"You say that I am right—so often right. But I was not right that day in Annandale. When I came to you, with the Lord Edward. I it was who urged Your Grace to lead this campaign in Ireland. In person. Lest the English win a swift and easy victory. Against *your*

187

judgement. I believed it to be the wise course. I much blame myself now . . ."

"We can all misjudge, Thomas. Ireland has confounded more hopes than yours. Or mine. It is a strange land, where no cause ever truly triumphs, I do believe. The English are finding it so, equally. I fear my brother is likely to discover the same. But that is his concern, not ours. Dear God—I could wish that Scotland seemed less far away . . .!" That was strange talk from Robert Bruce.

In the days that followed, as March turned to April, that wish of the King's became a litany with them all, a refrain often on their lips and never absent from their hearts, as the road home stretched out and seemed but to grow the longer. They were forced to turn partly west again, in their travelling north, for the English had now greatly reinforced the Pale, and mid-East Ireland was something of an armed camp. The point of fighting battles seemed highly debatable in the present circumstances; certainly the Scots were past the stage of looking for trouble—their empty bellies saw to that. The central counties of Leix, Offaly, Westmeath and Cavan which they were forced to cross, were good lands ruined, pastures neglected and covered with reeds and rushes, peat-bog spreading far and wide, lakes and tarns and swamps everywhere. These were the lands of the O'Farnells, O'Molloys, O'Regans, O'Mores and MacGeoghegans, and these tribes had been far too long fighting the English and each other to care for their land. All was in the fiercest grip of famine. Two nights after the Scots turned north-west from Kilkenny, they started to kill their starving horses. It was a grim but significant milestone on their way.

Thereafter, each day inevitably they covered fewer miles, and more slowly. The magnificent light cavalry host of the warrior King of Scots, one of the most renowned and potent striking forces in all Christendom, was no longer magnificent, scarcely even any longer cavalry. It had become a horde of hungry, silent, scowling men, dragging themselves northwards with only a dogged determination not to leave their prominent bones here in an alien land. It was perhaps as well that the enemy seemed no more inclined to fight than they were. Starvation may not make for peace and goodwill, but it certainly limits war.

At Rahan, on the 10th of April, they heard that Mortimer, with de Burgh's men, if not de Burgh himself, was as good as sacking Dublin, and that the savaged citizenry were wishing that they had opened their gates to the King of Scots. Widespread civil war appeared to be breaking out between the English and the Anglo-Irish. These, at least, were apt to have enough food in their stomachs to sustain the effort.

But even this news was insufficient, now, to distract Bruce and his people from their course. It did mean, however, that they could probably risk moving further to the east in their northwards march. They turned to cross the bare uplands of Westmeath, towards Trim, and, they hoped, fatter lands.

But now the concomitants of under-nourishment were taking their toll. Sickness and disease were growing rife, and men were dying in increasing numbers. Horses also, so that starving cavalry-men were now concerned to eat their mounts while still they represented sustenance. Only the sick rode, any more, and not all of them.

For Bruce to maintain a degree of discipline in his host, in the circumstances, was no small feat—especially as he was now a sick man himself. His old trouble of fever, vomiting and itching skin had come back—and on an empty stomach vomiting bore especially hard. Nevertheless he sought vehemently to retain his hold both on himself and on his men, to keep it a unified and manageable force, to uphold the morale of all. He had seldom had a more testing task. That he succeeded was in no small measure thanks to the sheer love his hardened veterans bore him, a love which let them accept from this man what no other, king or none, dared have posed.

They reached Trim on the 19th of April. Here they were only a few miles from Tara, Slane and Navan, a countryside they knew, with the new season's pasture beginning to sprout for their remaining horses, and a certain amount of food still available for men—at a price. And the Ulster border was only thirty miles away.

Perhaps the Bruce brothers were not so very different in all respects. Robert was not entirely free from the same damnable pride that made Edward so awkward a man to deal with. Here, at Trim of the de Clares, near the Ulster border, when he ascertained that there was little of real scarcity, that cattle and fodder were to be had for good Scots silver, and that no enemy concentrations seemed to be taking any special interest in them, he ordained a halt. A major halt, not of hours' but of days' duration, a full week of resting, eating and recuperation, followed by some modest raiding and spoliation in the Boyne valley, wherein men regained a considerable degree of strength, vitality and self-respect, and the horses became less like walking skeletons.

As a consequence when, on the last day of April, 1317, the Scots force crossed back into Ulster, with the bells of Dundalk and Carlingford celebrating the Day of the Blessed St. Ninny, it was as a dignified, disciplined if depleted body of men, at least half of them mounted, carrying along with them a number of highly-placed Anglo-Irish prisoners for hostage and ransom, with sundry enemy banners and standards displayed beneath their own. Also there was quite a sizeable herd of cattle driven along behind, as thoughtful contribution, gesture and parting-gift for his brother, even if these cost Bruce the last of his money to purchase. He was still less than well, but he would die rather than turn up at Edward's court looking like anything but a victor with largesse and to spare. He had brought a starving, disease-ridden army right across a famine-stricken, pestilence-devastated Ireland, from south-west to north-east, over 200 miles, mainly on foot—but that must not be obvious to any at Carrickfergus. He was still The Bruce, the First Knight of Christendom—God help him! Highheaded then, the Scots marched round Belfast Lough, conquerers, and even found breath to blow fanfares of trumpets to announce their coming. But, previously and privily, the King had sent messengers ahead to the Lord of the Isles, to have his galleys ready, if possible, for an immediate embarkation.

For this, and various other reasons, the final meeting of the royal brothers went off a deal better than it might have done. Edward did not wish to make explanations as to why he had hastened north and left his brother's flank entirely unprotected. Nor what had happened to his great resounding Irish host of foot. And Robert was determined not to reveal that he was sick and weary and indeed, for that man, dejected, at odds with himself, and preoccupied with his failure in this wretched campaign. They forbore mutual recrimination, for once.

On the 2nd of May, Festival of St. Begha, Bruce and about 4,000 men took to Angus Og's galleys, and sailed away from Ireland. Of the rest, those that were not filling nameless and hastily-dug graves across the length and breadth of the land, had elected to stay behind, accepting Edward's offers of large lands, titles, even knighthoods, for continuing and experienced armed support. Bruce put no hindrance in their way—but found it strange that any should so wish, after the experiences of these last months. Though such failure to understand, he told himself, was a sure sign of advancing years. Once, might he not have seen the thing differently?

For himself, all Robert Bruce looked for now was the sight of Scotland's hill-girt shores. And then the soft arms of Elizabeth de Burgh.

He still shivered and vomited and itched, however hard he sought to hide all three.

As they had done three years before on the high ground above Lanercost and the Vale of Irthing, after much longer parting, the two of them spurred urgently ahead of their respective parties, alone, to meet together this time on the heather moorland above Ballantrae where Ayrshire merged with Galloway, the King of Scots and his Queen. Eager-eyed, calling, they rode—but as they drew close, Elizabeth's face fell a little if the man's did not. But only momentary was her hesitation. Then they were in each other's arms, mounted as they were, the lean, haggard, sweat-smelling man, and the splendid, statuesque yet voluptuous woman, clutching, kissing, gasping broken, incoherent phrases.

"Robert! Robert, my love—God be praised that He gives you back to me! Bless you! But . . . oh, Robert—you are thin! Wasted. Drawn. You are sick, I swear! Mary-Mother—what have they done to you . . . ?"

"Tush, my dear, my sweeting—it is nothing! We are none of us fat, see you! Ireland is scarce a fattening land. But, you—you make up for us, by the Rude!" He held her away for a moment, the better to see her. "I' faith, you bloom, woman! You burgeon! You . . . you fill my arms most adequately!" And he reverted to their embrace.

He squeezed a strangled laugh out of her. "Lacking this riding-cloak, you would see me burgeoning indeed! Swelling. Fruiting, no less! I am quite gross . . ."

"You mean . . . ? Fruiting? You mean . . . ?"

"Aye, Robert—that is what I mean! Once more. I am six months gone. Now I have started, my dear, I swear there will be no stopping me!"

"Dear God—here's joy! Here's wonder! Another child. And you did not send me word . . ."

"Time enough for that. As you did not tell me that you had been sick! But you have. I can see it, trace it on you . . ."

"Smell it, belike!" he jerked. "But that is by with, now. Nothing. What of Matilda? The child? Is she well? Come, lass—here come the others. Greet them. But briefly. And then let us ride on together, alone. There is so much to say . . ." He looked past her shoulder. "Is that Walter?"

191

"Walter, yes. He has been acting the son to me. And I mother to both his child and my own. That is, between distinguishing himself, with Jamie Douglas. They have been doing great things on the Border."

"Aye. I will speak with him . . ."

When, presently, they were riding on northwards together, to Turnberry, and Bruce had treated his wife to a very foreshortened and carefully expurgated account of the Irish adventure, at length she interrupted him.

"Robert—what you are telling me scarce makes sense, unless there is a deal more to it than you say. You have starved and suffered grievously, have you not ? The campaign little less than a disaster ?"

He grimaced. "You could say so."

"The fault was not yours, I swear!"

"Whose, then ? Who do I blame ? Mine was the decision to go. I commanded. I it was who urged the move south from Carrickfergus, out of Ulster. I believe Edward would have been feasting there still, had I let him! It was I who changed, and refused to assail Dublin. I who elected to make for the West. If none of it was successful, who should I blame ? *I* misjudged. And when a king misjudges, lesser men suffer."

"But the famine . . . ?"

"I knew of the famine. And thought that I had its measure! In that I misjudged also."

"And Edward ? You have scarce mentioned Edward. What of the King of Ireland ?"

"Edward . . . is Edward!"

"He failed you, did he not ? Is that not the truth of it ? The gallant, dashing Edward failed you ?"

"He would tell you, belike, that I failed *him*!"

She shook her fair head. "Robert, my heart—I am a woman. But not, I hope, a fool! And I know you, know that it is not in you to fail anyone. Know also that you blame yourself too much. A strange thing for so potent a man. But I shall learn the truth of all this. From Thomas. From Sir Gilbert. They will not deceive me . . ."

Bruce changed the subject. "What is this of James Douglas ? And Walter ? On the Border. He is still besieging Berwick ?"

"Yes. After a fashion. The siege of Berwick continues. But Jamie is seldom there. King Edward, *English* Edward, hearing that you were gone, called a great muster of his armies, at Newcastle, to come and raise the siege and to punish Scotland. Save us—we were all prepared to send for you to come home, Robert. William Lamberton had the letter written. Then we heard that Edward himself had failed to come. To Newcastle and his host. All awaited him there, but he stayed in London. This second Edward is a strange man."

"He blows hot and cold. Unlike his sire, who blew only hot!"

"Perhaps. At any rate, when still he came not, the Earl of Lancaster, whom he had made lieutenant of the venture, would have no more of it. He dispersed the great army, saying that those who wished to relieve Berwick and punish the Scots could do so, and merrily. For himself, he was going home to his lady! And so we breathed again."

"This is none so different from Ireland!" Bruce observed.

"I would not have thought it. But, in the English array were some hardier spirits. Notably the young Earl of Arundel. And some Gascon knights the Plantagenet had brought over to fight for him. These were not to be put off from winning booty. So fragments of the great host came north—though most, they say, followed Lancaster's lead. It was not a great invasion, but savage and scattered raiding across the Border."

"And Jamie dealt with it to his satisfaction?"

"Ask Walter. Walter was there with him, much of the time. Let him tell you himself."

Bruce turned in his saddle to call his son-in-law forward.

That young man, modestly disclaiming any major prowess, attributed all to the lord of Douglas—whom he obviously hero-worshipped. He described how the Earl of Arundel had come first, with Sir Thomas de Richemont and many thousands, crossing the Cheviots at the Carter Bar. And how Douglas and he had ambushed them, by Jed Water, at Lintalee, making a narrow passage even narrower by plaiting and lacing together the scrub birch-trees so that scarcely even a rabbit could have got through, much less a cavalry force, ill-led. The slaughter had been enormous, Douglas killing de Richemont with his own dagger—though Arundel had escaped. Later a strong party of Edward's Gascon knights forded the Tweed at Coldstream, and were raiding and burning in the Merse and Teviotdale, when Douglas slipped down out of Ettrick Forest and waylaid them as they returned towards England, sated with booty, wine and women. Most of the invaders died there, at Skaithmuir, including Raymond de Calhau, Piers Gaveston's nephew, whom King Edward had made Governor of Berwick. Douglas said it was the hottest encounter he had ever known. On another occasion, near to Berwick itself, Sir Robert Neville of Raby, the Peacock of the North, with a strong squadron of English North Country knights, was routed, Douglas himself slaying Neville. These were only a few of the victories.

"Bless him—Jamie was ever my best pupil!" the King said. "But —what of defeats, Walter? Even Douglas cannot have *all* victories!"

"None, Sire. Save that we have not yet taken Berwick."

"Aye, Berwick is a hard fist to unclench. One of the hardest in the two kingdoms. It can be supplied by sea, and is protected also by the town and its walls. If a besieger is prepared to sack the town first, and slay its people—as was Edward Longshanks—then perchance he may win Berwick Castle. That I am not."

"There was another victory—but not of Jamie's winning," the Queen put in. "Despairing of getting past the Douglas, an expedition from Yorkshire, from the Humber, came by sea. They sailed up Forth, and landed at Inverkeithing, in Fife. The Sheriff of Fife made but feeble resistance, it is said, and the Englishmen drove them towards Dunfermline. But the good Master William Sinclair, Bishop of Dunkeld—he that is brother to my lord of Roslin—was at his manor of Auchtertool. Perceiving disaster, he grasped the Sheriff's spear from him, shouting shame, and with sixty of his own servants rode back to charge the enemy. It was more than the Fifers could stomach, and with or without their master, they followed on. The Yorkshiremen were driven back to the sea, with 500 dead it is said, and more were drowned in their boats. And the good Bishop none the worse!"

"They do say the Bishop told the MacDuff that Your Grace would do well to hack the spurs from off his heels!" the Steward added. "And cried that all who loved their lord and country should follow him."

"Ha! We must cherish my lord of Dunkeld—a cleric after my own heart. And, I think, find a new sheriff for Fife. A case of poor master, poor man—for though the Earl of Fife has been returned to my peace for two years now, with all his lands returned to him despite his former treachery, he still loves me not. Alas for MacDuff! We must consult William Lamberton on this . . ."

"I sent a messenger to him so soon as I heard of your coming," the Queen said. "If I know my lord, it will not be long before he is at Turnberry."

Bruce gazed around him as he rode, sniffing the scents of heather dust, pine resin, opening bracken and raw red earth, laced with the overall tang of the sea—which was for him the smell of springtime in Scotland. He would not have disclosed how glad he was to be back in his own land, how inexpressibly dear and sweet that land was for him. He had scarcely realised, until now, just how much it meant to him, the very growing, enduring land itself, not only the idea that was Scotland and its people—a land which, God knew, he had paid enough for, to call his own. If Ireland had taught him how much his own land, the actual soil of Scotland, meant to him, then perhaps Ireland was not all loss.

As ever, thereafter, Robert Bruce found the waiting until he could be alone with Elizabeth frustrating, almost intolerable. But he was the King, not his own man; not even, in this his wife's. At Turnberry Castle innumerable men waited to see him, officers of state, secretaries, ambassadors, churchmen, courtiers, kinsmen, deputations. A banquet had been hastily conjured up for the returned, tired and hungry warriors, and entertainment thereafter. Through it all the man forced himself to patient endurance, even apparent appreciation. At his side, Elizabeth watched him and understood. Occasionally she touched his wrist, his forearm, with gentle pressure—and grieved to feel him so thin.

At last, up in their own tower-chamber, at parapet-level, with the door closed behind them and the half-light of the May night about them, he held her in his arms for long, just held her, not speaking, not even kissing, gripping her splendid rounded body to him, face buried in her plenteous flaxen hair. Quiescent she waited.

Weary, strained, jangled as to nerves and emotions as he was, the desire rose in him. Smiling, she responded, aiding his suddenly eager fingers to unfasten and drop her gown, her shift; then, feverishly now, to throw off his own attire.

The great bed received them. Their urgency had become mutual.

When the fierce first passion was spent, and the man at least lay back, exhausted, Elizabeth raised herself on one elbow, to consider him, running light searching fingers over his hot, but not sweating person. And as he jerked and shivered uncontrollably, involuntarily pushing her hand away, she sat up.

"Robert!" she said. "What is this? You are burning hot. Your skin. I can feel it. And rough. Broken. What is this?"

"Only my old trouble, lass. You know of it. This itching . . ."

"But this is worse. Harsher." She peered, in the dim half-light, trying to inspect him. Then she jumped up and hurried, wholly naked as she was, to an aumbry near the door, where was kept a lamp and flint and tinder. Lighting it, she came back to him.

"Hold it up," he instructed. "No—to yourself, not to me. That I may see. I' faith, woman—you are magnificent!"

"And you are not! Robert—you are patched red! Patched like an old hide. Great marks. Rough. Flaking. My dear, my dear! And so thin, so desperately thin. Oh, my love—what has become of you?"

"Nothing that your presence and your fine feeding will not cure," he asserted strongly. "I have been in the saddle for months, lass. Eating poorly. And living less cleanly than I would. Give me time . . ."

"No! This is more than that. More than you say. Here is no mere chafing of the skin: No simple dryness. You are sick, Robert. Sick."

He was silent.

"This is worse than it has ever been, is it not?" she demanded, holding the lamp close. "Even the time you told me of. At Inverurie. And at Melrose. I think it was less harsh, less angry than this, was it not? It is a, scurvy!"

"It is only the skin. I was more ill then. Weaker. More fevered. It is but this skin affliction that is worse. Nothing of grievous hurt."

"How can you say that? This of the skin is like to be but the outer sign of inner sickness. The scum that rises to the surface of a pond speaks but of foulness beneath. This ailing of your skin keeps returning. When you are weak, weary, low in body. I do not like it, my dear . . ."

"And think you I do!" he burst out abruptly, harshly, surprising even himself.

Biting her lip, she eyed him. "You are concerned, Robert. Concerned for yourself. I can tell. Of yourself, you fear. Fear some worse sickness, do you not? I know you . . ."

"Have I said a word? You dream it all, woman!"

"Perhaps. Perhaps. At least, I can anoint it. Comfort you. With some salve. Did not Christina MacRuarie have some salve that greatly soothed? We must send to her. But, meantime, I have only what we rub on the children, the babes, when their skin is chafed. It may help a little . . ."

"God's death! Think you balm for babes can wash away *this* soiling!" he cried, sitting upright. "As well feed me mother's milk from these breasts! I am soiled, woman—soiled! You will not wash it off with salve!"

"So-o-o!" she said slowly. "It is as I thought. You conceive yourself to be sicker than you say. You admit it, Robert? You fear it."

"Aye, I fear. I fear that my sins have caught me up!" His voice was tense now. "Fear that I am not to escape the price of murder, of presumption before God, of excommunication!"

She stared. "What . . . what do you mean?"

"Elizabeth." He gripped her with both his hands. "You do not think . . . ? It is not . . . ? It could not be . . . leprosy?"

She drew a quick, gulping breath, speechless, appalled.

"Sweet Christ—am I a leper!"

As still the woman did not answer, save to wag her head, he sank back on the bed. But not in despair. Suddenly he was less tense. It was out, at last. This ghastly secret dread, this spectre that had haunted him for so long. He had put a name to it now, said the dire

196

word, shared the fearful weight of horror with another. He knew a kind of relaxation.

"No, Robert! No!" Elizabeth cried, when she could find words. "Not so. It is not true. Never think it. This is not leprosy. I swear it. You are wrong, wrong!"

"It . . . it is my daily prayer that I am. But I fear . . ." He paused. "It could be God's will. His punishment."

"No. You torture yourself. Just as you blame yourself too much. You punish *yourself*, Robert. For what was no fault. Or little. The death of a foresworn and dangerous traitor. The assumption of a crown that was yours by right both of blood and conquest. You punish yourself. God is less harsh, I vow!"

"Yet He punished full harshly others for less fault. For *my* fault. My brothers. My sisters. Marjory. Christopher Seton. Atholl. Isobel of Buchan. Your own self indeed . . ."

"Was that God? Or but the savagery of a man, a man crazed with hatred? Edward Longshanks is not God!" She shook her head. "Besides—this is not leprosy. The leper's skin is white, not red, is it not?"

"I believed so once, told myself so. But in a lazar-house at Cashel, in Tipperary, I saw two men with skins as red as mine. Saw them, forced myself to speak with them. I tell you, they itched as do I! Were fevered. One of them vomited. Not the other . . ."

"But were they lepers? You are sure?"

"They were in a leper-house. Believed themselves to be so. Tended by the Brothers of Saint Lazarus."

"That need mean little. Ignorance. The folly of neighbours. Have you spoken with a physician, Robert?"

"I have spoken with none. Until you. I . . . I dared not."

"And you were right, in that. I say you were right to speak of this fear to none. This is not to be spoken of. None must hear of it . . ."

"If I am unclean, my dear, shutting our eyes and ears to it will not cleanse me."

"Merciful Mary—you are *not* unclean! Oh, Robert, my heart—never say it, never think it! It is a folly, a sin! This is no more leprosy than is a rash of the fowl-pox, or the ruby-pox. Say nothing of it to any, Robert. Or all the world will have you leper by the next day, as good as dead and buried! Men shunning you. You, the King!"

"And yet I must know, lass. For certain. I cannot live with this sore secret, uncertain. I have done so for too long as it is, gnawing at my mind . . ."

"But I tell you it is not leprosy. That you are wrong . . ."

"Because you wish it so, Elizabeth. You are my wife, my other part. You cannot judge, I think, more truly than do I. I need another to tell me, another who loves me less. But who will not noise it abroad. With that I do agree. It must not be spoken of, until, until . . . God help me, until I am sure it is true! Or the rule of this my kingdom will become confusion impossible. A leper-king! Already dead under the law! Banished the presence of clean men. Who would succeed me? There is none. This also I have thought on, through the long nights, and over many a weary Irish mile. None must learn of this—until it is sure . . ."

"Myself, I would tell no man," Elizabeth said. "But if you must, ask William Lamberton. He is wise, knowledgeable—and discreet. He would be best."

"Aye—Lamberton. I will tell Lamberton. He should know, too, for he is my confessor, my spiritual adviser. He will tell me truly." The man paused, looking at her, surveying her, all her naked loveliness, and frowning. "Elizabeth," he went on, from stiff lips, as though forced to it. "And you? What of you, lass? If indeed I am leper. What of you?"

"What of me, Robert? I am your wife."

"You . . . you could not remain so."

"I am your wife," she repeated. "Your other part, as you said but then. Said truly. For we are one."

"But . . . no, lass. I could not be. Tied to a leper. It is against the law, besides. You know it. All marriage ties are dissolved, the law declares. The leper is dead, in the eyes of the law. A leper may not cohabit with a clean woman . . ."

"Robert—be silent! How can you say such things? I wed you for better or for worse, did I not? Before the altar in Linlithgow did we say aught about leprosy? Besides, you are no leper, I tell you. But if you were, think you I would leave you? I, Elizabeth de Burgh!"

"My heart—heed you. Would you become a leper too? Already—already it may be too late! Already I may have given you this evil thing. Lying here with you tonight. I should not have done it, I was weak, wickedly selfish. By fouling this dear flesh . . . ?"

"Mary-Mother—hear me! If you *are* leper, think you I would wish to be other? I waited eight years in English prisons—when I would not have cared whether I was leper or clean. Only waited for this, to be with you, *you*, once more. United with you. Your wife. Now, we are together—and I thank God daily. Think you that anything, anything under heaven, will part us now, save death itself? I, Elizabeth, am wife to Robert Bruce. I told you, on that island in Linlithgow Loch, that I would be a jealous wife. In this, more than in your casual taking of other women. Those whom God hath joined together let no man put asunder! No man, Robert Bruce—even you!"

"And the law of the land, woman?"

198

"You are the King. The law itself, and above the law. And even if you were not, I would say the same. God's law is above man's law, is it not?"

He sat up again, to take her in his arms. "My dear, my dear," he said.

Clean or unclean, they lay in each other's arms through that night, although there was no more of passionate coupling. Strangely, it was not long before the man slept, a sleep which he had been desperately needing. Hour after hour the woman lay at his side, staring up at the painted ceiling, an arm about his jerking, twitching troubled body. The cocks were crowing before her eyes closed.

. . .

The Primate, Bishop of St. Andrews, arrived there three days later, days in which a constant stream of visitors descended upon Turnberry, lords, sheriffs, councillors, officers, in great style or no style. William Lamberton came in a litter, not because it became his dignity, as did some clerics, with musicians and choirs of singing boys to mark their presence, but because he was now partly crippled with arthritis and found sitting a saddle almost as trying as walking. He had, in fact, walked the length and breadth of Scotland too much, in too much harsh weather, slept under too many dykes, suffered too much hunger, exhaustion, for even such a powerful frame as his; so that now he who was Wallace's friend before he was Bruce's, and whose service with both had brought pain and sorrow as their main reward, though not yet fifty, had to travel in a litter slung between pacing jennets—even though the pace, for jennets, was apt to be forced and uncomfortable. But if the great rawboned, lanky body somewhat failed the man, the spirit within, like the shrewd, searching, patient mind, did not.

Primate and King, in a corner of the parapet-walk that overhung the beach and the white lacework of the tide, sat on the rose-red, sun-warmed masonry and looked out across the sparkling waters to the dramatic skyline of Arran and the Highland hills behind Bute— that is, when they were not considering each other's appearance a little askance.

"It grieves me to see you so sore stricken in the joints, old friend," Bruce declared. "A hard burden for a doing man such as yourself. It should not have been for you to come all this way, from St. Andrews. Rather I should have come to you. I would—but Elizabeth had sent for you . . ."

"And think you I would have my liege lord waiting on me like some suppliant for a vicarage? I am not so far done that I cannot fulfil my duties, however halting my gait, Sire."

"We have a compact, do we not, William, that you name me by my name when we are alone? Have you forgot?"

"Not forgot, Robert. It is a graciousness I treasure but can scarce bring myself to invoke. But at least I can still cross a few miles of Scotland to welcome home her monarch—even though I do it in a bed of sorts!" The hollow, lantern-jawed features creased to a smile. "Mind, I would be better pleased to come less far than to Turnberry and the Ayr coast. Not for my old bones' sake, but in that I believe you would be better seated nearer the centre of your realm, Robert. Where your people can see you and savour your royal presence. Now that you need not watch the Border like a hawk. And Galloway and the Isles likewise. No Kings of Scots have made Ayr, this Carrick, their chosen seat heretofore. You are not, surely, to be a warrior all your days, my friend? Dwelling in an eagle's nest of a fortress. A royal palace in a kinder place, amidst your people, at Stirling or Dunfermline or St. John's Town of Perth? Where you may put aside your well-worn armour and live more gently. Besides being nearer to your old done William Lamberton!" He looked at the other keenly. "I think that such time has come, Robert. That you *need* such easement."

The King frowned. "I would remind you that there is still no peace treaty with England. Nor is our campaign in Ireland like to bring it much nearer. They are still set on conquering Scotland."

"Set—but now in the dogged, obstinate English fashion. And a deal less sanguine of success."

"Perhaps. But—you have been on this matter to me before. I fear that I am in no state, no frame of mind and body, to start building palaces, to settle to this easement you speak of. That is not to be for Robert Bruce, I think."

"Frame of mind and *body*?" the other took him up quickly. "What mean you, friend?"

Bruce shook his head, actually fearful, afraid to put this matter to the test, afraid of the possible sentence that spelt doom, afraid even of the impact of his revelation on their cherished friendship. Holy Church was stern in its measures towards lepers, men rejected of God. He sidestepped, put off, weakly.

"I ailed somewhat, in Ireland. It is a hard country to campaign in. There was much famine. I have been . . . less than myself."

"Aye, Robert—I saw it with my first glance at you. And felt a stoun at my heart. Here is sorrow, pain, trouble for us all. For all Scotland. A plague on it that you ever went to that unhappy country. That my lord of Moray convinced you . . ."

"A plague, truly! But I went of my own will. We cannot blame Thomas. The failure of judgement was mine. And many have

200

suffered for it. If *I* must suffer a little, it is but due." He faltered, at the sound of his own words. And then pulled himself together. "Forgive me, friend. I talk like a sickly woman, concerned with her health. When you, *you* sit before me, crippled and in pain, from hurts, wounds, privations, gained in my service. I crave pardon."

"Not so. I am bent, yes. I creak like an old door. But I am none so hard-used. I can still serve my time, serve my liege and his realm. I am still fit for my tasks. Although, God be thanked, my tasks, my true life's tasks, are near fulfilled now. I have been privileged in a small way to aid you in saving this realm. I have held the Church, in Scotland, free from domination. And I have near finished the re-building of the cathedral. At St. Andrews. Only months now, and it should be done. And very fine—even though I wickedly boast. A house to God's glory, which I believe Scotland may be proud to have raised in her prostration. Thanks to you who made it possible—as you made so much else. I make no complaints."

"You never did, man. But I am glad that your cathedral is near done. A noble work to have conceived, and concluded, while the realm was still fighting for its life. Only a man of your spirit, your faith, would have done it, could have done it. I rejoice for you, and with you, William."

"Bishop Arnold it was who conceived it, 150 years ago. I but finish his work. But, it is my hope, Sire, that you will come to St. Andrews and rejoice indeed with me, with all the Church, with half Scotland, to celebrate the work's completion. It will scarce be ready for St. Andrew's Day. But St. Rule's Day, perhaps. Next midsummer. God being willing, we will make a great jubilation, a solemn consecration. Not only to crown the long task, but to demonstrate to all, to all Christendom—and especially to His Holiness in Rome—that we are not just a small quarrelsome folk, as I fear he thinks us. Nor murderous rebels as King Edward seeks ever to teach him. But a proud and independent nation, concerned, even in our extremity, with God's work. We will invite embassages from far and near, Sire. From Rome—aye from England itself. We will make sure that they see a realm united and strong, which can turn its mind to other concerns than war. With a sovereign lord whose fame rests on more than winning battles . . ."

Bruce's finger-tips had begun to tap-tap on the stonework as the other propounded his great and politic conception. The frown had come down again.

"Do not build on it," he interrupted harshly. "Or, not on my presence thereat. A year hence. I may be . . . otherwhere!"

"Eh . . . ? Not, not another campaign? You are in no state,

Robert, for more soldiering, meantime. I swear it. Do not say that you contemplate more warfare ?"

"Not warfare. The warfare I fear is different—a battle I am not like to win! If it is as I fear." He was gripping the stone now, knuckles white. "William—if I was a leper, I could scarce attend your celebration!" That was rapped out.

"A leper! Saints have mercy—what mean you by that ?"

"What I say. I may be a leper. Unclean."

"Dear Saviour Christ! Sire—you do not mean this ? You cozen me . . . ?"

"I cozen none. But nor would I cozen myself. This sickness of mine—I fear that it may indeed be leprosy. Of a sort. I have feared something of this for years. But, in Ireland, I saw others. As myself. Lepers . . ."

"Robert—Your Grace's pardon. But this is folly. Beyond all belief!"

"Why ? Think you kings must needs be spared the ailments of lesser mortals ? Say you I *could* not take this evil? Because of my anointing, perhaps . . . ?"

"No. But . . ."

"Hear me, man. Before you are so sure . . ." Voice subconsciously lowered, Bruce leaned forward to tell the other the reasons for the dread that nearly came between him and his sanity.

His first shock over, the Bishop heard him out without interrupting, however often he shook his grizzled head. When the other had finished, he reached out and took the King's hand to place and hold it between his own two palms, a gesture as eloquent as it was simple.

It was Bruce's turn to shake his head. "You are good, William. Kind. But your kindness will not serve," he rasped. "It is the truth I need, not kindness. I need to *know*. Know my fate." He withdrew that hand.

Lamberton was silent for a little. "You have spoken of this to a physician ?" he asked, at length.

"No. I have spoken of it to none. Save Elizabeth. And now you."

"That at least is wise. Heed me, Robert—and say nothing to any. I am no physician. But I cannot believe that what you have told me truly signifies leprosy. A skin ailment, yes—but there are many. The true leper is much more wasted, stricken. His sores remain, they do not come and go. They grow worse. You have suffered this sickness, at times, for years. Ten years. That cannot be leprosy. When I took your royal hand between mine, Sire, it was not only in token of continuing fealty and love, whatever sickness you may have. It was that I do not, cannot, conceive your person as unclean, not to be touched. I truly conceive your fears to be groundless."

"You do?" The sudden rise, the hope, in his voice, was not to be disguised.

"I do, as God is my witness. And I urge that you put it from your mind. Say naught to any. Even those closest."

"And physicians?"

"No, Robert, my friend. Not unless your sickness grows the worse. I do not believe that we may trust any man with so dire a secret. Physicians have tongues like other men. Someone would whisper. Then there would be talk—and talk become clamour. And once there was such clamour, the Church would be invoked. Its laws on lepers. However firm I stood out against it, some would demand that the Church acted as ordained. You still have our enemies. You know how this, of all ills, frightens men. Faced with leprosy, the worst in men comes out. You know what they would demand?"

"I know enough."

"I pray that you know enough, then, to say nothing. To any. For Holy Church could be invoked to declare you lawfully dead. To conduct funeral obsequies over your empty coffin. To declare your throne vacant. Your marriage dissolved. Masses to be said throughout the realm for the benefit of your soul, as departed this life. Your child declared orphan. You could be ejected by bell, book and candle from the haunts of men. Debarred from entering any city or town or village, save at certain seasons, and then only sounding a clapper before you, that folk might avoid you. You, Robert Bruce! Thus until your dying day. Which could be years later. Sweet Saviour—think of it, Robert! You, Scotland's deliverer, Scotland's hope. I would sooner that you cut out your tongue, and mine, than that you spoke of this to any!"

For long moments the King stared out across the sparkling water. "As you will," he said, at last.

ELIZABETH DE BURGH and William Lamberton made a notable confederacy, and they had their way with Robert Bruce. And not only in the matter of keeping secret the King's fear of leprosy. On the subject of making a new home for the royal family, the Queen added her voice to the Primate's. She had never been particularly attached to Turnberry and since Marjory's death there she had frequently wished to be gone. The place spoke to her too much of alarms, fears and hurried journeys. Moreover she agreed with Lamberton that the monarch should dwell near the centre of his kingdom, not on the outskirts. And setting up a new home might well be a useful distraction for a man with a dark shadow on his mind.

Bruce, of course, was not really an enthusiast for castle or palace building. Throughout his life he had been more concerned with pulling down such places, either as enemy-held or as constituting threats to his security. He was not disposed to start erecting some new and ambitious edifice, therefore, especially in present circumstances. But he acceded to the others' advice that a move should be made to a more central spot—not the least of his considerations being that Turnberry was really Edward's house now, the seat of the earldom of Carrick which he had granted to his brother—and it went against the grain to be beholden to Edward for anything. Of the other great Bruce castles, none were any more central than this. Moreover, Lochmaben was largely in ruins, since the last English withdrawal; Annan little better, and almost in England; and Buittle, in Galloway, was also Edward's, as Lord thereof. While Inverurie, up in Aberdeenshire, had been demolished early on by Edward Longshanks, and was as remote in the other direction as these South-West houses.

The obvious choice lay between Stirling and Dunfermline, royal palaces both—for Linlithgow had been destroyed, on Bruce's own commands, as too dangerous a place to permit near the strategic battleground of Stirling. It was that vital strategic situation which told against Stirling itself, in this issue. He would have gone to dwell there readily enough; but Elizabeth was set against it. She coveted as home no fortress skied on a rock overlooking half a dozen past battlefields—and who knew how many more to come? She wanted

204

to wean her husband's mind away from war and strategy, in so far as this was practicable; and Stirling, with Bannockburn spread below, was scarcely the place to achieve it. With Lamberton's help, she influenced the King strongly in the direction of Dunfermline, therefore. After all, it had been the great Malcolm Canmore's capital, its abbey superseding Scone as the burial-place of the Scottish kings. Here were interred Malcolm and his beatified Queen Margaret, as well as their sons. Also the Kings Donald Bain, Eadgar, Alexander the First, David the First, Malcolm the Fourth and Alexander the Third. It was, next to Iona's remote isle, the most royal place in Scotland; moreover it was in Fife, the same county as Lamberton's St. Andrews. Elizabeth pointed out that the child in her womb might well be a son, the heir to Scotland. If it was, surely it was right that he should be born in this hoary cradle of the Scots monarchy?

So, with still nearly two months to go until the birth-date, the move was made, from Clyde to Forth, that midsummer of 1317, and the Court of Scotland came to settle in the modest grey palace above Pittendreich Glen, overlooking the widening Firth of Forth, with the ancient climbing town of Dunfermline in a horseshoe behind, and the great abbey towering close by. Edward the First had burned all on his departure therefrom in 1304; but less thoroughly than was his wont, and the churchmen had been busily repairing it, the abbey especially. Much more remained to be done at the palace, but there was still more habitable accommodation than there had been in Turnberry's fortified towers. The King and Queen moved into the Abbot's quarters while their own apartments were being made ready for them; and the Court settled itself to roost where it could. It was thirty-one years since last this had been the seat of government, when Alexander the Third had ridden away that stormy evening towards St. Andrews, to fall over the fatal cliff at Kinghorn.

Despite her condition, Elizabeth was in her woman's element. She had been married, and Queen of Scotland, for fifteen years, and at last she had a home which she might call her own. She busied herself from morn till night in supervising, planning, furnishing. She deliberately involved her husband in the business much more than was absolutely necessary, or considered suitable by many, Lamberton aiding and abetting. And Bruce, after a little initial resistance, became interested, even moderately enthusiastic, finding small challenges, problems, decisions on a domestic scale new to him. His physical betterment was evident, undeniable, his preoccupation with himself fading.

The sudden, slightly premature accouchement and, after only

four hours of comparatively light labour, birth of a second princess, was only marginally a disappointment. There was heartfelt relief too, not only in that Elizabeth, at her age, had had no difficulties of delivery; but that the child was perfect, small but entirely healthy, lovely. It had been Bruce's second, secret dread, from the moment of learning that his wife was pregnant again, that the child would be affected in some way by his feared disease, sickly, handicapped, even a monster. That she was not so engendered so great a joy and comfort that her sex seemed scarcely a major matter.

They called her Margaret, after the sainted queen who had made Dunfermline her home two and a half centuries before.

Bruce was busy at more than domestic matters. There was so much to be done, in the rule and governance of his realm, so much that had been neglected, not only during the Irish campaign but during the long years of war. He was not a man for idling and inactivity, however much his wife might urge a period of recuperation, and he threw himself into the business of civil administration with a will, almost as though in an effort to wear himself out with work. Dunfermline buzzed like a bee's bike disturbed, the old grey town on the ridge above the Forth fuller of folk, of clamour and colour, than it had ever been. Bernard de Linton, who perhaps had thought that the return of the monarch would lift some of the burden of administration from his shoulders, as Chancellor, instead had to find a deputy Abbot for Arbroath and come to take up residence at Dunfermline, there to labour harder than ever.

Bruce required his churchmen's help and advice for more than mere civil administration and the day-to-day running of the kingdom. After his military rebuffs in the Borders and at Donibristle, in Fife nearby, Edward of England, far from conceding the desired peace treaty, had turned to Rome for aid in his warfare against Bruce and Scotland. And the present Pope had found it convenient to pay heed. He was attempting to organise a crusade against the Turks, and desired the adherence of England. Scotland he appeared to consider as not worth including in the matter. He proceeded, therefore, at Edward's request, to fulminate against Scotland in general and Robert Bruce in particular. He ordained a compulsory two-year truce between the two countries, and addressed a Bill to the King of England and to "Robert Bruce who carried himself as King of Scotland". He also commanded that the Scots immediately stopped besieging the English in Berwick-on-Tweed—an unusual provision in a papal bull. And he sent two cardinals to present his commands—a subtle move.

Bruce had lived under the papal frown for years. But this new assault was serious, in that it specifically denied him recognition as true king before all the princes of Christendom, so implying that he was not a person with whom any Christian ruler could properly conclude any agreement or treaty. Not only would England, therefore, be sustained in its reluctance to enter into a peace treaty, but other and more friendly nations were also thus inhibited from establishing and maintaining relations. Scotland was to be a pariah amongst the peoples.

This was all a great blow, of course, not only to Bruce but to Lamberton the Primate, who had anointed him King and consistently supported him—as well as to all the other clerics of the realm. They were loth to rebel openly against the authority of the Holy See, from whom they drew their own spiritual authority. A policy of pressure and counter-intrigue at Rome, allied to a masterly inactivity at home, was their obvious recourse; but the former took time, and much money, to arrange intrigues at Rome as elsewhere being largely a matter of massive bribery. And this device of sending the two cardinals was a notably skilful move, since these Princes of the Church outranked Lamberton. They were heading for Scotland via London—where they collogued with King Edward—and Durham, where Lewis de Beaumont was about to be consecrated and installed Prince-Bishop of the Palatinate.

At a Privy Council at Dunfermline in September, Lamberton strongly contended that they must do all in their power to keep the cardinals out of Scotland, for against their rank and authority, his own authority must yield and go down.

"How can we keep them out?" the King demanded. "They have announced to the world that they are coming. You would not have me to use force against the representatives of Holy Church? *Such* representatives!"

"Not force, no. But a little guile perhaps," the Bishop suggested, "Prevail upon them to send, in the first instance, envoys, nuncios, of lesser rank. To prepare their way. Men whom I, as Primate here, can outspeak. So that I may seek to teach them their lesson, to take back to their masters."

"Aye, but how is that to be done, my lord?" Bishop Sinclair of Dunkeld, the hero of Donibristle, asked. "How to make these cardinals send nuncios? They are already at Durham for this Beaumont enthroning. What will halt them now?"

"We, the bishops of Scotland, could send them a message of welcome, my friend. Greetings to our illustrious brothers in Christ. But at the same time urge that they delay a little." He glanced at the King. "Say that we are uncertain as to how our liege lord Robert might receive their eminences. In view of the unkind, and we are sure incorrect, accounts that have reached Scotland. As to the Holy

Father's pontifications. Until these are put right, these misunderstandings cleared, we urge discretion. We are concerned that the Holy Father's lofty emissaries be received with the respect and honour due to their high office. So we advise that they send nuncios to prepare the way."

"Ha—guile indeed!" Lennox said. "And these envoys? How would you serve them, my lord Bishop?"

"Indifferently. Confusedly. Send them back to Durham in greater doubt than heretofore. As to their masters' reception in Scotland. But with an invitation for the cardinals to attend the celebrations at the consecration of my cathedral at St. Andrews next year. So that there is no hint of unwelcome. From Holy Church."

"I do not fully see the wherefore of this," the King observed.

"Time we need, Sire. Time for representations to Rome. Time for our friends there to serve our cause. Time to gather gold. Aye, time for Berwick to fall, if possible, so that this Bull is outdated. All this, and more. We must buy time. This device is to buy it."

Sinclair intervened. "If they agree to nuncios, then let us teach these a lesson. To pass on to their principals. If they travel north from Durham they must pass through Northumberland. You, Sire, have resumed the Lordship of Tynedale, and much of Northumberland now pays you fealty. Yet men still consider it to be in England. Some of Your Grace's Northumbrian lieges could surely be prevailed upon to waylay these nuncios before they reach Scotland. To somewhat mishandle them, rob them even—delay them, certainly. In England. So that the blame lies at England's door, not ours! That might help the cardinals to love the English less!"

Bruce actually slapped the table. "There's my Bishop!" he exclaimed.

"Better, Sire," Abbot Bernard added. "They could be relieved of their letters to you. These opened privily, the seals unbroken. Scanned and copied. Then handed back, but their contents sent to Your Grace hot-foot. So you would know before the nuncios arrived what their terms were. And be prepared to receive them aptly."

Grinning for the first time in months, Bruce looked at the Primate. That man inclined his grizzled head—as much perhaps in satisfaction at his friend's improved spirits as at the programme proposed.

"It behoves us, since the realm's safety is at stake, to play with such cards as we hold," he acceded.

"Spoken like a churchman!" the Earl of Dunbar and March declared, with sarcasm.

"Even churchmen may have their small diversions, my lord. So long as they do not cheat thereat!"

The Earl frowned.

"Save me from ever having to differ from the Lords Spiritual!" Walter the High Steward said fervently—and none of the Lords Temporal present thought to say otherwise.

It was a full six weeks later, therefore, before two indignant and unhappy clerics, in shabby, borrowed habits and high dudgeon, presented themselves at Dunfermline and the Court of the King of Scots—the Bishop of Corbeil and Monseigneur d'Aumery. They were civilly received—but not by the King—and kept kicking their heels for some considerable time before an audience could be arranged. Meantime, however, they were lent rich clothing, and given much sympathy over their dire experiences and shameful treatment at the hands of the North Country English. It seemed that when, with a splendid retinue, the nuncios were half-way through Northumberland, en route for Berwick, they had been rudely and savagely set upon by lawless hordes, at Rushyford, and despite their protestations and claims to sanctity, had been seized, insulted, stripped of their fine raiment, and carried off prisoner to the rude castle of one of these ruffians, by name Gilbert de Middleton, at Mitford. There they were thrown into dungeons, their baggage stolen, even the sealed letters they carried. They had been held in this horrid and distressing state for some considerable time, until eventually they were freed, but only the said letters given back to them. Since when, suffering grievous discomfort and privations, they had made their difficult way hence, to fulfil their charge and duty.

When Bruce found time formally to receive these ill-used and outraged envoys of Holy Church, he was courteous and sympathetic, seeking sad details and shaking his head. When at last they graduated from complaints to the object of their visit, and read the open letter that constituted their credentials, he still listened to them with attention—even though the tenor of their delivery was hardly flattering towards an independent monarch, and their references to the cardinals' requirements less than tactful. It was only when the Bishop moved forward actually to hand the sealed envelope to him that Bruce's expression changed to the stern.

"I rejoice in His Holiness's interest and care for my realm," he declared. "And I have, myself, long desired a firm and lasting peace with the kingdom of England. In this, we are agreed. But"—he tapped the sealed letter—"I fear that I cannot accept and open this letter. I see that it is addressed to 'The Lord Robert Bruce, Governor of Scotland'. It seems, my lord, that this is not for me!"

The nuncios blinked, and exchanged hasty glances.

"But . . . we do assure you that it is," the Bishop asserted. "The cardinals themselves gave it into my hand. For delivery to yourself."

"Then the fault, I concede, lies not with you, my friends, but with those who sent you. I cannot open, or reply, to a letter which is not addressed to me as King. It says but 'Lord Robert Bruce, Governor'. Amongst my subjects there are many bearing the name of Robert Bruce, who share with the rest of my barons in the government of the kingdom of Scotland. This letter may possibly be addressed to any of them!"

"No! No—it is not so. It is to you, sir . . . my lord . . ."

Bruce frowned. "Do you deny me the witness of my own eyes? The words are here written. But, enough. I have heard what you have had to say, permitted you to read aloud the open letter. To these, since they refused me my title of King, I will give no answer. Nor will I by any means suffer your sealed letter to be opened in my presence. Take it back to those who gave it."

"My lord—Your Excellency!" the Bishop protested, in agitation. "I . . . we regret it if this letter is not addressed to your liking. But it is not for our holy mother the Church either to do or to say anything, during . . . during the dependence of a controversy, which might, might prejudice the right of either of the parties. You understand . . . ?"

"So!" Bruce cut him short. "You acknowledge the controversy, and the rights of parties? *Two* parties! Both parties. Yet, in your open letter of introduction did you not read out more than once the style of Edward, King of England? Did you not? If, then, my spiritual father the Pope, and my holy mother the Church profess themselves unwilling to create a prejudice against my opponent by giving me the title of King, I am at a loss to see why they have thought proper to prejudice *my* cause by withdrawing that title from me. During—how did you say it? During the dependence of the controversy! All my subjects call me King. By that title do other kings and royal princes address me. My friends—if you had presented a letter addressed such as is this to any other kings, you would, I swear, have received a still rougher answer! You have mine —and less than roughly! For I do not fail to respect your calling and authority, and I entertain all reverence for the Holy See. Say so, when you return this unopened letter to your masters."

Monseigneur d'Aumery sought to retrieve something from the wreck. "Your Excellency—at least will you accept this two-year truce His Holiness requires? Command a temporary cessation of hostilities?"

Bruce shrugged. "To that I can by no means assent without the advice of my parliament. Aye, and while the English spoil the property of my subjects and invade my realm. My friends—convey my respects and good wishes to those who sent you. You have my permission to retire."

William Lamberton led the chagrined nuncios away.

The crestfallen emissaries had hardly left for the South before Bruce prepared to follow them, for at least some of the way. The surreptitiously-opened papal Bull had revealed that one of the specific demands was that the siege of Berwick should be raised forthwith. Actual and public disobedience to the Pontiff's express commands was to be avoided if at all possible. Therefore it behoved the Scots to get Berwick safely out of the arena of controversy before the Bull was officially broadcast, if by any means this could be effected. James Douglas had been besieging the place off and on, the last Scots territory in English hands, for well over a year—but it was a most difficult task, the castle surrounded by its powerfully-walled town, both of which could be supplied and reinforced by sea. Against siegery, in principle, as he was, Bruce decided on an all-out effort to reduce the place before the cardinals could trumpet forth their rejected Bull, from Durham.

On this occasion he did not intend to rely wholly on military threats, encirclement, starvation, and the like. A little guile might conceivably help. He sent a royal proclamation before him, which was to be conveyed somehow to the citizens of Berwick, by writings smuggled into the town by any means possible.

A few days later, he set out in person for the Border.

Siege warfare had never been really mastered in Scotland, by more than Robert Bruce—like military archery—for this was a concomitant of *aggressive* war, the conquering of other nations' fortresses, and hitherto the Scots had had no such ambitions. But in Ireland Bruce had had opportunity to confer with Sir Hugh de Lacy, Anglo-Irish baron, who had served extensively in foreign wars and engaged in much siegery. His advice and guidance, on proper engines and methods for the business, Bruce had sought and obtained. As a consequence he now had ideas to put into practice.

Much solid and mature hardwood was required for the construction of adequate engines and rams, and the neighbourhood of Berwick itself was not rich in old woodland. But the Earl of Dunbar and March, lord of this area, knew of some good oak forest at Aldcambus, on the north flanks of Coldingham Moor, near Cockburnspath, about a dozen miles north of the Tweed. Here the royal party repaired, to cut timber and build siege-machinery—and give time for the royal proclamation, perhaps, to make some impact in beleaguered Berwick. It was nearly Yuletide, and no time for this sort of thing; but time was of the essence, with those cardinals liable to sound off any day.

The cardinals in fact did make their presence – and their indignation – felt rather sooner than Bruce had bargained for; but fortunately in a less damaging fashion, at this stage, than might have been. They sent another intermediary, bearing a very stern open letter, plus verbal messages, to Bruce, with many threats should these be ignored; also they included once again the unopened papal Bull, to present. But this time they chose a Scot to do the presenting, one Adam de Newton, Prior of the Minorite Friars of Berwick, a former colleague and superior of Bernard de Linton when Vicar of Mordington. In some fear and trembling, this unfortunate cleric was brought north by James Douglas himself, to Aldcambus, after having sought a safe-conduct. Prudently, perhaps, he had left behind in Berwick both the Bull and the open letters, still inadequately addressed as they were, in the shrewd belief that the verbal messages would be more than ample to deliver, in the first instance.

Prior Adam's fears as to a dire confrontation with his monarch did not materialise. Bruce in fact would not see him. In his joyful reunion with Douglas, the King wholly ignored the cleric. It was their first meeting since Ireland, for Douglas had been away on one of his periodic deep punitive raids into England at the time of the royal return. Their delight in each other's company only increased with the years and their long partings. An arm around his friend's shoulder, Bruce led him away along a woodland path amongst the rustling fallen leaves – and only as an afterthought signed to Sir Alexander Seton, now the Seneschal, to take the Prior in hand.

Douglas was somewhat concerned at the King's appearance, although this was a great deal improved from what it had been a few months before. The younger man himself was beginning to show the signs of continual campaigning and command, the lines and bearing of authority, confidence, decision, implicit in his slender person and darkly handsome features. They had much to say to each other.

At length Bruce got round to questioning the other about the Prior.

"He brings fulminations and threats against you from these insolent cardinals, Sire," Douglas informed. "The man himself is leal enough, I think. He is in much fear – as he should be, by God! When I heard something of his mission, myself I near hung him up from the nearest tree! But he declares that he had no option but to obey these arrogant Princes of Holy Church, as he names them. They are his superiors, his masters. They sent for him, to Durham, and he could not refuse their command. But at least he left their letters in Berwick meantime, wisely deeming his life of greater value than them! One, he told me, is addressed to Robert Bruce, calling himself King of Scots!"

"Ha—*calling* himself! They learn but slowly, these Romish eminences!" Bruce shrugged. "I expected no better. So he comes with only verbal threats and pontifications?"

"Aye—but I believe they are strong enough! The man trembles at the thought of delivering them to Your Grace."

"Then we shall spare him that ordeal, Jamie. It is best that I do not see this priest. Do not hear these threats and fulminations. We shall get Seton to deal with him. Now—what of Berwick . . .?"

With Seton acting as go-between, the Prior's message was soon interpreted—interpretation rather than declaration being involved, the envoy being inhibited from speaking out, and Seton outraged that open threats should be made against his liege lord. Simply, the message was this—that unless an immediate two-year truce was concluded, all raiding against England stopped, and all English hostages and prisoners freed, the whole people of Scotland, as well as The Bruce personally, would be declared excommunicate, and the wrath of God and the castigation of Holy Church would descend upon a contumacious and disobedient nation. There did not seem to be any concessions required of the English.

"Sweet Christ—can they do this?" Douglas exclaimed, when they heard the terms. "Excommunicate a whole people? What of Bishop Lamberton? What of *all* the Scots bishops and clergy?"

"I fear that they can do it—in name at least," the King said. "If the Pope is Christ's Vicar on earth, he can withdraw Christ's holy sacrament. Whether he *should*, whether God accepts such harsh judgements, such sweeping condemnation of innocent folk, is not for me to say—I, who have lived under excommunication from Rome these many years."

"Aye, Sire—and is that not sufficient answer to this folly? You survive such censure passing well! Why not lesser men?"

The King bit his lip, and said nothing.

Seton nodded. "Who cares for these monkish cursings?"

"I do, Sir Alexander—I do!" Bruce answered tightly. "As must you. As must all. You and I may be prepared to defy the Holy See, in this. But that cannot be expected of all the people. Their faith in God is precious, and the Pope God's mouthpiece. *We* may say that he mis-speaks—but others will be less bold. Moreover, this cannot but weaken the authority of Lamberton. It is a grievous matter."

"What then can we do?"

"God knows—save seek to make time. To delay decision. As I

have been doing. So far, this is but a threat. We must seek to keep it only that. For so long as we may. Until we can make this Pope think anew . . ."

Both men looked at him blankly, at a loss.

"We can start by sending Prior Adam back to Berwick. For his papers, his letters. We will see that he is delayed. When he finds us again, with them, there will be more delay. We—or *you*—will find them to be wrongly addressed, so that we must debate and consider. Whether to receive them. Then send him, and them, back all the way to Durham. For amendment of superscription. Unopened. Once he is safely out of Scotland, evil men could again waylay the Church's representative—godless men caring nothing for the true religion! Rob him, shamefully destroying the letters, even this Pope's Bull. How say you—without that Bull, can these cardinals act? Make final denunciation? When the Bull has not been read by or to me? Or made known to the people?"

"I' faith—I would say not!"

"Here's a ploy, by the Mass!"

"No ploy, Sir Alexander. It is no game, I promise you. It is deadly earnest. Much may depend on it . . ."

Prior de Newton was detained at Aldcambus two days, and then sent back for his documents—but not before Seton wormed out of him much about the state of Berwick, the people's morale, the unpopularity of the harsh and overbearing governor of the town, Sir John de Witham, and what bad terms he was on with Sir Roger Horsley, governor of the castle. All of which Bruce heard with interest.

But that same evening there were tidings of even more immediate interest. A messenger came from Moray, who latterly had been aiding Douglas with the siege, to the effect that one Peter de Spalding, who claimed to be a kinsman of Sir Robert Keith, the Marischal, in view of the royal proclamation of mercy and in pursuit of a full pardon for past adherence to the English, was prepared to open a section of the town walling adjacent to the Cow Port, to King Robert's forces one night—he apparently being one of the captains thereof.

Keith, summoned, admitted that he had a cousin of sorts a mechant in Berwick, by name Spalding, although he had not heard of him for many a year.

This was news indeed—although there were many who smelled a trap, and the treachery on the wrong foot. But Bruce, with the need to capture this fortress urgent, was prepared to take the chance that it was a genuine offer. He sent Douglas back to the town's outskirts forthwith, with orders to contact this Spalding somehow. He himself would wind up this siege-engine building, and come on with the main force next day.

. . .

The following night, in sleet-laced rain driven by a salt wind off the North Sea, the King rode down the south-facing slope of the Lamberton ridge. The town of Berwick-on-Tweed lay unseen below and before him—for lamp-oil would be scarce in the belea-guered town and no lights showed, although it was not yet midnight. The land ahead, indeed, seemed darker than the sea; an indefinable belt of wan glimmer stretched all along their left flank somewhere, the phosphorescence of breaking combers on an iron-bound coast.

It was not an army that Bruce led down the long slow hillside; merely a motley company of lords, knights and men-at-arms, with the carpenters, wrights and smiths who had been constructing the siege-engines. These unwieldy, lumbering machines, dragged by oxen, their axle-trees screaming, their timbers creaking, had greatly delayed the royal progress that day; but they were much more important, in this context, than any thousands of men, and the high-born warriors had just had to summon their patience. Getting the things across the bogs and innumerable streams of Coldinghame Moor, for instance, had been a desperate, mud-slaister of a business. Proud lords would have left it to others more suitable for the task, and hurried on to Berwick; but that was not Robert Bruce's way. It had taken them fourteen hours to cover the dozen miles.

They were past Halidon Hill, the last prominence on the long green ridge, and were dropping to the farmstead of Camphill, only a mile from the north-western walls of the town, when suddenly lights began to appear ahead of them, lights that flared and blazed and sank, then blazed again, and at some distance. An indescribable noise also came to them, on the south-east wind, rising and falling likewise, but different from the distant thunder of the tide.

"Save us—have they started?" Gilbert Hay cried, at the King's side. "Jamie has not waited for us—for Your Grace?"

"Jamie is in command at Berwick," Bruce reminded. "Yet I would have thought that he would have delayed until I came."

"It may not be the assault. Just some disturbance in the town," Sir Hugh Ross suggested.

"I think not. Those are torches and fires. And at the far side of the town, where this Cow Port lies. Douglas has struck. Come—leave these engines. Irvine will bring them on." And he spurred his mount forward.

A courier met them as the hillside levelled off to the town meadows. "My lord King!" he shouted. "Word from my lord of Douglas. The assault is on. We are into Berwick. Over the walls . . ."

"I have eyes and ears, man! What are Douglas's tidings?"

"These, Sire. That my lord of Dunbar would not wait. Would not abide your royal coming. He and his were stationed to the east of the Cow Port. He must have given the signal. To those within. The three lights, two and one. Without word to my lords of Douglas and Moray, he advanced. Scaled the walls and over. With ease. And so on in."

"Curse the arrogant fool!" the King exclaimed. But it was himself he cursed, in fact; himself others would criticise. For in his efforts to hold together his warring, jealous nobles, he had allowed the Earl of Dunbar and March a command under Douglas. It was, after all, Dunbar's country, his earldom, and he could raise thousands of men hereabouts, in the Merse—had raised them, in the past, for the English. Here was opportunity to redeem himself. Instead—this! He was, of course, senior in rank and status to Douglas—although the latter was Warden of the Marches. Even senior to Moray, ranking only second to Fife in the hierarchy of Scotland's great earls, as descendant of Kenneth MacAlpin and the true Celtic line.

As others growled and muttered around him, Bruce rapped out, "And Douglas? And Moray? What of them?"

"With Earl Patrick into the town, my lord needs must follow. Or lose the surprise, lose all. He said to tell Your Grace. My lord of Moray took the left flank, the west. The walls were not defended, not there . . ."

"Aye. This Spalding, then, was honest in his treachery! Enough, then. Lead us down to this part . . ."

The uproar from the town was much louder now, the flames ever growing, heightening, buildings evidently afire. The area of battle was spreading, at least.

They reached the walls in the vicinity of the Cow Port. That great gate was still closed; but scores of scaling ropes and ladders hung from the parapets—and, unlike most siege-scalings, no layer of bodies lay inert at the foot. In the flickering light of the fires, Bruce was one of the first to clamber up.

The scene that met their eyes was dramatic as it was chaotic. All this part of the town was already ablaze, the sea-wind fanning the flames and causing them to leap the narrow lanes and vennels. Against the red and ochre glare, and amidst the rolling smoke-clouds, black figures were silhouetted, running, darting, wrestling, falling. Frequently steel flashed, reflecting the fires. Shouts and fierce laughter, screams and wails, penetrated the roar of the conflagration. Hell had come to Berwick that night!

Frowning, the King eyed it all. This was not as it should be.

Berwick was a Scots town, its greatest seaport, an important part of his realm however grievously it had been forced to co-operate with the enemy. Seventeen thousand had been massacred here by Edward Longshanks, in 1296, as an example to other Scots—hence perhaps the subsequent co-operation. It was no part of the King of Scots' policy to emulate.

"Find me Dunbar. Also Douglas," he ordered his companions. "And command this slaughter to cease. Our enemies are in Berwick Castle, not in this town. Quickly. I shall stand here."

Douglas was first found. He came running, eyes streaming, features blackened with soot. "Thank God you are come, Sire!" he cried, panting. "I can do nothing with the man Dunbar. Earl Patrick. Nor can Thomas. He will have the whole town ablaze. His men are sparing none. They heed no word of mine . . . ."

"I have sent for him. This slaughter of citizenry must be stopped. But—the castle, Jamie? What of the castle?"

"Thomas watches it. He holds the Castlegate. That before all else. They have not sought to break out. Into the town. Horsley's garrison. As yet."

"As well! And the other? This Witham? The town governor?"

"I have him. Captured. Drunken, and bedded with a whore. The town is mainly in our hands. A few pockets of Englishry still hold out, but not many. Mainly by the harbour. But, see you, our men are much scattered. Or Dunbar's men are. If there was a sally in force from the castle, and Moray could not hold it, all might yet be lost."

"I know it. Get your men gathered together, Jamie. How many have you?"

"Near 600. Moray has half that."

"And Dunbar?"

"Who knows? Perhaps 1,500."

"Aye. Well, leave Dunbar to me. Gather your men, and reinforce Thomas at the Castlegate. At all costs we must contain Horsley. He has the name of a fighter. And keep the remnants of Witham's force from reaching the castle likewise."

The King waited on the high wall, above the holocaust, where he could be found, while Douglas made off again, to dodge and double, threading his way to avoid the burning streets.

Hay brought the Earl of Dunbar and March to his monarch at length—as High Constable of Scotland his authority was undisputable.

"My lord," Bruce snapped, at once, "I am much displeased. Who gave you leave to burn this my town of Berwick?"

"Your Grace's town of Berwick is a nest of adders that should be smoked out," the other returned coolly. "That I do."

"Douglas commanded here, in my name, as Warden of the Marches. His orders were to spare the town. He has been besieging Berwick for a year—Berwick Castle. As you know well. At any time he could have contrived that the town should burn. Such was not my will. You knew it, my lord. Yet you have chosen to do this. You will tell me why, anon. Meantime, you will halt this folly, this carnage, immediately. Have your men withdrawn. All burning, and slaying of the citizenry to cease. You understand ?"

"If you wish Berwick Castle to fall, Sire, you will think again," the Earl declared thinly. "This town protects it like a breastplate. I remove that breastplate for you."

"Silence, sir! Do you debate my commands with me, the King ?" Bruce cried. "My lord Constable—see that the Earl of Dunbar calls off his men forthwith. No further delay. Have them assemble at the Salt-market. There is room there."

Bowing stiffly, the Cospatrick was led off.

But it was not so simple as that. Dunbar, it proved, had but little hold over his irregular force of Mersemen, many of whom had old scores to pay in Berwick town. Men inflamed with passion, liquor and rapine were not to be restrained, controlled, assembled, now scattered wide as they were. They continued to run riot, roaming where they would. In his efforts to bring them to heel, the King had to order the detachment of large numbers of Douglas's and Moray's veterans, thus greatly endangering the entire venture. Bruce made his own way through the inferno to the narrow, climbing Castlegate, which rose steeply from the town to the frowning fortress which dominated all from its rocky eminence high above the Tweed. If Sir Roger Horsley and his large garrison chose to clear this Castlegate with volleys of missiles flung from their great slings and mangonels—as they could readily do—and then sallied out in force, the depleted Scots force could by no means hold them. As cork for this bottle, Bruce knew his stopping-power to be quite inadequate.

That Horsley continued to hold his hand was surprising.

All that grim night the situation remained unresolved, with a confusion of fighting in narrow flame-lit streets, as much between Douglas's veterans and Dunbar's local levies as between Scots and English. Yet no break-out was attempted from the castle, no stones and projectiles were hurled down the Castlegate—which even in semi-darkness could not have failed to be effective, so narrow was the gullet. Bruce stood through the long hours, in the throat of the ascent, with a mere handful of men—although trumpet calls could have brought at least a hundred or two others fairly swiftly. Lights shone up at the citadel, but no stir of movement—that same castle where exactly twenty years before Edward Plantagenet had so deliberately humiliated him before Elizabeth, before all, at the Ragman Roll signing.

A chill grey dawn brought no immediate easement, for though the fighting and burning was tailing off, through weariness and satiety rather than any major imposition of discipline, the danger from the castle was heightened, since Horsley could now see how comparatively few he had to deal with; and missile-fire—and worse, arrows—could now be used accurately. But still no sally developed. Gradually Bruce began to breathe more freely. For some reason Horsley did not commit himself. To help matters along, the King ordered much blowing of trumpets from various parts of the smoking town, much unfurling and parading of standards. And he sent an impressive deputation, under the High Constable and the Warden of the Marches, to within hailing distance of the fortress gatehouse, to demand the immediate surrender of this Scots citadel to the King of Scots in person, offering honourable terms and a safe conduct for the garrison to Durham. Also he hanged a couple of score of Dunbar's looters and rapers, from beams made to project from Castlegate windows—as much to impress the garrison as to enforce his authority and punish the men, on the principle that any commander who could so afford to deal with his own troops must be very sure of his own strength. The Earl of Dunbar was constrained to officiate at these hangings, for sufficient reason; also it allowed the King to give it out that it was punishment for indiscipline against the Earl's own orders, a face-saving device that was important if this powerful noble was not to be totally estranged and thrown back hereafter into the English arms.

By midday, although there was no response from the fortress to the surrender demand, Bruce was satisfied that there was not now likely to be any break-out. Even with his siege-machines, however, he could not effectively assault the citadel, so secure was its position. But at least it was now cut off from the harbour, as from the town, and from reinforcement and supply by sea and land. Giving orders for such salvage and aid operations as were possible in the unhappy town, the weary and hollow-eyed monarch allowed himself to be persuaded to take a few hours' rest on the late Governor Witham's bed.

Prior Adam de Newton arrived back in Berwick that same morning, having been unaccountably delayed *en route*. His Minorite priory had been spared the flames, and his precious letters and Bull were intact. Wisely he decided that the moment was scarcely ripe for any attempt at presenting them to his difficult liege lord. First things probably came first, and there was ample for priests to do in

Berwick-on-Tweed for the moment. The lords Cardinal would surely understand.

. . .

It was not long before Sir Roger Horsley recognised realities, saw that if he had been going to attempt any counter-measures, he had left them too late, and decided to accept the terms of honourable surrender. It said something for the Scots King's reputation, as a man who kept his word, that the Englishmen were prepared to trust to it; for at the last siege of Berwick, Edward of England had likewise offered honourable terms to the Scots castle garrison, after the capture and massacre of the town; and when Douglas's father, Sir William, the governor, had submitted on those terms, the Plantagenet had laughed aloud, put him in chains, and sent him to walk, thus, with common jailers, all the way to London, for imprisonment in the Tower—thereby creating more than one deadly enemy. His son, grim-faced, watched the English garrison ride out from castle and town, swords retained and flags flying, a few days after the fall of Berwick, on their way to Durham; but he made no protest.

Berwick was a tremendous prize, in more than the mere cleansing of the last inch of Scots soil from the invader. It was one of the most renowned fortresses in the two kingdoms, and its loss a damaging blow to English morale. It dominated the Border, and all of Northumberland right to Newcastle. It gave the Scots a first-class seaport. And it endowed them with a mighty collection of warlike engines collected here, springalds, cranes, sows, ballista and the like, such as they had never had before. Above all, of course, Berwick's restoration to Scotland, before the Papal edict anent it had been made public, invalidated the said edict—which was Robert Bruce's urgent preoccupation meantime, in this strange contest of wits with the Holy See.

Ever a believer in striking while the iron was hot, and in order further to demonstrate to the Papal envoys that they were backing a losing side, Bruce sent for his son-in-law, the Steward, to come south with as large a mounted force as he could quickly raise. This, with Douglas's own Border contingent, was to form one of the swift, hard-hitting raiding columns beloved of the King, to stage one more deep penetration of England, for the cardinals' benefit mainly. Douglas and Moray would lead it—for though Bruce dearly would have liked to do so in person, he could not fail to recognise that in his present state of health this would be foolhardy and might endanger more than the operation itself. Walter Stewart would take over the governorship of Berwick meantime.

On learning of these preparations, Master Adam de Newton

summoned up his courage and once again presented himself at the King's door, this time complete with his letters and Bull. Sir Alexander Seton received him, as before, turning the sealed letters over in his hands.

"To whom are these sent, Master Prior?" he asked, as though coming new to the whole matter.

"To the King, sir. To King Robert."

"It does not say so. You have failed to address them properly, I fear."

"That was not for me to do, Sir Alexander. I am but the bearer. I cannot change the superscriptions. Nevertheless, they are written to the King, and none other."

"We have but your word for it, man. And you admit that you are but the bearer. I cannot take these to His Grace. All must be in the proper form, for King Robert. It is as much as my neck is worth!"

"But, sir—this is of vital import. This is the voice of Holy Church. From the Holy Father himself."

"The more necessary that it is properly directed and addressed. Take it back, Master Prior. Take it to those who gave it to you."

"I dare not . . ."

"You dare not do other, Sir Priest! It is the King's command. How think you he will look on one of his own subjects who contests his royal decision? In favour of a stranger's?"

"These . . . these are Princes of the Church. The spokesmen of Holy See. They will be very wroth . . ."

"More wroth than The Bruce, angry?"

The other swallowed. "I dare not counter them. They could un-priest me. Their patience is ended."

"Is it so? I wonder? For the man Witham, whose house this was, tells us that King Edward much consoles Their Eminences in their waiting at Durham, in many ways! In especial, he has conferred pensions upon them. Pensions for their lives. Why, think you?"

The Prior shook his head, wordless.

"Go then, Master Newton—and bring back your letters properly inscribed. His Grace will then read them. He does not reject the letters of His Holiness. Only requires that in so important a matter there should be no mistake." Seton shrugged. "If he wrote a letter and sent it to the Bishop John, calling himself Pontiff, at Rome? How then? Would the Pope receive it?"

"I know not. It is not for me to say. But . . . something other is." He drew himself up, as with a physical bracing. "Other than these letters to deliver, I have a second duty. A message to proclaim. To all. A verbal message, Sir Alexander. I have delayed too long in pro-claiming it. If King Robert will not hear it, his subjects shall."

He turned. Quite a crowd of citizenry and soldiers had collected, as at any development around the King's house. The Prior raised his hand.

"Hear me, good people—in the name of His Holiness the Blessed John, Pontiff and Vicar of Christ. His Holiness blesses you all. He desires and decrees that a truce of two years' duration is now in force. Between the peoples of Scotland and England, their rulers and councils. In this evil warfare which has shed so much blood, and defiled the fair face of Christendom. His Holiness decrees than none soever, be he named Robert Bruce or other, shall raise hand or sword against the English, from now on, for the space of two years. Nor any at his behest or command . . ."

Newton had been raising his voice as he went on, to counter the murmuring of the crowd. But he got no further than this. The murmur rose to a great and angry shout. The mob surged forward, gesticulating furiously.

With difficulty Seton extricated the alarmed Prior from the outraged crowd, pulled him inside the house and slammed the door. Then he hustled him through the building, past the kitchen premises, and so to its backdoor courtyard, and there ejected him into a lane.

"Off with you Sir Prior, before worse befall you," he said. "Happily, I did not rightly hear your message—which may well have been treasonable, I do very much fear! Thank you your saints that I did not. To Durham with you—and come back better instructed. Quickly—before they find you! See—you have dropped your Bull . . .!"

Master Adam's troubles were far from over, even though he did manage to escape amongst the warren-like burned-out streets of Berwick. Only a few days later, as King Robert rode south-westwards a little way with Douglas and Moray, on the start of their punitive raid into England, news was brought him that the unfortunate Prior had fallen into the hands of more broken men, some way to the south, in the region of Belford, presumably Northumbrians. Heathenish scoundrels, anyway. He had been most roughly used, his servants beaten, and all he had possessed taken from him, even his very clothing, so that he was left to continue his journey to Durham on foot, barefoot, and completely naked—a latter-day martyr, no less.

Gravely the King listened to these shameful tidings, and desisted from making anxious enquiries about the safety of the Prior's precious documents.

Bruce parted from his friends on the banks of the Till near Etal, to turn back for the ford at Coldstream and his return to Dunfermline.

222

"Go where you will—but take no greater risks than you must," he told them. "This is no invasion, see you, but only a demonstration. Take heed—for I need you both. More than you know. And do not be gone too long."

"How far shall we press, Sire? How far south?" Moray asked.

"I care not—so long as you press south of Durham! I would like to see my lords Cardinal make for London. In a hurry! But not *you*, see you! No probing for London, this time. Yorkshire will serve very well. If you seemed to move in eastwards somewhat, once past Durham, so much the better."

Douglas smiled. "Your Grace does not wish a captive Prince of Holy Church?"

"God forbid . . . !"

CHAPTER

16

ST. ANDREWS had known many stirring occasions in the past, not least Bruce's first real parliament nine years before, after he had completed his conquest of the Highland area, the Rosses and the MacDougalls. But this outdid all. Indeed it was probably Scotland's greatest spectacle and celebration ever, to date, both church and state combining to make it so, each with good reason. William Lamberton was as anxious as his monarch that far-away Rome should hear of this glittering event, be aware of the splendid edifice erected to God's glory and Holy Church's pride, in the ecclesiastical metropolis of Scotland, and to perceive that this far northern kingdom was no rude, impoverished wilderness, inhabited by semi-barbarians, but one of the most ancient, vigorous and cultured nations of Christendom and a strong buttress of Christ's Church. He had even invited the Pope's two representatives, from London, to be present for the occasion—after carefully ascertaining that they had already departed for France, on their way back to Rome, in high dudgeon, following upon their undignified scuttle south from Durham.

Bruce, while equally concerned over this aspect of the business, had further reasons of his own for making the most of events. He, the warrior-king, was at pains now to build up an image of a monarch of peace and prosperity, the father of his people, not just their shield and sword, the patron of things beautiful and enduring—above all, the founder of a dynasty. And his dynasty, obviously, was going to need every support and buttress it could possibly claim. This was his constant preoccupation, these days. Therefore, as well as out of gratitude and love for his friend, he had given Lamberton every available aid and encouragement in the lengthy, at times seemingly hopeless, task of completing the mighty and magnificent cathedral of St. Andrews; and now flung himself wholeheartedly into helping to make the opening and consecrating thereof an occasion which men would speak of for centuries.

To this end all Scotland had come to the grey city in the East Neuk of Fife, at the tip of the promontory between Forth and Tay—or all therein who were of any note, or conceived themselves so to be, apart from the vast numbers who were not. The royal summons had been clear and emphatic. The King had even had Lamberton hold up the celebrations until Douglas and Moray could get back from their successful and extended demonstration sweep of Northern England – and they had had to return from as far away as Skipton in Craven, and Scarborough. Now they were back, triumphant, with no losses to speak of and legendary exploits for their men to boast – as well as vast trains of booty, which had much delayed them, innumerable illustrious and valuable hostages for ransom, and indeed a magnificent collection of church plate, gold and silver vessels, fonts, crucifixes, chalices, lamps, candlesticks and the like, jewelled vestments and other treasure, as votive offerings for the newly-completed cathedral. Lamberton received this largesse, the cream of apparently no less than eighty minsters, churches, abbeys and monasteries, in Yorkshire and Durham, somewhat doubtfully – and wondered what sort of letters were speeding from Archbishop William Melton of York to the Vatican. But at least all this was probably better installed in the sanctified premises of St. Andrews than decorating rude barons' halls or melted down for money.

Even Walter Stewart had taken brief leave of absence for a couple of days from his onerous duties as governor of Berwick-on-Tweed, in order to attend. The King had insisted on this; for one of the secondary objectives of this whole affair was to bring before the people the infant Robert Stewart, Walter's son and Bruce's grandson, second heir to the throne and, in view of Edward Bruce's Irish preoccupations, of growing significance. The boy was now two and a half, a fine, sturdy, laughing child, seeming wholly to take after his very normal father – though Marjory Bruce had been a laughing normal child, indeed a poppet, once.

So, on a day of blustery wind and sunshine and showers, all rain-washed colour and contrasts, at noon two great processions set out into the crowded streets, the King's from the great Augustinian Priory, which he was making his headquarters meantime, and the Primate's from the episcopal castle. At the head of the first, behind a large company of musicians playing stirring airs, Bruce walked, splendid in cloth-of-gold and scarlet beneath the Lion Rampant tabard studded with jewels, bareheaded save for the simple circlet of gold with which he had been crowned at Scone when Scotland could not rise to better. But to compensate, Elizabeth who paced at his side, regal in purple and silver, wore a magnificent crown on her yellow hair, flashing with gems and pearls, especially made for the occasion.

Immediately behind stalked a distinctly embarrassed High Steward, leading his grinning, skipping son at his right hand, and the toddling Princess Matilda at his left – a thing that he would have died rather than be seen doing, for anyone else than his beloved father-in-law who, however, had been smilingly adamant on Elizabeth's advising. And she had been right, for the crowds went wild with delight at the spectacle. Thereafter a nun all in white carried the infant Princess Margaret in her arms.

Next came the heroes, Douglas and Moray, in gold-inlaid half-armour, bearing in the crooks of their right arms gold-plated and engraved jousting helms, plumed with their respective colours—although these latter were only recent replacements of English lord's crests. Sir Gilbert Hay, the High Constable, whose duty and privilege it was always to be close to the monarch, walked with them.

These were followed by the King's sisters and their husbands—Christian, with Sir Andrew Moray of Bothwell, son of the hero of Stirling Bridge, her third spouse and a deal younger than her still highly attractive self; Mary, now Countess of Atholl in her own right, and wed to Sir Alexander Fraser, the Chamberlain; and Matilda, with Sir Hugh Ross.

Alone, after them, grim, sour-faced and clad in little better than rags, for all the world like a witch, hirpled the Countess of Buchan, eyed askance by all yet condemned by none, a woman who had paid a more terrible price than most for that day's celebrations.

The man who, after a noticeable space, stalked next, handsome narrow head held high, weakly chin out-thrust, tongue ever moistening lips, was MacDuff himself, the Countess Isabel's brother—although she would by no means recognise his presence—Earl of Fife and senior magnate of the land, heir of a line older than the dynasty, making his first public appearance since his belated change of allegiance—and unsure of his reception. He led the Earls of Scotland, as was his right—although some of that splendid group would have voted to see him beheaded. But his presence, along with that of many another ex-traitor, represented not only victory for Bruce but the continuity and wholeness of his kingdom. The King's pardon embraced all. Only Mar was missing, Bruce's own nephew and Christian's son, who still preferred Edward of England's service, and was said to love that strange man. The Lord of the Isles strode, a little apart, inevitably.

Sir Alexander Seton, in the scarlet robe of Seneschal and King of Arms, led the resounding company of the lords and barons, with the colourfully-garbed Highland chiefs carefully mixed amongst them—for the King was concerned, as ever, to heal this grievous dichotomy between the Highland and Lowland polities—however much not a few of the proud Scoto-Norman barons resented being coupled with Erse-speaking barbarians with touchy tempers.

There followed the almost unnumbered host of the knights and

226

lairds and sheriffs, the lesser officers of state, the captains and chieftains, far enough behind to have their own band of musicians. Many of these were the veterans of twenty years of grim warfare, hard-bitten, tough, the most seasoned fighting men in all Christendom, with no traitors here. If Robert Bruce could have followed his own choice, it was with these that he would have marched, for it was on their broad shoulders that his throne rested. He had much ado keeping such out of the way of Fife, Menteith and their like. He was at pains to remind them that a kingdom, a realm, was not all composed of heroes and patriots.

Long before all this resplendent throng could emerge from the Priory, the King at its head had met the even more resplendent procession of the clergy, from the episcopal castle. Here was magnificence on an awe-inspiring, dazzling scale, with robes and copes and dalmatics, chasubles and tunicles, stoles, mitres, pastoral staffs and enshrined relics, in every colour under the sun, ablaze with jewels, coruscating, scintillating. Even Bruce was shaken at the magnitude and quality of this splendour, of its wealth and riches. Where had all this been hoarded away, hidden, during the long years of war and want? Certainly the Church had been his most faithful and generous supporter—but it seemed that it had been better able to afford that help than he had realised. Today, Holy Church had come into its own, and something of the accumulated wealth of the centuries was revealed—no doubt deliberately, as part of the lesson to be spelt out.

Even the Primate himself, who usually affected the plainest of garb, was magnificent in brocaded purple velvet, stiff with gold wire and rubies, his fingers sparkling with diamond rings, as, from his litter, he raised them to bless the genuflecting crowds. The King scarcely recognised his worn and shrewdly humorous friend. Behind him paced every bishop in Scotland—if in reality Master John Lindsay could be called Bishop of Glasgow. Bruce, and the Scottish clergy headed by the Primate, had appointed him to succeed old Bishop Wishart, who had died two years previously. But the Pope had refused to confirm; indeed had appointed an English Dominican, one John of Egglescliffe, who, though duly consecrated at the Vatican, had never dared to show his face in Scotland. Amongst all these splendid clerics was the odd shambling figure of the timeless Dewar of the Coigreach, from Strathfillan, wild-looking as ever, hobbling with the aid of St. Fillan's Staff; and, now looking middle-aged, stocky and ill at ease, the Dewar of the Main. Thereafter, Bernard de Linton, Chancellor and Abbot of Arbroath, led the cohort of abbots, mitred and otherwise, priors, deans, archdeacons, prependaries and canons, such as Bruce had not fully

227

realised even existed. When it came to making a demonstration, it seemed, Holy Church required lessons from none.

Fortunately the approach to the cathedral was broad, spacious, and the two processions could proceed side by side without confusion – although the King silenced his musicians in favour of the choir of one hundred singing boys, which preceded the prelates with chanted anthems of heart-breaking sweetness and purity.

Vast, lofty, massive, but perfectly proportioned, the mighty building reared before them, its huge central tower soaring over 200 feet, its steep roofs rivalling its spires, turrets and flying buttresses in their aspiration towards heaven. Cruciform in shape, 350 feet long by 160 feet wide at the transepts, of developing design from Romanesque to first-pointed Gothic, illustrating the 160 years of its building, it was the largest single edifice in the kingdom, and made all the other fourteen churches of the ecclesiastical metropolis look puny, dwarfed.

As they drew near, the great carillon of bells, brought at major expense from the Low Countries, rang out in joyous pealing harmony, vibrant, resonant but clear. And quickly, skilfully, the choir changed and spaced its singing and rhythm so that it blended and fitted into the bells' clangour in extraordinary fashion, something which must have demanded long practice and unlikely patience on the part of impatient boys. To this accompaniment the two processions branched apart again, to enter the mighty building by different doors, the clerics by the chancel to the east, the King's party by the great arched main entrance, deeply recessed and with triumphant wealth of mouldings.

Within, all was calm, hushed, even the filing in of large numbers of not very silent people seeming to create but little stir in the vast quiet of the towering forest of stone. Quite daunting indeed was the effect of it all, the richly ornamented arches crossing and recrossing to seeming infinity above the double rows of stately pillars, the soaring clerestory with triple rows of pointed and mullioned windows above, richly stained, with the brilliant hues of tempera paintings on the walling, lightening any claustrophobic effect of tremendous, overwhelming masonry. From mighty nave, built to hold 3,000, by transepts, choir and chancel to the High Altar, the place combined sheer beauty and strength with transcendent size, to an extraordinary effectiveness. Even David, Bishop of Moray, had to admit that it outdid his own beloved cathedral of Elgin, which hitherto had been called the glory of the kingdom.

The boys had not ceased to sing, and were now climbing winding turnpike stairs within slit-windowed pillars, from which their anthem came in strange, unearthly fashion, to join the ranks of older choristers and musicians who were already installed up there in the three lofty galleries which surmounted the clerestory, with open arcading inwards. To their harmonies, now reinforced by soft instrumental music, Bruce and Elizabeth made their way slowly up through the centre of the nave, to climb the choir and chancel steps to their thrones, set on the right side; while the bishops and senior clergy all but filled the rest of the chancel. Lamberton himself, leaning heavily on his golden pastoral staff, and supported by his acolytes, limped directly to the High Altar. It was ablaze with candles, their flames diffused by the rolling clouds of incense.

It took little under an hour to fill that tremendous place—although even so it presented no appearance of fullness, so noble were the proportions. Then, as at last the bells ceased their pealing, and in shattering contrast to the sweetly melodious chanting maintained all this time, suddenly the Te Deum crashed out, in splendour, with trumpets, horns, shawms, tambours, cymbals and men's voices, rich, deep, quivering with power. The Service of Thanksgiving, Dedication and Consecration began.

Bruce shook the tears roughly from his eyes. And not for the first time, his wife pretended not to notice. If emotion was an essential part of Robert Bruce, she was prepared to thank God for it.

The praise, prayers, singing and sonorous Latinities had given place to the Primate's address—for it was that, rather than any sermon—when the King's attention was distracted by some small commotion nearby, where a side-door opened from the dormitory, so that the canons might slip in to perform their midnight services. Two newcomers had entered there, no canons but notably richly dressed gallants, though obviously travel-stained. One was already beginning to move towards the throne, when Sir Alexander Seton hurried to halt him. The whispers of altercation could be plainly heard, through the Primate's richly harsh voice speaking on in strange power to be issuing from so gaunt and racked a body.

Bruce frowned—the more so as he suddenly recognised one of the intruders to be Sir William de Soulis, Hereditary Butler of Scotland, Irish Earl of Dundalk.

Sir Alexander, as High Seneschal and Herald King, was clearly urging the visitors to wait, to turn back—but de Soulis would have none of it. All but pushing Seton aside, he shouldered his way round him and came striding towards the King. All around, the ranks of the nobles seethed and stirred.

Bruce, for his friend Lamberton's sake, at this the climax of his career, was not going to allow any unseemly disturbance to break out. With an imperious hand he flicked Seton and the others back, and beckoned de Soulis on—but his brow was black.

The Lord of Liddesdale dropped on one knee at the side of the throne, and reached for the King's hand—but it was snatched away from him.

"Your Grace—hear me!" he exclaimed.

"Hush, man! Quiet!" the monarch jerked, below his breath. "How dare you!"

"Sire—you must listen. I pray you. It is your brother. His Grace, the Lord Edward. His Grace of Ireland. He . . . he is dead."

The King stared, suddenly still, rigid. Elizabeth's hand slipped over to find his wrist, to hold it.

All anywhere near could see that the King had received shattering news. Lamberton himself could not but see it; be very much aware of the interruption; yet he prevailed, in that most difficult of tasks, to keep his voice steady and even and to continue with his celebratory discourse seemingly undisturbed.

"Sire," de Soulis whispered. "You heard? King Edward, your royal brother is killed. Fallen in battle. At Dundalk. A great slaughter. Eight days ago . . ."

"Dear God—dead! Edward dead!"

"Aye, Sire. It was a sore battle. The English, under the Lord John Bermingham, were advancing on Ulster. His Grace moved to meet them. We camped at Tagher, near Dundalk. His Grace would hear nothing but that we attack the enemy—though they were ten to one. He . . . he was one of the first to fall."

"You have brought his body home?"

"Alas, no, Sire. The English—they took it. Dead. They beheaded him. Quartered the body. Sent it as spectacle to four parts of Ireland. The head to be sent to Edward of England . . . !"

"A-a-a-ah!" That strangled sound was not so much a groan as a snarl. And loud enough for many to hear. Even Lamberton paused for a moment in his delivery, brows raised towards the King.

But that last intimation of English savagery had made Robert Bruce himself again, the warrior he had always been rather than the gentler monarch and father of his people he now sought to be. The iron came back into his features, and he raised his head. He caught the Primate's eye, and gave a brief shake of his head to the latter's enquiry, sitting back in his throne, a clear indication that Lamberton should proceed. Still low-voiced, he said to de Soulis:

"Very well, Sir William. I thank you. Of this more anon. You may retire!"

"But, Sire—there is more . . ."

"Later, sir."

It was the other's turn to frown, as he rose, bowed stiffly, and backed away.

The celebrations continued, as planned.

Later, the long service over, and when the processions had wound their colourful way back to their respective bases, a great banquet, masque and dancing was arranged for the evening – more than one indeed, for all walks of men and women. Bruce cancelled none of it. But he did call a hurried Privy Council, for the hour or so intervening, in the refectory of the Augustinian Priory.

It was a larger Council than usual, for practically every member entitled to be present was already in the city. Sir William de Soulis himself was present, in his capacity of Lord of Liddesdale, if not Butler of Scotland.

"My lords," the King said, without preamble, when all were seated, Lamberton himself the last to hobble in. "I grieve to upset this great and auspicious day's doings, and to inconvenience you all thus. But you should know what tidings the Lord of Liddesdale has brought me. Some may already have heard. And to give me your counsel as to the necessary decisions. My brother, the Lord Edward, Earl of Carrick and latterly King of Ireland, is dead. My . . . my brother, the last of four. All slain. By the English. At least he died honourably. On the field of battle. Yet he was dishonoured in his death, in that the enemy's spleen triumphed, even so. They dismembered his body. Cut it up – as they did the others. To exhibit as trophies. Despatched throughout Ireland. His head sent to England. Such, my lords – such are they with whom His Holiness of Rome makes cause! These to whom he would have us submit!"

In the hubbub that followed the King waited set-faced. Then he banged on the refectory table.

"My lords – may I remind you that this is a Council, not a wives' gossip!" he declared, with a harshness that had not been heard in his voice for long. "My lord Edward's death I shall mourn, in my own way. We were not close. We much disagreed. But we were brothers. But – that is my business. Not this Council's. What is, is twofold, and to be considered herewith. The Lord Edward was appointed by parliament first heir to my throne. It therefore becomes necessary for parliament to appoint anew. For my bodily health is not of the best, and I need remind none that the succession is all-important." He caught Lamberton's eye, and the older man shook his head almost imperceptibly.

"So this Privy Council must guide parliament in the matter. A parliament to be called as soon as may be possible. As you know, forty days' notice is required. But effective decision cannot wait so long. So decide, my lords." He paused. "Secondly – there is to decide what to do about the Scots forces still remaining in Ireland. They are not so many, but still some thousands . . ."

231

"Sire," de Soulis interrupted—and men, however distinguished in blood or position, did not interrupt their sovereign. "They are fewer than that. Fewer than you think. For they were all at this battle. The spearhead of the King's army. Two thousand and more. Few now are alive. Of any degree, noble or simple."

Every eye stared at him.

"All are dead. My cousin, Sir John de Soulis. Sir Philip de Moubray. Sir John Stewart of Jedburgh, my lord Steward's cousin. Sir Fergus of Ardrossan. Ramsay of Auchterhouse . . ."

"Christ's mercy! All these—my good friends! How came they all to die, man? Here must have been utter folly!"

"The English were strong in cavalry. They were commanded by the Lord John Bermingham. With many notable captains. Sir Miles Verdon. Sir Hugh Tripton. Sir John Maupas. He it was who slew the King. I, and others, urged that we should retire. But His Grace must attack. They outnumbered us ten to one. The Irish levies fled. The King fell, early. The Scots would not flee. They died there, around their King."

"A-a-aye! God rest their souls! The brave ones. My men. But— the waste! The folly of it. Men who had fought with me on a score of fields. To die so!"

"They died honourably, Sire. Choosing death with their monarch."

"No, sir. Not their monarch. Their leader, perhaps their friend. But the Lord Edward was not their monarch. These were subjects of *mine*. I say that here was waste and folly. As was all the Irish adventure. But—what matter? They died. And you, sir, did not!"

"Eh . . . ?" De Soulis blinked, and flushed. "What means Your Grace?"

"What I say. These, you said, chose death with the Lord Edward. *You* did not, it seems, Sir William!"

"By God's good providence I was preserved. Unhorsed in a charge. Stunned. Led off the field by my esquire. And so preserved. I seem to mind Your Grace in similar case at Methven!"

"That is true. I stand rebuked. My claim is that these stout friends of mine, old friends—their deaths were waste, folly. You say not—yet you were less foolish. I commend your wisdom in this, at least!"

"Your Grace is not doubting my courage? My honour?"

"Your courage—no, sir. Your honour—who knows? It is a chancy commodity, honour! It is concerned with more than battles, Sir William. You have been privy to much that was against my interests—you, my Butler. You ever supported my brother in his Irish follies—against my known wishes. You worked against

232

my lord of Moray, my lieutenant, sent to Ireland to guide my brother. Your courage I do not doubt, sir—but let us leave honour out of this!"

De Soulis had half risen from his bench, glaring. It was most plain how these two men misliked each other.

"Sire—I do protest!" he exclaimed. "You wrong me, in more than in my honour. Without cause. Moreover, you miscall me. I would remind you that I am a peer of the realm of Ireland. Earl of Dundalk. I would request that you style me so!"

"Sir William de Soulis," Bruce grated, "in this realm of Scotland, you are Lord of Liddesdale—by my good favour. You are Hereditary Butler—by my good favour. These, and nothing else. You have not surrendered your Scots citizenship. Or not to me. For Irish. Or you would not be sitting at this Council. Do you wish to do so ?" That was rapped out.

The other sat back, biting his lip. He had great lands in Liddesdale and the South-West March. And his new Irish lands were already overrun by the English. "No, Sire," he said, thickly.

"Very well. Remember it. Remember also that at my Privy Council I expect to receive counsel. Not bickering and disrespect. In this realm no man trades words with the monarch—save in a privy chamber. Now—let us proceed, my lords. It seems that there is little that may be done anent bringing back of the Scots force from Ireland. Though what can be done, must. Therefore, our immediate concern is this of the succession."

"My good liege lord," Lamberton said, at once, "I speak for all when I say that we all do most deeply grieve for you in the loss of your royal brother. This, the last of your brothers. He was a brave man, and a mighty fighter. As are all of your race. He was perhaps over-bold. But who here will judge him, in that ? Is it Your Grace's wish that this night's feasting and masque be set aside, in mourning ? For the heir to your throne ?"

"I think not, my lord," Bruce answered. "I know—or knew—my brother, passing well, whatever our differences. His failings were those of a high spirit and a light heart. He would never wish this great day's celebrations to be curtailed—he who would most have found them to his taste. Nor do I believe it right. This day we celebrate not only the completion of a large work in God's name and to His Glory, but the final freeing of this realm from the invader. After the fourth part of a century, no enemy English foot defiles our soil. To this end Edward Bruce laboured, fought and suffered as much as did Robert. As have done so many. All here—or most! Therefore, since this day will not come again, let there be no damping of its joy. So Edward would say—of that I am sure. And all those, our friends, who died with Edward. So say I. Let all proceed. Now—to this sore matter of the succession."

"Lord King." Again it was William Lamberton who spoke. "I think it no such sore matter—by Your Grace's leave. All sorrow that your royal health has in some measure suffered the price of a score of years of war and privation. But it is none so ill that we must conceive the appointment of a successor to your throne to be of urgency. God willing, you will reign over us for long years yet. I pray you not to conceive otherwise."

Again the two men's eyes met, sharing their grim secret, as all around men cried acclaim and agreement.

"You have much recovered, Sir King, since your return from Ireland. Do not tell me that Robert Bruce has become fearful for his body, like some old woman—for I'll not believe it!" Only Angus Og would have dared to speak thus to the monarch, even with a smile, the independent Prince of the Isles.

"His Grace was more sick than you know, my lord," Moray declared stiffly. "Even though he was concerned to hide it from all."

Bruce glanced quickly at his nephew. He was a keen and observant man. Could he possibly know? Have guessed?

"I am less young than once I was," he said, shortly. "Sickness that in a younger man might be thrown off, might serve me less lightly now. I desire the succession to be settled."

There was a pause. Then Gilbert Hay spoke.

"Is there indeed any choice, Sire? Lacking a son from your own loins—which, pray God, may still be—there is only your grandson, the child Robert Stewart. No other of the royal line survives. Since the Lord Edward had no lawful issue."

The old Earl of Ross was not asleep after all. He cleared his throat, and looked at his son, Sir Hugh. Edward Bruce had indeed a son, by their daughter and sister, the Lady Isabella Ross—only he had omitted to wed her. As he had omitted to wed that other, the Lady Isabel de Strathbogie, the forfeited Earl of Atholl's sister, to the realm's cost. Neither of the Rosses spoke.

"There is surely more choice than this?" James Douglas pointed out. "Your Grace has two fine daughters. Although the realm has never had a queen-regnant—save for she who died at Orkney, the little Maid of Norway who never ascended the throne—is there aught to make such Queen impossible? Other realms have had such monarchs. Must Scotland be different?"

There was a muttering round that table, from many. Clearly it was an unpopular suggestion—although it was like loyal and devoted Jamie Douglas to have made it, for his liege's sake. And Elizabeth's.

When none actually raised voice to speak against it, Douglas reiterated, "I say is there aught against it? In fact? Other than prejudice? If, as God forbid, we should have a child as monarch, does it matter so greatly if the child is a female? Either would require sound guardians, regents. Does the law of this land say otherwise? I know little of these matters, of rights and laws of succession. My lord Primate—can you tell us?"

Lamberton spread his hands. "It is scarcely a matter of law or right, Sir James. I see it as a matter of choice. Two concerns bear on our decision—or, on parliament's, for we only do advise parliament on this issue. One concern is what is best for the realm. The other is His Grace's own desires. I agree that, as an infant, a princess might serve as well as a prince. But infants grow apace. And in a nation which must ever fight for its survival, a Queen would serve less well, I fear. And there comes the thorny question of marriage, and a new male strain to the dynasty. Too many would seek to supply it! A realm with a young Queen to marry, could be endangered, a bone of contention for dogs to fight over."

"There are dogs a-plenty to fight for this bone, it seems—Queen or none!"

"My lords," Bruce intervened. "I have thought much on this matter, in the past. I believe there is a side to it which we must needs consider. It may be as my lord Bishop says, that the succession is not a matter of right, of law. But I think that there is guidance, at least. Consider. My style and title is not as that of the King of England. Or the King of France. Or of Norway. I am, for better or worse, the King of Scots. Not the King of Scotland. Here is more than the mere form of words. It is so because of our ancient Celtic polity. From which this crown descends. Never forget it, when you think of Highlands and Lowlands. It was the Celtic support, which saved me, and the realm, at our lowest fortunes." And the King glanced over at the Lord of the Isles, Sir Colin Campbell, and other Highland chiefs present.

"In that language," he went on, "I am *Ard Righ. Ard Righ nan Albannach*, High King of the Scots. As in the Irish polity—also Celtic. And if High King, or King of Kings, there must be lower kings. In Ireland they so call themselves. Here, this has not been our custom. Save in the Isles. And in Man. The great Earls of Scotland were our lesser kings—the Seven Earls. But now more. All the land was divided between these. The *Ard Righ* was appointed by them, his line sustained by them. But, unlike the monarchs of other lands, the *land* of Scotland was not the High King's. It was, and is, that of the lesser kings, or earls, who support him. As an Earl himself, he has his own lands—but as King, no. So he is not King of Scotland, but of Scots. The people of the land, not the land itself."

235

Men nodded. "It is both the strength and the weakness of your throne, Sire," Bishop Moray said.

"Perhaps. But all this you know. It bears, however, on this of the succession. Our kingship is different—as you say, in some matters weaker than others. The *Ard Righ*, if he rests on the support of his earls, and other lords, must be their choice, their representative. Hence this Council; hence parliament's decision. And if this is our ancient custom, then it follows that the succession is one of *choice*, within the royal line. And where there is doubt, as here, the choice should be such as the lesser kings would select to be their strong right arm. Therefore, I say, it should be of a man, a male, a prince, where possible. As it ever has been hitherto."

There was a murmur of agreement.

"Spoken like a Bruce, Sire!" Malcolm, Earl of Lennox declared—as one of the original Seven Earls. "Your grandsire said the same. When Alexander, of blessed memory, lost his son and there was no heir. Save the princess in Norway. Your grandsire claimed to be named heir. Until a prince might be born. King Alexander acceding."

Bruce nodded. "So be it. We nominate to parliament, to be held so soon as may be, the child Robert Stewart, son to the High Steward, as first heir to the throne."

"Lacking a son to Your Grace," David of Moray put in. "But with regents. Good regents. Governors. Two. Other, my lord Steward, than yourself. I mean no disrespect. But this is necessary."

"I say the same, my lord Bishop," Walter Stewart agreed readily.

"What two better than my nephew, Thomas of Moray? And the good Sir James Douglas?" the King said. "In their strong hands Scotland would be safe."

Approval for that was fairly general—although inevitably some frowned or looked blank.

De Soulis spoke again. "And, Sire—what if the child Robert Stewart dies? Bairns are fragile stuff on which to build a kingdom! What then?"

Men, who had sat back, thankful for the business to be over, turned frowning faces on the Butler, annoyed that the thing should be further dragged out.

"The boy is lusty. That can wait," Angus Og jerked.

"Have you other suggestion, my lord of Liddesdale?" Bruce asked level-voiced.

"I would but remind this Council, Sire, that there are more strings to the royal lute, in Scotland, than that of Bruce. If male heir is to be found."

There were not a few indrawn breaths, at that.

236

"So Edward Longshanks took pains to show, at the Competition. In 1292," the King acknowledged grimly. "Do you wish another such contest for the throne?"

"By God—no!"

"A mercy—not that!"

"Better a Queen than that!"

"Are you crazy-mad, man . . . ?"

When de Soulis could make himself heard above the outcry, florid features empurpled, he said, "I made no such suggestion. I but reminded the Council of a fact. If a man to rule Scotland is vital, there are men to consider. With the blood-royal in their veins."

"Comyns . . . ?"

"Traitors!"

"Who, man—who?"

Bruce raised his hand. "We shall not forget it, Sir William," he assured, carefully.

Others were less calm, restive, scowling, eyeing each other.

"I move that we proceed to the next business, Sire," Lamberton said.

"Is there more business, my lord Primate?"

"It may scarcely be Council business. But it is of interest to all here, and should be made known throughout the realm. The two Cardinals, before they left England, I am informed, made pronouncement of excommunication against Your Grace, and against all who supported you. This latter, I say, was not within their power to do, without my knowledge and agreement. *I* represent Holy Church in this realm. And I support Your Grace to the full. No Cardinal, or other than the Pontiff himself, can excommunicate me, as Primate. Or over-rule me within my province. Therefore this pronunciamento is faulty. Faulty in one respect, faulty in all. It is to be ignored. These are my instructions, as Primate."

Bruce actually smiled. "I thank you, my lord Bishop. We all do, I vow. Not only that you remove such great weight from our souls. But that you end this Council on a light note. All shall hear of this. I thank you all, my lords, for your attendance and your advice. Let us now resume our celebrations. And mourn the Lord Edward, in our private chambers, anon . . ."

ROBERT BRUCE wondered how many times he had sat thus, in the saddle, at the head of a company of grim-faced armed men, great or small, and gazed southwards across the Borderline into England. How often they had looked, dreading what would sooner or later bear down on them from over there, the great enemy hosts, intent on the annihilation of Scotland. Lately, of course, it had been rather the other way, and it would be the folk over there, south of Tweed, Esk or Solway, who must dread and quake when the smaller but faster lines of steel appeared on the Scottish slopes. How much longer, he asked himself? How long before proud, stubborn men, in York and London and Rome, would accept hard facts, recognise his kingship, and come to a peace conference? How much longer before he could lay down his sword?

Not that July night of 1319, at any rate. It was still the unsheathed sword. The only question was in which direction to wield it. Along the gentle ridge of Paxton, above Tweed, only five miles west of Berwick, they waited, the great Scots cavalry host, stretched out along the escarpment behind Bruce for a full mile, ten thousand armed and horsed men, silent, menacing, the largest raiding-force that he had ever mounted. Waited for James Douglas, as the grey summer night settled on land and sea.

They had moved south through Lothian and the Lammermuirs and into the Merse, by quiet, little-known passes, by Garvald and Spartleton Edge and Cranshaws. At Edrom, Jamie had left them, four hours earlier, and raced ahead with half a dozen of his own mosstroopers. None knew Berwick and vicinity, nowadays, so well as the Douglas. He had spies and informants scattered all around the area. Jamie would gain the information they required, if anybody could. He had promised to bring tidings to the King, here at Paxton, by an hour before midnight. He was almost an hour late. Ten thousand men fretted and fidgeted.

"Shall I take a troop? To seek him?" the Earl of Moray asked, at his uncle's elbow. "I know many of the places where he would go. To gain news . . ."

"I think Jamie would scarce thank you, Thomas!" Bruce answered. "To play nurse. Give him time."

"He should have taken more men," Gilbert Hay, at the other side, declared. "He should be less rash. More careful of himself."

"Less rash ? Gibbie, we are getting old when we talk so! James Douglas remains young of heart."

"So did my uncle, the Lord Edward!" Moray murmured.

"No, Thomas. I said young of heart. Not young of head! Jamie's head is not so young. He will not take undue risks. And sound tidings we must have."

"You fear the King of England may have learned cunning, with the years ?" Fraser the Chamberlain asked.

"No, Sandy. Edward of Carnarvon will never learn cunning. It is the loyalty, or otherwise, of his lords, that concerns me. Notably one—Lancaster. That man's behaviour, of royal birth and five Earls in one as he is, could change all at this juncture. I must know his dispositions."

Edward of England, stung by the loss of Berwick, the repeated Scots raids deep into his kingdom, and the Cardinals' failed mission, had not proceeded to a peace-treaty, but had raised a new army and marched north to retake Berwick-on-Tweed, summoning all his northern vassals to support him there. But his unpopularity was as great as ever, as even in the days of Piers Gaveston—for he had elevated new favourites, the Despensers. The northern lords looked towards Lancaster as their leader. If Lancaster came to join his monarch before Berwick, as commanded, then the Scots host, tough and potent as it was, would look puny.

"Lancaster hates King Edward—all men know," Fraser was saying, when the drumming of hooves silenced him. All heads turned in an easterly direction.

It was Douglas and his half-dozen, lathered in horse-spume.

"My sorrow that I have kept you waiting, Sire," he exclaimed, panting. "But the English have got two great rings around the town. Earthworks. A double circumvallum. Thick with men. Winning through these is no light matter. It took time . . ."

"Double earthworks ? That bespeaks many men."

"Many, yes. Too many. Lancaster is come. He has joined the King. With unnumbered thousands. He came but yesterday."

"A curse on it! I had hoped . . ." Bruce frowned. "Did you learn anything of numbers, Jamie ?"

"Not that I could rely on. The King may have brought some 20,000. But Lancaster and the northern lords have many more."

"And you say that they have dug these trenches and banks. All round the town ?"

"Save at the harbour, yes. The King's force did that. He has brought a host of foreigners, Low Country men, versed in siege war.

239

With many great and strange engines and devices, I am told. He intends to have Berwick again. At all costs. The Steward must be sleeping but poorly!"

"Perhaps. But I am more concerned for ourselves than for Walter! Our own attack. These trenches and earthworks may have been dug to encircle the town. But equally, they will protect the besiegers against ourselves. To assail the English dug into these, their spearmen and archers, with our smaller force—and that cavalry —would be folly. That way lies disaster."

"So fear I. With Lancaster's host on the flank. To sweep us up," Douglas agreed. "We cannot do this by assault, Sire."

"What, then?" Hay demanded. "Must we sit and besiege the besiegers? Call for more men?"

"The English could call up more men more readily than could we," Moray pointed out. "There are more of them nearer at hand."

"They have brought a fleet of ships, with their siege engines, into the harbour," Douglas went on. "These also are a danger."

"I much fear . . ." Moray was saying, when the King cut him short.

"Fear nothing, Thomas," he said. "This is not the way. I have not come so far to throw my people into hopeless slaughter. As it would be. No—we adopt the other project. We seek to draw King Edward off, since he is too strongly placed for us to fight. Or *you* do. For this will take too long for me to be away from Dunfermline. You and Jamie will take the road south, once more."

To none did Bruce have to explain why he wanted to get back to Dunfermline quickly. The Queen was pregnant again, and nearing her time. The King was on edge, for more reasons than he would admit. This time it might be a son. But Elizabeth was getting past normal child-bearing age. And what effect might his sickness have on any issue now . . . ?

Douglas nodded. "Gladly. How far south this time?"

"York, I think, will serve."

"Would not further serve better, Sire? To draw King Edward after us?" Douglas suggested. "The nearer to London we win, the better. The South will lie unprotected, with his armies here."

"Perhaps. But York should suffice, I think. I have word that Edward's Queen, Isabella, is presently there. He left her at York when he marched north."

"Ha! You mean . . . ?"

"I mean that, unlike the English, I do not usually make war against women. But this lady, taken into your custody for a little— or even the threat thereof—would, I believe, fetch Edward south promptly, and shorten the siege of Berwick more swiftly than any other means."

240

James Douglas slapped his saddle-bow gleefully. But Moray shook his upright handsome head.

"I do not like it, Sire," he said.

"Of course you do not like it, Thomas! It conflicts with your honour—well known to us all! But it could, nevertheless, save many lives. Thousands, it may be. Perhaps this city itself."

"It was *your* honour, Sire, that I was considering—not my own," his nephew answered stiffly. "This they would hold to your blame. Not mine. Or the Douglas's."

"I could thole it! Jamie—I fear this must be your especial task, then. Unless you also scruple?"

"It shall be my delight. I have heard that the lady is . . . generous!"

"Aye. That is why I jalouse that her husband will hasten south when he hears! But, on your return, remember Lancaster. He may seek to cut you off." The King paused. "There is another matter that might bear on this. William Lamberton tells me that Archbishop Melton is now holding some great gathering of his priests at York—synod, convocation, chapter, I know not what. Churchmen have much sway with Edward. This may also help to bring him south."

"We shall attend on their deliberations, with pleasure!" Douglas nodded, grinning.

"How many men do we take?" Moray asked, rather emphasising the pronoun.

"Take all. I will go with you as far as my lordship of Tynedale. To Wark Castle. It is important that I treat it as part of my realm of Scotland. Receive fealties and homage, conduct an assize, show my writ to run there, as monarch. Something to bargain with, when I bring Edward to the peace-table. From there, I shall return to Dunfermline. And expect you both to rejoin me within the month."

"So soon, Sire . . . ?"

"So soon. I want Walter Stewart relieved quickly—since the English have these especial siege-engines. He may not be able to withstand them. So what you do must be done swiftly, or it may be to no profit. It is not a campaign that I send you on, but a single stroke. You are not going south to fight battles, only to draw Edward of Carnarvon away from Berwick. I am weary of bloodshed—even English blood. I want these thousands of stout lads back, my friends. Is that understood?"

The great mounted force moved on, quietly, down to the ford of Tweed.

* * *

Two weeks and a day later, again at midnight, in the bedroom which had been Queen Margaret's above the plunging ravine of Pittendreich, where her four fine sons had been born, all to be Kings of Scots, her descendant watched his wife in labour, and suffered each pang with her. He would not leave the chamber though she urged him to, and cursed the physicians and midwives as bungling incompetents. Emotionally wrought up, he equally cursed his own uselessness—and possibly, by his sheer helpless invalidity may have somewhat aided Elizabeth by distracting her from her pains.

When, after a moderately short labour, the child was born, a boy, and dead, Bruce was a stricken man. He left the bedchamber at last, set-faced, and went to lock himself into his own room.

Something had told him that this would be the son on which he had set his heart. Head in hands now, he crouched at the window, staring out into the blue night. Accursed, excommunicate, rejected of God, the refrain beat in his brain. And behind it all the still more ominous word, leper, leper . . .

It was that word which presently sent him hurrying back to his wife's chamber. It was not to Elizabeth's side that he went, however, but to the cot where the pathetic bundle lay inert, silent. Snatching up his son, he tore off the blood-soaked wrappings and carried the tiny, wrinkled, naked body over to a lamp, there to peer and examine.

From the great bed Elizabeth raised her voice, tired, husky. "What . . . what do you, Robert? I am sorry, sorry, my love. Again I have failed you. But—why torture yourself so?"

"I look . . . to see . . . if the finger of God . . . is on him also!" her husband grated. "The mark of my sin! To see if . . . if there is . . ."

"Hush Robert!" Despite her weakness and the sweat that started from her brow, Elizabeth de Burgh sat up. "Say it not, I charge you!" That was as good as a command. She looked warningly towards the women who still remained in the room. And as he paid no heed, and went on muttering, she deliberately swept down a goblet of wine which stood untasted on a table beside her bed. It fell with a crash.

That startled him. He transferred his stare to herself. Then curtly he dismissed the women, and laying the child down came to her side. "I am sorry, lass," he said, his voice sane again. "Forgive me." He took her hand.

"Robert—you must watch your words," she chided, sinking back on her pillow. "You might have let out, before all, your fear, your *wicked* fear!" For that strong woman, there was near-hysteria in her voice. "It is not so, I tell you. This has become a madness with you. Let the evil word once fall from your lips, into the ears of others, and hell itself will engulf Scotland. Hell, I tell you!"

"Hell, perchance, is here already!" he answered grimly. Then he shook his head. "But I will not say the word, Elizabeth my heart. Content you. God forgive me—if He has any forgiveness for such as Robert Bruce—I will act this out, keep silent. And thereby, it may be, further burden my soul. With others smitten, perhaps, from me."

"No! No, my dear—it cannot be so. Do not rack yourself so. If you were indeed . . . unclean, would not I now be so also? I, who share your very bed? Could I have escaped? And are others like to be smitten when I, your wife, am not? I tell you and tell you—your sickness is not what you fear. It is but a scurvy, an affliction of the skin, or some such. It cannot be the evil thing. You have been better these past months. Much better . . ."

"The redness is still there. I still sweat . . ."

"Yes. But in yourself you are stronger. More as you were. Think you I do not watch you? You cannot deny that you are better. Could it be so if it was what you dread?"

"I do not know. I am no physician. But those that I saw in Ireland were just as am I." He looked towards the cot. "And the child was born dead." Flatly, tonelessly, he said it.

"And are not other children born dead, Robert, and their sires in good health? Your own sister Mary bore one such. And my brother Richard. Oh, my dear—I am sorry, sorry for this death. Your son. *Our* son. After so long." She was panting with exhaustion. "But there was no mark on the child? No flaw? Was there? The women said it."

"No," he admitted. "No mark."

"You must see that you are wrong, my dear. Our daughters—they are both well. Perfect. Fine children. Yet they both were born since you have had this sickness. I pray you, put it from you. This fear . . ." Her voice tailed off, and her eyes closed, wearily.

He looked down on those heavy-lidded, blue-circled eyes, with sudden great compassion, and kneeled there beside her bed. "Oh, lassie, lassie," he said. "Here I cark and lament—while you suffer. You are worn, done, my sweet, needing my help, my strength. And I but make moan! Forgive, Elizabeth . . ."

"I . . . I am not done, Robert," she whispered, "Not yet." Her hand came out to touch his hair. "I will give you a son, yet—God willing. A living son. You will see . . ."

• • •

James Douglas and Thomas of Moray failed to conform to orders by exactly one week—which was accounted for by the vast amount of booty they brought back with them from Yorkshire, which had much

243

delayed them. Apart from that, they could claim that the expedition had been a success, indeed a triumph—even though they had not managed to capture Queen Isabella.

"She escaped us by a single day," Douglas told his monarch, who had come out to meet his friends at the foot of the palace hill. "She was warned, and fled to Nottingham from York." He glanced sidelong. "I have not charged my lord Earl with sending the warning—but who knows!"

Moray was not much of a smiler, but he at least raised his eyebrows. "My lord of Douglas was inconsolable," he said. "Yet, from all accounts, he should thank me. The lady would have devoured him quite, so tender a morsel!"

Despite their differences of character and outlook, these two were good friends, and the most able and effective joint commanders in Christendom.

"Yet Berwick was saved?" Bruce said, an arm linked with each, as they climbed the hill. "Walter Stewart sent me word, ten days back, that the siege was raised and King Edward gone."

"Yes. Perhaps the Chapter was even more effective a draw than his Queen!" Douglas suggested.

"The chapter . . . ?"

"Aye, Sire—we have been keeping strange company since we parted from you. You mind the convocation you told us of? At York? We were constrained to take some part." Douglas chuckled. "We made debate with their spiritual lordships and eminences! They are naming it, we heard, the Chapter of Myton!"

"A plague on you, man!" the King cried. "Enough of this—or I will have you both clapped in the pit on charge of *lèse-majestié*! Out with it? What happened?"

"Heed him not, Uncle," Moray advised. "As I do not. He has been deranged since his disappointment over the English Queen! The matter is simple. King Edward having scoured the North of England for soldiers to take to Berwick, there were none left at York to oppose us. Save churchmen and their soft levies. The Archbishop, at least, did not flee, with the Queen. He is a man, that—if something of a fool in the matter of warfare! He raised a motley host of clerks—bishops, abbots, monks, priests, acolytes and the like, with their servants, and sallied out to contest our passage. At a place called Myton-on-Swale, east of Boroughbridge, they sought to give battle."

"William of Melton did that? He chose to fight? Fight the two most redoubtable captains in these islands!"

"Aye, Sire—he might almost have been a *Scots* bishop!" Douglas put in. "Only, had he been so, he would have known better how to fight, I swear! His flock were as sheep to the slaughter."

244

"Save us—did you have to do it? Slaughter them?" It was at Moray that Bruce looked.

"We had little choice. There were great thousands of them—and more dangerous in their flight than in their fight! They streamed across a bridge, to our side of the river—and then quickly decided that they were better back on their own side. Some of our people had set some stacks of hay afire, and the smoke confused them . . ."

"You would have thought that priests would have been at home in smoke, incense!" the irrepressible Douglas asserted. "Naught would do but that they all should be back across the river. The bridge would not take them—since I held it—so they must needs swim! In future, clerks should learn to swim!"

"I think you make more of this than you ought, Jamie?" the King said. "Is it your conscience troubling you?"

"Conscience, Sire? Why, we were picking them out on our lance-points! Never have I seen such urge to the water. Nor such panic. The Gaderene Swine were not to be compared with the priests of York! More drowned than died in fight—but more still died of fright, I do believe! Of stopped clerkly hearts! It was a sight to be seen. And—we loaded a thousand horses with their spoil. It seems that they thought to fight more with golden crucifixes and croziers than with swords!"

The Queen, almost recovered, met them at the palace entrance. "Welcome back, my heroes!" she greeted. "I have missed you both. As has His Grace. Did all go well?"

"Your heroes have been distinguishing themselves by slaying priests. Not one, or two, but a host, it seems. A shameful massacre. God knows what they were at!"

"We spared all we could," Douglas protested. "They died like flies in a frost. There was no stopping them."

Bruce shook his head over his friends. "How many? How many died?"

Douglas glanced over at Moray. "Four thousand," he admitted.

"Dear Christ-God!"

"Not all priests and the like," the other hastened to assert. "The mayor and burgesses of York were there likewise. And their train-bands."

"Fit foes for Douglas and Moray!"

"There were more than 20,000 of them, Sire. What could we do . . . ?"

"We restrained our men as best we could," Moray put in. "But the confusion caused by the panic of so many was worse than anything I have ever seen."

"Did many great ones fall? Bishops, abbots and the like?"

245

"Some were wounded. Many roughly handled. But I do not think that many died," Douglas said. "They were the nimblest at escaping, first back across the bridge. We captured the Bishop of Ely – but he ransomed himself quickly and most generously, having a high opinion of his own worth!"

"Aye. You may smile, Jamie. But we are in bad enough odour with the Holy See, as it is. How think you the Pope will look on this? How will it be recounted to him? Not as panic and folly, but as a terrible and sacrilegious slaughter by the godless and rebellious Scots. The cry will ascend to heaven itself! For a year and more I have been at pains to fend off the Vatican's assaults and anathemas. Yet to preserve a face of respect and worship of Christ's Vicar. And now . . .!"

"His Holiness may perhaps be placated," Elizabeth put in, "by a display of the King of Scots' generosity and liberality towards Holy Church. Not Holy Church in Scotland or in England, but in Rome! Laying up treasure in heaven is, I am sure, his prime concern. But treasure on earth has its value also! You gained great spoil from this clerical host, you say, Sir James? Why not send part of it to His Holiness? As token of your humble faith and loyal worship?"

Moray swallowed, the King stroked his chin, and Douglas burst into laughter.

"By the Mass," he cried, "Your Grace has the rights of it! Here's a ploy! A selection of crosses, croziers and reliquaries – even Saint Etheldreda's thigh-bone! What more apt? Better than handing all over to Master Lamberton!"

"I do not like it," Moray objected. "It smacks of blasphemy, of irreverence . . ."

"Tush, man – leave such to the priests," Bruce told him. "It is their business, smelling out the like. It might serve – it might well serve. At least to give us time. Bless you, my dear! We will reinforce our envoys at Rome with a train-load of treasure-on-earth from Yorkshire. But I think not Ely's bone. To be of value, that must be named – and might prove a bone of contention indeed, an embarrassment. Even to His Holiness. But – come, my heart. You should be seated. You are not wholly yourself yet. You must preserve your strength . . ."

The two younger men hastened to apologise, to offer arms, to all but carry the Queen indoors between them.

"I am sorry, Sire. About the child," Douglas said, over his shoulder. "It was a sore blow. A prince at last – and then . . ."

"God's will be done," Moray said.

It was Elizabeth who answered, not Bruce. "We shall test God's will again," she declared. "Let us pray, with greater success."

246

There was a pause. Then Bruce rather abruptly changed the subject.

"Lancaster did not intercept you, on your road home ?" he asked.

"Not Lancaster, no. King Edward himself sought to do so—but we eluded him by striking westwards. Across the hills," Moray answered. "Saddled as we were with booty and prisoners, we were in no state to meet him. Besides, we had Your Grace's command."

"I am glad that you remembered it. Even belatedly!"

Hurriedly Douglas spoke up. "Lancaster was not there, Sire. Prisoners told us that he had quarrelled with King Edward. When the news of our raiding southwards, and our defeat of the Archbishop's host, reached Berwick, there was trouble in the King's camp. Lancaster had words with him. Probably he would have had him march south with him. Or continue the siege alone. Whatever the cause, he marched off to the south-west, to his own territories, taking near half the force with him. But he gave *us* no trouble."

"Aye. There is a lesson there, for any monarch!" Bruce nodded grimly. "Too great and powerful a noble. Of the king's own blood. On such, a realm may founder. You note it, Earl of Moray and Lord of Nithsdale ?"

His nephew looked shocked. "*Me*, Uncle ? You do not suggest . . . ? I am your loyalest servant . . ."

Bruce laid a hand on the other's arm. "I know it, Thomas. I but cozen you. Nevertheless, you heard de Soulis, at that last Council. There are other strings to the Scots lute than Bruce, he said. It behoves us not to forget . . ."

247

IT was to be doubted whether the old Dewar of the Coigreach fully understood the honour that was being done him. Certainly he did not appreciate it. But then, he was a very ancient man, now, and had always been difficult; though far from senile, he was distinctly set in his strange ways, and found anything new deplorable. His next junior, the Dewar of the Main, probably had not the wits fully to grasp the significance of the occasion; but at least he approved of his fine new clothes, and the handsome croft of land he had been granted further down the glen. He was cheerful now, if a little drunk, and indeed adopting a definitely superior if not patronising attitude to the other three Dewars of Saint Fillan, custodians of the Mazer, the Bell and the somewhat mysterious *Fearg*—which, being wholly encased in silver was of unstated composition but the greater worth. These three had done nothing to aid Bruce in his hour of need, preferring to follow their chief, Patrick MacNab of that Ilk, Hereditary Abbot of Glendochart, who was a kinsman of Mac-Dougall of Lorn, and so pro-Comyn and anti-Bruce. The King had forfeited MacNab, after Bannockburn, and given his barony to Sir Alexander Menzies of Weem, a loyal supporter. However, the three junior Dewars, hereditary custodians of the other relics of St. Fillan, were in a different case. Humble enough men of the hills, however significant their office in the old Celtic polity, it was unthinkable that the Abbey of Glendochart should be reconstituted without their presence—or, at least, the presence of their relics, from which of course they were by no means to be parted. So there they were, hanging about in a wary and somewhat suspicious group, scarcely prepared to believe that they all had been forgiven and indeed granted crofts likewise, for the maintenance of their office, out of the former MacNab lands—for they were now dignified as prebendaries or canons of the restored Abbey.

For that was what was being done this blowy spring day of sun and shower of the year 1320; reconstituting the ancient Culdee Abbey of Glendochart. It had taken nearly six years to see this fulfilment of Bruce's vow, taken before Bannockburn, that if he had the victory that vital day, he would renew this renowned shrine of the Celtic Church. Building such a place, comparatively modest an ecclesiastical establishment as it was, in such a remote Highland glen, had been slow and difficult, especially with so much else on the King's mind. At Bannockburn, the Dewar of the Main had carried his relic, the saint's arm-bone in its silver reliquary, ever close to Bruce and so in the thickest of the battle. The King, excommunicated by Rome but blessed in despite by the strange representatives of the former Celtic Church, was now showing his gratitude.

Although the Culdee Church was long gone as an entity—Queen Margaret had seen to that, in her burning zeal for Rome—the memory of it and its practices and attitudes was by no means lost, especially in the Highlands, where it was an undying influence. After all, it had flourished for 700 years, and as late as 1272 it had retained an establishment at St. Brides, Abernethy, the old capital. Therefore, this restoration was not wholly an anachronism, however much the Romish clerics felt bound to frown on it. Glendochart could not now be a Culdee establishment in fact, of course, since no such persuasion existed any more, even in Ireland. But Bruce had done the best he could, setting the Abbey up as part of the Augustinian Order, the nearest in attitude and sympathies to the Celtic ideas of worship. Moreover he was placing it under the general supervision of Abbot Maurice of Inchaffray, now Bishop of Aberdeen nominally, but not confirmed by the Pope, a fighting cleric of similar spirit—who indeed had been the young Dewar's mentor at Bannockburn, fighting and praying as lustily.

So, in the same green glen of Strathfillan, under the towering and still snow-capped giants of Ben More and Stobinian, where fourteen years before the fugitives had worshipped in the cabin-like chapel, and then gone out to their defeat at Dalrigh at the hands of MacDougall, the King and Queen now with a great company, splendid but almost wholly secular, watched Abbot Maurice consecrate the new chapel and bless the new and simply-pleasing whitewashed conventual buildings; supported by the five Dewars, however out of place and uneasy they seemed. All was done in the open air—for three good reasons; the new place of worship would not hold one-tenth of the company; the Celtic Church had always been very partial to the open air, caring little for buildings; and this would tend to prevent any embarrassment to such clerics as were present and who might lack Maurice of Inchaffray's rugged independence of spirit. Most, of course, had diplomatically been engaged otherwise this March day. Even Bishop David of Moray, who had been one of those present fourteen years before—although even then he had refused to enter the chapel—found it reasonable to absent himself.

The fact was that this was wholly Bruce's affair, and he was glad enough to excuse the Romish clergy. In essence, it was but a way of saying thank-you to the strange creature who had blessed him when no other would or could—perhaps saving his reason at the same time—and who later had equally saved his life by getting him across Loch Lomond when trapped by his foes. He owed a lot to the Dewar of the Coigreach and his Saint Fillan. The fact that the saint's Gaelic name was *Faolain an Lobhar,* Fillan the Leper, was very much to the point—though some doubted if this was the same Fillan.

So a highly unorthodox consecration service was followed by an outdoor celebration of the Eucharist, dispensing both elements to all who would partake, in the old Celtic fashion, using fistula to suck up the wine. Thereafter a banquet was spread there beside the rushing peat-brown river beneath the mountains. The people of Strathfillan, Glen Dochart, Glen Falloch and other surrounding valleys, were there to watch and participate, along with the more splendid folk of the Court and nobility. Even Patrick MacNab himself was there, from the rump of his lands up on Tayside, forgiven but by no means restored; for he was still Hereditary Abbot of Glendochart, to the Highlanders. And there was the MacGregor, too, Chief of the Children of the Mist, who had surprised all by re-appearing from Ireland, after being presumed dead at Dundalk, lame now but very much alive, and more fiercely proud then ever.

It was on this scene of *al fresco* feasting, after the ceremonies, that another abbot appeared, Bernard of Arbroath, Chancellor of the realm. De Linton was fattening up nicely with the years and responsibility, as was entirely suitable for so important a prelate; but the eager brown eyes were still those of the young vicar who had acted Bruce's chaplain and secretary on many a rough and bloody campaign.

"You have timed your arrival nicely, i' faith," the King greeted him smiling. "All the sacrileges and barbarous rites are now safely past. Yet you are not too late to partake of the provender! Holy Church may now unbend!"

The Abbot coughed. "I fear not, Sire," he said, low-voiced. "Holy Church is scarcely unbending yet! From further afield than Arbroath. Or St. Andrews. That is why I am here now. May I have Your Grace's private ear?"

Head ashake, the King took him aside.

"A nuncio has arrived at Dunfermline, Sire. Unannounced. From Rome. Or, at least, from Avignon. From His Holiness, personally. He landed at Dysart, and the first we knew, he was chapping at your palace door, in Dunfermline. No Cardinal, this but a papal secretary. Bearing no letter addressed, or mis-addressed, to any. Carrying instead an open paper, a pronunciamento signed and sealed by Pope John, declaring that he is there to speak with the voice of the Supreme Pontiff."

"M'mmm. So Pope John learns cunning! We have taught him this, at least!"

"We have taught him only the *need* for cunning, Sire. Nothing else. For the nuncio is directed to pronounce, from the Cathedral of St. Andrews, the excommunication not only of your royal person, but of all and sundry who support you, clergy as well as lay. Not only so, but my lords Bishop of St. Andrews, Dunkeld, Aberdeen and Moray, are especially cited as excommunicate. It is, therefore, the entire realm which he is to declare excommunicate. Without question or delay. In the name of the Vicar of Christ and God's Vice-regent."

"The bishops! The whole realm! Surely not?"

"The whole realm, Sire."

"But, 'fore God—this is impossible! The clergy, too? They are part of the realm, yes. But can it be so? It means *you*, man! You support me. It means every priest. And Lamberton. By the Rude, he cannot excommunicate Lamberton! The Primate. This cannot be."

"The nuncio is specific. There is no mistake. The Scottish realm *is* excommunicate, in its entirety, since it supports Your Grace. Already is, since the anathema was pronounced at Rome before the nuncio left. He is but to acquaint us. Not only so, but His Holiness has commanded the Archbishop of York, and the Bishops of London and Carlisle, to repeat the excommunication on every Sabbath and saint's day throughout the year. Against every man, woman and child, clergy and laity, of this people. Until, as he says, we submit and put ourselves under the proper rule and governance of King Edward of England, as Lord Paramount of Scotland."

King stared at Chancellor, for once at a loss. "The folly of it!" he cried. "The wicked, purblind folly! Here is heresy, surely? To pronounce such sentence. Even for the Pope. He cannot do it."

"He has done it, Sire. And who may declare that the Holy Father himself commits heresy? Not you. Nor I. Nor any man. Since the Pope it is who rules what is heresy and what is not."

"But to excommunicate, to cut off the sacraments from a whole nation. Including its bishops and priests. For the sins of one man. Or what he claims are sins, in his ignorance. Ignorance—that is what it is. Are we to be at the mercy of one man's blind ignorance? The eternal souls of a whole nation endangered because this

Frenchman in Avignon does not know the truth? Believes English lies. Are we, man? Are we?"

De Linton spread his hands helplessly. "The Pope, ignorant or other, is still the Pope, the voice of Christ on earth . . ."

"You say that? This is blasphemy, man! Would you make Christ-God a liar also? Make him speak lies, trumpet forth the falsehoods of men? Watch *your* words, I charge you!" the King cried, his voice shaking.

Robert Bruce, in anger, was a terrifying sight. De Linton actually backed away. All around, eyes watched the pair anxiously, not knowing the trouble but concerned.

The King took fierce grip of himself, turning to pace a few steps away and back. "What says Lamberton to this?" he demanded thickly, at last.

The other could barely find words. "I . . . I do not know, Sire. I sent word to him. As I came here, to tell Your Grace. The nuncio—the nuncio himself was for St. Andrews. When he discovered you absent. I know not what my lord Bishop will say . . ."

"William Lamberton will not take kindly to being excommunicate! Dear God—have you considered what this means, my lord Abbot? It means that neither he, nor you, nor any priest who supports me—and that should be every priest in this land—may give or receive the sacraments! Does it not? If you are excommunicate yourselves, you are, indeed, no longer priests. You are no longer Abbot of Arbroath. Lamberton no longer Bishop of St. Andrews, or Primate of Scotland. Save us—the thing is beyond all in madness!"

"Such thoughts have not escaped me, Sire. I have had ample time to think of them, riding here from Dunfermline." De Linton was recovering.

"M'mm. No doubt. Forgive me, my friend, if I spoke you too harshly. But—what are we to do?"

"We can only do the one thing, Sire. Labour to change the Pope's mind. So that he withdraws this anathema."

"At least, you do not suggest obeying him! Submitting, as humbled rebels, to the English."

The other drew himself up. "Did you think that I would, my lord King? I, or any?"

"No, Bernard—I did not. But changing the Pope's mind will be a sore task, I fear. And long. He is set against us. Our envoys to Avignon have not moved him. Nor our treasure, sent in October. Although he has not sent it back! What else can we do?"

"I was thinking, as I rode here. Of more than the consequences, Sire. We could send him a letter. Not your Grace—for that he would reject. But the whole community of the realm of Scotland. A letter from the nation. Signed by all who have any authority in this kingdom . . ."

"A letter? Is he going to heed a letter, at this pass? A piece of paper? You know how we treated *his* letters!"

"This would be more than a letter, Sire. A statement of a people. A declaration. The signed declaration of a nation. His Holiness could scarce ignore such. Not if it was signed and sealed by hundreds, great and small. You said that he had acted in ignorance. That the Pope was ignorant of the true facts of our independence as an ancient realm. Let us inform him, then. Let us dispel his ignorance, declare the truth of our history and our polity. That we have never been subject to the English, or any other in Christendom. That we love freedom above all things, and will submit to none. Though we would be friends with all."

Bruce eyed the younger man, in his eagerness, keenly. "Think you he would read it? Heed it? Where silver-voiced envoys, and silver in treasure have failed?"

"I believe that he might. Pope Boniface heeded the letter of the English barons against us, in 1301. This would be better, greater, the voice of a people. If the names of a whole realm subscribe it. Never before has there been such a letter, I think. From so many. His Holiness could not but heed it."

Bruce shrugged. "I am less sanguine, I fear. But it is worth the attempt. It can do no harm. And I can think of nothing else we may do. But . . . how shall we get men to subscribe it? This will be difficult. If we could hold a parliament . . . But there is no time for that. Since a parliament requires forty days of warning. We cannot wait. Yet a Privy Council would not serve, I think."

"No. It must be greater than that. Councils are of picked men. Our enemies would say that such men are creatures of Your Grace. To be of value, this must stand for all your realm. Not just Your Grace's friends. A Convention? Would not that serve? Not a parliament, but a Convention of the Estates. A meeting. Call such forthwith, Sire. And if we do not have sufficient attending, we can have others to sign elsewhere. In their homes, if need be."

"Aye, a Convention. You have it. And for another matter also. I need something of the sort. Too many lords and chiefs are coming to blows over who has what lands in this realm. During the years of war, many have won or taken themselves lands. Many of one faction or the other. Those who held them formerly dispute. There is much bad blood. Even here, this morning in Glen Dochart, Sir Alexander Menzies and the MacGregor, both my friends, all but had their swords drawn. Over a mere parcel of land in Glen

Falloch. A Convention called to settle such matters. An assize of lands, before judges. All holders of disputed land to show by what title they hold them. Then, when they are assembled–this letter. They will come–for lands! There is nothing like a little soil and rock to bring men out of their chimney-corners! See that this matter is made known, my lord Chancellor."

"Gladly, Sire. It is well thought on. It is excellent reason for calling a Convention. So we shall have no lack of signatories."

"Draw up some such letter for all to sign, then, my friend. Word it so that the Pope learns how well-established and ancient is our kingdom, how long our line of kings. How ever we have been independent. And how freedom is our very life. That above all. For if freedom fall, all falls. Say that no power on earth shall make us subservient to the English–and the powers of heaven would not try! Say that if I, the King, were to countenance any such subservience, the realm would drive me from its throne. To my proper deserts. Tell the Pope that, Bernard. Write it down. And then bring it all to me, that I may approve it. And to Lamberton also. His is a wise head."

"With all my heart, Sire. And this Convention? Where shall it be held? And when?"

"So soon as may be. So soon as messengers can carry the word. We must not delay–or the country will be in a turmoil. Unless your priests will reject the Pope's anathema, and dispense Mass as before. Will they?"

Abbot Bernard looked unhappy. "Not . . . not on their own authority, Sire. That would be apostasy indeed. Not to be countenanced. But . . . it is not for me to decide. I am but an abbot. This is for the Primate."

"The excommunicated Primate! Yes, it is Lamberton's business. I must see him quickly. But the need for haste, in the matter of the Convention, is the more evident. Seven days? Ten? Can it be done?"

"It must, Sire. And where?"

"Not at Dunfermline. Nor yet at St. Andrews. I do not wish to meet this nuncio. Yourself avoid him–since he claims to speak with the Pope's voice. I have promised to attend young Scrymgeour's marriage, at Dundee, on St. Ambrose's Day. That is eight days from now. Make it there, at Dundee."

"My abbey of Arbroath, Sire, is nearby. Accept the hospitality of my house for this meeting. It is larger than any in Dundee . . ."

"Ah, yes, my princely abbot! So it is. Next to Dunfermline, the greatest abbey in the land. So be it. Call the Convention for Arbroath, the day following St. Ambrose's Day, the day after the wedding . . ." The King paused, blinking. "Dear God!" he said, "Can there *be* any such wedding? Lamberton was to officiate. But if he is excommunicate? If you all are excommunicate? Must we stop marrying now? And burying? As well as Mass?"

Abbot Bernard wagged his head, lost in consternation.

. . .

William Lamberton was made of sterner stuff, ecclesiastically, than Bernard de Linton. Or perhaps it was but that he had more experience of churchmen's politics. At any rate, he celebrated young Scrymgeour's nuptials as planned, before a great and splendid if somewhat uneasy congregation. But he did more. After the bride and groom had passed out of the Church of St. Mary, Nethergate, for the banquet to be held in the Greyfriars Monastery, the Primate, with the royal permission, asked the congregation to remain a little longer. And there, from his throne, in full canonicals, he read out a curious announcement, his harsh voice resonant with great authority.

The pronunciamento of the Papal Nuncio from the Cathedral of St. Andrews no doubt had been heard of by all, he said. He himself had listened to it sadly. But as senior bishop and Primate of this realm, it was his simple duty to advise his flock on the situation. He had consulted with other bishops, and now made declaration that, while he, and the whole Scottish Church, was in most filial obedience to the Holy See in all things, there was, at this present time, some dispute as to the position and validity of its present incumbent, His Eminence the former Monsignor Jacques d'Euse, hitherto Archbishop of Avignon, and these past three years styled Pope John the Twenty-second.

After a sort of corporate gasp, not a sound was heard from that huge company, every eye fixed in an apprehensive fascination on the bent wreck of a man up there beside the High Altar.

The dispute was on two grounds, Lamberton proceeded. One, that being forced by French might to dwell in Avignon, not in Rome, the said John was indeed under the pressure and influence of the King of France, who at this time was in alliance with the King of England. And so unable properly to exercise due rule and justice within Holy Church. And two, that he had himself been declared heretic by certain authorities for maintaining the doctrine that the blessed do not in fact enjoy the vision of God until their resurrection, contrary to the teachings of the fathers. Until these doubts and disputes were resolved therefore, he personally, William, Primate of Scotland, could not accept any sentences of excommunication, or other assaults upon his spiritual authority, not specifically promulgated by the College of Cardinals in full consistory court—which he learned from the Papal Nuncio aforementioned had not been done.

The long sigh of breath exhaled was like a wind over a heather hillside, as the company perceived relief, remission, at least a temporary lifting of the dark shadow which had come to loom over their lives.

It was inconceivable, in the circumstances, that church government and worship of God should be allowed to break down, Lamberton rasped, at his sternest. In consequence he required all bishops, priests and deacons, all abbots, priors, friars and monks, all who owed obedience to himself in this Province of Holy Church in Scotland, to continue steadfast in their said offices, to perform their full duties, and to ignore all utterances and commands from other ecclesiastical authorities than himself. On *his* head, heart and conscience, rested the full responsibility. And so, let all go forth, in God's peace, from that place.

They all went forth indeed, but hardly in God's peace.

That night, after the feasting at Dundee, Bruce, Elizabeth and the Primate sat together alone in the abbot's study of the vast Abbey of Arbroath, over a well-doing fire of logs, grateful for the warmth after the long ride in the face of a chill wind off the North Sea. They waited while Abbot Bernard went to fetch the papers of his draft of the projected letter to the Pope. It was their first opportunity for private talk that day.

"How dear did that announcement in St. Mary's cost you this day, old friend?" the King asked. "It was as brave a deed as any I have known. Braver than any done on a field of battle. To take upon yourself, your own shoulders, the entire burden of this rejection of the Pope's commands and anathema. To accept the responsibility for a whole nation's disobedience to the Holy See, to the head of the Church you represent. This was truly great, truly noble William. I know of no other who would have dared it."

"Noble is scarce the word I would use, Robert my liege," Lamberton said, shaking his grey head. "What I did was expedient, lacking in scruple, cynical, maybe. But not noble."

"Yet you perhaps jeopardised your own soul to do it. For the nation. That is, if you believe what you profess."

"Aye—and there's the rub! Do I, William Lamberton, believe what I profess? Sometimes, I confess to you, my friends, I do wonder! I fear that I have become but a wavering leader of this flock."

"Wavering? After today? I would I had more such waverers!"

"Wavering in what I believe, and should teach others, Robert. Which is no state for a bishop to be in. The older I grow, I find, the less of accepted doctrine I truly respect. Save for the faith of Christ crucified. And the all-embracing love of God."

"Is that not enough?" Elizabeth asked quietly.

"For you, perhaps. For most. But—for me? For the Primate? The foremost representative of the One, Holy, Catholic and Apostolic Church, in this land? The fount of doctrine, the source of dogma? I would not have our nuncio, or indeed any priest anywhere, to hear me say it!"

"Perhaps you do not altogether accept the doctrine of papal infallibility!" Bruce observed gravely. "Even if the said Pope is truly Pope."

The other looked into the fire, as gravely. "Would my liege lord have me to burn as an heretic? To deny so essential, so vital, a doctrine!"

"Deny nothing, then. But . . . I think you do *not* indeed consider that you have placed your immortal soul in jeopardy, by this day's work?"

"My soul, I fear, has been in jeopardy all my days! For my many sins. But such faith as I cling to assures me that Christ's sacrifice and God's infinite mercy are sufficient to save it, nevertheless." Lamberton raised his head. "But, see you—this of the Pope's position. I but prevaricated, quibbled, there at Dundee. God forgive me. This Pope is truly Pope—of that there is no real doubt. His residence at Avignon is by his own choice, not by *force majeure*. Even though the Curia does not like it. And he is said now to be much less hot on his doctrine of resurrected bliss. Moreover, such would not invalidate his appointment, whatever Philip de Valois may say. No—I but used subterfuge, used these things to gain time, to soothe anxieties, to enable the rule and charge of the Church in this land to continue. To have accepted the papal ban would have meant the breakdown, not only of the Church, but of all Christ's work, in Scotland. Therefore I did what I did. But there is no substance in my doubts as to His Holiness's authority— as many of the clergy at least must know. And the College of Cardinals will endorse Pope John's anathema—nothing is more sure. Unless we can change their minds. And his. We have but gained a breathing space."

"A costly breathing space for you, William—which we must use to good advantage. This of the letter—de Linton's letter. The declaration, from all the realm. You think well of it?"

"Well, indeed—very well. So be it that it says the right things. And is signed by the right people."

"The *right* people? Not all the people? That is, the people who have any rule and authority in the realm?"

"That as a principle, yes. But in fact we must be careful. To give His Holiness no excuse to ignore it. By including signatures which he must reject."

"*Must* reject?"

"Must, yes. He may have no relations with an excommunicate. Therefore excommunicate's signature on such letter could be held to invalidate it, I fear. He has, in a fashion, excommunicated the entire nation. But that is different, a mere form. Those who have been excommunicated by name—these should not sign. Your royal self. Myself. The Bishops of Moray and Dunkeld and Aberdeen. These, I fear, he could reject as offensive, in the present circumstance. And therefore claim that he could not read or accept the letter."

"I had never thought to sign it," Bruce said. "Since it is from my subjects, not myself. But you? If you and the other senior bishops do not sign, it could be claimed that there was division amongst the clergy. That the most important might not be in favour of what was written."

"True. I think, therefore, that *no* clergy should sign. Let it be a letter from the temporality of Scotland. It might have the more force. Seem less of a disobedience to the Church's supreme Pontiff. See you—the clergy have already sent a manifesto to the Vatican, on the subject of Your Grace's right to the crown. From Dundee. In 1309. Asserting Scots independence. This new declaration would come better from the laity. It could be couched in stronger terms than would be seemly for the clergy to use towards their Pontiff!"

"That is true . . ."

Abbot Bernard came back with a great sheaf of paper. "I fear that there is overmuch writing here, Your Graces," he apologised. "A great plethora of words. But there is so much to be said. So many matters to cover. I have written and scored and written again. Many times. I cannot make it shorter, with all said. Your Grace, and my lord Bishop, may do better than my poor efforts . . ."

He spread his papers out on the table, and lit a second lamp. "Here is the start:

"*To the most Holy Father in Christ our Lord, the Lord John, by Divine Providence, of the Holy Roman and Catholic Church Supreme Pontiff, his humble and devoted sons and servants, the earls, bishops, barons, abbots, priors, priests, freeholders and whole community of the Kingdom of Scotland, send all manner of filial reverence with devout kisses of your blessed feet . . .*"

"Not servants, my friends—not servants," Bruce intervened.

"Sons, perhaps. Sons in God. But I will not have my good Scots subjects servants to any. Not even to myself! And is it necessary to kiss the man's feet? If the Lord Christ Himself was content to *wash* others' feet, I do not see why we should kiss the Pope's."

"In letters to the Pontiff it is the customary style," Lamberton said. "No doubt it is fulsome, unsuitable. But this he expects. And it costs us little—since the signatories will never have to do it!" And, as the King shrugged acceptance, "But this of bishops and priests, my good Bernard. His Grace and I have come to decision that this letter should not seem to come from the clergy at all. Only the temporality. To avoid sundry pitfalls. It will lose nothing thereby, and be the less rebellious towards His Holiness. And after your devoted sons, I would leave space for the names of the signatories. Rather than have all signed and sealed at the end only. It must needs be a long letter, as you say. Therefore, to ensure that His Holiness reads it, he should know from the start the quality of the signatories."

"As you will, my lord . . ."

The Queen spoke. "But, my friends—do you forget? If it is not the priests and clergy who sign, then most of the barons and lairds will not be able to sign, at all! Since they cannot write. Only make marks and append their seals."

Bruce smiled. "Trust a woman to see the thing clearly!" he commended. "It is true. In the main it will not be signatures we send. But names, written by clerks. With their seals. The more reason, then, to have the names at the start. But, proceed, my lord Chancellor."

"Yes. I then recite something of the history of our race, as recounted by the books and chronicles of ancient writers. How our nation came out of Scythia and through the Mediterranean Sea, by Spain, to Ireland. And thence 1,200 years after the outgoing of the people of Israel, acquired for themselves the land of the Picts and Britons in Dalriada, naming it Scotland, from their one-time princess. And how, from then, we have had 113 kings . . ."

"Save us—have we indeed? So many?"

De Linton coughed. "So the chroniclers and seannachies have it, Sire. And who am I to disprove it? Since it is our concern to convince His Holiness of the ancient establishment and continuing independence of our realm. Do you wish this altered?"

"No, no. By no means. The more the better. Save that most of them must have been heathens!"

"Aye, Sire—I have considered that. I put it thus:

". . . 113 *of their own royal stock, no stranger intervening, have*

259

*reigned, whose nobility and merits, if they were not clear otherwise,
yet shine out plainly enough from this that the Kings of Kings
even our Lord Jesus Christ, after his passion and resurrection,
called them, though situated at the uttermost parts of the earth,
almost the first to His most holy faith, nor would have them confirmed
in this faith by any one less than His first Apostle, although in
rank second or third . . ."*

The Abbot paused. "I walk warily here—for, of course, His
Holiness occupies the throne of St. Peter . . .".

"Very wise, Bernard," Lamberton nodded, straight-faced.
"Precedence is most important!"

"Yes, my lord. So I say:

*" . . . to wit, Andrew the most meek brother of St. Peter, whom
He would have always preside over them as their Patron. Moreover
the most holy fathers, your predecessors, considering these things
with anxious mind, endowed the said kingdom and people, with
many favours and very many privileges. So that our nation, under
their protection, has hitherto continued free and peaceful, until
that prince, the mighty King of the English, Edward the father of
him who now is, under the semblance of a friend and ally, in most
unfriendlywise harassed our kingdom, then without a head, and
unaccustomed to wars and attacks . . ."*

"I would put in there that we were guiltless of offence towards
Edward," the Primate said. "That it be clear that the English
invasion was wholly one of aggression by Edward."

"To be sure. So:

*"The injuries, slaughters, and deeds of violence, plunderings, burnings,
imprisonments of prelates, firing of monasteries, spoliations and
murders of men of religion . . ."*

Abbot Bernard looked apologetic. "You understand, Sire, why I
stress that Christ's Church suffered so greatly? It must be made
clear to His Holiness that the English are the enemies of the Church,
not its friends."

"The point does not escape me, friend. But—I think that we
might leave all this of history to yourself. Let us on to the point
of today."

"I come to that now, Sire. To where Your Grace comes into it.
I say:

*"From these evils innumerable, by the help of Him who, after
wounding, heals and restores to health, we were freed by our most
gallant Prince, King and Lord, our Lord Robert who, to rescue his*

260

people and heritage from the hands of their enemies, like another Maccabaeus or Joshua, endured toil and weariness, hunger and danger, with cheerful mind . . ."

"I swear we could dispense with that . . .!"

"No, Robert," Elizabeth declared. "That must go in. It is no more than the truth. My Maccabaeus! My Joshua!"

"M'mmm. Proceed then, my friend."

"Him also the Divine Providence and, according to our laws and customs which we will maintain even to the death, the succession of right and the due consent and assent of us all, have made our Prince and King; to whom, we, for the defence of our liberty, are bound, and are determined in all things to adhere. But, if he were to desist from what he has begun . . ."

The Chancellor's voice tailed away, as he swallowed, and looked up apprehensively.

"Well, man? Go on. What will you do if I desist in my duty? I told you to make it clear that the freedom of the realm is above all things precious. Be not mealy-mouthed in this."

"Aye, Sire. But it sounds ill, coming from your most leal servant. I put it so:

"If he were to desist from what he has begun, wishing to subject us or our kingdom to the King of England or the English, we would immediately endeavour to expel him as our enemy, and the subverter of his own rights and ours. And make another our king who should be able to defend us."

Appalled, de Linton looked at his liege lord.

"Bravo! Well said, my lord Abbot! This is simplest truth. Look not so like a dog expecting a whipping, man! If this letter is to mean anything, it must declare without a doubt that the Scots make their own masters, and that freedom is all."

"That is what I say next, Sire:

"For, so long as a hundred of us remain alive, we never will in any degree be subject to the dominion of the English. Since it is not for glory, riches or honours we fight, but for liberty alone, which no good man loses but with his life."

There was a brief silence in that lamp-lit room, as the words burned themselves into their consciousness. Then Bruce actually rose from his seat, and put his hand on de Linton's shoulder.

"I thank you, Bernard, for those words," he said, his voice thick. "No man spoke nobler, or truer. Here indeed is the message which we declare. Not only to this Pope, but to all Christendom, to all men everywhere. I thank you. And I thank God that I chose you to write this letter!"

"Amen," Lamberton added, simply.

Quite overcome, the younger man shook his head.

"Abbot Bernard," Elizabeth said gently. "You make me wish that I was born a Scot, I vow!"

Bruce cleared his throat. "After that, my friend, the rest cannot but suffer descent, decreasement. Read no more. But tell us the sense of what remains."

"There is still much, Sire. Perhaps too much. For I am wordy, I fear. But we have to make our needs and requests clear. I therefore beseech His Holiness, who must be no respecter of persons, to admonish and exhort the King of England to desire no more than his own, and to leave us in peace. I say that it derogates from His Holiness himself if any part of the Church suffers eclipse or scandal — as does this part, in Scotland, through English avarice and lust for power. And I urge, Sire, that he, His Holiness, rather stir up the Princes of Christendom to better warfare than attacking their weaker Christian brethren, by leading a great crusade against the heathen, for the succour of the Holy Land—to which, if the English will leave us in peace, we will adhere with our whole strength. And the King of England also be able to aid the better, for not warring with us!"

"Splendid! Excellent!" Bruce cried. "Here is shrewd work, indeed. Is that not sharp steel, William? Your Pope can scarce deny that—since he has declared such crusade to be his aim and ambition. Master Bernard has him there!"

"It is a notable thrust, yes. I say I served Your Grace well when I recommended this young man to be your secretary. Is this your closing note, Bernard?"

"Not quite, my lord Bishop. I . . . I have made very bold in this letter, already. Regarding His Grace. But this was on his own royal command. I make very bold again. If your lordship thinks too bold, I will score it through. But . . . in the name of this people and nation I have seen fit to rebuke His Holiness. Is this apostasy?"

"I shall tell you, friend, when I hear it. But, to my mind, His Holiness could perhaps do with some rebuke! What say you?"

"I finish by declaring that . . . where is it? Here it is:

"that if trusting too much the reports of the English, Your Holiness do not give to this implicit belief, and abstain from favouring them, to our confusion, then the loss of life, the ruin of souls, and other evils that will follow, will we believe be laid to your charge by the Most High!"

He looked up. "Is it . . . is it too much ?"

The King slapped the table-top, making the heap of papers jump. "By God, it is not! Apostasy, or what you name it, it may be. But it is true, and just, and requires to be said. You are a bold priest, Bernard de Linton—but praise the saints for it! Let it stand."

Lamberton nodded. "Never before have I heard a cleric, even Abbot of Arbroath, charge the Supreme Pontiff with the ruin of souls!" he observed. "But it is not before time for Pope John, I think. I almost wish that I was signing this declaration after all!"

"I say that it makes a most splendid end to a splendid letter," the Queen added. "You are a priest after a de Burgh's heart!"

The King pushed the papers away. "Better than anything I could have asked for," he said. "But, now—how best to gain the necessary superscriptions and seals ? After tomorrow's Convention, my lord Chancellor, I will have you to read aloud this letter to the assembled company. I will declare that its every word meets with my approval. And you, my lord Primate—will you say likewise ? Then, I will ask if any present makes objection to any of it. Not this word or that, or we should spend the day at it. But with its sense and purpose. I cannot believe that any will speak contrary. Then I shall ask that all who will put their names to it, affix their seals. It will take time, so many. But your clerks will see to that. No clergy, but all earls, lords, barons and freeholders, in their due order."

"All, Sire ? Surely not all ?" de Linton protested. "You would not wish certain names on this letter, I think ? Those of traitors. Men who have worked against you . . ."

"There you are wrong, my friend. This is a letter from the realm of Scotland. The whole realm. Therefore all of any degree must subscribe it, friends or unfriends. If it is headed, as it should be, by Duncan MacDuff, Earl of Fife, premier earl and noble of this land, whom all know is no supporter of mine, so much the more effective a letter it is. Is it not so ?"

"Indeed it is," the Bishop agreed. "I have no doubt but that His Holiness at Avignon knows well enough who are Your Grace's unfriends. Yet, I think, the said unfriends will not refuse their names tomorrow! That would be next to proclaiming their continuing treason and treachery. Moreover, not only will this test their new-found loyalty, but it will serve as a chain to bind them to Your Grace hereafter. Their seals and superscriptions on this great document. Do you not see it ?"

"Ah, yes. Yes—you old fox! This I had not thought on. But it is so. Only—this letter will go to Avignon. To the Pope. So I will not hold those seals and superscriptions."

"Then there must be two copies, Sire. One to be sent, and one to hold in your Chancery. Both subscribed and sealed. Bernard —you must needs have your clerks work on it. Two copies. All night, if need be. For tomorrow's meeting. Busy pens, indeed—but it must be."

De Linton nodded. "Myself, I shall check each word, my lord."

The Queen smiled. "Poor Abbot Bernard!" she said. "I fear that he will get but little sleep this night."

"The Chancellor has spent harder nights than this will be, in my service," Bruce said. "Till tomorrow, then, my good friends."

· · ·

Strangely, it was not the subscribing and sealing of the famous Declaration of Arbroath which went partly agley that next day, the 6th of April, but the superficially unimportant preliminary. Bruce had conceived rightly that a summons to show title to all lands held, would be an excellent, almost foolproof means of ensuring a full attendance at his meeting, since land-holding was the vital concern of all; but he had not foreseen the reaction to its inquisition and assize on land-titles. In the great refectory of Arbroath Abbey, when de Linton, as Chancellor, made formal announcement in the Kings' name that all who held land of the Crown in this realm of Scotland should now show by what right and title they held it, for the good will and better administration of the kingdom, he was answered by a great shout, and the shrill scream of steel. All over the hall swords were whipped out and held high, while their owners cried aloud that it was by these, their swords, that they held their lands— good and sufficient title.

Bruce half rose in his throne, set-faced. Behind him his great officers of state clapped hands to their own sword-hilts, glaring, astonished. Appalled, Abbot Bernard turned to look at the King.

Although the sword-barers were fairly numerous, and scattered about the hall, they did not in fact represent more than a quarter of those present, it could be seen after a moment's scanning. Some indeed were quick to sheathe their weapons again, when they perceived the frowns of the majority. Those who persisted with the naked steel and shouting were mainly younger men, hot-heads. But not all. There were some notable and more mature figures amongst them.

Sinking back in his chair, though his brows were black, Bruce gestured to de Linton to hold his peace, and then turned, to nod to Sir Gilbert Hay, at his other side.

That man, Lord High Constable of Scotland, was nothing loth.

His hands had been itching on his hilt. With a sweep he now drew his own great brand, and held it out straight before him, menacingly.

"Hear you!" he cried. "I, Gilbert, Great Constable of this realm, alone may carry a naked sword in the presence of our liege lord the King. All others who do so can be held guilty of *lèse-majesté*, even treason! Put back your steel, every man. In the name of the King!" For so modest and normally quiet a warrior, Gibbie Hay's voice sounded almost like thunder.

None disobeyed. But one spoke back—Sir William de Soulis, Lord of Liddesdale, recently appointed Governor of Berwick in place of the Steward. This had been one of Bruce's innumerable attempts to create unity and harmony in his realm—for de Soulis held that he should be Warden of the Marches, instead of Douglas, since Liddesdale formed part of the Borderline while Douglasdale did not; moreover, as Hereditary Butler and distantly of the blood-royal, he was senior in rank as in age.

"His Grace the King has no reason to fear *these* swords, my lord Constable!" he called. "All have been drawn in his service times a-many. Which is more than can be said of some of those present! But they are good, just and sufficient title to the lands which we hold, nevertheless, gained by the sword and held by the sword. As, indeed, is His Grace's kingdom!"

There was a breath-held silence at such bold words, until Hay answered.

"That is as may be, Sir William. But you know well, as do all here, that it is not lawful, indeed is a notable offence, to draw sword in the presence of the monarch, unless commanded to do so. Only the Constable may do so, for His Grace's protection. Must I protect His Grace from *you*, sir?"

"That will not be necessary, Sir Gilbert. As, equally, all well know," the other returned coolly.

"Sir William is right, nevertheless, Sire," another voice spoke up—and a significant one. For this was Sir David de Brechin, the King's own nephew, like Moray, by another half-sister, a daughter of the Countess of Carrick and the Lord of Kilconquhar. He was a highly popular individual, winsomely handsome, champion at games and tourneys, and sometimes styled the Flower of Chivalry. "By sword we took lands from the King's enemies, while fighting in his cause. Should other title, mere papers, be required of us?"

"Aye, Sire," still another cried, "and why is our title to such lands being now questioned? From those who have shed their blood for you!" That was Sir Gilbert Malherbe of Dunipace, who, indeed, had shed no blood of his own.

"Is it to take these lands back from us, to give to highly-placed traitors who now surround Your Grace's throne?" Brechin shouted.

Uproar shook the abbey refectory.

Bruce, who preferred as far as possible to leave the conduct of such meetings to the officers concerned, and not to interfere, nevertheless raised his hand towards the Chancellor.

"Since you have addressed *me*, Nephew, with my lord Chancellor's acceptance I shall answer you," he said calmly—however inwardly he raged. "This assize into title is necessary, for the common weal of this my kingdom. The holding of much land is in dispute, claimed by more than one liege or vassal, fought over, to the disturbance of my peace. Marches between lands and estates are often undefined. Tenants know not to whom to pay their rents. Some are paying twice over, threatened by these same swords you shamefully brandished! *My* subjects, whom I, the King, am sworn to protect. As I shall. Loyal barons of mine are at each other's throats over handfuls of acres of ground, brave fighters acting like hucksters! To the troubling and weakening of this realm, and the harassing of my judges. This must not continue. The purpose of this Convention is not to take land from any. That will be for parliament to decide, if it is necessary. It is but to establish who can show best right and title to what. I will not have my lieges snarling over my land like curs over a bone!" He paused, gazing round him sternly. "Nor will I hear talk of traitors in my royal presence—for past trespasses which I, in parliament, have forgiven and wiped clean. Understand it—or bear my most sore displeasure."

There was a long silence. Even though the King had not raised his voice, and spoken almost conversationally, none there failed to recognise the steely grip on the royal temper, and what it could mean should that grip weaken. As Robert Bruce grew older, his anger was demonstrated less and less; but it was sensed the more alarmingly beneath his self-imposed restraint. And was the more terrifying. These were brave men, fighters who had spoken; but they would have been foolhardily so indeed had they pressed their case further, there and then.

"So be it," Bruce nodded, sitting back. "Sir Gilbert—overlook the drawn swords this once, if you please. Let all proceed in order. My lord Chancellor—continue."

Moistening his lips, Abbot Bernard went on to outline the procedure whereby every landholder would present himself, in due order, before the earl and sheriff of whatever earldom and county his lands were situate, with his proofs; and all who might dispute such claims should likewise so present themselves. All

266

in different chambers of the abbey. Clerks would take due and proper note of all. Where dispute still prevailed, and the claimants could not accept the earl's or sheriff's ruling, appeal could be made to judges appointed by the crown. And in final instance, if such was necessary, to the King himself. Such decisions and judgements to be laid before a parliament to be called for later in the year, at Scone, where was the Moot-hill of the Scots realm, traditional scene of landed exchange, tenure and grantage. This by order of the King's Grace.

This businesslike statement had the effect, as intended, of calming tempers and damping down histrionics. There would undoubtedly be much debate and many hot words in the various abbey apartments thereafter; but meantime, and in the presence of the monarch, order prevailed.

As de Linton, finished, looked towards the throne, Bruce raised his hand again, to still the murmur of talk.

"My lords, my friends, my comrades all," he said, in a different tone. "Before you disperse about this business, there is another matter which requires your attention. A matter of great import. As all know, our neighbours of England, whom we have given cause to heed our love of liberty and freedom, have turned in their extremity to the Pope for aid in their assault on our realm. Unfortunately His Holiness, insufficiently informed as to our history, our ancient kingdom and our independence, has believed the lies told him by King Edward, and . . ."

His voice was drowned in the growl of men, a menacing sound.

"Hear me, my friends. His Holiness, I say, believing these things against us, has pronounced his anathema against us, as a people and nation. I say, hear me! Your turn comes. While my lord Bishop of St. Andrews makes due and proper enquiry as to the present Pope's appointment and authority, it is nevertheless necessary that he should be fully informed of the truth as to Scotland's state. Therefore the Chancellor has drawn up a letter, a declaration, to send to His Holiness. It is long, but resounding. And I, and the Primate, have heard and agree every word. Now it is for you to hear it. And, if you agree, to append your names and seals. All of you. For this letter is from *you*, the temporality of this kingdom, to inform the Pope of who you are and what you are, and who you have freely chosen as your king. But, above all, what you will pay for liberty, freedom, the freedom to live your lives according to your own land's laws and customs, and to choose your own rule and governance . . ."

The crash of acclaim and applause and feet-stamping shook the abbey, and continued.

Bruce gave them their head.

"My friends," he went on, at length, smiling a little, "I perceive our temper agrees. We demand to be allowed to belabour each other – but woe to him who seeks to belabour *us* from outside the realm! This we have sufficiently demonstrated. Now it is your turn to enlighten, to declare. My lord Chancellor will read out this letter. Heed it well. Each word has been well chosen. It is my hope but not my command – never my command – that all here will subscribe it. That it may go as a united declaration from this Scottish nation, since you, in your persons, represent all the people of the kingdom. But if you wish not to subscribe, to lend your names to it, you must not do so. If our vaunted freedom means anything, then each is free *not* to agree. No steps will be taken against any who abstain. This on my royal word. My lord Chancellor – pray read your letter."

Never, undoubtedly, had so many hardened warriors and men of action listened to so long a composition and with such close attention. But after a few snarls at kissing the Pope's feet and suchlike, there was a notable and complete silence. That is, until the item about expelling even the King himself, should he fail to uphold Scotland's liberty, was reached, when there was a considerable commotion, exchange of comment, staring at the throne, and nodding of solemn heads; and when that dealing with their willingness to die for freedom came up, and the refectory throbbed with vehement chorused assent. The final indictment of the Pope himself, should he ignore all this, raised not a few eyebrows, but the majority swallowed it without objection, some with glee. At the end, a positive storm of affirmation broke out, and maintained. For a non-letter-writing and not very literate company, the enthusiasm for this lengthy epistle was extraordinary.

Exchanging glances with Lamberton, Bruce at last raised hand. "Who, then, will lend his name and seal to this letter?"

A forest of hands shot up, many with fists clenched, and a roar of "I will! I will!" resounded.

"Those of contrary mind, to declare it."

No single arm or voice was lifted.

"It is well. Very well. The clerks will take names, and instruct in the business of sealing. Two copies. To work, my friends. This convention stands adjourned . . ."

EGGED on by Elizabeth, the King was planning both a new house and a ship. He was less than keen on either, to tell the truth, but the Queen was urgent and persuasive. She was anxious to have his mind occupied with forward-looking projects, plans assuming that there were many long years of active life ahead of him yet. For the fact was that, when the pressures of national emergency and immediate crisis of one sort or another lessened, as now, and Bruce had time to brood, his attitude to the future tended to become dark and cloudy. Indeed, whether it was the need for action which kept his recurrent sickness at bay, or the lack of it which made of his mental state more apt breeding-ground for the distemper of body, such times as he was not occupied with vigorous activities and urgent demands on his attention, his illness regularly grew worse. Not merely in the mind. The red itch spread in ever larger patches on his skin, vomiting and shivering became more frequent and violent, and the accompanying lassitude and weakness grew. It was Elizabeth's concern, therefore, to keep her husband involved in activity—since it was equally true that, the more demanding the problems, the more was required of him, the less evident became his bodily troubles. She could not engineer crises of state; but at least she could try to entangle him in domestic preoccupations.

She used the fact that Bruce had never really taken kindly to Dunfermline—although she herself liked it well. Brought up amongst hills, by the more colourful Western Sea, he found Fife too green and tame for his liking. Moreover, the older he grew, the more Celtic in sympathy he became, his mother's strain getting the upper hand. And Fife, like Lothian, was scarcely Celtic in its aura. He could hardly be said to pine for the Celtic West; but undoubtedly his preferences lay there. Shrewdly, therefore, Elizabeth fostered them.

He should build a new house. Not another great castle—since his policy still was rather to demolish all such, in case they might be used against him—but a comfortable house to live in, graciously, by the Western Sea, where he could look out over the colourful skerry-strewn, weed-hung bays and sounds rimmed by blue mountains, where he could hunt and fish and hawk, and talk with the seannachies and bards and story-tellers of the Celtic environment. She was at pains not to make this programme seem like that for an ageing man–for he was, in fact, still not forty-seven years old. So she stressed the activities which could conveniently be carried on from such a base–the sailing amongst the Western Isles and Highland coasts in especial, for it was one of Bruce's great dreams to fully integrate his Highland and Lowland divisions within the realm. He should have a special ship built, large enough to carry him and a small court–including herself–in reasonable comfort; yet small enough and suitably designed to wheel across the narrow isthmuses and tarberts with which that seaboard abounded. In it he could sail all the Hebridean seas he loved, keep in closer touch with Angus of the Isles and other island chiefs–even with Christina MacRuarie. She was cunning, was Elizabeth de Burgh.

Because he was still the monarch, however, such western domicile of delight could not be too far away from the core and centre of his kingdom, the Stirling-Scone-St. Andrews triangle. At need, he must be able to travel quickly thence, and others from there reach him readily. Therefore, with mountain passes, rushing rivers, winter snows and the like to consider, the nearest Highland seaboard was indicated. Bute, his son-in-law the Steward's island home in the Firth of Clyde, was thought of, and its Rothesay Castle was in better state than most; but actually to be confined to an island was risky, and the King could be storm-bound at some most inconvenient moment. Nearby, however, on the northern mainland shore of Clyde, looking towards the mountains of Cowal, Gareloch and the Kyles of Bute, might serve. This was Lennox territory–and his old friend Earl Malcolm eager to co-operate.

So, this July evening, four men sat on the platform roof of one of the flanking-towers of Dunfermline Palace, overlooking the deep, steep, tree-filled ravine of the Pittendreich Burn, as the sun sank over the Stirlingshire hills far to the west, and discussed designs for house and ship both–Angus of the Isles, greying now, Malcolm of Lennox, and Walter Stewart, with the King. The house, it had been decided, was to be at Cardross near Dumbarton, where the royal fortress, of which Lennox was Hereditary Keeper, could protect it; for it was to be no stone castle or stronghold, but a rambling, pleasant manor-house, perhaps within a far-flung stone wall of enceinte. Bruce had always had a nostalgic fondness for Christina MacRuarie's house of this sort, at Moidart, and was seeking to have the new building modelled on such, Lennox and Walter Stewart suggesting modifications and improvements. Angus Og was not interested in houses, only in ships, and was impatiently, indeed scornfully, pressing claims for a design of his own.

The caphouse door opened, and the Queen came out. The men rose from their benches, Stewart and Lennox each seeking her approval for suggestions of their own. But, smiling briefly, she shook her head, and looked at her husband.

"Sire, we have a visitor," she said. "A lady. The Countess of Strathearn."

"That woman! What of it, my dear? I do not greatly like her. Whatever she wants, she may wait a little."

"I think that you should see her, nevertheless," Elizabeth said. "And . . . not here."

At the gravity of her voice, the King eyed her quickly, and nodded. "Very well. Await me, friends . . ."

Going down the twisting turnpike stair of the tower, Elizabeth spoke. "Robert—I fear that there is trouble. Sore trouble. If what Joanna of Strathearn says is true. She comes from Berwick-on-Tweed. And talks of treason. A plot. Against you, my heart. Against your life."

"Joanna of Strathearn in a plot? That empty-head! I'll not believe it! None would trust her with a part in a masque . . .!" He paused. "From Berwick, you say?"

"Yes. Hotfoot, she declares."

"M'mmm. De Soulis! I heard that she had become his mistress."

"She was more ambitious, I think! See—I have her in my own chamber . . ."

The Countess, a somewhat over-ripe and vapidly pretty woman in her late thirties, of slightly royal birth, only child of the late and weakly Malise, Earl of Strathearn, who had been so notable a weathercock during the late wars and died seven years before, was pacing the floor in evident agitation. She dipped a perfunctory curtsy, and burst forth without preamble.

"Your Grace—you are in danger of your life. Of your life, I say! From a wicked, evil man. He plans to slay you. William de Soulis. To slay you, and seize your throne. He is a monster! You must move against him. With all speed. Take him. Hang him, the forsworn wretch! Rack him! No fate is too bad for him. He must die, I say . . .!"

"You may be right. But calm yourself, Lady Joanna," Bruce interpolated. "Do not distress yourself so. I swear matters cannot be quite so ill as you fear . . ."

"They are, I tell you—they are! He is a devil, a satyr! A betrayer. A betrayer of . . . of . . . of Your Grace, Sire. His King." That last fell distinctly flat.

"And of you, I think? Which is perhaps more greatly to the point!"

271

She bit her lip. "He . . . he plans to slay you, Sire. And then to mount your throne. It is the truth. I swear it. By all the saints of God!"

"Then he is a bigger fool than I esteemed him!" Bruce snorted.

"Fool he is, yes. But scoundrel more. Lying wretch! Ingrate . . .!"

"How can this be?" Elizabeth asked, more to halt the other woman's humiliating vituperation than for information. "What claim can William de Soulis have to the throne?"

Bruce answered her. "His grandsire, Sir Nicholas de Soulis of Liddesdale, was one of the original fourteen competitors for the crown, in 1291. Before Edward. He claimed in the right of his maternal grandmother, Marjory, bastard daughter of King Alexander the Second, married to Alan the Durward. All knew her as bastard—but the Durward sought to have her legitimated. And when he failed, claimed her as legitimate daughter of King William the Lion, Alexander's own father! On such claim, de Soulis made his stand, saying, in consequence, that he was indeed nearer to the main royal stem than either Bruce or Baliol! But he could produce no proof or papers of legitimation. And all agreed, besides—save himself—that no child born bastard, even though legitimated later, could in fact heir or transmit the crown."

"He says that is not true. William de Soulis says," the Countess declared, impatient of any diversion of interest from herself. "He says that is but the invention of others. He says that once Your Grace is dead, men will be glad to have him as King, rather than any puling infant."

"Then he little knows his fellows!" Bruce commented grimly. "What support does he expect to gain? Who will rally to such a cause?"

"Already many do. He has much support."

"I'll not believe it! Name me names, woman!"

"For one, your nephew, Sir David de Brechin."

"Dear God—no! Not he. He would never so betray me. My own kin. He is headstrong, but loyal . . ."

"Then why, Sire, has he been accepting a pension from King Edward these last years? If he is so loyal!" Her face contorted. "As has the precious Sir William!"

Bruce stared. "Not that! I cannot accept that . . ."

"I have seen it. How, think you, can your Butler, Governor of Berwick, pay 360 esquires, in his own livery, to ride in his train? As he does today. Not on the rents of Liddesdale, I vow!"

Shaken, the King looked at his wife. "De Soulis—of him I could believe it. But not my own nephew . . ."

"And why not?" Shrilly the Countess spilled out her hate.

272

"Many another is in the plot. Why not he? You have, it seems, offended many. By your assize of lands. There is Sir Gilbert de Malherbe. Sir John de Logie, Sir Eustace de Maxwell, Sir Walter de Barclay, as well. Aye, and Sir Patrick Graham likewise . . ."

"Sweet Jesu! That these, my own lieges, men I myself have knighted, every one, should turn against me! For the sake of a few miserable acres of land."

"Sir William has promised them great things. In his kingdom. Great estates and high office. As he promised me . . ." The Countess caught her breath, and her words, blinking rapidly, as though that had slipped out unawares.

"Ah, yes, Lady Joanna? And what did Sir William promise *you*?"

The woman looked from one to the other, uncertainly. "Marriage, Sire," she said, at length, almost defiantly.

"Marriage, heh? So—you were to be the Queen!"

"I, I never approved his plotting, Your Grace. I swear it."

"Of course you did not! Yet you would have married the Lord of Liddesdale, in despite of it?"

"We . . . we have been close. In . . . in an association. For many months. Since he returned from Ireland."

"And you are no longer?"

"He is a deceiver, I tell you! A miscreant! He has become embroiled with a chit of a girl. Daughter of some mere Northumberland squire! All paps and calves eyes! But she has him cozened and bewitched, the fool. Naught will do but that he weds *her*. A man old enough to be her grandsire . . ."

"So this squire's daughter is to be Queen in Scotland!"

"Not if I may prevent it, by the saints!" That was almost a whisper.

"Do not distress yourself, lady! I think the chances are but small. Sir William will have to dispose of Robert Bruce first!"

"But you are to be slain, Sire. It is all plotted. He says that the Pope has accepted your letter. The great letter of Arbroath. And has agreed to recall his excommunication and to urge a peace upon the English. He is sending a messenger, an envoy—I mind not what they call them—to Berwick. To have a truce signed, preparatory to peace. Before yourself and the King of England . . ."

"I' faith—de Soulis is well informed! I myself but learned of this a week past. The coming of this nuncio."

"He learned it from the King of England, Sire. I told you, he serves England. On your way to Berwick, for this, you will be attacked and slain. In the Pease Dean, where the hills come down to the sea. It is all arranged for. Men chosen . . ."

"Robert—the shame of it! The foul and filthy shame!" Elizabeth exclaimed, coming to grasp his arm. "Oh, my dear—that men, your own men like these, should be so vile!"

"Aye. Shame, indeed. De Soulis never loved me. He was ever my brother's man, not mine. But these others—David Brechin, Logie, Maxwell, Barclay. Graham—Graham whose father died gallantly fighting the English at Dunbar!" The King shook his head. "What is this evil of treachery, this canker that ever and anon grows in the heart of this people?" He drew himself up and pointed at the Countess. "And you, madam! You say this was all plotted. For long. You must have known of it, in part. The grasp for the throne. To be so advanced, it must have been plotted for long. Yet only now do you come to me! Because—because you are no longer to be the Queen! This is the worth of *your* loyalty?"

Joanna of Strathearn shook her head, wordless.

"Very well. Is there aught else that I should know, woman? No? Then you have my permission to retire. Go. I shall not thank you for what you have done, I think! Remain meantime in this house. But—keep out of my sight! Now—I want Walter Stewart . . ."

When the Steward came pounding down the stairs, Bruce was calm, specific, but harsh.

"Walter—there is a plot against my life and crown. William de Soulis. At Berwick. I want him. I want him taken, forthwith and brought in custody. For trial. This parliament called for Scone, on the 4th of August. Twelve days hence. I want him there, to stand trial, before all. And not only he. I want David Brechin, John Logie, Walter Barclay, Eustace Maxwell, Patrick Graham, and so many others as are in their fell company. A large party. Therefore you will need many men. Go to Douglas, Warden of the Marches. At Roxburgh. Berwick is his responsibility, de Soulis governor under him. He will aid you. It is understood?"

"By the Mass—a plot! Against Your Grace? I will not believe it, cannot conceive it . . ."

"You are not asked to believe it, man! But do as I command. Forthwith. You have the names? Soulis, Brechin, Logie, Barclay, Maxwell, Graham. And all such others as may be implicated. I want all such before parliament at Scone, twelve days hence. But be discreet about it, Walter. I do not want any to get word that their schemes are known, and escape over the Border into England. See to it . . ."

.   .   .

And so there was another great assembly in the refectory of another great abbey, in slightly smaller hall if more ancient, Scone of the Moot-hill and the Stone of Destiny, dynastic heart of Scotland, on the 4th of August 1320. Again it was hugely attended, since this

274

parliament was to hear, consider and pronounce upon the holdings and titles of lands in dispute. But before this judging, another was thrust unexpectedly upon the delegates.

Trial before parliament was quite a normal procedure, for treason, where the accused could be assured of a fair hearing and not be at the mercy of the Crown—although sentence on any condemned was usually left to the Crown. The King presided, but he seldom took any active part in the proceedings, content to leave all to his officers. The accused spoke for themselves and could attempt to sway the assembly as best they might.

On this occasion those in charge were distinctly surprised that there was little or no attempt by the prisoners to excuse themselves, or even to seek support and sympathy. All the principals to the plot had been captured and were present, save for one who had been implicated later, and then had been found to be seriously ill at his own house of Methven, not far away—the same Sir Roger Moubray who had betrayed Bruce at the Battle of Methven soon after his coronation. Also the Countess of Strathearn was not present; her attendance would have been off-putting and unsuitable; and fortunately, her evidence was not necessary.

The fact was, William de Soulis had confessed readily enough to the entire indictment. He was ever a fiercely proud man, and found it beneath his dignity, once things had gone unredeemably wrong, to deny, argue or plead. Throughout the hearing at Scone he kept a lordly silence. The others in some measure took their cue from him, as leader—although Sir Gilbert de Malherbe, Lord of Dunipace, always a shifty character, broke down after a bit and disgraced the knightly code, shouting and beseeching wildly, to the distaste and embarrassment of all present, his co-defendants in particular. David de Brechin, around whom most interest centred, as the King's nephew and because of the esteem in which he was held for gallantry on Crusade as on games-field and tourney-ground, contended briefly that he had taken no part in the conspiracy; but admitted that he had known of it and had taken no steps to controvert it. There was some sympathy for a fine and handsome young man led astray—until it was revealed that he had in fact been in English pay for years, whereupon all turned against him and his fate was sealed. Maxwell, Barclay and Graham all strenuously denied any involvement in the plot. All they admitted was that they were friends of de Soulis, and had been approached, in some fashion, to take part in a protest against the King's policy on the assize of lands; but none knew of any plan to kill or replace the monarch. De Logie, and a Liddesdale esquire named Richard Broun, who was said to have acted as principal go-between, maintained only a rigid silence.

So, much more quickly than might have been expected, the thing was over. Maxwell, Barclay and Graham were acquitted. The rest, including the absent Moubray, were found guilty, and worthy of death, the accepted penalty for high treason, and turned over formally to the King, for sentence at his pleasure. Then, relievedly, the parliament moved to the next business.

This was an announcement by the Chancellor of the reported comparatively favourable reaction of the Pope to the Declaration of Arbroath, and the proposed truce with England. Men heard the first with satisfaction, but the second with doubts. Truces were of little interest to the Scots, since they were so regularly and wantonly broken. But the withdrawal of the papal anathema was something different, a major success and an augury for the future.

They passed on to the vexed and prolonged business of land titles and tenures. Many had come prepared to fight the entire policy; but the conspiracy against the King, shaking all, had the effect of deflating the opposition. The difficult and controversial business went through with the minimum of trouble and delay. By such extraneous influence did a major land reform go through.

Later, with time unexpectedly to spare, Bruce called a Privy Council, to aid him decide on the sentences to be imposed. The decision had to be his own, however.

By common consent, all waited for William Lamberton, the senior of the Lords Spiritual, to answer the King's question first.

He shook his head. "In sorrow I must say it, Sire. But for the weal of the realm, and the security of our nation, there can be but one due decision. All should die. Mercy is godly—but for a people embattled, treachery, the hazarding of all that we have fought for and gained by infinite bloodshed and pain, is too great a danger for mercy. Here is evil, which must be stamped upon before it poisons the realm."

Most present nodded agreement.

"My lord Earl of Fife ?"

The thin-faced, uneasy-eyed Duncan MacDuff, premier noble of the land, who had consistently taken the English side in all the troubles, and not even lifted a hand to save his sister when she hung for years in her cage on Berwick Castle's walls, shrugged stooping shoulders. "Who am I to disagree ?" he said.

Men noted that answer.

"Does any say otherwise ?"

Sir Ingram de Umfraville, one-time Guardian of the realm, uncle of the absent Earl of Angus, English by birth and always anti-Bruce and pro-Comyn—but an honest man enough—spoke.

"Mercy may be too costly, Sire—but discretion should not be. Must all these be treated alike ? De Soulis should die. De Malherbe

276

and de Logie likewise. And the man Broun. But David de Brechin, your kinsman and my friend—he is in different case. A younger man, and an ornament to your kingdom. Beloved of many, honoured by the Holy See for his crusading zeal. He was in grievous error in not making report of this wicked plot. But he refused to take part in it. He might well, in the end, have used his guilty knowledge to save Your Grace. He is not to be judged as the others. Banish him your realm for a time, Sire. But do not hang him."

"I hold with Sir Ingram," Patrick, Earl of Dunbar and March said.

"As I do not!" Douglas asserted. "He has been receiving English gold. A paid traitor."

"It was not for that he was tried, Sir James."

"Hang all, and be done," the Lord of the Isles advised briefly.

Bruce turned to his other nephew, Thomas Randolph. "My lord of Moray—your guidance in this? You are of like kinship to me as is Sir David. And you also once embraced other cause to mine. This man is your cousin. What say you?"

Moray took long seconds to answer. When he looked up his noble features were drawn. He spoke almost in a whisper. "What he did is unforgivable. He contemplated the murder of his liege lord, of his own blood, the man who had forgiven him his error. He it was who, by every law of God and man should have come and made known this wickedness to Your Grace—not that woman in her bitterness. Those nearest the throne bear the greater responsibility to support it. I cannot say other than that my cousin should die."

There was silence for a little.

The King broke it. "Very well, my lords. I thank you for your counsel. But the decision remains mine. Mine only. If I decide ill, I take the blame—not you. I speak, *must* speak—and think—for the realm. Not myself. I have decided. Sir William de Soulis should die. But because he is of the royal descent, one of the few who are, for the realm's sake it should not be said that the King took the life of a rival to his throne. Many would so claim. I sentence him therefore to perpetual imprisonment. I can do no other. In this I do him no kindness. He will not thank me. Nor would any here. Better a quick death than to rot in a cell in Dumbarton Castle. That proud man will suffer the more. This, for the realm's sake."

Gravely men nodded. None questioned.

"His paramour, the Countess of Strathearn, was content that I should be slain so long as she was to be de Soulis' Queen. Only when supplanted did she turn. Not for my sake, or the realm's, but to spite her betrayer. It is not suitable to execute a woman. Or to cast her in a cell. She shall be banished the kingdom. For the rest of her life."

All approved.

"De Malherbe, de Logie, and this Richard Broun, have nothing in their favour. They are proven traitors who plotted my death only for gain. De Soulis at least believed he had a right to my throne. These would have plunged Scotland into war, internal war—and English domination thereafter, to be sure—for their own gain. They die. They shall be hanged. As for Roger de Moubray, I will not hang a dying man—as they say he is. Let him be."

Again there was no dissentient voice.

Then Bruce leaned forward and spoke differently. "David de Brechin, my sister's son. Here is a stab at the heart! He chose to support Comyn, not me. He refused to attend my coronation. He fought against me at Inverurie. But these could be forgiven. Others did as much, and more. But . . . he signed your letter at Arbroath, a solemn declaration. While yet he was in receipt of English gold. Now, within weeks, this! He is the fruit of my mother's tree, a fair and goodly fruit to seem—but rotten at the core. When I condemn others to the gallows, should I spare him?"

There was not a word spoken, although Umfraville nodded head.

"I cannot, my lords. I will not. David de Brechin hangs with the others. It is my royal decision." The King's jaw was set, his lined and craggy face like granite.

Umfraville leapt to his feet. "It is not right! Unfair!" he cried. "You must not do it, Sire! Stain your honour so. Will you, the First Knight of Christendom, hang the Flower of Chivalry? And let de Soulis live! Here is shame . . . !"

"Shame, yes, Sir Ingram. Shame that the Flower of Chivalry is cankered in the bud! Shame to spare him because he is my own kin."

"I esteemed you greater than this, Robert Bruce! I have fought against you, yes. But I ever esteemed you noble. This young man is my friend . . ."

"As all know but too well, man!" That was Fraser, the Chamberlain, with a coarse laugh.

Umfraville, spare, grey, but flushed, ignored him, and the murmurs of others. "If you do this wicked thing, Sire—I shall leave your kingdom. Leave this Scotland I have chosen to dwell in for thirty years. Wipe the dust of it from my feet. For ever!"

Curiously, compassionately, Bruce eyed the strange man. "That I shall regret, Sir Ingram. You must do what you will. But you have great estates in Northumberland. Go to them. Like your nephew, Angus. None will hinder you. But this alters nothing. Sit, sir—or leave my Council table. My decision stands. The matter is closed. Now, to this of the proposed truce . . ."

PART THREE

PART THREE

CHAPTER

20

ON a slow rise of ground above the wide, sluggish River Ribble, to the north-east of the town, and so clear of the billowing smoke-clouds, Robert Bruce, in mud-spattered, travel-stained armour, sat his horse and watched Preston-in-Amounderness burn. The sight gave him not even a grim satisfaction; Wallace's burning of the Barns of Ayr, and the times without number when he himself had been forced to set afire his own Scots towns, villages and countryside, to deny their food, shelter and comfort to the invading English, had left him with a revulsion against the sight of blazing towns and fleeing, unhappy citizenry. Nevertheless, this deed was necessary—or so he assured himself—if Edward of Carnarvon was to be dissuaded from his new invasion of Scotland; just as burned Lancaster behind them had been necessary.

If the King of Scots did not display any satisfaction, most of those around him certainly did. And with some reason. For the burning of Preston and Lancaster was only the culmination of the most brilliant piece of raid-warfare yet to be demonstrated against the stubborn English who would not come to the peace-table. Never had there been anything like this, even under Douglas at his most inspired, the hardened veterans averred—and led by the King himself, indeed entirely planned by him. This should prove, if anything could, that there was no truth in the rumours of a sore sickness that was said to be eating into the Bruce and debilitating him. If this campaign was the work of a sick and failing man, then pray the gods of war for more of the sort, they said!

The plunder had been phenomenal—for this area was rich, and had never before been ravaged, the County Palatine, Furness, Amounderness, almost down to the Welsh marches. For all that, they were not weighed down, as so often, and dangerously, with booty; for Angus Og's galley-fleet had kept them company, off-shore, and now lay in the Ribble estuary nearby, laden with treasure, hostages and prisoners for ransom. They had had to fight nothing like a pitched battle throughout—Bruce had seen to that; but such skirmishes as had developed, they had won with ease. This was coolly planned, strategic warfare, with a vengeance, and no mere rough raiding.

Preston's smoke was intended to blow eastwards indeed, right across the Pennines, to York itself, where King Edward was mustering hugely; and to Teesdale, where Douglas and Moray waited, left in dangerous isolation when Thomas, Earl of Lancaster's revolt collapsed at Boroughbridge, yet reluctant to retire on Scotland while they might yet menace Edward's flank and hinder his advance.

For the entire strategic and military situation had changed, these past three months of 1322. It had all come about by what might seem utterly irrelevant happenings. King Edward's new favourite, Sir Hugh le Despenser, had finally become so obnoxiously arrogant and greedy that many of the old aristocracy had been driven to take arms against him and his father, led by Thomas, Earl of Lancaster, and the same Humphrey de Bohun, Earl of Pembroke, who had played a less than glorious part at Bannockburn. In this civil warfare, Lancaster, who was of English royal blood and had an eye on his unpopular cousin's throne, got in touch with the King of Scots, seeking his support, with promises of peace and friendship when he won the crown. Bruce, who neither admired nor trusted traitors, however much he had been forced to work with them, did not rate Lancaster's chances highly; but it suited his tactics meantime to fish in troubled waters, and the moment the Pope's two-year truce expired, he sent Douglas, Moray and the Steward south, not so much to aid the revolt as to take advantage of King Edward's preoccupation—always with the objective of bringing that obstinate weakling to a peace-treaty at last.

After Hereford had won a victory over the Despensers on the Welsh marches, he marched north to effect a junction with Lancaster, in Yorkshire. Now it was outright rebellion against their King. Edward mustered a loyalist army at York, and was fortunate indeed in that Sir Andrew Harcla, recently made Earl of Carlisle, decided to switch his allegiance. Harcla was a fine soldier if an unreliable man, and had hitherto worked in co-operation with Lancaster, his patron. In March, he moved south with the levies of Cumberland and Westmorland, caught the rebel army by surprise and in the rear, at Boroughbridge, where they were penned against the River Ure with the King's forces in front, and defeated them entirely, with great slaughter. Hereford was slain in the battle, and Lancaster captured, with many other lords. For once, thereafter, Edward acted decisively. Lancaster and the others were summarily beheaded—Lancaster, who had slain Piers Gaveston.

Douglas, Moray and the Steward, operating independently in Cleveland, to the north, with a force of about 4,000 only, found themselves in a potentially dangerous position.

The King of England, for his part, suddenly was in a stronger position than any he had known since Bannockburn, at the head of an enormous and victorious army, with the defeated rebels anxious to flock to his banner and prove their new loyalty, and his main internal opposition discomfited, the Despensers carrying all before them. Out of the blue Edward announced that he would proceed north, to punish the rebellious Scots at last and wipe out the stain of Bannockburn.

In this abruptly transformed and unexpected situation, Bruce flung aside all his preoccupations, and acted with his old dash and verve. He sent couriers to order Douglas and the others to remain as a threat to the English host on the north-east, but to retire discreetly before it; he himself would make shift to pose another threat on the west. Fortunately Angus Og's fleet was mobilised, indeed at its old game of raiding the Antrim coast. Bruce sent urgent pleas to his friend for help, and offered vastly richer pickings on the North-West coast of England than anything he could gain in Ireland. Himself, with a hastily-raised light cavalry force of about 8,000, raced south by west.

West indeed they had raced, in a fashion never before attempted, Bruce using knowledge gained as a youth in wildfowling expeditions on the Solway marshes and coasts. At low tide, the great shallow West Coast estuaries, in North England as well as South Scotland, all but dried out; and the King now risked a great series of gambles with sea and tides. Avoiding all the normal and necessarily slow routes by the Border passes and the Cumberland mountains, he had led his galloping horsemen splashing across the successive daunting shallows of the Solway estuary, then south round the West Cumberland coastline by Silloth, Workington and Whitehaven, across the estuarine sands of the Esk, at Ravenglass, and the Duddon at Millom, into Furness. Then on over the levels of Leven-mouth near Ulverston and so into Cartmel, finally thundering over the Kent-bank sands of wide Morecambe Bay and down upon Lancaster itself. By taking enormous risks with racing tides, quicksands and mud-banks, and the fording of innumerable channels, by the most skilful calculations of tidal-timing, the Scots force had descended, totally without warning and at an almost unbelievable speed, upon an area in the heart of England thought to be entirely immune, more than one hundred miles south of Carlisle—and, at Preston, slightly south even of York. All this in the course of a few hectic days.

So now Preston burned and Robert Bruce watched it, sitting like a hunched eagle in his saddle. He hoped that he had come as far as need be, that Edward would take fright at this brazen intrusion on his right flank, and would call off the declared invasion of Scotland. With any true soldier and sound commander, he could have wagered on it; but this Edward Plantagenet was none such, an un-predictable law unto himself. Before the Scots the land lay soft, green and open to the Mersey—the late Lancaster's territories, lordless now and in confusion. There was nothing to stop Bruce between here and Wales. But he had not come south for such conquest. He awaited couriers from Douglas. He had indeed been waiting for three days, since Lancaster burned. Preston was as much a filling in of time as added warning for King Edward.

"There are rich towns on the Mersey, Sire," Sir Alexander Fraser, his sister Mary's husband, suggested hopefully.

The King said nothing.

"Give me but a thousand men and I will burn them all for you, my liege!" That was Sir Andrew Moray, his sister Christian's latest spouse, fiercer fire-eater than his father.

"No."

His third brother-in-law, Sir Hugh Ross, Matilda's husband, was more diplomatic. "If we turned east here, Sire, and made for the passes between Ribble and Aire, and so into mid-Yorkshire, we would meet Douglas's messengers, and also save our time."

"To no advantage," the King replied. "Our purpose is to make Edward of Carnarvon call off his plans to invade Scotland. That only. We shall do it better by remaining a threat of unknown strength here in his West. The nearer we move to him, the more like he is to learn our true numbers. He has ten times our force, man. We wait here until we hear from Douglas. The further south we drive, the greater danger of being cut off. Remember that we are dealing with Harcla now—a shrewd and able captain. If Edward heeds Harcla, we must needs watch our every step."

"An upsprung Cumberland squire!" the Chamberlain snorted. "I do not see the Despensers touching their caps to *him*!"

"He fought Boroughbridge as I fought Bannockburn—and won. With like tactics. The Despensers lost *their* battle. Even Edward Plantagenet must heed Harcla now. As I do. We wait."

They had to wait until early evening of that day, in fact, before the looked-for couriers arrived, exhausted, on foundered horses, having had to ride half as far again as contemplated. This was because Douglas, Moray and the Steward were now far further north than Cleveland, they explained. They were retiring steadily towards Scotland. For King Edward was not to be distracted. Against Harcla's advice, it was said—against even the Despensers' advice—he was determined on his invasion of Scotland, the more so in that the rebel Bruce was not there to stop him. He and his main force were marching north with all speed, by the east route, Douglas retiring before him, as commanded.

"And Harcla?" Bruce demanded. "What of Harcla?"

"Harcla is sent, with 20,000 men, back to the West, Sire. Through the dales and the passes, by Wensley and Dee. To ensure that Your Grace does not get back to Scotland."

"So-o-o!" The King beat a mailed fist on his saddle. "The fool—the purblind fool!" he exclaimed. "And myself as great a fool! To have believed that Edward of England would ever act as a man with wits in his head! I have wasted my time and strength on a royal dolt! You—how far north was King Edward when you left Douglas?"

"Near Darlington, Sire . . ."

"Then he is sixty or seventy miles nearer Berwick-on-Tweed than am I! With Harcla between us. See you how a misjudgement of one man's temper may endanger an entire kingdom!" That was thrown at his companions. But Bruce's glance was not on them. It was turned westwards towards the sunset and the sea. "How far ebbed is yonder tide?" he demanded, in a different voice.

"You mean . . . you mean . . . ?" Ross asked.

"I mean, Hugh, that we go now. Go as we came. But faster. Much faster!"

"But . . . the ships, Sire? MacDonald's ships . . . ?"

"We cannot load 8,000 men and their horses on Angus's galleys, man. And I shall need every man and every horse, in Scotland. I mean to meet Edward Plantagenet when he crosses my march! So we ride. Day and night. Across the sands again. Even if we must swim for it! Sound the trumpets, I say . . .!"

.   .   .

Time may indeed be made to seem to wait for a sufficiently determined man; but the tides will do so for none, even kings—as another had found out before Bruce. The Scots did indeed cross the Border slightly before King Edward did, having avoided Harcla by keeping to the sea, practically *in* the sea, all the way. But they crossed Solway, whereas Edward crossed Tweed, the one a hard day's riding south-west of the other, and some eighty miles apart.

In consequence, although Douglas and the others gallantly sought to delay the English host all through the Merse, they could do little against twenty times their number. It was *only* some slight delay that they achieved, before the Lammermuir Hills passes, where a comparative few could hold up a legion. This Douglas did, Moray and the Steward hurrying on ahead to try to raise a defensive army at Stirling. But such delay could be only brief, inevitably. Numbers told, and Douglas had to fall back amongst the round green hills, to burn Lothian before the invaders, buying time for his monarch and friend.

Bruce and his desperately weary host—or most of it—arrived at Stirling two days after Moray and the Steward. Drawn and gaunt with fatigue as he was, the King was by no means exhausted, nevertheless; indeed he seemed able now to draw on some hidden and scarcely believable fund of nervous energy, setting an almost impossible example to his lieutenants. Gulping down food and wine as he questioned Moray and others in Stirling Castle, he was rapping out orders the moment the tactical position began to become clear.

The situation he uncovered was thus: Lothian was ablaze, and much of Edinburgh with it—this at Scots hands. Already the English advance-parties were in the city, with the main body pushing forward in the Haddington-Gladsmuir-Tranent area, a vast horde of over 100,000. A large English fleet had sailed up the Forth, and was now at Leith, the port of Edinburgh. Douglas, who had contested every pass of the Lammermuirs, had now fallen back, via the Moorfoot and Pentland Hills, organising the burning of all grain, food and forage stocks in the low ground as he went, and the fouling of wells. King Edward had travelled far and fast—for so huge a force —and therefore had far outdistanced his heavy baggage-trains. Food for man and beast was now his great, his only problem.

"Scarcely his only problem, Thomas," Bruce said. "He has still to cross Forth. It has stopped better soldiers than he!"

"Those ships, Sire. At Leith. The word is that they are transports. Not food ships. Little food is being landed from them— desperately as it is needed. It seems that they have been sent to ferry the army across the estuary. The English will not be coming up here, to cross Stirling Bridge. Or not all of them. Two prongs, it may be. One on either side of Forth."

"Then we must prepare to receive them. In Fife, and here. How many men have you gathered?"

"All too few, as yet, Sire. A general muster is ordered—but it will take time. There are some 5,000 here. Lennox has 2,000 on the way. Sinclair, Bishop of Dunkeld is raising Strathearn. Menteith is marching. MacGregor and the nearer Highland clans are coming. And no doubt Bishop Lamberton is raising Fife—since its Earl is not like to!"

"Aye. Then you will command here, Thomas. Hold Stirling and the bridge. I will take Fife. You will send on to me the forces as they come in. We do not know where Edward will choose to land, if he crosses Forth. But I cannot think that he will use wide crossings, with so many to transport. Moreover he will wish to take my seat of Dunfermline—that you may be sure. He will not cross east of Aberdour, I think. I will base myself midway between there and Stirling. At the port of Culross—that would be best. From there I could quickly come to your aid, if need be. Or strike east along the Fife coast. Or even cross to the south shore, in small boats, to get in the English rear, should there be opportunity. And it is but a few miles from Dunfermline. Keep your 5,000 here, and have all other sent there."

"How long, think you, have we ?"

"Not long—if it was I who commanded. Only days. But with Edward of Carnarvon—who knows ? The English must be desperate for food. Because of the speed of their advance, and the land burned before them. Waiting in Edinburgh will serve them nothing. Unless they have more ships coming north, with provision and fodder. Their strategy is to attack us quickly, while they are strong and we are not. So we must use what forces we have—and thank God for every day He grants us for more aid to come up. I sent commands to Galloway, Annandale and Carrick, to muster, as we came up. Many thousands will come from these—but not within a week."

"Walter Stewart has ridden on, Sire. To Dunfermline. To be with the Queen and the Court. To have all ready to flee northwards. We did not know how long Your Grace would be . . ."

"That is well. But we will not have them to flee yet awhile, let us hope. This English army is great in numbers. But I cannot think that it is great in much else! It has been too swiftly put together. Insufficiently ordered. And I cannot believe it better led than that which failed at Bannockburn—for it has even less able commanders. Edward and young Despenser are babes in warfare! Had Harcla been in command, I would have been more fearful."

"The Despensers do not love Harcla, it is said. And King Edward does not trust him."

"For that the good Lord be praised! But—enough of this. I ride for Culross. My lord Chamberlain—I want messengers sent to every Fife burgh and provost, every village in South and East Fife. All shipping, boats and fishing-craft to be sent up-Forth to Culross. And fires to be lit everywhere along the shore. Inland also. Great fires, with much smoke. Burn straw, thatch, brushwood—what they will. So that from Edinburgh and the Lothian coast it will seem as though all Fife is being burned, as Lothian has been. That there will be no food for the hungry English there! It may discourage Edward from his sailing. Aye—but tell the Fifers to be ready to fire the food and forage in truth, if and when the enemy sails. But meantime, let the smoke serve . . ."

. . .

August 1322 was wet and cold and windy. In it, East Scotland smoked, while still King Edward sat in Holyrood Abbey, at Edinburgh, and did not move. Every chill, rain-soaked day of it the Scots forces grew in numbers and preparedness, at Stirling and Culross. Probing English sallies were made south and west, into Ettrick Forest's outskirts and North Clydesdale, in especial – but these were in search of cattle, sheep, even deer, and grain and hay, sustenance for 100,000 hungry men, and rather fewer hungry horses, since the latter were now being eaten. The Scots' grim joke was that the invaders were settled down to wait for this year's harvest.

It was no secret in Edinburgh – and therefore to Bruce's innumerable spies therein – that Edward was in fact waiting for a provisioning fleet to sail up from the Humber. A wiser commander would surely have organised this somewhat earlier.

When Bruce heard the reason for the English delay, he sent immediate word to his Lord High Admiral, Angus Og, now recruiting legions of Islesmen, amongst the Hebrides, to send to the aid of his friend. The King's request – he never sent commands to the Lord of the Isles – was that he cease these activities forthwith, and drive with his galleys, with all their famed speed, up and round the north coasts of Scotland, through the Pentland Firth, and so down the eastern seaboard, to intercept Edward's victualling fleet if at all possible. How many days it would take these wolves of the sea to make the difficult 500-mile circuit depended on the winds and tides, as well as on strong men's sinews. But the MacGregor, himself an expert on galleys, come limping from Loch Lomondside with his Children of the Mist, declared that *he* could do it in five days and nights of even winter seas. Though MacDonalds, of course, were not MacGregors . . . !

Be that as it may, on the 10th of August a single long, low galley came racing up Forth from the open sea, its great square sail painted with the black Galley of the Isles, its double-banked oars raising a curtain of spray on either side. On board was young John of Islay, Angus's son and heir, little more than a boy but splendid in antique Viking-style winged-helm and golden chain-mail. He announced that his father's full strength, in ships, now lay in the Tay estuary, hidden, with scouting craft as far south as Berwick and the Farnes. There had been no sign of any English fleet – save what they had glimpsed, in passing, in Leith harbour. Did the Lord Robert want that routed out, and sunk?

Laughing, in his relief and satisfaction, Bruce declined this particular service meantime, and knighted the young man there and then.

By the third week in August there was still no sign of the victualling fleet. The cold, wet and unseasonable northerly winds continued,

288

and the Islesmen's protracted vigil must have been a sore one. Presumably it was the said contrary winds which delayed the English ships—or else treachery at home, from whence rumours of new revolts of rebellious barons came daily. King Edward ventured neither upon the Forth nor along its Lothian shores, westwards. The tales from famine-stricken Edinburgh were harrowing.

Bruce had now some 25,000 men assembled, the majority at Culross, some 8,000 at Stirling. He had even sent a couple of thousand Highlanders south to reinforce Douglas in the Forest, from which that stalwart was assailing the English lines of communication and preventing food-trains and cattle-herds from winning northwards through the hills.

On the 2nd of September, Holyrood Abbey went up in flames, and a valedictory slaughter took place in unhappy Edinburgh. It was the equally unhappy Plantagenet's leave-taking. He turned his petulant and haggard face to the south, and led—if that is the word—his now semi-mutinous host homewards. Knowing too well the burned and smoking desert of East Lothian and the Merse, they took the hill road this time, by Soutra and Lauderdale and the eastern skirts of the Forest—but found neither food nor comfort there, for now Douglas gave them no rest. Out-of-hand, unruly, the English were easy prey for that hardened scourge of their kind. He and his slew and slew, but seemed to make only little impact on the vast, sprawling, starving thousands. There was nothing like a battle, nor even a standing fight. The nearest to anything of the sort was when Douglas came rushing to the rescue of Melrose Abbey, that lovely fane where Leader joined Tweed—but not before most of the rose-red buildings were ablaze and Abbot William Peebles and many of his monks crucified or otherwise shamefully slaughtered.

It was a disorganised and demoralised rabble, of barely half the numbers that had gone north, which crossed the Border on the 5th and 6th of September, the King and the Despensers spurring far ahead. Northumberland thereafter wilted and cringed under the infamous influx. Douglas followed on, direly busy.

It did not seem so long since Elizabeth de Burgh had been concocting activities to keep her husband's mind off himself. Now, despite her pleas that he hold back, rest awhile, himself was not to be considered. The words sickness and leprosy had not passed his lips in months. He saw opportunity wide before him, and was not the man to fail to take it. He had an unblooded army standing impatient, and an enemy in hopeless rout and confusion, their land defenceless. He sent some mounted reinforcements for the busy Douglas; besought Angus Og to continue down the English east coast with his ships; and, saying goodbye to his protesting Queen, left Lamberton,

Lennox and Abbot Bernard in charge of his kingdom and set off with Moray and Walter Stewart for England once more, with a picked force of 20,000 light cavalry and Highlanders.

The iron was hot, he said. He would forge a lasting peace out of it, for Scotland, if it was the last thing he did.

. . .

It was early October before Bruce and Douglas joined forces. They met deep in the North Riding of Yorkshire, indeed just three miles from Northallerton, on the same hill where, nearly two centuries earlier, the King's ancestor, David the First, had suffered resounding defeat at the Battle of the Standard. Bruce had come, more slowly this time–for now his host was an army, even though a small one, and no mere swift raiding force–once more by the tidal sands of Solway and Cumberland, since he had no wish, at this stage, to try conclusions with Harcla, sulking at Carlisle. Then, hearing that King Edward was in the neighbourhood of York again, and joined by his doleful cousin John of Brittany, Earl of Richmond, with a new English army from the south, the Scots had turned eastwards through the Pennine passes, warily–for here they could, indeed should have been ambushed. But they encountered no opposition, and proceeding down Wensleydale towards the lowlands of Swale and Ouse, they saw once again the familiar sight of burning towns, villages and farmsteads in the plain below, and recognised that Douglas was there before them. So, presently summoned from blazing Northallerton, the now saturnine Sir James came cantering up to meet his liege lord on the Hill of the Standard, their first encounter in eight months.

"Jamie, Jamie–what an executioner, what a brand of destruction, I have made of the gentle chivalrous youth once I knighted!" Bruce said, clasping the other to him. "Wherever I go, I hear tell of you. Every prisoner brought before me whispers dread of the Black Douglas! My courtly friend has become the very Angel of Death!"

"Only to the King's enemies," the younger man said. "And until such time as these proud and stubborn English acknowledge your kingship, and my right to be ruled by none other."

"Aye. It is eight long years since Bannockburn, and still they will not learn their lesson. Nor ever will while Edward lives, I think. Strange that so weak a man should, in this, be as obstinate as was his strong father. So different, yet both equally blinded with hatred and the lust to dominate other than their own. When they have so much. To the terrible cost of their own, as well as of ourselves." Sombrely, Bruce looked around him at the fair but burning plain of Swale.

"Harcla, Sire? What word of Harcla?"

"None. He has not emerged from Carlisle. He is holed up in that fortress like a fox in a cairn. Thomas, here, thinks that he sulks. That Edward preferred the Despensers to command the Scots venture, rather than himself. He now will teach his silly liege a lesson!"

"He is a strange man," Moray said. "Able, but no more to be trusted by friend than by foe."

"So I have sent him a message," the King went on. "Offering my lord of Carlisle . . . an accommodation. To Thomas's much disapproval!"

"I say that there is no good to come of dealing with traitors," his nephew averred. "He was Lancaster's feudal vassal, yet betrayed him. Effected his death. Now he withholds his service from his king. Why should *you* trust him ?"

"I do not. I would but instil in his treacherous but nimble mind that it might pay him better not to offend both the King of Scots and the King of England at the same time! So that he does not seek to interpose his Cumberland army between us and Scotland. For such accommodation I am prepared to treat even with such traitor. You are still too nice, Thomas—after all these years and bloodshed. Unlike Jamie here, who has learned my lesson all too well! Praise your God that you are not King!"

"I do, Sire—I do!"

"So speaks Saint Thomas!" Douglas laughed, but affectionately. "Praise, I say, the other saints that his niceness does not extend to his sword-hand! I have missed you of late, friend."

Moray nodded in stiff embarrassment, and found no words.

Bruce looked from one to the other of his two most brilliant captains and most valued lieutenants. "What news have you for me of Edward, Jamie ?" he asked. "And this of John of Brittany, that soured fish! Where are they ?"

"Yonder, Sire!" Douglas pointed south by east. "Not far off. I have kept on King Edward's heels ever since Melrose. Never more than a score of miles behind him and his rabble. We are less than that, here. They say he bides at Rievaulx Abbey. Just behind those Hambleton Hills. Beyond the plain. Fifteen miles."

"A-a-ah!" Bruce gazed narrow-eyed at the smoke-hazed line of low green hills. "So near ? Only two hours' riding. Edward Plantagenet so near." He looked thoughtful.

"Aye, Sire—but Richmond is in the way. The Lord John of Brittany. He occupies a strong position on the hill ridge."

"How many ?"

"His own force, some 20,000. The remainder of the King's army —who knows ? And local levies . . ."

"But not all up on this ridge ?"

291

"No. Richmond holds the ridge, watching us. Or watching *me* hitherto. He has sat up there these three days, and seen me burn this Vale of Mowbray. Not ventured down, although many times my numbers. Therefore, I think, he but holds a line, behind which King Edward may rebuild his broken host. At Rievaulx in the Rye valley. He is but giving the King time."

"Can we turn his flank? Richmond's? Reach the King's horde behind. Without taking the ridge. I do not know this country."

"I think not. Northwards, these Hambleton Hills run into the Cleveland Hills. Where I campaigned before Boroughbridge. No route through for an army. South are more hills, to Ampleforth. Not high, but steep escarpments, easily defended. Between, there is but the one gap, by Scawton and Helmsley, to the Rye. But my scouts declare it strongly defended."

"M'mm. We are well used to mightier hills than these. We have thousands of Highlandmen. It ought not to be so difficult . . ."

"What would you, Sire?" Moray asked. "A battle? Or just a stratagem?"

"I never fight battles, Thomas, unless I must. If we can gain our ends without a battle, that is best. Edward Plantagenet is but a few miles away. It is not likely that he, nor Richmond, yet knows that I am here. Jamie, yes—but not ourselves. If we struck swiftly, we might surprise Edward. Who knows, even capture him!"

"*Capture* the King!"

"It might be the quickest way to win our peace-treaty!"

"God in heaven—here's a ploy!" Douglas cried. "Could we do it, Sire?"

"Who knows? But we could try. Only, it would have to be done swiftly. Today. By tomorrow's dawn Edward will know that there is more than Douglas on his heels. He will flee southwards, I swear. We have but four hours of light—and, not knowing the country, we cannot here fight well in the dark." Bruce was peering across the three-mile-wide Vale of Mowbray, south-eastwards. "Is that not a break in the escarpment? Yonder, south of that village. Beyond the knoll. A stream comes down there, for a wager. From the high ground."

"I see it, yes," Douglas nodded. "It drives up towards the ridge. Shallowly. A steep, dead-end valley, I'd say. You think . . . ?"

"It is wooded in the lower parts, I'd say. A plague on all your smoke, Jamie! I cannot see clear."

"As neither can Richmond see clearly over here, Sire! To perceive your coming."

"True. How far north of your gap through to Rievaulx is this break? This corrie? How far north of the defended pass by the places you named?"

"The Scawton Moor and Helmsley gap. But a couple of miles, I'd say. Less, it may be."

"Good. Richmond, then, sits up on the ridge facing us, with this Scawton gap on his left. If an attack was mounted up the smaller valley, the corrie, directly on to his escarpment—what would be the result?"

"Massacre, I'd say, for the attackers!" Walter Stewart put in from behind, grimly.

"Only if the attack was pressed home. To the end."

"Ah! A diversion only?" Douglas said.

"More than that. A true attack. But in stages. And for special purpose. What result, I say? If Richmond believed it the *main*, the only attack?"

"I' faith—I see! He would withdraw his men out of the Scawton gap, to aid him and protect his flanks. I see it . . ."

"Only if he believed his flanks threatened," Moray interposed. "And if he was sure that there would be no secondary assault, through the gap. By a larger force."

"As you say, Thomas. But if he does not know that there *is* a larger force—my force—in this vale? And Douglas, whom he knows of, attacks with his full strength up this corrie? And nimble Highlandmen climb both flanks of the corrie, north and south? And are seen so to do. What then?"

"It might serve . . ."

"There looks to be much woodland over there. If my main force was hidden in those woods. With scouts out to watch the Scawton gap. Then, if Richmond withdraws his people from it, I rush down and through with my cavalry, we are into the Rye valley behind him, cutting him off from the King. And Rievaulx is at our mercy."

"Sweet Mary-Mother—a joy! A delight!" Douglas slapped his thigh.

"Scarce a joy for you, in that shallow valley, under Richmond's nose! Acting bait for this trap. And only possible if Richmond does not know Your Grace is here," the cautious Moray pointed out. "How can we cross an army to the shelter of those woods, over the open plain, without being seen? Which would ruin all."

"Jamie has already shown us. His smoke. Even now it obscures the view. It is a west wind. If there was greatly more smoke, if Jamie set his torchmen to fire everything that would burn down there, all along the vale—hay, straw, reeds, thatch, brush, scrub— then this would roll towards Richmond's escarpment, to the east, and he would see nothing of what went on below. If done skilfully."

"He would guess that an attack was being mounted . . ."

"To be sure. But it would be *Douglas's* attack. And when Douglas appeared indeed in this corrie below him, it would all fit well enough. He would have no reason to fear that another and much larger host was still lying below, in the woodland."

Moray had to admit that this was so.

"Now, then. Time is our enemy," Bruce declared. "Only four or five short hours, to do so much. But tomorrow it will be too late. I fear we will be fighting in the dark, this night. You have it, Jamie? Yours is the heavy weight of this task. You can have so many more men as you need. Richmond may charge down on you. It may be sore fighting, there in the bed of the corrie—although then, the Highlandmen on the heights could come down on his flanks. Are you content?"

"Content," Douglas nodded. "It is a ploy after my own heart. Save that it will not be I who rides to capture King Edward! That I would wish to see."

"That we none of us may see. Now—to work. The fires first . . ."

"Sire—you do not need me, in this," Moray said. "Your permission, I pray, to ride with Sir James?"

The King looked quizzically at his nephew. "You consider his to be the dangerous part, and needs must share it?"

The other shrugged. "I am like to see more fighting with him than with Your Grace, I think!"

Wryly Bruce grimaced. "How true, Thomas—if scarce your most courtly speech! Go, lad—go, both of you. With my blessing. I will see you, I hope, at Rievaulx . . ."

*   *   *

Two hours later Bruce stood within the shelter of the last of the trees, and gazed eastwards, upwards, blinking away tears from smoke-reddened eyes. Visibility was still not good—although the billowing smoke-clouds had thinned greatly now—and the smarting did not help. All around him men were sniffing and coughing, and horses snorting and blowing through inflamed nostrils.

The viewpoint was as good as any they would get; yet it was markedly inadequate to see what went on up in the upper corrie of that southern spur of the Hambleton Hills. Indeed the King could see only the tail-end of Douglas's force disappearing, for this hanging valley of the escarpment mounted in steps, and from his lowly position in the wide skirts of it, he could not see into the upper section. Though above and beyond it, the ridge itself was clear enough—or as clear as the smoke-haze allowed. Wide as it was down here, half a mile at least, up there it tailed away into a fairly narrow but shallowing gut, flanked by lofty and prominent green shoulders. At least he could see what went on up on these, where swarms of

Highland clansmen climbed quite openly, their drawn broadswords glinting in the westering sunlight.

But that was the least of the glinting. Along the escarpment edge itself, just about a mile away, the afternoon was ablaze with flashing steel, reflecting from armour, helmets, lances, swords, maces, battle-axes. The Earl of Richmond's splendid southron host was drawn up there, in full view on the skyline, stretching as far as eye could see, from here, under a forest of banners, pennons and spears. It made a magnificent and daunting sight. Yet it was with satisfaction that Bruce eyed this part of the picture—for this was what he had visualised and planned for. What did make him anxious was not all that glinting steel and martial chivalry, but how many archers Richmond might have, and where, and what he might do with them. Archers were the great imponderable. Used to pick off those Highlandmen on the open shoulders, they could be enormously damaging to the entire strategy. And if the English chose to use such on Douglas's packed host in the corrie below, once they came within effective range, there could be a terrible slaughter. Bruce was gambling that this they would not do—not out of chivalry but out of a different kind of knightly pride. It was apt to be only up-jumped men like Harcla who would allow base-born archers to steal the day when high-born knights stood by. In near-defeat or serious crisis it would be different. But this should look like neither.

Bruce had his thousands of light cavalry hidden in the scattered woodland which clothed all these hillfoot skirts. Two miles to the south, still in the foothills, a small detachment under Walter Stewart were as well hidden on a wooded knoll at the western end of the road through the pass-like gap in the hills, which led over the Scawton Moor to Helmsley. From here they could see if and when the forces holding the gap were withdrawn.

The King rather envied Douglas and Moray. He too would have preferred to be riding up that corrie, even though in full view of the enemy and with the risk of unanswerable archery attack from above. It would at least be action, better than waiting here, a prey to the misgivings of the commander who plans a battle and then must leave its carrying out to others—and who may see all his visions and forecasts made nonsense of by events. Not that he feared greatly for his friends; he had sent them into a dangerous situation, admittedly —but they were as well able to look after themselves therein as any men living. And, because he knew John, Earl of Richmond, he did not believe that the worst would happen.

John of Brittany had been Edward the First's nephew, and one-time Lieutenant of Scotland, in 1305, the year of Wallace's death. Even then he was a sombre, gloomy man, prematurely grey. Seventeen years later he was not likely to have become any more fiery or apt to take risks. No fool, but over-cautious, conservative, he was the sort of man who could be relied on to do the obvious, conventional thing; and if he erred in doing so, it would be on the side of delay, of prudence, of circumspection. Nor would he allow in others the rashness he himself abhorred—for he was inordinately conscious of his rank. But he was no craven, and of a bull-like stubbornness of purpose. Taking all this into account, Bruce had planned the day.

He was jerked out of his introspection by the thin high ululation of trumpets blowing up there on the summit ridge, many trumpets, the first peremptory bugling taken up by others right and left along the escarpment. And before these had died away, the entire centre of the steel-clad line seemed to buckle and bend. Instead of a line, a front, it became slowly a moving wide V, as deliberately, without any excited charging, the English mounted chivalry surged forward and over the lip of the escarpment of Roulston Scar, and on down the steep slope, in perfect order. As far as could be discerned from below, not a single arrow had preceded them.

"There rides a confident commander!" Hugh Ross commented, at the King's side. "As well he might be. He has all the advantage. Height. Ground. And four times the number of men. Can Douglas hold him, think you, Sire?"

"Would I have sent him up there if I did not believe so, man?" Bruce snapped. "Use your wits!"

Abashed, Ross bit his lip, silent.

The King relented, more on edge than he hoped to appear. "See you, Hugh—that narrow place hems in Douglas, yes. But it also prevents Richmond from deploying, from bringing his superior force to bear. There is just no room on the floor of the corrie for large numbers. The very ground will force Douglas into a long schiltrom formation, a hedgehog of spears. The English will only be able to attack in any strength at the head of the formation. If they swing round the sides, they will be on steep and difficult ground. And Douglas will retire, slowly. My orders were that he retires down the corrie, drawing Richmond after him. The further the better."

"It will be strange fighting for the Douglas!"

"Jamie's turn will come." Bruce turned. "Young Campbell there. Colin—your turn now. Off with you! And Ranald MacRuarie. God speed—and watch for their bowmen."

Nothing loth, the two young Highland chiefs, impatient this last half-hour, raced off, dismounted and in opposite directions. Right and left, but half a mile apart, their two large groups of clansmen waited, as eager as themselves.

For a little there was nothing to be seen from the King's position, not only in new developments but in the main cockpit of the corrie. For now the leading ranks of the English chivalry were low enough therein to be hidden, as were Douglas's men. Only to be seen were the new and seemingly endless ranks of advancing steel-clad horsemen, coming over the skyline and down the slope—a daunting enough sight. Detachments of enemy infantry were now striking out along the shoulders of both flanking hillsides, to engage the Highlanders already up there. These, their part largely played, were falling back somewhat.

Dependent on their ears now, the King and those around him fretted. It was galling indeed not to be able to see the drama up in the corrie. But at least something of the noise of it came down to them, the shouts and screams, the clash of steel, the whinnying of horses, the trumpeting.

Sir Alexander Fraser, the Chamberlain, an impatient man, stamped about on the fallen leaves of the wood, cursing their inactivity—until Bruce, rounding on him, outcursed him into muttering quiet.

Gilbert Hay, the Constable, touched the King's arm, and pointed upwards, to the left. "Stones," he said briefly.

High on the northern of the flanking shoulders, the English infantry, spreading quickly along in the wake of the retiring Highlanders, were beginning to prise loose stones and rocks, large and small, and send them hurtling down into the gut of corrie.

Bruce nodded.

"Campbell and MacRuarie should have been off earlier," Fraser growled.

"How could they, man? Seen from up there too early, and Richmond might never have moved. He had to be committed to the descent before I dared send them. Douglas will have to thole the stones meantime. Besides—so long as they roll stones down, it must mean that Richmond is not seeking to attack Douglas's flanks. Or the rocks would hit their own men, first."

With that doubtful consolation they had to be content. They waited.

Presently, again it was Hay who pointed. This time downwards, not up. He pointed at the stream which ran close by, and which came tumbling out of the corrie. It was running red.

None commented.

At last, when inactive watching and waiting and listening had become almost insupportable, there was a diversion. On the same northern shoulder of hill, Campbell's clansmen came into view, from the far side, in their hundreds, running and leaping and yelling over the skyline – to the obvious alarm of the stone-rollers. Quickly a new infantry battle developed up on the high ground.

"Thank God for that!" Fraser jerked.

It was less easy to see to the top of the right-hand and southern shoulder, from here; but within minutes noise was coming from up there also. Presumably there was less available loose stone there, for the fighting seemed to be taking place on the crest of the hill, as Christina MacRuarie's nephew attacked.

Now trumpets were blowing again, up on the main escarpment, in a crescendo, as the English rear saw a new and utterly unanticipated menace developing. Bruce sighed his relief.

The trumpeting continued. Somebody in command was in major alarm – Richmond himself perhaps, if he had not ventured down into the corrie personally. Thereafter a novel feature could be discerned in the confused picture – a distinct trend of some few horsemen spurring *uphill* out of the corrie again, back to the escarpment, against the stream, as it were – although this itself was now slackening notably. Recalled captains, undoubtedly.

"There!" Bruce cried. "There is what I looked for, schemed for! They are confused now. Where have these new Highlandmen come from! More than ever Douglas had, in the vale. We have them in doubt." He turned. "Willie Irvine – now!" he ordered, playing his last card in this game of bluff. "Up there, to Douglas's aid!"

Thankful for action at last, Irvine, the former royal armour-bearer, led his 300 mounted men out of the cover of the woodland, straight uphill towards the corrie, at the canter, yelling as they went. They had been sitting their horses amongst the trees all this time, for this moment. Their own three trumpets brayed their lustiest, to draw attention to themselves.

The braying was more than echoed from above, as this surprising cavalry reinforcement for Douglas appeared on the scene. Indeed the English buglers sounded almost hysterical.

"Pray that is sounding in the Scawton gap," Gibbie Hay said.

"If it is not, what then?" Fraser demanded.

"Then we move up to rescue Jamie Douglas," the King answered. "And say farewell to any chance of capturing Edward Plantagenet. But – wait you. Learn what it is to be a King, Sandy! Who commands – and then waits."

Even Bruce's apparently steely resolve was wilting before, at last, a young Stewart esquire came crashing his horse through the woodland glades, shouting for the King.

"Sire!" he called, "Sire – word from the Lord Walter! The enemy are riding out of the gap. Back to the east and north. Up the hill. In force. They leave, he says–they leave. They draw out, towards yonder fight, up there . . ."

"All the saints be praised! My lords–to horse! Our's the opportunity now . . .!"

The change from frustrating idleness to hectic movement was crazily dramatic. The entire woodland burst into feverish activity, and in only moments the King was leading the way in a headlong dash by thousands, due southwards along the foothills. Avoiding the thicker cover now, since it delayed them, he accepted the certainty that they would be seen from above, for only a mere haze of smoke remained caught by the trees, and led out by the higher and open braesides. Speed was everything–speed, allied to the effect of appalled surprise and confusion above.

They had almost two miles to cover, and did so in a wild, strung-out gallop, more like an enormous deer-hunt than a disciplined cavalry advance, Bruce caring nothing. Never had the shaggy, sure-footed garrons of the Scottish hills better demonstrated their qualities.

Just before they reached the knoll where the Steward had lain hidden and watching, with his 200, another messenger met them. The Lord Walter had ridden on, up the Scawton road, he reported. To take it and hold it, at all costs. Not many of the enemy had appeared to remain . . .

Without so much as drawing rein, Bruce swung his mount round, eastwards, into the gap.

For those enthusiasts demanding more militant action than mere hard riding, there was disappointment in that shallow groove through the escarpment and the moorland behind–no pass by Scots standards. Obviously, by the horse-droppings, the still burning fires, and abandoned material such as cooking-pots and horse-blankets, quite a large force had been guarding it, and presumably settling down for the night, not anticipating any large-scale assault so late in the October day. Their withdrawal had been sudden, and any numbers left must have been small, for only one or two bodies of men and horses lay scattered along the roadway, indicative of a running fight, a mere chase on the part of Walter Stewart's 200. There was nothing here for the King's force to do, save ride after, at speed.

As they went, however, Bruce's glance was apt to be as much preoccupied with the rising ground to his left, as to the front. His host's emergence from hiding, in force, could not fail to have been observed; and Richmond, or whoever was now in command on the escarpment, must surely recognise the extreme danger to his left flank. He was almost certain to send the former gap-stoppers hastening back, and with reinforcements. It was a race, then.

The little watershed between Swale and Rye was only three miles wide, with the hamlet of Scawton at the far end. Over it the King's force streamed, no impediment developing from the left flank. Where the land began to drop, from tussocky moorland to the gentler levels of the Rye, less wide a vale than Mowbray but very fair, Walter Stewart waited. Wordless he pointed northwards.

Behind the escarpment, the Hambleton Hills sank much less dramatically, in rolling green waves of downland, to the riverside. Stretched along these, over a wide front, a large cavalry host was in process of advancing southwards, at right angles to the valley, its ranks less than a mile off. Bruce looked from it, eastwards, across the levels, to where, about three miles further, the mellow stone buildings of the great Abbey of Rievaulx stood out clear amongst copses, orchards and gardens. A sigh escaped him.

"I must attend to these others, Walter," he called, reining up only partially. "I had hoped . . ." He shrugged. "I fear that Edward will be warned. He is fleet of foot! Go you, and try to take him. Take another 200, 300, of swift riders. Enough to grip him, if he is not gone. You understand? To Rievaulx. If he is gone, do not pursue too far. In darkness, you could run into trouble. Myself, I have work to do here!"

"Aye, Sire— I will bring King Edward, if it may be done."

The King waved his son-in-law off, and turned to his brothers-in-law and Hay. "Three divisions," he barked. "Quickly. Each to make arrowhead. And all three in another arrowhead. Sandy—the right. Hugh, the left. Gibbie, with myself in the centre. You wanted fighting! Quickly, I say. No marshalling. Work into formation as we advance. We will teach these Southrons how we fight in Scotland!"

It was all, necessarily, a very hurried and rough-and-ready division and forming up. But these men were, in the main, hardened veterans, and their captains amongst the most experienced cavalry commanders alive. Moreover, they all knew the Bruce's methods, and had complete confidence in his leadership. In only a brief minute or two, out of seemingly hopeless, streaming confusion, two distinct divisions appeared in the still turning Scots host, divisions which grew wider. It would be foolish to assert that the three resultant groupings approximated to any recognisable shape or order, or even were roughly equal in numbers; 15,000 mounted men cannot be so readily marshalled. But at least the advance uphill, northwards, began in triple formation, the centre foremost, and gradually its composite arrowheads began to form.

That they had time to do so was the measure of their foe's uncertainty and indecision. They should, of course, have been swept down upon at once, the English using their advantage of height and impetus, though probably not numbers. But this did not happen. It might be that there was in fact no overall and accepted commander up there, if Richmond and his chief captain were over in the corrie dealing with Douglas and Moray. These people would be mainly the formation which had been recalled from the Scawton gap, and then hastily turned back again, with, probably, the rearguard left up on the escarpment—a hurriedly patched-up company. Moreover, they were strung out in a wide line abreast, covering a lot of the downland country, a sensible formation enough for an assault on an enemy threading a long pass through hills; but unmanageable as to unified command, and hopeless for dealing with a tight-wedged charge aimed at one point.

And it was such that Bruce was mounting. An uphill charge is almost a contradiction in terms; but the slopes at this side of the hill were comparatively gentle, and the Scots' garrons bred to the hills. Gradually, from a fast trot, the King, at the very apex of the central arrowhead, lashed his own mount into a heavy canter—and none behind him were prepared to allow their middle-aged and allegedly sick monarch to outdo them. Gilbert Hay and young Scrymgeour, now standard-bearer, with the great Lion Rampant banner of Scotland held high, vied with each other to be closest to the King, so near that their knees rubbed his at each side. "A Bruce! A Bruce!" the famous, dreaded slogan rose from thousands of panting throats, as men savaged their beasts forward and up.

It was hardly to be wondered at that the English line lost its momentum, indeed faltered, and those who found themselves in the unenviable position of facing directly the spearhead of the charge took thought as to how to be elsewhere. Efforts were being made to concentrate, to draw in the spreading horns of the long line; but obviously this could not be done in time.

In the event, Bruce was not even involved in a clash, did not so much as swing his battle-axe. The enemy flung themselves aside right and left, to avoid the dire impact—and the Scots point was through. The ever-broadening wedge behind thereafter inevitably created its own effect. Sliced in two, the English front was rolled up on each side, without any real fighting developing, outmanœuvred rather than defeated.

Fraser and Ross did not require their liege lord's urgent trumpet-signals to tell them their duty. As with one accord they wheeled their respective commands around, outwards, east and west, to double back on the confused halves of the enemy front which was thus abruptly no front. Now they would have their bellyfuls of fighting—but it would be a great number of close-range, hand-to-hand tulzies rather than any tactical battle. Bruce had seen to that.

The King himself, with his 5,000, rode directly on, content to leave that matter to his lieutenants. Before him now was approximately a mile of slightly rising ground lifting to the escarpment, and thereon only scattered groups of infantry, spearmen, archers and a few horsemen and wounded men come up from the battle in the corrie—nothing that even a genius of a commander could whip up into a coherent and effective force in a few minutes. The spearmen could form themselves into one or two hedgehogs, schiltroms, and the archers could do some damage before they were overwhelmed; but they could by no means halt or break the charging mass of light cavalry.

That infantry, nevertheless, earned any renown available to Richmond's force that evening. Some, but only a few, fled. Most formed up to face this dire and unanticipated threat, in tight groups—it would be too much to name them schiltroms—and stood their ground nobly until ridden down in the rush of pounding horses and yelling men. There were no very large numbers of bowmen, but these acquitted themselves well—and almost all such Scots casualties as fell were the victims of these. But they had no backing and there was no unified command. Gilbert Hay lost a horse shot under him, and was in dire danger of being trampled to death by his own oncoming followers. The standard-bearer took an arrow in his shoulder, but his chain-mail and the padded leather doublet he wore beneath saved him from serious hurt. Bruce himself was untouched. They plunged on and past the scattered and heroic infantry, leaving them for the rear ranks to deal with.

And now, in front, was only the escarpment edge and empty air. Bruce indeed saw himself in real danger of being forced right over the lip of it by the charging press of so many behind, and yelled to his personal trumpeter to sound the halt. Only just in time the pressure relaxed, as the arrowhead's flanks swung outwards, amidst savage reining in of pawing, rearing, slithering, colliding horses.

And there, lining the edge, the Scots sat their panting, snorting, steaming mounts, and stared down into the already shadow-filled cauldron of the corrie, at the quite extraordinary sight of a separate and quite self-contained battle, a tight-packed struggle, concentrated by the shape and dimensions of that hollow of the Roulston Scar, where in a huge U-shaped conformation Richmond assailed Douglas's elongated schiltrom, 15,000 men locked in a death-struggle—or as many of such as could get to grips with each other, which was no large proportion at any one time. Some subsidiary activity was still going on along the flanking shoulders, distinct smaller battles of Highlanders and English infantry.

Bruce did not plunge down that slope to the rescue, as all impulse dictated. Instead, he called orders to be passed along for every trumpeter and bugler in his host to sound the Rally, and to keep on sounding it. Ragged and scarcely recognisable as such, the call began to blare out, along the escarpment edge, and went on, gaining in power, coherence and authority.

The effect down in the corrie was quite electrical, almost comic. Suddenly the contestants therein seemed to become the merest puppets, toys that abruptly ceased to be manipulated. As with one accord, friend and foe left off belabouring each other to pause, to stare upwards.

Douglas and his Scots recovered first, since they were the less surprised. Raising a tremendous, spontaneous shout of triumph, they renewed their efforts with redoubled vigour and entire confidence. Their tight-pressed ranks surged outwards. There was little corresponding renewal of the conflict on the English side. Their fate was writ altogether too clear.

In fact, the battle ended there and then. So obvious was it that they were trapped between the upper and nether millstones that, whatever Richmond himself might decide, his people unanimously recognised complete and ineluctable defeat. Escape was the only recourse now, all perceived.

But that corrie was a difficult place to escape from, hemmed in steeply on all sides save the west and lowermost. On either flank the mass of the enemy, as with one accord, sought to stream away westwards, around the Scots. Douglas saw it, and ordered his men to press still further right and left, well up the enclosing braesides, to stop the escape routes. And Bruce despatched contingents slantwise down both shoulders of hill, to aid in the business. Men still got past, but only individually and in small groups.

Otherwise everything was over, to all intents and purposes. Fighting died away, save for isolated incidents. At the head of the corrie, the Lord John of Brittany, Earl of Richmond, sourly yielded his sword to James Douglas, his lieutenants with him. Or such as remained on their feet.

Not a few had died, and died bravely, with their men. Fully a score of knights lay amongst the slain, there in the gut of the hanging valley, for it had been a fierce and prolonged struggle. Douglas's own casualties were not light.

He and Moray, the latter slightly wounded, his sword-arm roughly supported in a sling made by his golden earl's belt, brought their prisoners slowly up the steep slope, to present to their monarch, who had sat motionless in the saddle from the time of his arrival at the escarpment edge.

"A notable victory, Sire!" Douglas cried. "Hard smiting—until you came. As stark a tulzie as I have known since Bannockburn. But —it all fell out as you judged. I have here the swords of sundry lords, for Your Grace."

"Aye, Jamie—a notable victory. And all yours. You have borne the brunt—as I said you would, lad. And you, Thomas. Myself, I have not struck a single blow! Has it cost you dear, Jamie?"

"Dear enough, Sire. For this fight. But, if all is won elsewhere, a great victory—then the cost is light indeed. Our fallen are not yet counted—but I would say 500 perhaps. With many more but lightly wounded. As my good lord here."

Moray grimaced. "A pike-thrust meant for another! Nothing more honourable. What of King Edward, Sire?"

Bruce shrugged. "Walter went seeking him. In haste. But, I fear that he would be warned, in time to flee. He did not come to aid his cousin, at least!" And he looked at Richmond at last where that thin and tall individual, dressed all in black armour, stood in sullen and depressed silence, with sundry other notables. "I cannot congratulate you on your liege, my lord!"

The other inclined his long, grey head stiffly, and said nothing. He looked an old man, although in fact only a couple of years senior to Bruce.

"It is many years since we met," the King went on. "That day you gave us the tidings, at Stirling, of what your then King did to *his* prisoners! Sir William Wallace in especial. You considered it well done, then, I mind."

"A rebel, he died a rebel's death," John of Brittany said, almost primly.

"And do you, sir, expect better treatment?"

"I am no rebel, my lord of Carrick."

"So! You still hold to that folly, man!" Bruce shook his head. "Are you wise, think you? If I am but Earl of Carrick, and a rebel to your English King—then may not you, and these, expect the treatment a rebel would mete out? To hang you all from the nearest trees! Whereas, were you prisoner of the King of Scots, you might look to receive more courtly treatment! How say you?"

Richmond, in fact, did not say anything to that.

The King turned from him. "And these others, Jamie?"

"This is the Sieur Henri de Sully, Grand Butler of France, Your Grace. And these behind him are French knights also."

"Indeed. And what do Frenchmen fighting for a monarch who will not fight for himself? In a strange land?"

De Sully, a florid, powerfully-built man in splendid armour gold inlaid, bowed low. "We but visit, on our liege lord's command his sister, the Queen Isabella, Sire. The King of England being our host, we must needs fight for him when he is beset."

Bruce nodded. "True, sir. That is our knightly code. Your master, the King of France, is I hope my good friend. I accept therefore, that you are present in this battle not from enmity to myself. I think that I can serve him, and you, better than does His Grace of England! Remain you with my Court awhile, my friends. Come back with me to Scotland. Not as prisoners but as honoured guests. And I will send you home to France, in due course, wiser men! How say you?"

To a man the Frenchmen expressed entire satisfaction with this sudden turn in their fortunes.

James Douglas presented the other prominent captives. "This is Sir Ralph Cobham, Sire—called by some the best knight in England. He led the English van down upon us. And fought bravely."

"Then we welcome him to our company. I have known of Sir Ralph. Make his stay with us comfortable, Sir James. And this?"

"Sir Thomas de Uhtred, Keeper of the Castle of Pickering. He cost us dear, but fought nobly."

"Such knights are an honour to encounter. My lord of Moray—see well to Sir Thomas's relief, I pray you. Like yourself, he has taken some hurt. But—hold my lord of Richmond close I charge you —since he esteems himself in rebel hands! The rest I will speak with anon. Now—to see to our own hurts . . ."

The Scots set up camp down where the corrie joined the woodland, where was shelter, fuel and water. And there, hours later, Walter the High Steward came to the King, riding out of the darkness into the firelight. Save for his Stewart esquires, he was alone.

"Too late, Walter?" the King said. "I feared it. Edward of Carnarvon has as long legs as his father, but uses them a deal differently!"

"He was not long gone, Sire. From Rievaulx. Departed in much haste. His meal left on the Abbot's table! All his guard not yet gone. These we cut down—but got out of one that the King had fled for Bridlington. To take ship to London. Fifty miles. We took that road after him, by Helmsley and Nunnington, ten miles and more. Near to Malton. But he had fresh horses and we had not. And in the darkness, not knowing the land, we took the wrong road at Slingsby. So, in obedience to your royal command I turned back. I am sorry, Sire. I know that your heart was set on this. That all was planned to this end . . ."

"With any other King but Edward, you would have been successful, Walter, I swear! Never heed—none would have done better against this fleet-foot monarch, who yet calls himself Lord Paramount of Scotland!"

305

"At least I have brought Your Grace something," the younger man said. He drew from within his steel breastplate a golden casket, shaped like a double saucer, richly jewelled and engraved. "A token, Sire. The Privy Seal of England, no less! Left behind, in its keeper's, Sir Hugh Despenser's, haste!"

"Dear God! Their Privy Seal of the realm! Abandoned in craven haste? What shame is here! Humiliation. Save us—this day Edward Longshanks must be birling in his grave at Westminster!"

"More than that, Sire. We captured great treasure in gold, silver and jewels. Rich raiment, the King's own clothing. His tabard, with the Leopards of England. Horse-trappings and harness. We have a hundred horse-loads of rich spoil."

"Aye." That, strangely, was almost a sigh, as Bruce looked round in the firelight at all his lords and knights and captains, the Frenchmen also, and other knightly prisoners—although not Richmond himself, who was being kept rigorously apart, out of the King's circle. "You hear, my friends? This day a great and proud realm eats dust! This day is sorer in proud England's story than was Bannockburn. The day of Byland Ridge—as they tell me is the name of this hill—will go down in a people's annals as the very depth of shame. Because of the unreasoning hate, the stubborn pride and the craven hearts of those who led her. Bannockburn was grievous defeat followed by shameful flight—but all honour was not lost. Today, beaten deep in the heart of his own country, by lesser numbers of those he elects to call rebels, yet without himself raising a hand to strike back, or aid his fighting subjects, the King of England flees in abject fear, leaving even his Privy Seal behind. From this, his name and repute can never recover, I say. But I grieve not for this craven fool, Edward. I grieve for England, the greatest realm in Christendom, laid low for its lord's dastard fault. Mind it, my friends—mind it. The Battle of Byland, that was indeed no true battle, is not England's shame, but Edward's. Mind it, lest you come to crow overloud! And mind, too, how ill served may be even the greatest realm by its leaders—lest Scotland be ever likewise! Mind this day, I say."

There was silence around the great fire, as men heeded those words, and the stern tones in which they were spoken.

Then Fraser spoke up. "So? Do we drive on to London then, Sire? There will be little to halt us, I vow!"

"No, Sandy, we do not! Have you not learned yet? The conquest of another's realm is a hateful thing, a shame on the conqueror as on the vanquished. I am not here for conquest. I am here for one purpose only—to force a peace treaty, lasting peace, between the realms of Scotland and England. That only. What we have achieved today

306

may serve. Pray God it will. But setting all the English South afire and in arms, in largest war, as it would be, would breed only hate, bitterness, needless bloodshed. And probably defeat—for be it never forgotten that they are ten times more numerous than are we. No, friends—*I* turn face for Scotland tomorrow. Although some of you may remain here in Yorkshire a little longer. To recoup the cost of burned Edinburgh, Lothian and the Merse! From these rich, undamaged towns. As is but fair. Tax-gatherers, my friends—that is your role, now, not conquerors! And, who knows—you may teach the proud English a sharper lesson thereby . . .!"

CHAPTER

21

IT was long since Bruce had visited his castle of Lochmaben, in Annandale. Nor would he have chosen to visit it now, in early January 1323 – for this was no time to be travelling across Scotland, with snow on the hills and the passes choked. Moreover, the Yuletide celebrations were not yet over. Again, Lochmaben was still largely in ruins, and inadequate shelter for a winter visit – for the King, holding to his policy of having as few castles as possible for invaders and traitors to occupy against him, had never repaired it after its last battering by the English. However, Sir Andrew Harcla, Earl of Carlisle, had sent most urgent word, via Bishop Lamberton whom he had known, requesting a secret meeting with the King of Scots, and so soon as might be, at some spot which the Englishman could reach from Carlisle in a day's riding; and Bruce, intrigued, preferred to have the meeting sooner rather than later, for Elizabeth was, beyond all expectation, pregnant again, with delivery expected in only six or seven weeks. He was not going to risk being absent from his wife's side in the event of any premature birth. So he had settled for this early date of the new year, and at Lochmaben, remote and ruinous, as a suitably secure venue. There were not many men the King would have travelled so far to meet – but Andrew Harcla of Carlisle, in present circumstances, was one.

The new Earl was already waiting, in the castle's former brewhouse, the only building still intact, when Bruce, with Moray and Douglas and a small escort, clattered into the grass-grown courtyard on the green peninsula of the loch. Beating their arms against their sides, to warm their frozen fingers, they stamped into the brewhouse, where Lochmaben's keeper, Bruce's own illegitimate son by his second cousin, Christian of Carrick, entertained the Englishman with meats and wine before a roaring fire of logs.

The King embraced this other Robert Bruce briefly, a young man of whom he was not particularly fond, and who seemed to take after his late Uncle Edward rather than his father, fruit of the enthusiastic and comprehensive hospitality shown to the fugitive monarch at Newton-of-Ayr eighteen years before, but whom he dutifully cherished, as it were from a distance.

"Ha, Rob – so you are growing a beard already! On my soul, they

308

start younger each year! To make me feel the older, i' faith!" he greeted. "How is your lady-mother, lad?"

"Well, Sire—and sends greetings. And hopes that Your Grace will honour her house at Newton hereafter. But, Sire—yourself? You look but poorly. Thin. Is the sickness back again?"

Douglas coughed hurriedly.

Moray looked away. "This will be my lord of Carlisle, I think, Your Grace," he said.

"Ah, yes." The King turned, smoothing the quick frown from his brow. "My lord—your forgiveness that we are late. The snow blocked the pass by Beattock, and we must needs make circuit by Moffat. You would have little difficulty, coming up Annandale?"

"None, Sire. And I crave your royal pardon and patience in bringing you so far. But the matter is vital, and my position . . . difficult."

Andrew Harcla was a short, stocky, powerfully-built man of early middle-age, plain, heavy-featured, jerky of manner and without obvious graces, not unlike one of his own Cumberland bulls. But his small darting eyes were notably lively, and shrewd.

Bruce inclined his head. "That I understand, my lord. I came, since it was the best soldier in England today who besought me."

"I thank Your Majesty. More's the pity, I think, that I need not to be very able, and yet that! For these are sorry days for England."

"I do not deny it. And what would you with the King of Scots?"

The Englishman looked at Bruce's companions. "Your Majesty will understand how delicate is my situation, how secret is my visit. And how for your royal ear alone are my words."

The King shook his head. "My son, here, will leave us. But these —no. My nephew of Moray is now as my right hand in the governance of this my realm, since my lord Bishop of St. Andrews, to whom you sent your letter, is sore stricken, bedbound. Anything that you have to say to me, he should hear. And my good friend Sir James of Douglas is Warden of the Marches. Any matter which concerns the Border—and surely this must—is within his bailiewick. These remain, sir."

The other shrugged. "As you will." But he waited until the young man had left the brewhouse before continuing. "My head could fall, for what I say now, Sire. I beg you, and these, to mind it well. It could be called treason. My very presence here. Yet I am no traitor."

"That we will judge when we hear you, my lord. Yet, it comes to my mind that you once betrayed the Earl of Lancaster!"

Harcla set a heavy jaw. "I prefer that you use another word, Your Highness!" he said thickly.

"Perhaps. Let it be. What is your urgent matter, then ?"

The Englishman took a deep breath. "This, Sire. Because of the follies, failures and misgovernance of King Edward and his friends the Despensers, England is in sore straits, and in a state of revolt. Not yet open revolt, but near it. The country has never been so mismanaged and disgraced. Your own defeat of the King at Byland, and his shameful flight, has lost him all support. Especially in the North. The North, I say, has had enough of Edward of Carnarvon!"

"So! And you are King Edward's commander in the North!"

"The better to know the temper there. The better to take steps to improve the position."

"*You* take steps ?"

"Yes, Sire. I, and those who think as I do. Which is the greater part of the lords and barons of the North. We know well that Your Majesty has long sought a peace treaty and recognition of your sovereignty and independence. We would undertake to urge this course upon King Edward by every means in our power – and such means are not little. And if he will not listen, then to ally ourselves with Your Majesty against him!"

Bruce stared at the man. "Ally . . .! You ?"

"Aye, Sire. I, and others. Many others."

"You would turn your coats ? Turn traitors. Against your own realm ?"

"Not traitors. Not against our own realm. Only against Edward, who cannot and will not preserve us, our lands, people and goods. He is incapable of defending the North of England – nor does he care to do so. For years, Sire, you and yours – these same lords of Douglas and Moray, indeed – have raided and devastated and held to ransom our entire North. As far south as York. Has the King of England ever sought to aid us ? Never! He has invaded Scotland – but that was for his own pride and glory, not our help. We have pleaded with him for what should be our right, the right of any part of a kingdom – protection, aid, governance. And received none. So, we say, it were better that the North of England came under the King of Scots' protection than his enmity! We are too far from London, Sire. And once, Scotland reached as far as Lancaster . . ."

"You are proposing that I annexe the North of England – with your help, man ?"

"I am. If King Edward will not heed our last demand for a peace treaty."

Bruce looked at Douglas and Moray, at something of a loss. They appeared only astonished, and offered him no guidance.

"How much of substance is there here ?" he demanded. "I do not doubt your serious intent, my lord – or you would not have come

310

here at the risk of your head. But–how much of backing have you? Few can know of your move–or King Edward's spies would know of it also, by this!"

"I know the temper of the North, Sire. I am Governor. And I am no fancy fool sent up from the South. I am a Cumbrian. See you, the North has been in a ferment for years. The Earl of Lancaster knew it. But he acted foolishly, and too soon. Nevertheless, his execution grievously offended the North, where so many were his vassals. I heard cheers for Edward's defeat at Byland in Carlisle's streets! Northumberland is ready to revolt–for they have been harder hit by the Scots raiding than has Cumberland and Westmorland. Indeed, many there believe that Your Highness intends to annexe Northumberland to Scotland anyway. After your claim to Tynedale. That it is in your realm."

"There could be a grain of truth in that," the King admitted. "I *have* considered it. And I will so do–if it will bring King Edward to his senses and the peace-table."

"It is my belief that it would fail to do so. Even this. Never was a king so set in his folly. I say, Sire, that you will have to reckon without Edward of Carnarvon! He will not negotiate with you, because to do so he must recognise you as King of Scots, equal with himself, and independent. This he will never do. All the defeats and raids since Bannockburn have not brought him to it. Annexation of Northumberland to your realm in itself will not do so either. Other steps Your Majesty must take. You will only gain your peace treaty with another king on England's throne!"

"M'mmm." Bruce took a pace or two over the flagged floor of the brewhouse, in a quandary. In his heart, he knew that this man was probably right. Yet it went against the grain, against all his instincts, for himself, a king, to plot with a traitorous subject to bring down another king. Not that such qualms had ever affected Edward or his father. He swung on Moray.

"How think you, Thomas?" he demanded, to gain time for decision. "Is there to be no peace while King Edward reigns?"

"It is now nine years since Bannockburn, Sire. And you have done all that man can do to gain a treaty. In this I fear my lord of Carlisle is right. King Edward will not change now. Yet both realms need peace above all things. It seems that other means must be used to bring it about. Has my lord firm suggestions?" Recognising his uncle's difficult position, Moray asked the question himself.

Harcla responded without hesitation. "I have, my lord. I propose that King Robert should give me firm terms to lay before King Edward. If he rejects them–then we make armed revolt in the North, assisted by the Scots, to have the King deposed and his son

311

appointed in his place, with a regency. On understanding and agreement that the first act of the new sovereign would be the conclusion of a treaty of peace with Scotland, accepting the independence of that realm and the authority of King Robert."

"Firm terms, you say. From King Robert. What terms have you in mind?"

"Fair and honourable terms. Which King Edward, were he honourable, could accept. More important, which an English parliament could accept. Each realm to maintain its own king, laws and customs, unthreatened by the other. Each to promote and advance the common advantage of the other. All English claims on Scotland to be withdrawn, and all Scots claims on England. Arbiters to be appointed, of equal number and rank on both sides, to settle all differences between the realms, and subjects of the realms."

"These are fair conditions, sir," Bruce acknowledged. "But scarce inducements! There is nothing here to *induce* King Edward to agree."

"I do not believe that anything will so induce him!" the other returned. "Whatever terms you send, he will reject, I think. But these would commend themselves to a parliament. And give the lords and barons of England good cause to unite against the King, when he refused. Which is important."

"Yet inducement there should be, surely," Moray said. "To make it *possible* for King Edward to accept."

Harcla shrugged. "Anything such must come from you, the Scots."

"Long I have sought for, fought for, this treaty," Bruce said slowly. "Therefore I would give much to see it concluded. For my people's sake, who need peace. I have thought much on it. I would agree that one of my daughters should wed King Edward's heir, now some ten years of age. And I would make some payment in gold in reparation. For injury done to the realm of England these last years, some generous payment. If such would aid in the acceptance of these terms."

Douglas stared. "*Pay* the English . . .!" he exclaimed.

"King Edward is said to be short of moneys. All his treasure gone on his favourites. He might listen to the chink of gold, where other persuasion fails."

"Very well, Sire. Such generous offers I will make to the King. But still I fear he will not heed, and we shall require to take to arms."

"It may be so. But, see you, I will not now commence a war against the might of England. It is peace I seek, not large war. Revolt by Edward's lords is one matter. Invasion by my Scots host is another."

"Not war for you, Sire. Only support, we seek. No greater force than you have sent raiding into England times unnumbered. With captains such as these to lead that support!" Harcla nodded towards Moray and Douglas. "For I do not deny that England is short of able captains. However many great lords she has!" And the new Earl sniffed his contempt of all such.

"That is true, at least. But—these lords? How many would rise against the King?"

"Many. Most, indeed. Those whose stomachs King Edward has not turned, the Despensers have . . .!"

"Names, man—names!"

"The King's own brother, for one—the Earl of Kent. The Earl of Norfolk. The Lord Berkeley. The Bishops of Ely, Lincoln and Hereford. The Earl of Leicester, who is my lord of Lancaster's heir . . ."

"Kent would turn against his own brother?"

"He is hot against the King. The Despensers slight him. And not only he. The Queen herself, I think, would not be sorry to see her husband deposed and her son king. Her lover, young Mortimer, is one of those strongest for revolt—and he does nothing that displeases Her Majesty."

"So-o-o! England is in sorry state, I see!" Bruce looked at the stocky man shrewdly. "And you, my lord? What will be *your* place in the new kingdom?"

Harcla was nothing if not frank. "In the said revolt, I command. For none of these others is fit to lead an army. And when we win, I expect to be one of the regents of the young King."

"You do! You fly a high hawk, my lord—for one who but a year or so past was but a Cumberland squire!"

"My hawk has strong wings, Sire."

They eyed each other like wary dogs. Then Bruce inclined his head.

"Very well, my lord. We shall have a compact. I have a clerk out there, who shall write us the terms you are to put before King Edward. For the rest, if he refuses, it is between ourselves. On the day that you rise, with major force, a Scots cavalry host of 5,000 will join you, under my lord of Douglas. To remain under his command. You understand? I will have no Englishman commanding my Scots subjects. And, before then, I want proofs of your support, in more than in the North."

"That Your Majesty shall have. In abundance. I thank you. Give me but six months, and you shall have your peace treaty . . ."

.   .   .

Two of those months were passed before the King heard more of

Andrew Harcla. And, when he heard, Bruce was in little state to pay fullest heed, in a turmoil of emotion, agitation, joy, concern, inextricably mixed. For the very night before, or in fact the same dawn, Elizabeth had given birth, at Dunfermline, to a son—a living and perfect son. But the birth was a dreadful one, lasting over twelve hours and almost killing a woman too old for normal child-bearing. That the Queen survived the desperate night was indeed something of a miracle—just as the production of a hale male child at last, after twenty-one years of marriage, was a miracle.

So now all Scotland rejoiced in that an undoubted heir to the throne was born, and the bells that had celebrated Bannockburn now pealed and clanged and jangled as endlessly. But Bruce himself sat, a prey to anxiety, fears, self-blame—indeed could have wished the child unborn that his Elizabeth should have been spared this. For she was more than exhausted. She was direly weak, her features woefully waxen and drawn, her eyes dark-circled. She had lost great quantities of blood. She had lain, only part conscious, all that March day, whilst Dunfermline throbbed to the joyful clangour of the bells, and the King watched her every shallow breath. So he had sat hour after hour—and fiercely repelled any who sought to intervene, console, consult or otherwise distract.

It was a brave man, therefore, who entered that bedchamber above the Pittendreich Glen that late afternoon, unbidden—but then, this *was* a notably brave man, as all Christendom acknowledged whatever else it might say of him. James Douglas, come from the Borders, stood with his back to the door and looked at his friends.

Hollow-eyed, hunched, the King stared at him dully for long moments after he had recognised who was there—for he had not slept in forty hours, and was all but dazed. He did not offer a single word of greeting.

"I . . . I have heard all, Sire," Douglas said, low-voiced. "An heir. And Her Grace in sore state. But—God is good. He will aid Her Grace."

"Is He? Will He? What makes you so sure, James Douglas?" That was said thickly, in a monotone.

"Because He gave the Queen a notable spirit, Sire. That is why. It is that spirit will save her."

It was not the King who answered. Just audible, from the bed came the whispered word, "Jamie!"

Douglas came forward, then, and Bruce sat up. It was the first word Elizabeth had spoken, for hours.

She did not say more. But before her heavy-lidded eyes closed again, she mustered a tiny smile for them both. It lifted the King's heart.

314

"Oh, lassie! Lassie!" he said brokenly.

She raised the long white fingers of her left hand in brief acknowledgement, and his own rough and calloused hand reached out to grip and grasp.

So these three remained, silent.

At length, when it was clear that the Queen slept, Bruce spoke softly. "An heir for Scotland was not worth this, Jamie."

The other made no comment.

"But it was not this that brought you from Roxburgh Castle, I think," the King went on. "Word of it could not have reached you in time."

"No, Sire. It was other."

"Grave tidings ? To come yourself, not send messenger ?"

"Harcla, Earl of Carlisle, is dead. Tortured, half-hanged and disembowelled, after the Plantagenet fashion! There will be no revolt, Sire."

Bruce looked at the other heavily. "So Edward was not . . . agreeable!" he said. "Harcla went to him, with the terms ?"

"Yes. And King Edward esteemed it high treason. To have approached Your Grace, without his royal authority. No subject of his will have truck with rebels, he said! He dealt so with Harcla, as a warning to others."

The King drew a hand wearily over his brow. "How above all stubborn can be your weak and stupid man! Shall we never see peace, because of this royal fool ? What of all the others, the great lords who were to support the revolt ? Are these all taken also ?"

"No. Harcla went alone to the King – and was requited thus. Your Grace will wonder at how I had the news. It came from Umfraville. Sir Ingram himself brought me word, at Roxburgh."

"Umfraville! So we have not heard the last of that strange man. He ventured into Scotland again ?"

"Aye, Sire. His Northumberland lands march with yours at Tynedale, as you know – none so far from the Border. He was not illpleased at Harcla's death, esteeming him up-jumped traitor. But he is for a peace treaty between the realms, nevertheless. He says that he believes King Edward to be nearer to it than ever before. That he, Umfraville, seeks to prevail with the King to conclude such . . ."

"Ha! He would regain those great lost lands of his, in Scotland, if he might!"

"It may be so. But, whatever his reasons, he is working for a peace treaty. And is hopeful – despite Harcla's execution. Harcla died, he says, not because he favoured a peace, but because he chose to negotiate without his master's authority. Umfraville said to tell

Your Grace that if you sent an embassage to King Edward to discuss terms, it might be favourably received. He suggested Bishop Lamberton, since King Edward had a liking for him once. I told him Lamberton was too sick a man to travel . . ."

"Aye. It is as much as he may do to come to Dunfermline. But—this of an embassage. Will Edward receive an embassage from rebels, as he names us ? I think not. Has Umfraville forgotten this ?"

"No. He says that the embassage must not seem to be that. Just travellers on their way to another land. France, or the Low Countries, perhaps. Who could call at London in passing. And see the King privily. Through Umfraville himself. He has Edward's ear, he says . . ."

"That would be difficult. Whom could I send, that I could trust in this, whom Edward would not take and slay out-of-hand ? In his stupid arrogance and hate. William Lamberton would have served, yes. But you, or Moray, or Hay—such he would never tolerate. He has put prices on all your heads. We deal with no reasonable man."

"Some other cleric, Sire ? Whom he would scarce slay . . . ?"

Bruce looked at his sleeping wife thoughtfully. "Umfraville believes there to be hope in this ? True hope of Edward's acceptance ?"

"He says so. The King is alarmed at the enmity of his nobles. So he made example of Harcla. But he would wish the Scottish entanglement over, the better to deal with these others."

"Aye. Then I have thought of a way. David, Bishop of Moray, has long sought to go to France. It has been his desire to found a college there. In Paris. For Scots. A cherished project. I will send him, with the Sieur de Sully, Grand Butler of France, and the other French knights taken at Byland. Time they went home. Edward will give them safe-conduct, since they were captured fighting for him. On the way to France they will call to pay their respects to the King, in London. And carry with them such terms as I can offer." He nodded. "Harcla was too ambitious, too fast. But it may be that he did not die in vain . . ."

The Queen stirred, and opened her eyes. Both men sat forward. But, after another faint flicker of a smile, she closed her eyes again. Her breathing deepened a little.

"In that smile is your hope, Sire," Douglas said gently. "Her Grace is of all women both finest and fairest."

Bruce looked at the younger man keenly. "Of all women . . . ? *I* say so, yes. But you, Jamie ? You have never wed, my friend. You have never given your heart to another ?"

"Given long years ago, Sire. To one man—yourself. And to one

316

woman—who lies there. And smiles!" Douglas rose. "Have I Your Grace's permission to retire? I have travelled far and fast . . ."

. . .

Some eight weeks later, with the broom abloom and the first cuckoos calling hauntingly in Pittendreich Glen, and with the Queen on her feet again, although pale and frail, only a shadow of her former proud womanhood, but the new Prince David thriving lustily, Bishop David Murray of Moray sent word back to Scotland, not from London but from York, where King Edward had returned. He and de Sully had been received by the King, in Umfraville's company. Edward would not hear any terms from him, the Bishop, whom he declared to be both rebel and excommunicate. But he had been prepared to listen to de Sully, as a Frenchman and man of honour. Sully had announced the Scots terms. Later, the King had summoned only Sully to his presence, and told him that he favoured peace and could accept all save two of the Scots proposals. But these two were the basic independence of Scotland; and the kingship of Robert Bruce. These he could never accept. Therefore there could be no peace treaty, since the King of England could never sit down at such table with rebels. But, for the sake of peace, he was prepared to accept a prolonged truce—with the Leader of the Scots people, not the King of Scots, of which there was and could be none. He suggested a truce of thirteen years. He was prepared to send commissioners to sign such a truce at Berwick, on intimation that the Leader of the Scots people would meet them to endorse it.

"God in His heaven!" Bruce groaned to his wife, as this was declared to them. "The man is crazed! Run wholly mad. Will nothing teach him, nothing open his eyes? Must two whole realms remain for ever at war because of one man's insensate vanity? His own kingdom falling about his ears, and all he can think of is to deny me the name of mine!"

"It is beyond all in folly, yes," Elizabeth agreed. "But—this of a truce? Why thirteen years?"

"God knows! The man is deranged. In one *half* of thirteen years all could be changed. *Will* be changed. Neither he nor I alive, it may be! How can a man deal with such as this . . . ?"

"His Grace of England says that he will send his commissioners to Berwick, Sire. Next month," Bishop David's courier went on. "To sign the terms of the truce. With Your Grace . . ."

"Not with my Grace! Only with the rebel leader of rebellious Scots! As though I would sign anything on those terms. The crass fool! Small wonder that his lords are in near revolt, that England is riven and prostrate. With such a monarch . . . !"

"And yet, my heart, is the case so ill?" the Queen put in, gently. "Edward's pride is all that is left to him, empty, profitless pride. So he assails yours. Withholds all, for a couple of words, king and kingdom. Yet gives all nevertheless, in fact . . ."

"Gives all? What do you mean? He denies all. This treaty of peace—without it, I can never build up Scotland to what the realm should be, must be. All our treasure and strength is wasted in maintaining armed men, ever and again having to burn our own country in the face of invaders, living in our armour, horses saddled, our trading ships attacked on the seas. Near on thirty years of war! Scotland needs peace . . ."

"Yes, Robert—peace. But, see you—you blame Edward for flinching at a word. Your kingship, the realm's independent name. But are you not in danger of a like fault, my dear? This word treaty? What is it but a word? It is not the treaty that is important, but the peace. The peace that Scotland needs. And what is a thirteen-year truce, but peace? Bannockburn was but twelve years ago. So long a truce is as good as a peace, is it not? Since it is the peace you want, not the treaty, let not *your* pride deny it, Robert."

Biting his lip, the man stared at her.

"Moreover," she pressed him, "Edward's folly will not permit that he reigns for thirteen years. Or three, I think! Why wait for the peace which may follow, when you can have it now? Peace, whether in the form of truce or treaty, is the same, is it not? Both can be broken, or kept. I say, Robert—go to Berwick, and sign this truce. You will be none the less king."

"It may be that you are right . . ."

ELIZABETH DE BURGH smiled into the early afternoon sunshine, at the picture they presented, the man and the two boys, the stocky, sturdy ten-year-old and the toddler of not yet three, walking up from the shore together hand in hand, with the ribs of Robert's fine new ship in the foreground, and as background all the weed-hung skerries and headlands of the Clyde estuary and the heart-catching, colour-stained loveliness of the Western mountains. It was a fair and satisfying scene—but there was pain as well as pride and love and satisfaction in the woman's smile. For the man who held the children's hands walked with a clumsiness that was far different from his accustomed sure stride, and held himself with a stiffness that was almost the posture of age—although he was in fact but fifty-three. These last years his legs had been tending to swell; and although she had not said anything, Elizabeth feared the dropsy. The long years of stress, privation, hard-lying and irregular eating, were telling on Robert Bruce.

But it was not only the sight of the man that affected her. The two boys, uncle and nephew as they were, brought a lump to her throat at times. The good God only knew what trials lay in store for those two. Their two-year-old David was the child of ageing parents, like to be a king long before man's estate—no desirable fate. And Robert was an orphan now, Walter Stewart having died suddenly, unaccountably, five months before, at the age of thirty-three, leaving this ten-year-old boy High Steward of Scotland.

Bernard de Linton, at the Queen's side on the grassy terrace before the house, did not see the trio quite as did she. "A fair picture, Your Grace," he commented. "The King and his heirs. The succession assured. Concerned with the things of peace, not war. These ships. It is well."

"Well, yes." Elizabeth agreed, whatever her personal reservations. "I do not know who wins most delight from this ship-building—the princes or His Grace! Or, indeed, my lord of the Isles! They are all children together, in this, I do declare. I hear nothing but talk of ships and shipping, of keels and bulwarks and draughts, of beams and timbering and cordage, from morn till night. Cardross, I vow,

319

is no place for a woman, my lord Abbot—unless she be a Hebridean woman perhaps!" She said that with a smile.

The Chancellor coughed, wondering whether the Queen was indeed referring to the Lady Christina MacRuarie of Garmoran. He did not concede, as he might have done, that Cardross was no place from which to rule Scotland, either; and that he, the Chancellor, had to spend an unconscionable part of his time traipsing between Dunfermline and here, or Arbroath and here, or Scone and here—less than suitable employment for a mitred abbot and chief minister of the kingdom. His unannounced arrival, this sunny afternoon, from Dunfermline, was only one of many such occasions, when events demanded that he should see the monarch personally rather than just send messengers and clerks, with papers for scrutiny, signing and afixment of the Privy Seal. Abbot Bernard was a patient and shrewd man, if inclining towards pomposity in a small way with the years.

"Your Grace mislikes this new house?" he asked.

"No. I like it very well. As a house. It is more comfortable than all the great stone castles. But I have scarce my liege lord's passion for the sea, these islands and mountains. Nor indeed for his Highlandmen! They are well enough—but I cannot think that they conceive women to have any place in God's world, and theirs! Other than in their beds, to be sure!"

The Chancellor coughed again, rather disapprovingly for so stalwart a fighter. Where women were concerned, de Linton was slightly prim—and Elizabeth seldom failed to tease him, although mildly.

The two royal daughters, Matilda and Margaret, came running, laughing and shouting aloud, from the braes of Carman Hill behind the house, where they were tending to run wild, these days, with the herd-boys and milkmaids—unsuitable upbringing for princesses, but in tune with the King's frame of mind. After the tragedy of Marjory, Bruce had vowed that no other child for whom he had responsibility should have his or her youth spoiled, and young freedom denied, for any trammels of state and trappings of royal position. About this he was adamant. All too soon the demands and coils of their high estate would entangle his offspring. Meanwhile, let them have their fill of freedom, and learn to know their fellows, of all ranks and classes—especially these Highlanders. It rejoiced the King's heart that both girls, and Robert, already spoke the Highland Gaelic as well as they did French. Elizabeth was less sure that this was the way to train princesses—but her own strength was not what it had been, for she had never fully recovered from David's birth, and she tended to assert herself less.

"We need cakes. Cakes. And wine," Matilda cried, now aged ten, and an eager tomboy, all arms and legs. "It is a wedding-feast. A great feast. Up in the sheep-stall yonder. I am marrying Seumas. Am I not lucky? He is the best! We are going to have seven children. All boys. Seumas says we will not have any girls. Seumas says we must have cakes and wine. He would rather have *uisge-beatha*, but . . . wine will do. I said we would not get *uisge-beatha* . . ."

"You did not! *I* said it," Margaret, a year younger, and slighter, prettier, objected. "I said we would not get wine either. Only milk . . ."

"Milk is of no good for a wedding, silly! Only wine will serve, Seumas says . . ."

"I am marrying Ranald," Margaret revealed, but with less pride than her sister's announcement. Seumas Colquhoun was the head shepherd's son, while Ranald was Angus of the Isles' second.

"Ranald is not so strong as Seumas . . ."

"Hush you, hush you, shameless ones!" the Queen told them. "Can you not perceive that you outrage my lord Abbot? Make your reverences to him—and then be gone. Or your sire will hear you. Here he comes. Tell Mistress Kate in the kitchens that you may have oaten cakes, and a little watered wine. Watered, mind you! Now—off with you . . ."

"Ha, Bernard—I never know whether to rejoice to see you, for your own sake, or to fear for what brings you!" the King exclaimed, as he came up. His voice was strong as ever, at least. "Welcome to Cardross, whatever. These ones have been down with me inspecting the new trading galliot we build. They declare that she is too heavy and will surely sink. How think you?"

"I know not a galliot from a gallimash, Sire. I prefer God's good firm land . . ."

"Like Her Grace. I grieve for you both! Well—where have you ridden from today, my friend? Dunfermline?"

"Aye, Sire. With news. Grave news. Yet—perhaps none so ill. For us. For Your Grace. Concerning . . . concerning His Grace of England." The Abbot glanced down at the small boys, warningly.

"Edward, heh? I have never heard good news from that quarter, alack! Rob—take Davie. Go with the girls, there."

"I would rather stay with you, Sire," the Lord High Steward of Scotland objected. "The girls care only for that sheepleader Seumas Colquhoun!"

"Tush, man—you will not be outdone by a Colquhoun! Away with you both. And do not let the bold Seumas blood your nose again!"

The Chancellor looked after the small and reluctantly departing backs. "King Edward is dead, Sire. And . . . evilly!"

Bruce caught and held his breath, his eyes narrowing. He did not speak.

"Dead, Abbot Bernard? The King?" Elizabeth whispered. "Edward of Carnarvon dead! You are sure?"

"Yes, Madam–dead. Slain. And beyond all evilly. And the Despensers, father and son, likewise. All dead. England has a new king–Edward the Third. And a new ruler–the man Roger Mortimer!"

"Mortimer? That puppy! The Frenchwoman's paramour!" Bruce frowned. "Edward Plantagenet was a fool, and a grievous thorn in my flesh. I cannot weep for him. But . . . may he rest in God's peace, now. Like his dire father. How came he to die, Bernard?"

It was the Queen's turn to be glanced at by the hesitant Chancellor. "I think perhaps, Sire–alone?" he suggested. "It makes ill telling . . ."

"I am no blushing maid, my lord Abbot. And Ulster's daughter!" Elizabeth reminded. "Say on."

De Linton inclined his head. "Queen Isabella returned from France. Where she has dwelt these last years, away from the King. She brought a French force, under the man Mortimer. And the Count of Hainault. Henry, the new Earl of Lancaster, and the Earl of Norfolk, the Marshal, and others, joined her. The standard of revolt was raised against the King. And swiftly all was over. He did not fight any better against his wife and Mortimer than against ourselves, Sire! He fled to Wales, making for Ireland. He surrendered to their army, and was immediately deposed. And Edward the Third, aged fourteen years, declared in his stead."

"But was not killed? Deposed? Yet you say he is dead?"

"Aye. Murdered. Thereafter. Most terribly. By Mortimer's creatures. They . . . they thrust a red-hot iron up into his vitals. By the back passage. That he should die without evident wound. Secretly. But one boasted of it. And then confessed . . ." The Abbot's voice tailed away.

"Sweet Christ Jesu!" Shaken indeed, Bruce looked at his wife. "That men . . . should be . . . so vile! 'Fore God–Edward! Their King! To die so! He was young, yet . . . ?"

"But forty-three, Sire. But old in folly and misadventure . . ."

There was an interruption. Malcolm, Earl of Lennox, an elderly man now, put in an appearance. He came over from nearby Dumbarton almost every day to see his friend and liege. Always a hater of violence, told the grim tidings, he was greatly upset.

"What is it that is in these English?" he demanded. "This savagery, butchery? That they break into. To speak with, they are like ourselves. More careful, indeed. But scratch their fine skins, and they are thus beneath!" Pure Celt himself, he paused, a little

322

alarmed at what he had said, remembering that Bruce, at least on his father's side, was of the same basic stock as most of the English nobility; and Elizabeth was wholly so.

"Mortimer is from the Welsh marches, is he not?" The King shrugged. "I know not, Malcolm, what makes them so. We Scots have sins enough. But . . ."

"It is conviction, straight from God, that they are superior!" the Queen said quietly. "Always, they are assured that they are superior, right. There is no question. Therefore others must be wrong. And if wrong, inferior. All men are inferior to the English. They do not require to say it, even think it— they *know* it! And inferior creatures are lesser men, scarcely men at all! They cannot conceive themselves in place of such— and so can inflict these terrible savageries on others. For they cannot feel it in themselves, being otherwise. Being a different creation, superior, English!"

The men looked somewhat askance at the sudden unexpected vehemence of that outpouring. It was not often that Elizabeth de Burgh revealed something of the hurt and battened-down hatred which long years of imprisonment and scorning had bred in her.

Her husband changed the subject. "So what now?" he asked. "How shall these tidings affect us in Scotland? The new King is little more than a child. *He* will not refuse to sit at a peace-table with me, I think! But those who control him? His mother is a vixen, an evil woman. And this Mortimer an insolent popinjay. There will be a regency. Is there word of its members, Bernard?"

"Only that Henry, Earl of Lancaster, is chiefest, Sire."

"A weak man. Weaker than his brother Thomas, whom God rest. I' faith— they could have done with Harcla, now! So much the better for us. The old Lancaster was always of a mind to talk with us. He was kin to me, far out. His brother may think the same. We may yet win our peace treaty."

"Pray that it is better kept than the thirteen-year truce, then!" Lennox exclaimed. "I swear that meant little enough to Edward. First he brought young Edward Baliol to his Court, to set up as a puppet-king for Scotland! Within months of signing the truce! He seized our ships on the sea. Commanded the warding in prison of all Scots in England . . ."

"Aye— it has been a travesty of peace," the King agreed. "Two years of pin-pricks . . ."

"Yet it has given you breathing-space," Elizabeth insisted. "Time to think of other things than war. Trade, see you— and ship-building! There has been no invasion, no major raiding. I say that it was worth the signing. As says Thomas— my lord of Moray. And he has the wisest head in this land, I think."

"It may be so," Bruce allowed. "But what now ? The truce was made with Edward the Second. It does not bind his successor. It is now at an end. I want no more truces, but a true peace. An embassage to the new regents . . . ?"

"I think not, Sire–not first," the Chancellor advised. "It would smack of too great eagerness, perhaps. On the part of rebels! Better some less open move first, lest we be rejected, to our hurt. Do as Your Grace did with the Frenchman, de Sully. Send an embassage travelling to France. Or to the Pope. If to the Pope, then such cannot be denied a safe-conduct by the English. Then, in passage, it could sound out Lancaster and the others, privily . . ."

"Aye–that would be wiser, Bernard. You are right. Moreover, a treaty with France would be easier to forge than with England! But since the King of France's sister now controls the King of England, the one could well aid the other! Since the Pope now recognises me as king–since our great letter, and Moray's visit to him–if he could be prevailed upon to urge on the King of France, and the new King of England, to recognise my kingship, the thing might be achieved. An embassage therefore, first to the Pope, and then to France. Moray again ?"

"Assuredly, Sire. Send my lord of Moray–since it seems the Pope liked him well. But we require more than this peace treaty. We require that his offence against the Church in Scotland be lifted by His Holiness. It still remains, and is a grave inconvenience, if naught else! For it means, as you know, that new appointments within the Church, new bishops and abbots and the like, cannot be approved from Rome. And so do not carry full weight. Send a churchman also, therefore, to convince His Holiness of our true obedience and duty."

"M'mmm. Obedience and duty! Words I like not, my lord Abbot!"

"Yet in matters ecclesiastical we must use them, Your Grace," the other declared. "Since only in obedience to the Pontiff do we gain full authority for our offices in the Church."

"Very well, Bernard. Whom shall we send ? Yourself ?"

"No, Sire–not me. I am still in His Holiness's disfavour. As is my lord of St. Andrews. It must be one who did not defy him. In 1318."

"But you all did, man. All the bishops and senior clergy."

"Then it must be a younger man. Yet in high office. Send my lord's Archdeacon, Sire. James Bene. Archdeacon of St. Andrews. He is young, but sound, and no fool. The best of the new men. My lord's right hand . . ."

"Very well. So be it. Moray and Master Bene shall go. To the Pope, and then to King Charles of France. But by London. Send for a safe-conduct for them, from the new King Edward. We shall sound out this new rule in England . . ."

. . .

"You are not the only one to make a vow, Robert," the Queen said, one day the following spring when the King, confined to the house of Cardross with badly swollen legs, was bewailing many things but in especial that he was never likely now to lead that Crusade which the Pope was so anxious to sponsor, and which he had vowed to make that time in the Galloway cave when the spider had inspired him to his duty. "I also made a vow, once. And of late I have been minded to fulfil it."

"You? A vow? A woman, on a Crusade? That I'll not believe . . . !"

"Not a Crusade, no. But still a vow. And a pilgrimage. Is it so strange ? Cannot a woman, in her extremity, also call upon God and His saints for especial aid ? And promise to make some reparation should her call be heard, her requirement granted ?"

"No doubt but you are right, lass. It is but that vows seem scarce a woman's part. But then, Elizabeth de Burgh is no common woman! When did you make this vow ? And on what terms ? What pilgrimage do you speak of ?"

"I made it all those years ago, at St. Duthac's sanctuary, at Tain. Before the altar. When William, Earl of Ross betrayed us to the English. When all was at its blackest, after the defeats of Methven and Strathfillan, the fall of Kildrummy, you a hunted fugitive and Nigel captured – then I vowed that if God, hearing perhaps the intercessions of your Celtic Saint Duthac, would one day grant me a safe return to my husband's arms and make me the mother of his children, then I would make a pilgrimage of thankfulness to this far northern shrine. It has been on my conscience that I have never done it – and I grow neither younger nor stronger for journeying. I think the time has come to fulfil my vow, Robert – if you will give me leave ?" She did not add that, since Duthac had proved effective once, she might well seek to enlist his aid a second time, for the same husband, whose physical state was now much concerning her. She had never taken his leprosy fears too much to heart; but this trouble with his leg-swellings and breathlessness worried her greatly.

Not a little touched by her revelation, Bruce put an arm around his wife's shoulders. "My dear – you never told me. We would have gone together."

"When have you had time, opportunity – or latterly the strength – to spare for such lengthy pilgrimage into the Highland North ? With the saving and governance of this kingdom on your shoulders ?

325

Moreover, this was for myself alone. I would not, will not, be taken on such errand by you, Robert. You understand?"

"Aye, lass. As you will. And you think to go now?"

"Soon. Now that I may leave little David. And you all. The snows are melting in the passes. With May blooming, and the cuckoos calling, I shall go. A woman's oblation."

"Yet you must not go alone. That I will not have. You are the Queen. If I may not go with you, another shall. Whom will you have?"

"I would choose James Douglas. But since I know this to be impossible, I would have Gilbert Hay. He has ever loved me, in his quiet way. And makes undemanding companion."

"No—I could not spare Jamie. I but await Thomas's return from France, to send them both south once more. On their old ploys! Deep raiding into England. You know it. This cannot wait. But Gibbie you may have."

Elizabeth nodded. They were back to that—Scotland and England at war. The Queen-Mother, Mortimer, and the Regency Council had at first unilaterally confirmed the thirteen-year truce, to the Scots' surprise; but latterly it had become clear that this was merely a convenience to gain time to assemble their strength against Scotland. Spies informed that secret orders had gone out all over England for a May muster at Newcastle, where Count John of Hainault, the noted commander—to whose niece the young King had recently become betrothed—was to command with his fine force of heavy Flemish horse. Bruce intended to strike first, as of yore, with another of the Douglas-Moray swift cavalry drives, as dissuasion. But it was depressing to have to return to such tactics.

When Elizabeth went off about her own affairs, Robert Bruce smiled a little, to himself. He was not quite so moribund and immobile as she seemed to think him—even though horse-riding nowadays did tend to make him breathless and his heart to beat irregularly. He was damned if he was going to be carried about in a litter, yet—but there were other methods of transport. The new trading galliot he and Angus Og had been building, to be the first of a trading fleet, was all but finished. It would be a good opportunity to test its qualities out, while Elizabeth was elsewhere—for nothing was surer than that she would insist that he was not in a fit state to go sailing. He loved her dearly—but he was not going to be coddled. And he had been wanting to go to Ireland again, for some time, to Antrim, where the Irish chiefs and kinglets were once more wishing to enter into a league for the expulsion of the English. Since his brother Edward's death he had consistently refused to consider any suggestion that he should assume the highly theoretical and nominal High Kingship of All Ireland; but he was not against using his undoubted influence with the Irish to bring pressure on the new English régime, parallel with the Douglas-Moray expedition.

Once Elizabeth was safely off on her pilgrimage, he would go sailing.

. . .

The Queen gone, the galliot's trials satisfactory, the Irish agreement usefully concluded, and Bruce tired but not displeased with his physical state, the galliot returned up the Clyde estuary in late August, that year of 1327, escorted by a squadron of Angus Og's galleys. Thomas, Earl of Moray, himself was waiting for his uncle on the jetty at Cardross.

Moray had stirring tidings to relate. Douglas and he had twisted the English leopard's tail, with a vengeance. Not content with raiding and making diversionary gestures deep into England, they had had a confrontation with the young King Edward himself; indeed they had sought to capture him, and Douglas had been within yards of succeeding, the youthful monarch's personal chaplain being slain in the skirmish. They had defeated a forward force of the main enemy army at Cockdale, in Durham. Then slipped over the high moorland to Weardale, forcing the cumbrous English array to make a great and tiring detour in wet weather with rivers in spate, on terrain where the Hainaulters' heavy cavalry was bogged down. At Stanhope, a hunting-park of the Bishop of Durham, they had taken up a strong position on the hillside, for all to see, and waited, leading the enemy to believe that they would do battle there—despite the enormous difference in size of the respective forces. Presuming that a full-scale confrontation must develop the next day, the English leaders had camped for the night on the low ground. This was when Douglas had tried his audacious night raid, for a capture. They had collected many prisoners, including courtiers, before the camp was roused—though the King unfortunately escaped. And thereafter, since they had never intended to do set battle with a host ten times their size, in enemy country, they slipped away northwards in the darkness, and returned to Scotland forthwith. Douglas was now back on the Border, and he, Moray, had come for further orders.

"I' faith, Thomas—here is excellent news!" Bruce cried, his limp weariness forgotten. "On my soul, you make a pretty pair of brigands! That youth begins his reign with a notable indignity, indeed. Like his father! Perhaps it will teach his advisers that the Scots would make better friends than foes! With my Irish arrangements, just completed, I swear they will have to come to the conclusion

327

that a peace treaty is the only way in which they will win respite in their own realm!"

Moray coughed. "Unfortunately, Sire—it may prove otherwise. As I said, we captured prisoners close to the King. One, a Thomas Rokeby, esquire to King Edward, declared that it was common knowledge that Your Grace was dying! And that the English need not trouble—that once you were gone the rebel Scots would soon come to heel, with no need for any treaty . . ."

"By the Rude—they think that! So I am dying, am I ? 'Fore God, I will teach them otherwise!" The King's eyes blazed with all their old fire.

"We told Rokeby so, Sire—and let him go free, to convey the facts to his King. But—I doubt if he will be believed. Or even believed us."

"Then we will show them, beyond a peradventure! Hear you that, Angus my friend ? I am dying. The English have only to wait! So—they will learn differently, and swiftly! By two days from this I will be on English soil, by God! And we shall see who dies . . .!"

Robert Bruce was as good as his oath—however much it cost him, in bodily fatigue, pain in his legs and at his heart, and such exhaustion that he had to be propped up in his saddle by esquires, one on either side of his horse. Nevertheless, two days later and ninety weary horseback miles south-eastwards, he led James Douglas and Moray and their host over the Coldstream ford of Tweed, and on to besiege the Bishop of Durham's castle of Norham. Also he sent lieutenants to invest Warkworth Castle, and even the Percy stronghold of Alnwick, while others went further south still, and west, to waste Northumberland—saving always Tynedale—North Durham, Cumberland and Westmorland. Even though Bruce conducted this warfare largely from a tent under Norham's walls, the King of Scots' presence was made abundantly clear to all the North of England. He sent heralds to announce to the King of England, wherever he should be found, the Earl of Lancaster, the Archbishop of York and the Bishop of Durham, that he, the King of Scots, intended to annexe the county of Northumberland to the realm of Scotland forthwith.

It was in these circumstances, on a mellow autumn day of October, that Sir Henry Percy of Alnwick, Lord of Northumberland, with Sir William de Denham, of the English Chancery, came riding under a white flag to the Scots camp at Norham—an unhappy and nervous delegation. This was Bruce's first meeting with the son of his old enemy—for the previous Henry Percy had died the same year as Bannockburn. He was, in fact, very much a replica of his father, tall, thin, foxy of face and prematurely stooping, balding. Eyeing him,

Bruce knew a little disappointment. This man was not worth his vengeance. He had dressed himself in full armour to meet the envoys. It mattered not, after all; but he was glad that his swollen legs were hidden beneath the steel, uncomfortable as it was.

The Englishmen brought a request for a peace treaty, from King Edward and his regents. They wanted to know King Robert's terms.

"Have you writing to show me, my lord?" Bruce barked at Percy. "From your liege lord?"

The other nodded. He handed over a sealed missive, addressed to the Lord Robert, King of Scots.

The sigh that escaped from the Bruce was eloquent as it was long. He had waited and worked for thirteen years for that simple superscription.

The day following, the envoys were sent away with the Scots terms. They comprised six points—and were more favourable, generous indeed, than even Moray advised. Nothing must stop a settlement now. The points were: (1) That the King of England, and parliament, must acknowledge that King Robert and his heirs for all time coming should rule the independent kingdom of Scotland, without rendering any service or homage to any. (2) That the King of Scots' son and heir, the Prince David, should have for betrothed bride the King of England's young sister, Princess Joanna of the Tower. (3) That no subjects of the King of England should hold lands in Scotland; nor subjects of the King of Scots hold lands in England. (4) That King Robert and his heirs should lend military aid, if requested, against all save the French, with whom Scotland was already in alliance; likewise English aid should be available to the Scots, if required. (5) That the King of Scots would pay the sum of £20,000 within three years, as reparation for damage done to the kingdom of England. (6) That the King of England should use all powers to persuade the papal curia to repeal the sentence of excommunication against King Robert and his Council and subjects. And this forthwith.

If the King of England would confirm these terms, under the Great Seal of England, King Robert would send his commissioners to Newcastle, to negotiate the peace. And promptly.

Bruce had himself hoisted into the saddle again, and turned his horse's head for home.

They had not long crossed the ford of Tweed when a small party, riding hard, came galloping across the green levels of the Merse, to meet them. The King perceived that it was his Lord High Constable, Gilbert Hay, and reined up. And at his friend's grim, unhappy features, the royal heart missed another beat.

Pulling up before him, Hay flung himself down, knelt, looked up, opened his mouth to speak—and said no word.

"Well, Gibbie—well? You are back, from your travels. How is the Queen?"

Hay moistened his lips, and dropped his glance again. Still he knelt.

The scene swam before the King's eyes. "Out with it, man! She is not sick? In trouble . . . ?"

"Sire . . . my good lord! Oh, my friend, my liege—the Queen . . . she is dead! Dead!" Hay's voice broke completely. He rose, turning away, stumbling, blinded by his tears.

For long moments there was silence. After a stricken pause, Moray and Douglas urged their horses close, to support the King's person. He waved them back.

As from a great distance he spoke, levelly, evenly, his voice steady. "Speak on, Sir Gilbert," he said, staring straight ahead of him.

The Constable made two or three false starts, the King waiting patiently. At length, mumbling disjointedly, he got it out. The Queen had made her pilgrimage to Tain successfully, although it had taxed her strength sorely, the weather so ill, the rivers all in spate. But returning, at Cullen in Banffshire, near Sir Alexander Comyn's house, whilst fording a flooded stream, her horse had slipped and thrown her. She had fallen on rocks, in the water, and grievously injured herself. Within. An issue of blood, which would not staunch. She said that it was from her womb; after the prince's birth it had never fully recovered. They had carried her, wet and cold, to the nearest house. From thence to the Comyn's castle of Cullen. But nothing could aid her. The bleeding, from her woman's parts, would not staunch. She died there, calm, composed, kind, a Queen to the end, sending warm messages of love and devotion to her lord, her children, her friends . . .

Gilbert Hay, once started, was jerking and mumbling on. But he had lost his main audience. Robert Bruce had set his horse in motion, and was riding slowly away, head up, straight of back, jaws sternly clenched. Some yards on, without turning, he called back, and strongly.

"See kindly to Sir Gilbert," he said.

CHAPTER

23

THE King was stubborn. He would not be carried in a litter. Against all advice, he rode all the way from Cardross to Edinburgh, although by slow stages—and gained some small satisfaction to set against the pain, discomfort and exhaustion when, at Cramond near the city, he caught up with the train of Bishop Lamberton, himself lying in a litter, after crossing the ferry from Fife. Riding alongside his old friend's equipage the few remaining miles, he was perversely pleased to be upright in his saddle and so able to condescend to the other—however shocked he was by the wasted and emaciated state of the Primate.

Nevertheless, Bruce had to take to his bed on arrival at the Abbey of Holyrood, at Edinburgh, since he could by then by no means stand on his feet. This was a humiliation, and perhaps deserved; for not only was all the world coming to Edinburgh these March days of 1328, but the city had organised a great pageant and demonstration for the King and his guests—anxious no doubt to establish its loyalty in the end. Not that Bruce cared overmuch about disappointing the fathers and citizens—for Edinburgh was a place he had never loved, always looking on it as almost an English city, which had taken sides against him more often than for him; but it must emphasise to all that the King was a sick man, when the pageantry had to take place without his presence, with Moray and young Prince David deputising for the monarch—for he flatly refused to view the proceedings from a litter, as the Primate did, rain nonetheless.

His infirmity could not but be obvious to the Englishmen also, of course—although he kept them from his room, and only appeared before them on occasion, and briefly, fully clad and making an almost pugnacious attempt to appear fit and hearty.

To all intents, it was a parliament, on the Scots side, Bruce having summoned everyone of standing in the kingdom, to witness this consummation of a life's work. The terms of the treaty had been thrashed out at York; but despite objections by the English, Bruce had insisted that the actual signing should be done in his realm. There were a few outstanding details to be settled, but it was entirely evident that nothing now would hold up the ratification. It was to be the Treaty of Edinburgh, not of Newcastle or of York or any-where else—whatever the English chose to call it thereafter.

King Edward had sent up a resounding team as commissioners, headed by Henry de Burghersh, Bishop of Lincoln, a most able prelate and Lord High Chancellor of England. He was supported by the Bishop of Norwich, Sir Geoffrey le Scrope, the Chief Justice, and de la Zouche, Lord of Ashby, along with Sir Henry Percy again. It was noteworthy that both Percy and Ashby formerly held large lands in Scotland. Some trading was obviously envisaged.

Bruce was glad to leave the wrangling over details to others—although he and Lamberton were kept informed of every point, and maintained their fingers firmly on the pulse of the negotiations. The main difficulty was the matter of the betrothal of Prince David and the Princess Joanna of the Tower—or at least, the date of such marriage contract. The English renunciation, as they called it, of all claims of sovereignty over Scotland, was dependent on this marriage, it seemed. And David Bruce would not reach the age of fourteen, legal age for consent to actual marriage, until 1338, ten years hence. Much might happen in ten years—and the King of France was already suggesting that David Bruce would be better married to a French princess. Mere promises were insufficient for the English, on this score—since they, if any did, knew the worth of mere promises. It was not until Bruce offered the enormous and quite unobtainable sum of £100,000, to be paid by the Scots if by 1338 David was *not* married to Joanna, that this matter was settled. Money always spoke loud, in the South.

A second point of difficulty was the matter of military aid, in alliance. The situation if France attacked England was thrashed out. It was eventually agreed that if their French allies drew Scotland into war, the English would be free to make war in return, without infringing the treaty. The Irish position was equally troublesome. In an effort to get the Scots to agree that they would not aid any Irish rebellion, the English commissioners offered the return to Scotland of the Black Rood of St. Margaret and the Stone of Destiny, stolen by Edward the First from Scone in 1296. This, needless to say, was a grave embarrassment, since the true Stone had never left the Scone area, but had been kept in secret at various places there-abouts. Evidently the Hammer of the Scots had kept to himself his undoubted knowledge that his Stone was false, and the English fully accepted it as genuine. Bruce certainly did not want Edward's lump of Scone sandstone back; but nor was this the time to reveal the presence of the authentic original, he decided. He had plans for the Stone of Scone. So the Scots showed no interest in this offer, and instead obtained a promise that if anyone in Man or the Hebrides made war against the King of Scots, the English should not aid them. This matter had rankled in Bruce's mind ever since Lame John MacDougall of Lorn had been made English Admiral of the West, and had had to be driven out of Man by Angus Og and Moray.

At length, all was settled, and the great ceremony of the signing took place in the refectory of Holyrood Abbey, crowded as it had never been before. For this occasion Bruce was fully dressed in his most splendid cloth-of-gold, under the jewelled Lion Rampant tabard of Scotland—even though he sat on his day-bed, and could raise and rest his swollen legs thereon when necessary. Lamberton was also present, in his litter. And if these two seemed, by their obvious physical disability, to lend an atmosphere of invalidism and infirmity, there at least was nothing of senility or weakness about it, as their eyes, speech and bearing made abundantly clear. For these two, head of State and Church in Scotland, were indeed the most mentally alive and determined men in all that great company. Beside them, Percy was a drooping, hesitant ineffectual, Bishop Burghersh an anxious fat man eager to be elsewhere, and le Scrope a stiff, parchment-faced lawyer, niggling over words.

Before the actual signing, the English Lord Chancellor was to read out the Declaration of King Edward, written at York and to be incorporated in the treaty as preamble. As he was about to begin, Bruce intervened.

"My lord Bishop and Chancellor," he said, "it seems to me meet and suitable that your liege lord's pronouncement should be read by Sir Henry, my lord of Northumberland. His father was, to our cost, Lieutenant and Governor in Scotland, once! All knew him well, had to heed his voice! Let us be privileged to hear his son's, on this occasion, if you please."

And so it was that the son of the man who had hectored, lectured, reproved, deceived and harried the Bruce on so many occasions through the years, had to read aloud the words which were the justification and coping-stone of the hero-king's thirty years of striving and suffering, indeed of his entire career. That he did so in an undignified and scarcely intelligible gabble, was neither here nor there.

"Whereas we, and some of our predecessors, Kings of England, have attempted to gain rights of rule, lordship or superiority over the Kingdom of Scotland, and terrible hardships have long afflicted the realms of England and Scotland through the wars fought on this account; and bearing in mind the bloodshed, slaughter, atrocities, destruction of churches, and innumerable evils from which the inhabitants of both realms have suffered over and over again because

333

of these wars; and having regard also to the good things in which both realms might abound to their mutual advantage if joined in stability of perpetual peace, and thus more effectually made secure, within and beyond their borders, against the harmful attempts of violent men to rebel or make way; we will and concede for us and all our heirs and successors, by the common counsel, assent and consent of the prelates, magnates, earls and barons and communities of our realm in our parliament that the Kingdom of Scotland shall remain for ever separate in all respects from the Kingdom of England, in its entirety, free and in peace, without any kind of subjection, servitude, claim or demand, with its rightful boundaries as they were held and preserved in the times of Alexander of good memory King of Scotland last deceased, to the magnificent prince, the Lord Robert, by God's grace illustrious King of Scots, our ally and very dear friend, and to his heirs and successors.

EDWARD REX"

There was no cheering, no exclamation, no spoken comment at all, in that great chamber, as those words tailed away into a long and pregnant silence. All men considered them, on both sides, and the price paid for their pronouncement, and held their peace.

Robert Bruce took up the quill in a hand that trembled very slightly.

.   .   .

On an impulse, Edinburgh emptying of the distinguished company, the King did not return direct on the uncomfortable horse-back journey all the way to Cardross, but instead accompanied William Lamberton by sea from Leith to St. Andrews—this on the Primate's quite casual mention that he would not survive the transport by road in a horse-litter; and when the King remonstrated that this was no way to talk, the Bishop as factually announced that he would be dead within the month anyway. In the circumstances, the King remained with his friend.

Lamberton was too exhausted during the journey to talk at any length. But, in his own room of St. Andrew's Castle the day following, he was strong enough to speak with Bruce—and eager to do so. They had much to discuss. The Primate was particularly concerned about the future governance of the Church in Scotland, a matter that was now urgent. He advised that, much as he valued most of them, none of the present Bishops should be elevated to the Primacy. Not even the good Bernard, Abbot of Arbroath—who might well be given the bishopric of Man and the Sudreys, just become vacant. But the national leadership of the Church demanded a strong, sure and experienced hand. His own was about to be removed, and he

334

urged the appointment of his Archdeacon of St. Andrews, the vigorous James Bene, who had so distinguished himself as diplomat and negotiator in Moray's French and papal embassages, and who had in fact been administering the metropolitan see for long. The canons of St. Andrews had faith in him, and would elect him. With the King's support he would serve Church and realm well . . .

"Yes, yes, my friend," Bruce agreed, concerned that the other should not tire himself thus. "He it shall be, never fear. But there is no such haste. Leave it now . . ."

"There is so much to say, Sire. Haste indeed. For my time is short."

"You mean . . . ? You in truth meant what you said at Edinburgh, William ? That you do not expect to live out the month ?"

"To be sure," the other said, his voice weak, but only his voice. "My fear has been that I should not last thus long, to speak with you."

"That is grievous hearing, my old friend."

"Why grievous, Robert ? *I* grieve not, I promise you. I am more than ready to go. I am much blest. My work is done – all I have lived for. To few is so much granted. Scotland free. Your royal state recognised by all Christendom. Your succession assured. The Church here sound, in fair order, sure of its place, united. And this great cathedral completed." Gaspingly he enunciated these satisfactions.

Bruce nodded, understandingly.

"Life should mean achievement, in great things and small," the other went on, picking his slow words. "Without achievement, life is merest existence, of neither virtue nor relish. *You* know it well, Robert. I shall achieve nothing more here. Beyond – I believe that I shall. If the good God will find work for me in His greater purpose. I pray that He will. I long to be at it – not a bed-bound hulk here. Do you understand ?"

The King nodded again. "That I do, my friend. Indeed, you could be speaking from my own heart, from my own mind. For . . . such is my wish also."

For long these two colleagues and comrades considered each other.

"I thought that it might be so," Lamberton acknowledged quietly. "I am the happier in going. Happy for you, that such is your spirit. For here is joy, Robert. Although you have longer to wait for it than I."

"Not so much longer, I think."

"No ? Have you more reason to say that, Robert ? You believe your days here short ? This is not the matter of the leprosy again ?"

"No. It is strange. The leprosy—all these years I have lived with it. And kept it close. That none should know. At your behest. And Elizabeth's. I believed that it would kill me. But, no. It was not to be. That was the finger of God, only—not the sword of God! Now I have the dropsy. Have had it near two years. It strikes surer, deeper. At my heart. I have had many warnings. One day, soon I think, I shall receive my last. Perhaps before you do, old friend. But—I pray not before I am ready—or have *made* ready. *My* work is not fully done, I fear—but most of it is. Like you, I have no desire to linger, as less than myself. And like you, I hope to do better, hence."

They considered the future, in silence.

"You do not fear death, William," the King went on presently, not a question but a statement. "That I see—and rejoice in it."

"No, I do not fear it. Nor should any true man. Only those who have striven for nothing, buried their Lord's talent. The dying itself may be unpleasant—but let us hope, short. Being dead—that foolish word we use—that must be otherwise. An excellence. Fulfilment."

"You rate it so high as that? Excellence?"

"I do. For it is part of God's ordained progress and purpose with men. God's, not men's. And all such is excellent." The other raised an open hand, frail but eloquent. "What has God been doing with us this while, Robert, think you? In all our joys and sorrows, our achievements and defeats? What, but building—making *us* build. As I built that cathedral. Stone by stone, building our character. Heart, mind, will, understanding—aye, and compassion, above all. These things we have been attaining unto. Their fullest flowering in us. The body is as nothing, compared with these. All our years, these have been building up, for better or for worse. Now, they are at their height. Think you the All Highest ordained it thus for nothing? The patient moulding, ours and His, the secret strivings of the heart, this edifice that is our life's essence. Just to cast it away, discarded, unused, spurned, like a child's bauble? In all His creation, this is the height of His achievement—not the tides of the oceans, the lands, the sun, moon and stars. Man, at the summit of his earthly character —which is when he dies. Here is God's achievement—and man's, in His image. Purpose and order are in all His works—that is plain to all. Should, then, the greatest work of all be purposeless?"

This urgent profession, declaration, whispered but intense, had taken much out of the Primate, so that he lay back, panting, eyes closed.

Much moved, Bruce waited.

"This is fulfilment, therefore," Lamberton resumed, after a long interval. "God has given us reason. To use. If we cannot see this, we are fools. Failures. We move on, to *use* what has here been built up—

336

of this I have no doubt. And, Robert—I would be about it! About it, man!"

The King gripped the other's thin hand. "Then, I rejoice," he said, deep-voiced. "With you. No mourning, William. I have never heard greater sense spoken. For you, then, all is well. You go on, joyfully. Prepared. But—*you* have not murder on your conscience, my friend! What of me? I murdered Comyn, at God's own altar. What of me?" There was intensity there also.

"What of you, then, Robert? Are you different from other men— save in that you have had greater testing? That was sin, yes— although the man deserved to die if ever man did. But it is repented sin. And paid for a thousand times in the years since. I say, without that sin, and the need to expiate it, who knows—would Robert Bruce ever have achieved what he has done? For a whole nation? Would this character you have built up be so sure, so sharp and tempered a sword for God's use in His purpose hereafter? I think not."

"I would that *I* could be so sure of God's forgiveness!"

"Then use your wits, Robert! Use them. God is purpose, order, power. But, forget it not—love, also. Else where comes love? Love, the force which drives all else. Love is compassion, understanding. If *you* can forgive—and you have forgiven many, too many for your nobles—then do you deny it to God? Dare you?"

"No-o-o . . ."

This time the Bishop's eyes remained shut for long; and thinking he slept, Bruce lay back, thinking, thinking.

But then the weak-strong voice spoke on, as though there had been no pause. "If life has taught me anything, Robert, it is that love is of all things great, powerful, eternal, the very sword of God. Not weak, soft, pap—as some would have it! Love is God, there-fore it is eternal. Cannot die—God's, or yours, or mine. Here is the greatest comfort in all creation. Love cannot die with the body. It must go on, since it is eternal. See you what this means, my friend?"

"I think I do, yes. Elizabeth . . .!"

"Aye, your Elizabeth. She is loving you still. As you love her. Scorning, straddling this hurdle we call the grave! And not only she. Your Marjory. Your brothers. All those who have loved you, to the death. Whom you mourned for, unneeding. And I, who have loved you also—I take it with me. But its chain will link us still. And God's love, of which it is a part, will see that it grows and burgeons. In the fuller life to which we are headed. This . . . this is what I had to say to you, Robert Bruce. Thank God . . . He has left me time . . . to say it."

Those last words were barely distinguishable, spoken beneath the

337

shallow breath, yet with a certainty to them that spoke of strength not weakness — William Lamberton's last service to his two masters.

Bruce remained beside the bed for some time thereafter, but there was no more talk. Once the dying man moved his lips, but no words came; a faint smile, that was all. They were content. When, presently, the other closed his eyes, the King pressed his hand for the last time, and walked slowly from that room, leaving his friend to the hush of the waves far below, and the seabirds' crying.

"GIBBIE," the King said, a little thickly, "it is time. There is not long now. Bring me these three. And thus. Thomas Randolph. Angus of the Isles. And James Douglas. These three only do I wish to see, now. And, man—of a mercy, lighten your face! Have you vowed never to smile again? Here is nothing so ill. Another pilgrimage, and a lighter one—that is all. Less wearisome than that we have just completed. William Lamberton taught me how to die, a year ago. Now, get me my nephew Thomas—and not on tiptoe, 'fore God!"

Bruce's voice was surprisingly strong, however thick, and as vehement as ever—when he could speak—even though scarcely any of the rest of him could move. When, at times, overwhelming pain at his heart blacked out all things for him, he knew fear—not fear of the next step, but that it should come upon him before his tongue could enunciate what still had to be said. This had been Lamberton's fear, and then final relief—time to give his message to his friend.

So, while Hay fetched Moray, Bruce lay in the great room of Cardross, bathed in the bright June sunshine, and prayed that the roaring blackness would hold off sufficiently long, and that nothing should tie and hamper his tongue. He was the King. Pray God he could remain the King to the end—until he became just another new pilgrim . . .

Moray came quickly, with the Constable—for none of them was far away. All knew the end was near; indeed most of his friends had not expected their liege lord to survive the long pilgrimage to St. Ninian's shrine at Whithorn, at the tip of Galloway, and back, the astonishing epic itinerary of a dying man, out of which none had been able to dissuade him, litter-borne indeed as it had had to be.

"It is Thomas, Sire," his nephew said.

"I am not blind, man!" his uncle asserted. "Not yet. Come close. Do not go, Gibbie—you shall listen to this also. As witness. Thomas —hear me. You have good shoulders. You will require them. On them I now place my burden. Of rule and governance in this land. I leave a bairn as king—a child of five. An ill thing. For a dozen years, God willing, the rule of Scotland must be yours, in his name. You are regent, with James Douglas as co-regent. But yourself chiefest.

Jamie is the greatest fighter—but yours is the wisest head. I have instructed Bernard de Linton, and signed all that is necessary. You understand? From this day, Thomas, this hour, you take up my burden."

"This day, Sire . . . ?"

"This day. The gate stands wide for me. I will not hold back now, I think. Not of *my* will. But, be that as it may, from now, Scotland is in your strong hands. I thank God for them. You know my mind, what I would have for my son and his realm. See you to it."

"That I will. You may rely on me. And . . . I thank Your Grace. For all things. But, above all, for your faith in me. I, who betrayed you once . . ."

"You never betrayed me, Thomas. Only set too high a standard, to which I could not aspire—and feared to betray yourself. Since you learned that kings, and yourself, are but men, and men are finite, you have served me better than any. Now the decisions are no longer mine, but yours."

"It will be my endeavour to make them as you would, Sire . . ."

"No! Not that. You have a better head than I, in some matters. And a stout heart. Make your own decisions now. And for my son. They will often enough be hard decisions, and men will not love you for them. You will have a King's work to do, yet not be a King. I do not envy you your task, Thomas."

"I take it up willingly, proudly, Sire."

"Aye. Only, remember this, Thomas. All men have not your stature, your integrity of spirit. Be merciful. Particularly towards a fatherless and motherless laddie, who sits in a lonely throne—God knows how lonely! That alone I counsel you—be less unbending. Much proud uprightness, such as yours, must be swallowed for a realm's unity. I learned it, and so must you. That—and trust not the English. In matters of statecraft. However fair-seeming. Now—let us say God-speed. For my time runs out . . ."

Moray knelt by the great bed, to take and kiss his uncle's swollen, stiff hand. "Your servant, now and for ever," he said simply, and stood.

"Aye, lad. See, Gibbie—here is a man who knows how death is to be treated! No moping and long faces. No tiptoes! Now—Angus. Farewell, Thomas . . ."

The Lord of the Isles came in, greying but still the stocky, assured figure on which Bruce had always relied so heavily. He eyed his friend with his accustomed calm and practical gaze, his reserve innate even yet.

"I said that foolish pilgrimage would kill you," he observed dispassionately.

"It was meant to, man! Think you I, Robert Bruce, would rust away, like an old sword in a sheath? Besides, I had to see Carrick and Annandale and Galloway again. Before I moved on. But—here, Angus. And listen well." The King's voice was urgent, now, as in haste.

"I listen . . . Sire," the other said, coming close.

"Ha! You say it! You have never said that word until now, man! Long years I have waited for it—from the Prince of the Isles!"

Angus smiled grimly. "I can afford it—now! Can I not, Your Grace?"

"Aye—Angus Og, as ever! You do not change. But thank you, nevertheless, my friend. Now, heed. Moray I leave as regent. With Douglas. This you knew of. You do not love him, I know. But, for my sake, give him your sure support. For my son's sake. This I charge you, if our friendship means aught. He will need all your strength. The English will not be long in showing their teeth, treaty or none. When I am gone, they will be at Scotland's throat once more. Edward and his regency are cherishing this Edward Baliol, at their Court. Not for nothing, you may be sure. A child of five years, on my throne, and they will not delay in recollecting past wrongs and humiliations. Moray is going to require your strong right arm—and your galleys, Angus!"

"I shall not fail your son," the other assured quietly.

"That is what I desired to hear, my friend. I thank you. But—there is something else. The Stone. The true Stone of Destiny, at Scone. Baliol knows of it, if the English do not—that their stone is false. His father was crowned on the true Stone. I prophesy that it will be Edward Baliol's ambition and desire to be likewise! And the English are grooming him for some great role, nothing more sure. Pray God Moray can keep him, and them, at bay. But, if he comes, I want that Stone hence. That he, and the like, may never sit thereon. Take it, Angus—take it. After my son's coronation. Take it to your Isles, where none shall be able to follow it. And keep it safe, on some fair island. Until one of my line, or whoever is true King of Scots, requires it again for coronation. Will you do this for me, old friend?"

"It is as good as done."

"Praise be! Then—farewell, Islesman! Your isles were my sanctuary once, your stout arm my strength, your Celtic folk my saving. You have my thanks. And, Angus—when you sail next by Loch Moidart, carry my last salutation to Christina MacRuarie. I owe her much—not the least of my debt to the Isles. Now, go, my friend—and send me Jamie."

For the first and last time in his life, Angus, Lord of the Isles, knelt and kissed another man's hand.

341

"Quickly, Jamie— quickly!" the King muttered, to himself.

That darkly graceful man, still youthful-seeming, did not keep him waiting. He came in almost at a run, went straight to the bedside, and dropped on his knees, reaching for the King's hand. Obviously he had been waiting at the door, in a fever, for this moment.

"My dear liege! My beloved lord!" he cried. "Tell me that it is not true! That this is . . . this is . . ." His voice broke.

"Jamie, Jamie— this is not you! The Black Douglas! He they frighten bairns with!" Bruce said, seeking a smile. "Have I not taught you better than this— you, my especial pupil! This is not the end."

"You mean . . . ?"

"I mean that I but take a new road. The road your Queen took. And my brothers, my daughter, Lamberton, my friends. *Your* friends. So many of them. Do you grudge me this? Now that this gross body has failed me?"

The other shook his head, wordless.

"Come. You are as bad as Gibbie Hay, Jamie! Thomas and Angus Og knew better, I vow! What mumble you there?"

"I but pray, Sire, that I may follow you . . . along that road. And soon! As I have always done . . ."

"That you will do, most assuredly!" Bruce agreed. "How soon— who knows? That is in God's hands. But, the same God willing, I will be looking back for you. I . . . I . . ." The thick voice choked to silence.

"Sire! Sire!" Douglas started up, eyes wide. Gilbert Hay moved in, at the other side.

As from far, far away, in a few moments, the King's voice returned.

"Are you there, Jamie? You are . . . still with me? Give me your hand. It is not, not this time, I think. Not yet."

"Dear God— are you in pain, Sire? Great pain . . . ?"

"No. Little pain. It is the darkness. The waters. A great darkness of waters. Roaring loud. Little pain."

Distracted, helpless, his two friends watched him.

"Ha— I see you again, now. Both of you. The tide ebbs a little. Look not so affrighted, Jamie. And you, Gibbie. Who ever was afraid of dark water, save bairns? We, who have faced together the worst that men can do to men, a thousand times? Here is naught for hurt. Only— time. Time is short. Hear then, Jamie. I have a vow unfulfilled. You know of it. I made promise once, in a Galloway cave. That, given my kingdom, given peace, my cause won, I would draw my sword again. And go against the Infidel. Who defies God's holy places. A Crusade. I swore it there . . ."

342

"But how could you do it, Sire? How fulfil it? You have had to fight and battle, always. Until this last year . . ."

"Wheesht, man—wheesht! Let *me* talk—for I have not long. *You* have time enough! You, Jamie, must be my lieutenant in this, as so often. Warden of my March. *You* shall ride for me against the Saracen. Fulfil my vow. This I charge you. When I go hence, so soon as I am on my way, take this useless body. Cut out my heart, from within it. Part of it was ever yours. Cut it out, and place it in a casket. And take it with you. Against the Infidel. Wherever he may best be struck. We shall go crusading together . . . after all. You understand?"

Douglas's lips moved, but no words came.

"It is my . . . my royal command, Jamie—my last, here. My body you shall place beside Elizabeth. Under the fair tomb I had made for her in Paris. In Dunfermline Abbey. Side by side lay us, in that place. But . . . my heart goes on to war! In God's cause, this time. And in your company. Close company, Jamie. You have it?"

The other could only nod.

"It is well, then. God be thanked—all now is done. I want for nothing. The tide may come again, when it will. I am ready. Bide with me, Jamie. Gibbie—fetch the children. My son, my daughters, young Robert. For but a moment—then away with them. Here is no place for bairns. I would but bid them . . . good day. Jamie and you . . . will bide . . . thereafter. To see me on my way, my good way . . ."

Sir James Douglas raised steel-gauntleted hand to shade his narrowed eyes against the glaring Mediterranean sun, under the upraised visor of his great war-helm.

"I fear that I have led you but ill, my friends," he said. "These Moors have outwitted us. They think, and fight, differently from the English, I perceive! Too late I perceive it. It seems that I have led you into a trap. Were the wits here which belonged with this royal heart, it would have been different. Forgive me."

His companions, at the head of the small Scots host, protested as with one voice.

"Who could tell that they had these numbers hidden in this hellish valley?" Sir Alexander Fraser, the Chamberlain, said.

"The Castilians are at fault, not you," Hugh Ross averred—Earl of Ross these last two years, since his father's death. "They declared these valleys clear."

"Your strategy is still right, my lord," young Sir Andrew Moray of Bothwell, the third of Bruce's sisters' husbands, declared stoutly. "Were there fewer, as we believed, we still needs must cut our way through them."

"Aye—there you have it, friends. We cannot turn back, with these on our flanks, and the great canyon to cross. This cliff-girt valley will not let us climb out. We can only go forward, southwards—and cut our way through. Despite odds. King Alfonso will not come to our aid—that is sure!" Douglas shrugged, under his armour. "Arrowhead formation, then, my lords—the formation *he* loved well! Bruce's wedge! We will drive his wedge through them, and teach the Saracen how the Bruce fought! Pass the word—Bruce's wedge!"

He raised his hand again, and drew over head and helm the silver chain and casket that hung before him and never left his person, day or night.

The trumpets shrilled their commands, and the 500 mounted Scots of the Northern Division of the army of Alfonso the Eleventh of Castile and Leon, hemmed in in the bare, baking, hostile Spanish valley of Tebas de Ardales, reined and sidled and prepared to marshal themselves into the driving spearhead formation which their late monarch had perfected, and which, given sufficient impetus, was the hardest man-made force on earth to halt. Far ahead, half a mile at least, the vast host of the main Moorish cavalry completely blocked the widening mouth of the dry valley, southwards towards the open plain; while to east and west the rocky heights of the sierra were lined by the serried ranks of the Infidel foot, stretched as far as eye could see on either side.

Douglas, at the apex of the wedge, rose in his stirrups. "God, Saint Andrew and Saint Bride be with us, now, my friends." He raised the chained casket high. "And the Bruce!" With a snap he shut his helm's visor. "Come!"

Out of seeming chaos the great arrow-head developed and took shape. Heedfully Douglas gave it time, restraining his own and the other leaders' impatience to attain swiftly the necessary momentum. Fortunately they had that half-mile—and as fortunately, the Moors did not ride to meet them, content to wait in solid phalanx for the impact of this suicidal charge of 500 against 5,000.

Half-way, peering behind him in the saddle, and cursing the helmet which so restricted his view, Douglas was approximately satisfied. He dug in his spurs, and gestured to his personal trumpeter. Jerkily but unmistakable, the Full Charge call rang out.

They had just the time and space to achieve the outright gallop. Thundering on the dry, sun-baked ground, they bore down on the waiting palisade of mounted spearmen and curved-sword warriors, some of the fiercest cavalry in the world, and crashed headlong into them like a battering-ram. But crashed at only one point in the long front, a point where only two or three dark fighters would not have been human had they not wilted somewhat, reined aside, drawn back.

With a resounding crash, the screaming of men and horses, and a lance-tip glancing harmlessly off shield and armoured shoulder, Douglas was through the first and second lines, thrust and driven on by the hurtling weight behind. Ignoring the waving swords of the enemy, attempting no swordery of his own, he swung the chained heart round and round in windmill fashion, right and left, and beat and beat with his other clenched fist at his mount's flank, through the splendid heraldic trappings, to keep up the impetus. Impetus, momentum, thrust—that was all, that was everything.

"A Bruce! A Bruce!" he shouted, as he rode, and all behind him cried the same.

Their tight-packed formation in the bottleneck of the valley was both the Mohammedans' weakness and strength. They presented an almost solid barrier to the Scots drive, however much individuals in the way sought to draw clear—but could not. On the other hand, they were so close ranked, drawn up to oppose the conventional cavalry attack on a wide front, line behind line, that they had no room for manœuvre, to bring their weapons to bear; and, of course, because of the narrow-fronted penetration by the wedge, not one in a score of the enemy could be in contact with their swift-moving assailants.

So long as it remained swift-moving. There was the difficulty, the danger. Strive as Douglas and the Scots leaders would, their speed fell, the press too thick. And as their pace slackened, so increased their vulnerability. Sundry blows of lance and scimitar set Douglas reeling in his saddle—yet he scarcely noticed them. All his attention was concentrated on the way ahead, forcing the wedge through.

And there *was* a way ahead, space, a thinning of the tight-packed host. That was ever more apparent. If they could win through to it . . .

Their fine gallop reduced now to a mere lumbering, stumbling trot, Douglas broke through into the open, Fraser and Ross close at his flanks, still the head of the arrow, however misshapen it was behind. But now the impetus was gone. And immediately in front, not seventy yards off, was not another rearguard line but a single large group of white-robed Saracen notables, emirs, imams, the enemy high command, under a great Crescent banner. Beyond was practically empty plain.

The dark chiefs did not hesitate. With a mighty shout they spurred forward to the assault.

Douglas knew a strange, fierce exultation. This, then, was the end. The way was open for escape—but not for Douglas. With the enemy leaders before him, not for Douglas to waver or dodge or bolt. He stood in his stirrups, dizzy from the blows he had received, and drew his great sword at last. But with his left hand. His right still swung the chained heart. Higher he raised it, and plunged forward, at a canter now, to meet the foe.

"Lead on, brave heart!" he cried. "As ever—was your wont. Douglas follows! Or else dies! A Douglas! A Douglas!" And with all his strength, he hurled the glistening silver casket and its chain before him into the midst of the Saracens, just before they closed on him.

He went down, horse beneath him, under a hail of lance and sword thrusts. The arrow-head was disintegrated. But the mass of the Scots were through. In their hundreds they swept out of the great mêlée, and down upon the Moslem leadership. In the chaos of those final moments, with their own people milling and streaming past, Ross, Fraser and Sir William Keith of Galston reined round and back, smiting, to where Douglas lay. Keith, an enormous man, leapt down, while his companions, now joined by others, circled and

347

caracoled and slashed protectively. Keith grasped the slighter and limp body in the black armour, and with a mighty effort hoisted it right on to the front of his own saddle. Beneath the body lay the gleaming casket-heart. Grabbing this also, he clambered up behind the Douglas.

"A Bruce! A Bruce!" they all cried, as they spurred after the others, out into the open plain.

The good Sir James left his last battlefield, following in his liege lord's road.